Someone Who Was

by the same author

Let's Go Somewhere
Stumped for a Tale
The Wit of Cricket
Armchair Cricket
It's Been a Lot of Fun
It's a Funny Game
Rain Stops Play
Brian Johnston's Guide to Cricket
Chatterboxes
Now Here's a Funny Thing
It's Been a Piece of Cake
Brian Johnston's Down Your Way
45 Summers

Brian Johnston

Someone Who Was

*Reflections on a life
of happiness and fun*

Methuen London

First published in 1992 by Methuen London
Michelin House, 81 Fulham Road, London sw3 6rb
Reprinted 1992

Copyright © 1992 Brian Johnston

A CIP catalogue record for this book
is available from the British Library

isbn 0 413 65490 7

Printed and bound in Great Britain
by Clays Ltd, St. Ives PLC

*To Pauline and all my family
in gratitude for their love,
tolerance and laughter.*

Acknowledgements

My grateful thanks to Ann Nash for her presentation of my manuscript so that at least it *looked* good!

Contents

Illustrations

Preface

For the last twenty years my wife Pauline has run the St Marylebone branch of the Royal National Lifeboat Institution.

In addition to many other activities, in March there is an annual flag day. One of Pauline's main collecting points is Paddington Station. Every year I go along to help at about 4.30 p.m. and try to sell flags to the hundreds of travellers rushing to catch their trains to rather posh counties such as Royal Berkshire, Buckinghamshire, Oxfordshire and Gloucestershire.

People are very generous and many of them say that the RNLI is the *one* charity which they always support. Inevitably, with my nose and the fact that I have been around for a long time, I am recognised by quite a few of the donors. This perhaps encourages them to give the odd pound coin instead of fifty pence or less.

In March 1990 I was there as usual. Collectors are meant only to rattle their tins but I am afraid that I break the law and exhort my 'victims' to give generously, telling them that one day they might be grateful to be rescued by a lifeboat.

I had all the usual enquiries as to how I thought that England was doing in the West Indies, and did I like Geoff Boycott? I was feeling quite chuffed with all this friendly recognition when a lady came up, stared at me and said, 'I think I recognise you, don't I?' I replied politely that yes, she possibly did. To which, after another hard look, she said, 'Oh, yes, I know now. Aren't you *someone who was*?'! It nearly ruined my evening and I cannot remember how much she gave me!

Later, however, when I got home, I realised that although at the time I was still very active, in two or three years she would almost certainly be right. I thought what a splendid title it would make for a book, looking back on my eighty-odd years.

Rather than write a normal book I decided to make it an alphabetical look back. It makes an easy format to read, and I was inspired by the famous alphabet which Bud Flanagan and Chesney Allen used to recite in their act:

A for Horses	N for A Dig
B for Mutton	O for The Wings of a Dove
C for Highlanders	P for A Penny
D for Rential	Q for a Song
E for Adam	R for Mo
F for Vescence	S for Ranzen
G for Police	T for Two
H for Respect	U for Got My Birthday
I for Novello	V for La France
J for Oranges	W for A Fiver
K for Café	X for Breakfast
L for Leather	Y for Mistress
M for Sis	Z for Breezes

So here goes. This is my alphabet:

A for Actors and Actresses	N for Newspapers
B for Boat Race	O for Oxford
C for Coffee	P for Prep School
D for *Down Your Way*	Q for Questions
E for Eton	R for Religion
F for Family	S for Sport
G for Grenadier Guards	T for *Test Match Special*
H for Health	U for U or Non-U
I for *In Town Tonight*	V for VIPs
J for Jokes	W for 'The Wood' (St John's)
K for Knowledge	X for Ex-Commentators
L for Lord's	Y for Yorkshire Pudding etc.
M for Music-Hall	Z for Zany

A

for Actors and Actresses

N.B. This category does not include
music-hall or variety artists.

I became stage-struck one night in either 1919 or 1920, I cannot
remember which. I was staying with an aunt who had a house
in Lowndes Street. Her husband was Colonel Freddy Browning,
a well-known sportsman and man about town, and father of
General 'Boy' Browning of Airborne fame.

One night they had a bridge party at which one of the guests
was Dame Clara Butt. When she was dummy she asked the
butler, Ford, to telephone one of the West End theatres where
the Co-optimists were performing. In those days by calling up
a theatre it was possible to listen to what was going on on the
stage. How they worked out the performing fees for the players
I just don't know. Anyhow she was soon connected, and sat
listening to the Co-optimists singing the Canadian folk song
'Alouette'. She let me listen and at the end of the song there
was tremendous applause from the theatre audience and shouts
of encore. It was magic to think that this was coming live from
a theatre and I was completely captured by the atmosphere
which came across the line. I was 'sold' on the theatre from
then on.

It was at this dinner party that Freddy Browning played a
practical joke on Ford. As Ford was handing round the
vegetables, Freddy turned to his next-door neighbour at the
table and said in a loud voice, 'Do you happen to know of a
good butler? We are thinking of making certain changes here.'
Ford nearly dropped the vegetables!

This same aunt took me to two theatres, which further
whetted my appetite. We saw Gerald du Maurier in a play
called *Interference* which, incidentally, included Gracie Fields in
the cast – her first straight part. Du Maurier was fascinating to
watch. He didn't appear to be acting at all, just moving and

behaving in a completely natural way. There were long pauses in the dialogue as he moved about the stage, lighting a cigarette, patting a cushion, picking up a book or using the telephone. I was to meet him in later years when, as an old Harrovian, he brought his daughter Daphne to the Eton and Harrow match at Lord's.

In complete contrast, but very much to my taste, were Fred and Adele Astaire in *Funny Face* with Leslie Henson supplying the comedy. They were a superb singing and dancing partnership, and I particularly remember their 'Oompah Trot' where they trotted round and round the stage, getting faster and faster as they went.

So I had seen a straight play and a musical, and my next yearly treat was a visit to the Aldwych theatre to see the Ben Travers's farces with Ralph Lynn, Tom Walls, Robertson Hare, Mary Brough and Winifred Shotter.

These farces usually ran for about a year and I used to catch them on my way back to Eton. I was always given some journey money to get myself a meal, but I used to spend it instead on a seat in the stalls. Lynn and Walls were a great partnership with perfect timing – the secret of all farces.

During the thirties I switched my allegiance to the music-hall, and saw only a few plays and musicals, one of the latter being *Anything Goes* with that lovely Yorkshire comedian Sydney Howard in the part of the gangster/clergyman. For some reason (which I always regret) I never went to see any of the Ivor Novello musicals at Drury Lane – *Glamorous Night, Careless Rapture* or *Crest of the Wave*. It wasn't until the war started that I went to see *The Dancing Years*, and was enchanted, and of course then saw his remaining shows *Perchance to Dream* and *King's Rhapsody*. I was lucky enough to meet him one night at supper in the Savoy Grill. Zena Dare was one of the regulars in his shows and her daughter arranged the supper after we had seen *Perchance to Dream*. The hit song was of course 'We'll Gather Lilacs' which I had first heard Ivor play at an open-air concert in an orchard in Normandy in 1944. It seemed to me that in the show this essentially romantic love song was rather thrown away, sung as a duet by Olive Gilbert and Muriel

2

Barron. Right at the end of the show Ivor sat playing nothing in particular at the piano, while Roma Beaumont slowly walked up a staircase as the curtain dropped.

I had the temerity to suggest to him that Roma should stop halfway up the staircase and sing a chorus of 'Lilacs' to him before disappearing from sight. He didn't seem to mind my cheek and unbelievably a fortnight later the change was made.

There was one other actor I met before the war when I was staying down in Bude during a vacation from Oxford. A girl called Marjorie Thomas told us that an impoverished actor from the Liverpool Repertory was coming to stay with her, and that we were to be nice to him, and see that he didn't have to stand any drinks. He duly arrived with a monocle and sleek black hair and played quite a good game of table tennis, in spite of being terribly short-sighted. Just before the war he married Marjorie who promptly changed her name to Colette and became the first of Rex Harrison's wives.

For a few years before the war I shared a house with William Douglas-Home who had been to RADA and was doing a bit of acting in the West End, as well as starting to write plays. He was appearing in Dodie Smith's *Bonnet Over the Windmill* and became engaged to Ronald Squire's daughter who was also in the cast. The engagement didn't last long and it became extremely embarrassing for William once it was broken off. The trouble was that every night in the play he had to propose to her which, after all the publicity they had had, got a few titters from the audience.

In 1938 I thought I might follow William and try to be an actor, instead of working in the family coffee business. I had only ever acted in one play, when I played the part of the silly-ass detective in *The Ghost Train* by Arnold Ridley. I thoroughly enjoyed myself but had no real illusions that I was any good. However, I had got some laughs in the play, and learnt what a marvellous tonic laughter can be.

I thought that before making any decision I would go to a fortune-teller to find out what my prospects would be. I read about a lady near Olympia who had just read the hand of the Duchess of Kent. So I went along to see her and she went through all the paraphernalia of cards, examining the lines on my hands and even taking a look at my stars.

When she had finished she said that one day I would be well known and recommended that I should have a go at being an actor. She even asked me to sign a 'future celebrity' book because she was so certain that I would be successful.

I was delighted at the time and left her determined to try and go on the stage. But in the cold light of day I realised what a big step it would be for me to leave a good job in my family firm and risk being a failure as an actor. So to my eternal discredit I decided to continue with my humdrum city life. I just hadn't got the guts to change.

When I joined the BBC in January 1946 I fell on my feet. I joined the Outside Broadcasts Department and was allotted to help John Ellison with live broadcasts from theatres and music-halls. My job was to arrange these. It meant getting in touch with the managements to see if they wanted to have a broadcast from their show, and the only refusal – due to some complicated contractual rights – was from *My Fair Lady*. The theatres realised the publicity value to be gained from radio when, if the BBC audience liked what they *heard*, they would then go along to the theatre and pay to *see* it.

This meant that I had two very important things to do. It was essential to pick the best part of the show to broadcast, i.e. with plenty of the hit songs, supported by some of the comedy. If this was visual the second thing I had to do was to give a descriptive commentary on anything happening on the stage, in order to make it clear to the listeners at home.

It was a splendid job and meant that I had to deal directly with producers, managers and the stars of the shows themselves – people like Val Parnell, Emile and Prince Littler, Jack Hylton, Harold Fielding, Lee Ephraim and Bertram Montague. We needed 100 per cent cooperation from the stars because it was essential that they 'favoured' the microphones when singing or talking. There were also occasions when for timing reasons, or even censorship, we might have to ask for certain cuts.

The first show in which I was involved was *Song of Norway*, followed by *Under the Counter* with Cicely Courtneidge and Jack

Hulbert, which started a long friendship. Jack was a very strict producer who worked his choruses very hard until they reached perfection. Cis was as lively and funny off stage as she was on stage. I have never met anyone with greater vitality, something recognised by Ivor Novello when he wrote a musical called *Gay's the Word* especially for her, with a hit song called 'Vitality'. (Incidentally, could Ivor have been able to use that title today?) After that show followed shows such as *Oklahoma!*, *Annie Get Your Gun*, *South Pacific*, *Carousel*, *Call Me Madam*, plus a pantomime each year from one of the big London theatres.

Later on television entered the scene and I used to sit in a box and introduce the shows – mostly comedies, not musicals, and a number of Brian Rix's farces from the Whitehall Theatre.

Brian had gathered around him a regular team under Wally Douglas the producer. It was like the old Aldwych days – a repertory of farce.

One of my favourites in his team was Leo Franklyn, father of William Franklyn, and an old-time musical comedy comedian in the style of Leslie Henson, Laddie Cliff or Stanley Lupino. I remember in one farce when he was a hotel porter, one of the guests rang down and asked indignantly, 'Where's the chambermaid?' to which Leo replied, 'I don't know, sir, but probably in Stoke-on-Trent or somewhere else in the Potteries.'

All these live theatre shows gradually became far too expensive due to the increased demands from the Musicians' Union and Equity.

My association with actors and actresses has continued right up to the present day in a number of interview programmes for both television and radio. On TV, Channel 4 had a programme called *Years Ahead* which was primarily for the elderly or 'wrinklies' as we call ourselves. I was given an interview spot in this with elderly artists, most of them still working, as an encouragement to the older viewers not to retire completely but to ensure that they had some hobbies or interests to keep their brains alert and working.

ITV in conjunction with MENCAP put on another interview series called *A Chance to Remember* in which I invited famous actors and actresses to recall past memories, helped by a little gentle jogging of their memories by me (see p. 11). And then on Radio 3 during the Saturday luncheon intervals of the Test matches we invite lovers of cricket – not necessarily good players – to come and have a chat in the commentary box about themselves and their love of cricket. This we call *View from the Boundary*, and the BBC have published a book of that name with transcripts of the conversations.

I have thus been privileged to meet and make friends with a large number of theatrical people and have made a list of them all to show what a large variety have taken part (see p. 203).

There are many stories about the stage, and here are just four of my favourites.

Two actors were sitting talking on a sofa during a play when suddenly the telephone in the room started to ring. This was not in the script so the actors ignored it and just went on with their dialogue. But the ringing went on and on. Neither wanted to get up and answer it as it would mean ad libbing when they took off the receiver. Finally something had to be done as the audience were beginning to roar with laughter. So one of the actors finally had to get up and go to the telephone. He lifted the receiver as the audience went silent, anxious to know who this mysterious call was from. He listened for a few seconds and then turned to his fellow actor and said, 'It's for you!' (Collapse of actor on the sofa.)

Dulcie Gray told me a marvellous story of when she was once appearing in the Regent's Park open-air theatre. It was a glorious summer and during one matinée the audience were basking in shirt-sleeves under the hot sunshine.

It was the custom at the theatre that when it rained, the audience and the actors would take shelter in a large marquee, where the performance would be continued under cover.

Robert Atkins was the producer at the time and had had occasion to give notice to a young actor for some

6

misdemeanour, and this matinée was his last performance. He had a very small part and only had a few words to say at the beginning of one scene.

He made his appearance on cue but instead of delivering his short speech, he stepped forward and announced to the perspiring audience in a loud voice, 'Due to the inclement weather the producer has decided that the performance will now be continued inside the marquee.' Being an English audience, they just gathered up their things and went off to the marquee without a murmur!

I was told this same story by both Googie Withers and Dulcie Gray of what happened during a matinée performance in the Chichester theatre. I am still not certain to which of them it really happened.

Anyway, one of them was acting a scene in a drawing-room and carrying on a conversation with an actor. Suddenly from the front row of the stalls an elderly lady in a Miss Marples hat got up and made her way onto the stage. She sat down in an armchair, took out her knitting and without saying a word listened to the conversation between the actor and actress. There was great excitement from the prompt corner but there was really nothing they could do except ring down the curtain, which they obviously did not want to do. However, after about five minutes the lady picked up her knitting, got up and walked back into the auditorium and out of the theatre. The audience were amused and also bemused. They couldn't work out if it was all part of the play. What happened to the old lady, who she was, and why she did what she did was not revealed.

An old Shakespearian actor was on tour playing King Henry VI in *King Henry VI, Part Two*. He was well known for his liking for the bottle and was frequently the worse for wear on stage. There was an up-and-coming young actor on the tour playing the part of the Duke of Buckingham.

One morning the old actor persuaded the young actor to meet him for a pub lunch before the matinée. As usual he imbibed freely and plied his young friend with glass after glass of whisky.

By the time they had to go to the theatre they were both in a pretty poor state. At the start of the play the King enters a stateroom accompanied by the Queen and various Dukes. After a short welcoming speech by the Duke of Suffolk, the King has to reply and on this occasion he staggered forward and began to lurch around the stage, slurring his words. He was more or less incomprehensible and the audience began to boo and barrack him. He began to shout and his words became completely lost. There were odd cries from the audience of 'You're drunk. Get off!' This infuriated him and drawing himself up to his full height he blurted out, 'If you think *I'm* pissed, wait till you hear the Duke of Buckingham.'

Lord's Taverners

One of my main contacts with actors has been through the Lord's Taverners. This philanthropic body of cricket lovers was founded in July 1950. Because – except for matinées – actors work in the evening, many of them had the time to go to Lord's to watch cricket. Their inevitable meeting place was outside the old Tavern from where, with their glass of beer in their hands, they were able to enjoy the genius of Denis Compton in his halcyon and pre-knee-trouble days.

They enjoyed their cricket so much that they thought they should share this enjoyment and enthusiasm for the game in a practical way. Under the initial leadership of the founder, Martin Boddey, they decided to form a club made up of members of the arts – actors, writers, journalists, poets, musicians, broadcasters and so on. Their modest object at the start was to provide cricket gear and equipment for small clubs and youth organisations especially to encourage youth cricket.

This grew to helping build pavilions and laying down concrete pitches for practice in schools and/or village grounds.

After HRH Prince Philip had agreed to become Patron and Twelfth Man they channelled their funds through the National Playing Fields Association for the benefit of youth cricket. The funds were generated from an annual ball at Grosvenor House, cricket matches, boxing evenings, golf days and so on. Members paid a £1.00 entrance fee and in the first year I believe the Taverners distributed £18,000. In 1990 the sum was £1,500,000.

Thus have the Lord's Taverners grown in forty-one years. Their membership from the original few has now grown to 1,500, made up not just from the artistic world but from all walks of life, especially businessmen who have contributed so generously. One of the main targets for their money these days is the provision of minibuses for the mentally and physically handicapped.

But to be a Lord's Taverner there is still one vital qualification needed. You must be a lover of cricket. The Taverner's saga is yet another example of the extraordinary bond between cricket and the world of entertainment which has existed for so many years. Both aim – or should do – to provide fun and entertainment. Long may they continue to do so.

As a matter of interest I have included on p. 11 a list of some of the first hundred or so actors who joined the Lord's Taverners over forty years ago. Great names and an awe-inspiring collection of talent and artistic skills.

I must also add that in the past – I'm not so sure about today – this love of cricket was not just confined to *actors*. In the old Q stand – now the Allen stand – Gladys Henson and Celia Johnson were often to be seen, whilst I am reliably informed that the late Dame Peggy Ashcroft listened avidly to *Test Match Special* when on a film set or during rehearsals for a play.

Alas, I cannot boast of ever treading the boards with any straight actor or actress – unlike in the music-hall (see *M for Music-Hall*) – but I did once appear in a film. In 1950 I received a telephone call from Herbert Wilcox's secretary asking whether I could go down at short notice the next day to Shepperton Studios.

Herbert was filming *Derby Day*, and suddenly discovered he needed an interview with Peter Graves in the paddock at Epsom Races. I leapt at the idea and was told to report at some ghastly hour at Shepperton Studios the next morning wearing – if I had it – my own morning suit. Luckily I had one and on arrival was greeted by Herbert who said he wanted an interview of roughly one minute. Peter and I could work out the initial dialogue but in the final ten seconds or so I had to be sure to put a certain question to Peter.

It was all delightfully vague and all the technicians were very helpful and friendly and keen to know how good the visiting West Indies team was.

The one trouble was that Peter was a tremendous giggler and I'm afraid we had to do one or two retakes because we started to laugh. I am very bad at this and over the years have often broken down laughing during an interview. I have now found that the secret is not to look the interviewee in the eye.

Anyway, Herbert seem quite pleased with the result and when to my horror BBC 1 showed the film in 1972, I was amazed to see that our interview had not been cut in any way.

I was also proud and delighted when on one MCC tour in Australia where Anna Neagle was appearing in *Charlie Girl* Herbert introduced me to someone as follows: 'This is Brian Johnston. He played for me in one of my films!'

In 1990/91 the BBC decided to revive a sort of *In Town Tonight* on Saturday nights on Radio 2. I say 'sort of' because in fact they decided not to do it live like *In Town Tonight* but to record it on the previous Friday evening. It was called *Bob Holness Requests the Pleasure*, and was a mixture of interviews, comedy and music provided by a Big Band. They kindly asked me to take part in some way and accepted my suggestion of something which I had always wanted to do. I have visited eighteen West End theatres and interviewed various stars in their dressing-rooms. The title of this ingredient was *Stage Door Johnners* and on p. 12 is a list of those whom I interviewed.

I list 'theatre' as one of my hobbies in Who's Who and Pauline and I go as often as we can afford it. We favour comedies, farces, thrillers and musicals. We are not too keen on the more serious side such as Shakespeare, Ibsen and Chekov. Our main complaint is that the modern musicals have so few good tunes. Lloyd-Webber produces two per show but the fashionable Sondheim rarely composes anything which one can hum or whistle. *Follies* was billed as 'the musical of the year' but I successfully defied anyone who had seen it to hum me a single tune. This was also true of the successful and spectacular *Miss Saigon*. I always feel so sorry for the singers trying to sing a non-tune. Oh for Kern, Berlin, Rodgers, Porter and Lowe, who usually supplied four or five hit songs in every show. Their melodies certainly linger on.

Early Lord's Taverners	Martin Boddey	Bruce Seton
	John Snagge	Tony Britton
	Richard Attenborough	David Tomlinson
	Ian Carmichael	Donald Houston
	John McCallum	Guy Middleton
	Nigel Patrick	John Mills
	Stephen Mitchell	Jack Hawkins
	Richard Hearne	Ronnie Waldman
	Denholm Elliott	Richard Burton
	Robertson Hare	Terence Rattigan
	Naunton Wayne	Garry Marsh
	Bernard Lee	Frank Lawton
	Carleton Hobbs	Roger Livesey

Actors and Actresses Who Took a Chance to Remember	Donald Sinden	Brian Rix
	Christopher Lee	Glenda Jackson
	Richard Todd	Anthony Quayle
	Leslie Phillips	Michael Hordern
	John McCallum	Lionel Jeffries
	Googie Withers	Bryan Forbes
	Michael Denison	Nanette Newman
	Dulcie Gray	Sylvia Syms
	Hayley Mills	Phyllis Calvert
	Gordon Jackson	

B
for Boat Race

No one was more surprised than I was when in 1947 my boss in the Outside Broadcasts Department of the BBC (Seymour de Lotbinière – known as Lobby) asked me to take part in the annual radio broadcast of the Boat Race.

I had only joined the department in January 1946 and except for commentaries from theatres, the only *sporting* commentary I had done was for television at cricket, in the two London Tests against India. So I was very much a dry bob and always had been. The only time I ever rowed was at Oxford in an annual contest for Old Etonians against Old Harrovians. We would get the college boatmen to take up two eights to the Trout Inn at Godstow – almost a mile and a half up stream. We would have an uproarious supper, and then just before it got dark, stagger out to our boats and race back to the boat-houses in Oxford. As Eton was a rowing school and Harrow was not, the Etonians invariably won. I somehow got myself elected as 'President' so always chose to row at stroke so that if I got tired I could slow things down.

I don't think Lobby knew anything about this but he had somehow discovered that my father had been an Oxford blue, and had rowed in the Boat Race in 1899 and 1900. This has always been a bit of a joke among my colleagues as they were not very successful years so far as Oxford was concerned. They lost in 1899 by 3¼ lengths and so ended a run of nine consecutive victories. But 1900 was even worse. Oxford lost by 20 lengths – still the biggest distance ever recorded in any of the Boat Races, though up to then the distance of victory was also occasionally recorded as 'easily'.

Lobby somehow imagined that as a son of an old blue I would be a natural to commentate on the race.

So began forty-two enjoyable years in which I got to know well all the rowing fraternity. They are a very friendly lot of people and kindly made me welcome, though they must inwardly have wondered what on earth a cricket commentator was doing in their midst.

That first year Lobby stationed me on a small floating platform just alongside Hammersmith Bridge. The idea was to get the full flavour of the crews shooting under the bridge. I think I had about a minute to try and describe what I saw before handing back to John Snagge on the launch.

From then on I broadcast from a number of positions – from the tow-path, the top of Harrods and after 1952 mostly from Chiswick Bridge just beyond the finish. The reason for this was that in 1952 the BBC launch broke down at Duke's Meadow and was almost swamped by the flotilla of steamers who always follow behind the official launches.

This was a tragedy for poor John as it meant he could not see the end of the race. As his launch got further and further behind he tried valiantly to cope and came out with his immortal line, 'I can't see who is in the lead – it's either Oxford or Cambridge.' At this point Lobby who was directing affairs from the studio decided to switch to the TV commentary by Michael Henderson, which was admirable if you also had a picture to watch, but quite inadequate if you were just listening.

The whole thing was made worse by the fact that it was one of the greatest and closest races ever, Christopher Davidge's Oxford crew winning by a mere canvas, which had never been done before and only once since – in 1980.

Lobby decided that from then on there must always be someone on Chiswick Bridge so that if the launch ever broke down again, there would at least be someone in a position to describe the finish. It was to be my commentary position for most of the next twenty-five years, though I see in my diaries that for some reason I worked for TV in 1955, 1956 and 1957, interviewing experts on the tow-path at Putney before the race.

The job for the Chiswick commentator was strictly laid down. After Barnes Bridge there is a big bend towards the Middlesex side and as the crews row round the bend, they come within sight of Chiswick Bridge. Just before they reached the Mortlake Brewery John would hand over to the Chiswick commentator who would have about a minute's commentary before handing back to John to describe the finish from the launch.

The position was a safety valve, and not really necessary unless there was a crisis. There were *two*. The first was in 1978 when Cambridge sank shortly after passing under Barnes Bridge. For one or two years I had been following the race in the launch to act as a link man with the various commentary points along the course. This took the weight off John so that he did not have to worry about when to cue over or to whom. He could just concentrate on the race.

As we saw the Cambridge crew struggling in the water we obviously had to stop to help them, and I was able to cue over to Peter Jones on Chiswick Bridge to commentate on the rest of the race, which was Oxford coming home alone and winning in the fast time of 18 minutes, 58 seconds.

The second occasion was in 1990, the year following my retirement from the race. Peter Jones had taken my place in the launch with Dan Topolski doing the main commentary. Peter was a brilliant commentator with a Welsh flow of language matched by his descriptive powers and enthusiasm. He was best known of course for his soccer commentaries, but in recent years had become the big events man, gradually taking the place of Robert Hudson.

He had been on the Boat Race several times, either from Chiswick Bridge or once on the launch just after John retired. He sounded in his usual good form as the crews raced towards Hammersmith Bridge. For the first time for forty-two years I was at home listening to the race. I heard Dan saying 'Oxford are just shooting Hammersmith Bridge and we'll get the time . . .' There were then some mumbled words barely distinguishable though the words 'stopwatch' and 'say something' could be heard in the background. There was a moment's pause when all we heard was the rush of water as the launch shot the bridge. Dan, sounding slightly shaky, took up the commentary and in a few seconds cued over to David Mercer on the Middlesex bank nearly opposite the Chiswick steps.

I had suspected that something had gone badly wrong when we didn't get the time at Hammersmith Bridge. Now I knew for certain, because at that point David Mercer could not possibly get a good view of the crews. He carried on gamely until eventually the crews did draw level with him, after which he handed back to Peter Jones on the launch.

Instead of Peter we heard Dan who after a brief commentary cued over to Tony Adamson and Tom Boswell on Chiswick Bridge. I was then even more certain that something was going seriously wrong because it would be at least seven minutes or so before they could see the crews from Chiswick Bridge – after they had come round the bend after Barnes Bridge. Tony and Tom stalled for a time with Tony interviewing Tom about the race so far. They had of course been listening and also had a small TV monitor so they knew that Oxford were leading by about three lengths.

After a few minutes they (significantly) handed back to Dan who carried on the commentary until he said the launch was dropping behind, and called up Tony and Tom to describe the last two or three minutes of the race. When they had given the result they quickly handed back to the studio without waiting even for the official time of the race.

What had happened was that just before Hammersmith Bridge Peter suddenly collapsed, his voice tailing away. The producer in the launch quickly let the main control point know what had happened and told Dan to hand over to David Mercer.

The BBC team at all points did a magnificent job trying to carry on as if nothing had happened, and Dan Topolski deserves a special pat on the back. There was an ambulance waiting for them at the Ibis boat-house, and Peter was rushed to hospital where he so sadly died. It must rank as one of the most dramatic broadcasts ever and a perfect example of 'the show must go on'. I immediately telephoned the BBC as soon as it finished and was told what had happened. I felt terrible about it. Not only was Peter a very good friend and colleague of long standing, but he had taken my place in the launch. He has been sadly missed not only for his enthusiastic, authoritative and descriptive commentaries, but for himself – a modest, amusing, friendly and thoroughly nice man.

The Boat Race itself is a unique, totally illogical and typically British event. In contrast to the smooth straight stretches of the Olympic and National courses, it is raced over four and a quarter miles of twists and turns on the Thames. If you have ever looked down from an aeroplane onto the course, it looks like a giant corkscrew.

The crews have to contend with currents, tides and sometimes impossibly rough water. They have to train for it throughout the winter months, regardless of snow, frost or rain. It calls for tremendous guts and physical endurance and dedication beyond all reason. It is not just brute strength that is required, though it does help. Sometimes it proves just too much for a human being and I have seen two men – both for Oxford – who collapsed during the race, though strangely in spite of the handicap Oxford won on both occasions.

Lobby had known that both John and myself had been to Oxford but relied on our BBC training to sound completely impartial. Mind you, to start with it wasn't too easy not to sound depressed as Cambridge won for my first five years.

1980 was a sad year because after fifty years John Snagge retired, having commentated on forty-four Boat Races. But he went on with a bang. He was able to describe the thrilling finish when once again Oxford just won by a canvas. John had rowed at Pembroke College, Oxford but did not get a blue. He broadcast his first Boat Race in 1931 and continued except for the war up to 1980. He personified all that was good about the Boat Race with his deep unmistakable voice, his great knowledge of the history, the course and the technicalities of rowing itself. Everyone knew him and respected him, and every year before the race he would be asked to dine with each crew. They felt that they could trust him. He showed his thanks by presenting to the Presidents a golden sovereign dated 1829 – the first year of the race – and this coin is always used for the toss before the race.

John became such a part of the Boat Race that a lot of people thought it would stop when he retired. Luckily it didn't as I had the honour of taking his place in the launch until I retired in 1989. What fun I have had and what wonderful people I have had to work with. I must make special mention of the two Toms – Sutton and Boswell.

Tom Sutton was the Bill Frindall of the Boat Race, a statistician steeped in the history and records of the race. For years he kept John and myself – and seemingly everyone else either on TV, radio or the press – with the minutest detail of everyone and everything to do with the race. He was invaluable and an unfailingly cheerful companion.

So was Tom Boswell who so sadly died in 1990. He gave us tremendous help behind the scenes, with advice about launches, and his great knowledge about the Tideway. He was usually the 'expert' on Chiswick Bridge to help the likes of me and Christopher Martin-Jenkins. We couldn't have done without him, and he is sadly missed.

It was Tom to whom an enthusiastic lady came up during one broadcast rehearsal on the Friday before the race. 'Do tell me something,' she asked. 'I'm a great supporter of the Boat Race and I come to watch it without fail every year, and I shall be on the tow-path as usual tomorrow. But please explain one thing to me. Why are the same two teams always in the final?'

Appropriately the best story of the Boat Race concerns John Snagge. Every year when his launch approached Duke's Meadow, John would look at a flagpole where every year a man ran up a dark blue or light blue flag according to which crew was in the lead. By separating the flags he also tried to indicate the distance between the two boats.

John found this a very useful guide as at this point his launch was possibly fifty yards or so behind the boats. Since the man had a sideways view of the race he had a better idea than John of the exact distance between them. So John would say, 'I can see the flags going up on Duke's Meadow. It looks as if Cambridge is definitely in the lead by two lengths.'

At some rowing function someone pointed out this man to John. Neither of them had ever met. So John went up to him and said, 'I'm told you are the man who operates the flags on Duke's Meadow.' 'Yes, sir, I am,' he replied. 'Oh, do tell me then, how do you always get the flags in exactly the right positions? You must have very good judgement.' 'Oh no,' said the man, 'it's quite easy really. I just listen to John Snagge on the radio!'

Quite out of line with the sporting character of the Boat Race was the amazing behind-the-scenes mutiny by a group of Americans during the winter of 1986/87. The whole story has been dramatically told in a book by Dan Topolski and Patrick Robinson, called *True Blue*. It's one of the most gripping stories I have ever read. I was given it for Christmas and had finished it by the end of Boxing Day.

It tells how Dan and the Oxford President Donald Mac-Donald fought off the mutineers, and with a depleted Oxford crew and with the bookies making Cambridge 6–1 on favourites, won an emotional and totally unexpected victory in the race.

Thanks to the brilliant coaching of Dan, Oxford had won a record ten consecutive victories, until being beaten in 1986. It was then that the group of Americans, including blues and international oarsmen, decided to challenge Dan's methods of training. They didn't think that the long hard winter grind was necessary. They thought he had too much authority, and tried their best to oust him and the President, and so take over the Boat Club.

I had been particularly busy that winter recording my last *Down Your Way*s and having many speaking engagements. It wasn't until after the race that I really realised exactly what had been going on. I remember seeing MacDonald standing up in triumph as the winning Oxford boat passed under Chiswick Bridge. I realised then that victory meant something very special to him. Exactly how much, I learnt when told how he had waited at the boat-house to greet Dan when he came ashore from his launch. He gave him a great hug and uttered words which brought tears to my eyes when I was told them.

'We could have been disqualified out there, Dan.'

'What on earth do you mean?' asked Dan.

'Because we had ten men in our boat, and they only had nine.'

A tribute to their great friendship and partnership which had overcome the mutiny and won the race for Oxford.

Just one final thought about the Boat Race. As an Oxford man, how sad I was to see the boorish and unsporting behaviour of the Oxford crew – especially by their President – at the end of the 1991 race which Oxford won so easily by 4½ lengths. The main justification for the continuance of this private match between the two universities is that it should be conducted in a sporting and chivalrous way. One of Oxford's complaints was that Cambridge did not reply to their 'three cheers' at the end of the race. Considering that the whole Cambridge crew were in a state of collapse – heads between knees – it's difficult to see how physically they *could* have returned the 'three cheers'. And some of the remarks made afterwards were totally unnecessary and spoilt the whole image of the race for many people. Of course there has to be competitive needle before and during such a contest but for goodness' sake when it's all over at least shake hands and either congratulate or commiserate.

C
for Coffee

The song was quite right. There *is* an awful lot of coffee in Brazil. There was in 1842 too, when my great-grandfather Edward Johnston founded the firm of E. Johnston to export coffee from Santos in Brazil.

The firm went through the usual periods of success and depression common to all businesses. It was later formed into a group of companies under the name Brazilian Warrant, and in the late twenties and thirties suffered badly from the collapse of the Brazilian currency and such overproduction of coffee that much of it had to be burnt.

The family business, in which we still had shares, was always in the background of my early life. There had, however, not been a member of the Johnston family in it since my father died in 1922. They always tried to tempt myself or one of my two brothers back into the fold.

This was the position in 1934 when I was due to come down from Oxford with no other job prospect in mind. I secretly had no wish to join it, but as there was no immediate alternative – I had toyed with the idea of being a schoolmaster or even an actor – I weakened and started my business career with the Brazilian Warrant in October 1934.

So I became a white-collar boy, and each day like countless others I put my bowler hat on my head, my umbrella on my arm, and caught a tube train at the same time each morning from South Kensington station. Each day as I got into the train there was always one thought on my mind – was I in the same carriage as the 'Nodder'? I had given this name to a man who always travelled to the City at the same time. Whether the poor chap had a disease or not I don't know but I used to watch him, fascinated. He just sat reading the paper, sometimes nodding his head vigorously up and down as if in agreement with what he was reading, at other times shaking it from one side to the other as if he couldn't disagree more. It was very funny to watch and brightened those otherwise dull and crowded journeys.

For the first year in the City I started at what is known as 'the bottom'. That applied to my salary too! I learnt to type with one finger (or two if in a hurry), I made up contracts, decoded cables, and was introduced to such financial intricacies as 'draft at ninety days' sight' or 'cash against documents less 2½ per cent'. I know that some people understand these sort of things, but I never did. I was also taught how to taste coffee. A fascinating business – one dips a spoon into a cup of piping hot coffee (no sugar or milk!), swills it around in the mouth and spits it out into a huge spittoon. I must admit I have often wanted to do this to some of the coffee one gets in England – even with sugar and milk! I soon learnt to nod my head wisely and pretend I knew which was good and which was bad. This constant sipping, alas, played havoc with the digestion. Although I enjoyed myself during this time I'm afraid I cannot pretend I enjoyed my job.

One of the other chaps who shared an office with me used to toss me for sixpence a time. We'd put down all the coins we had in our pockets and call heads or tails on the lot. One day we had all the coins down on the desk when we heard footsteps from the Chairman's office two doors away. I quickly covered the coins with an important letter and pretended to be discussing it with my colleague. Of course it was just this letter that the Chairman had come along to read. He came in and picked it up and there were all our coins lying guiltily in front of him. What he thought I do not know, but were our faces red!

After a year in the City I went to an agent in Hamburg for three months to learn a little German and something about the coffee trade there. This was in 1935 and even then our agent and his staff had to be members of the Nazi Party or (so they said) they wouldn't be given an import licence for coffee. I learnt a little German, and also to shake hands all round in the office on arrival in the morning, on going to and coming back from lunch, and again when we went home in the evening. One evening I was taken by these Nazis to a Party rally in a huge indoor sports hall to hear Goebbels speak. I didn't understand what he was saying but my friends translated from time to time. It was his famous 'guns or butter' speech and it was really terrifying to be a very obvious Englishman in civilian clothes, standing there among those shouting and cheering Nazis in uniform. At that time the small country of Memel was annoying the Nazis. I remember Goebbels saying it was just like a fly on one's nose: 'We shall flick it off when we can't stand it any more!'

After Hamburg I was packed off in 1936 to Brazil to learn the business at that end. It was a lovely voyage of seventeen days or so, calling at Lisbon on the way. It was my first time out of Europe and I revelled in the sunshine which became hotter and hotter as we went south. My destination was Santos, where our head office was, and the day before arriving there we had the thrill of entering Rio harbour at night with the magnificent illuminated figure of Christ looking down from thousands of feet above the entrance of the harbour. Rio itself is a lovely city – bathed in sunshine, with luxurious shops and hotels, beautiful women, golden sands, lively nightclubs – all right, I'll stop, but it's true. You ask anyone who has been there.

Santos is very different. It's a busy port, exporting coffee and cotton in fantastic quantities, but with little to offer in the way of entertainment except a beach, and few people live there for fun. It's a place for work, and Americans, Europeans and Brazilians alike did work very hard. There was a small English colony there, and quite a few Americans, and I soon settled down among them to learn more about coffee and quite a lot about life.

While there I had my first experience of acting and producing. I had always loved the theatre, especially revue and variety, but had never performed in public, reserving my attempts at being funny for my friends. In Brazil there were no other distractions except work, so we produced several revues and cabarets, and I even acted the 'funny man' in *The Ghost Train*.

This was produced by James Joint who was the British Consul in Santos at the time. He later became the Commercial Attaché at Buenos Aires, and the man who, by a strange coincidence, negotiated with the Argentinians over the meat question! When I knew him he unfortunately had no children, or else I'm sure they would have been known as the 'two veg'!

Besides playing quite a bit of cricket on matting, our American friends initiated us into the art of baseball and every Sunday morning the Limeys used to play the Yanks on the beach. Then came the great day when an American cruiser visited Santos and we challenged them to a proper game on the cricket ground. Imagine what a thrill I had when I went in and scored a home run. What a different game from cricket. When I went in the catcher kept up a running commentary: 'Come on boys, this Limey's no good, he'll never hit a thing, he's easy meat, heck I believe he's nervous. . . .' and so on. Naturally enough I missed the first two balls the pitcher sent down, but the constant chatter spurred me to better things, and at the third (my last chance) I let fly and luckily connected. The ball went soaring to where in cricket mid-off and extra cover would be fielding. For some unknown reason the Americans had no one out there, and by the time they retrieved the ball I had completed a home run, or rounder to anyone who doesn't know baseball. But oh, if only the wicket-keeper was allowed to talk like that in cricket. It would be too easy – I believe I would have played for England!

There was a large German colony there, who were most aggressive at the time. One man we particularly disliked used to travel to work on the same tram and we suspected him of being a spy. Herr Kurl was his name, and imagine our delight one day when he took his hat off and we saw that he was as bald as a coot!

I made several journeys inland to visit fazendas and coffee and cotton plantations. Except for the big towns, São Paulo, Rio, Santos, Bahía, etc., the country is very primitive and some of the main roads are little better than sand tracks. In the really hot weather (December to April) journeying by car was a nightmare because of the terrible dust. I didn't know this when

I was given a job soon after I arrived, to meet a very important American buyer at the docks. His liner was only calling in on its way to Buenos Aires and we'd been warned that he and his family would like a trip inland. So I ordered a car for them, and as it was a lovely fine day made sure it was an open tourer. They set off happily enough, smartly dressed, the American buyer in white panama and Palm-Beach suit, and his wife in the latest model from New York. I was waiting for them when they came back in the evening and I got the shock of my life. It might have been the Ink Spots going to a funeral. Their faces were black with dust and their clothes just one dark mess. I'm afraid we never got another order from that American buyer.

I had my first experiences, too, of the Carnival – when everyone goes mad for three days on end. All business is stopped and the streets are crowded with singing, dancing people. It is a fantastic and quite unbelievable sight to English eyes. They just never stop, in spite of the terrific heat, often nearly 100 °F in the shade – if you can find the shade. The revelry goes on all night too, with bands playing non-stop, no intervals and everyone just dancing round the room in long or short lines, like the Palais Glide. All the dancers, too, carry scent sprays which they squirt continuously over each other.

It was after one of these Carnivals when I had been in Santos for about eighteen months that I was struck down by a disease, quite common out there, called acute peripheral neuritis. I found my legs and arms gradually becoming paralysed, and in about two days was completely immobile.

I had to recuperate for six months before rejoining the firm in London round about the time of the Munich Crisis – I was given the title of London Manager, but still knew little about coffee, nor, to be honest, cared about it. I was sent on a short tour of our European agents which enabled me to visit Norway, Sweden and Denmark as well as France, Belgium and Holland. But the trip also included Hamburg just before Christmas. My friends in the office there still made me welcome but there was a nasty feeling of militancy and aggression in the attitude of everyone I met. I was glad to get back to my usual Christmas stocking.

D
for *Down Your Way*

Luck played a big part in my BBC career, and my participation in *Down Your Way* was no exception. It was not a programme to which I had regularly listened, though I had always enjoyed it when I did. I remember thinking of it as a worthy programme with entertainment value. It set out to promote the ordinary people of Great Britain and gave them the chance to air their views and tell the rest of the country all about their own particular city, town or village. It was very much *their* programme. They were the stars of the show and not the presenter however famous he might be as a broadcaster.

It started in December 1946 when the boxing and ice hockey commentator from Canada, Stewart Macpherson, recorded the first twelve programmes in different parts of London – the first one coming from Lambeth Walk. The format was roughly the same then as it was when I finished in 1987. Basically there would be six people interviewed, and they would each be asked to choose a piece of music. At the start the emphasis was more on the music than speech. The planners had seen the idea of the programme as providing them with music but interspersed with conversation in order to save needle time. This was a precious commodity at the BBC, as they were only allowed to play so many hours of recorded music over a year.

When Stewart started there was no preliminary contact with the place or people to be interviewed. His producer, John Shuter, would choose a particular district in London, look in the Post Office street address book and pick people out at random. Stewart would then go unannounced and knock on their door and do the interview.

This went quite well until the twelfth programme when a Mrs Brown had been picked out of the book as a possible victim. He went and knocked on her door which was answered by a large and ferocious-looking man. 'Is Mrs Brown in?' asked Stewart. 'Ah,' said the man, 'so you're the person who has been after my wife,' and threatened to slug Stewart, who beat a hasty retreat.

That was enough for him and he decided to stick to boxing and ice hockey – they were safer! Lionel Gamlin then recorded a few and Wynford Vaughan-Thomas the odd one. But they were only stand-bys although both famous as broadcasters.

It was decided that it would be the ideal vehicle for the friendly Richard Dimbleby and he recorded 300 programmes, until his TV commitments forced him to give it up. There was a slightly hiatus for about a year before another popular broadcaster took over. He was a newsreader and presenter of a variety of programmes, Franklin Engelmann, known to his friends as Jingle.

For the next nineteen years he recorded 733 programmes, not every week throughout the year, but with occasional breaks for him to present *Gardeners' Question Time* and a holiday programme.

On 1 March 1972, he had recorded his programme for the following Sunday. Phyllis Robinson and her co-producer Richard Burwood never kept a recorded programme in reserve in case of accidents. They took a tremendous gamble but it had worked. That night at home Jingle died of a heart attack but his programme was safe for the following Sunday. However, because they had no reserves, someone had to be found to take over and present the next recording due to be made the following Wednesday. And this is where my luck once again came in.

On Thursday I was walking down the corridor of our Outside Broadcast Department when the overall producer of the programme – Arthur Phillips – popped his head out of a door and asked if I had heard the sad news about Jingle. I hadn't, so he told me and asked whether I would like to take over the programme temporarily starting next Wednesday in Hyde in Cheshire.

There was no way I could refuse although I realised what a

28

tremendous challenge it would be to follow Jingle. It had become his programme and he had a large and faithful following. So it was with some trepidation that I undertook my first assignment in Hyde, Cheshire. I straight away apologised to listeners for my intrusion and promised that I would try my best not to let the programme down, and do it in my own way.

As it turned out I could only do ten programmes before my duties as BBC Cricket Correspondent took over during the summer. Four different interviewers were asked to fill in, until I was able to take it up again full-time from the beginning of October. By this time, aged sixty, I had had to retire from the BBC staff, and from then on I have worked as a freelance.

The procedure for recording the programme stayed roughly the same for the fifteen years in which I was in it. It went out on Sundays at 5.05 p.m. every week of the year, so with fifty-two programmes it was possible to cover most of Great Britain, the idea being to spread our recordings around the country. The producer, usually in consultation with me, would choose our location, often because we had received an invitation to pay it a visit.

He or she would then contact the Town Clerk or his equivalent and ask out of courtesy whether we might come. Of course they never refused. The producer would ask for a guidebook and for as much information as possible about the history, the industry and any annual traditional ceremonies or events which took place. The local press, and later local radio, were also useful providers of bits of news about the place or of any particular characters, or people with strange jobs or hobbies.

Armed with all this the producer would spend the Wednesday on location, finally choosing six 'victims' by the time I arrived about teatime. Only very occasionally did anyone not wish to appear, possibly because of shyness or some physical disability like deafness or a stutter. But mostly they were very happy to be chosen to represent their town or village, though sometimes our selections didn't meet with 100 per cent approval. 'Why didn't you have so-and-so, he's a great character.' We found to our occasional cost that many of the characters only came alight in a pub after having had a few – not ideal for broadcasting. We also tried to avoid too much officialdom such as the Mayor or Mayoress, admirable people though they undoubtedly were. We also had to take into account that in the previous week's programme we had had the local vicar, so took care not to have another for a week or so.

One thing we emphasised. We chose six people and we only recorded those six. Some programmes would have tended to record eight or ten people, and only to have broadcast the best six. But we thought that was unkind and humiliating to those left out. Only once did we break that rule. We decided to record the local schoolmaster about the history of a town. The interview was a disaster. I had only read the guidebook and I found myself having to prompt him about facts and dates.

He gave us a very good tea afterwards, which made it worse when on leaving we decided it would be unfair to his reputation to put it out. So Tony Smith had the inevitable task of going back and telling him. I think actually he was very relieved as he, better than anyone, knew how inadequate he had been.

People have often suggested that the programme ought to have been live and not recorded. It's also true to say that many people continued to think that it *was* live. But that would have of course been impossible to do because of the choice of a record after each interview. We couldn't carry around with us hundreds of records, and even with the tens of thousands which they have, the BBC gramophone library could not always immediately supply some of our requests. So just before each interview started we would ask the person what piece of music they were going to choose. If we were in any doubt the producer would ring up the BBC record library *before* the interview to check that they had it.

We were only caught out twice. Once a retired army officer asked for what he said was a famous military march. We both assumed that he knew what he was talking about, and pretended that we knew it well. When Tony Smith returned to Bristol he found that there was no such march in the BBC library, nor had the Military School of Music at Kneller Hall ever heard of it. So we had to substitute something else.

30

We had to do the same thing at Salisbury Cathedral one Christmas time, but for a different reason. We were interviewing the man responsible for the refabrication of the Cathedral's walls. He asked beforehand whether one of his young apprentices could choose the music. We agreed and when told what the choice was, stupidly did not check with the library, its title sounded so holy and Christmassy. In spite of this it turned out to be a particularly rude song which the BBC had banned from the air. So we chose a comparatively unknown carol instead and hoped the listeners would think it was what he had asked for.

Sometimes if I got to our place early enough we would record one interview on the Wednesday evening and do the other five on Thursday. The programme took about six and a half to seven hours to record, including lunch. We allowed an hour for each person and visited them in their home, office, factory, farm or shop – wherever they were. They always made us most welcome and offered us a variety of refreshments, depending on the time of day. Knowing me they often baked a special cake. One had to be careful not to overindulge in any place, otherwise we might insult the next person by having to refuse their hospitality. My main embarrassment was in Scotland where they were always apt to offer us 'a wee dram'. Unfortunately I loathe whisky but felt I had to say yes. Tony Smith luckily liked it so when he had quickly swilled his, I surreptitiously swapped glasses when no one was looking.

Each visit took the same pattern. We would chat for a few minutes, have our refreshment and then if they wanted or we felt it would help the interview, we would make a short tour of the shop, farm or factory. I would be chatting them up all the time in what I hoped was a friendly way, so that after about forty minutes or so I felt that I had got to know them and that they trusted me.

I would then say, 'I'm feeling broody now – what about us recording our conversation?' You will note that I called it a conversation and not an interview because I tried to be a friend and not an interrogator. We would then record about seven or eight minutes to which Tony – with his back turned to us –

would listen intently. At the end if he thought that there was something interesting which we had not covered, he would ask us to record another minute or so to include it.

We would then say goodbye and thank you, and set off for the next place. We got it off so pat that we never looked at our watches throughout our stay and nearly always ended up a couple of minutes either side of the hour.

The only exception to this procedure was when we were talking to a very old person. They tended to ramble on and had we kept to a tight timetable we might have missed their best story. So we would often record up to twenty minutes so as to capture every titbit.

After completing the six interviews my part in the programme was finished. The producer took the six tapes back to the BBC and spent Friday editing down the interviews to about four and a half to five minutes each, and slotting in the chosen pieces of music at the end of each interview. For most of my fifteen years the programme went out every Sunday, fifty-two weeks in the year. So occasionally we recorded two programmes in a week, going on to another place about fifty miles away for the second recording on Friday. This enabled us to stock up some reserves so the producer and I could take time off for holidays.

It was a lovely programme to do. I also visited places in Great Britain to which I had never gone, nor probably would have done, but for *Down Your Way*. In spite of urbanisation, motorways and pollution, we are still a beautiful country with spectacular scenery in addition to the green fields and picture-postcard villages. So I learnt a lot about the history, traditions, ancient ceremonies and customs. I wish I could swear that I remember it *all*, but I do have many happy memories.

But it was the *people* who made the programme so worth while. We read every day in the newspapers and see on the telly muggings, rapes, robberies and alas many murders too. But going round the country I realised there is a huge silent and unsung majority of people who spend much of their time caring for others – Round Table, Rotary, Lions, Mothers' Union, Women's Institute, Meals on Wheels, Mentally Handicapped, Help the Aged and so on. I met some marvellous people – over

4,500 – and they were so friendly and always made us feel at home. I still hear from some of them, or people will come up to me in the street and say, 'you won't remember, but you interviewed me on *Down Your Way* at such-and-such place.' I can't pretend I always remember them, but if they mention the town or village we met I can usually manage to remember two or three of the places we visited in them.

It's impossible to make a list of even a fraction of the characters I met and talked to, but there are one or two who stand out. There was Mrs Emily Brewster of Radcliffe-on-Trent. She had just had her 100th birthday when I visited her in her home surrounded by great-grandchildren. I asked her if she had enjoyed her birthday, and she said she had. I then asked if she had received a telegram from the Queen. 'Oh yes, I have,' she said, 'but I am a bit disappointed. It's not in her own handwriting!'

Then there was the old spinster of eighty-five who lived all alone in a house in Penkridge. It had been her father's farmhouse, but the land had long been built over. Remarkably she still did a milk round every day. But even more remarkable, she said she had slept every night of her life in that house. She had been for day trips to London or Great Yarmouth, but always came back home to sleep. Amazing really when you think how many nights the average person now spends away from home either on business, holidays or visits.

There were some people with unusual hobbies. One man in Kent collected prams. He had over 300, two-wheelers, four-wheelers, Victorian, modern, an extraordinary variety from all over the world. They were on his lawn, in all his living-rooms, and even in the bedrooms and bathroom. Just a wee bit eccentric perhaps, like the man who had a pipe museum consisting of (so he said) 20,000 different pipes, or the bottle collector in Alston who had 8,000 of all shapes and sizes in his small shop, which was visited by other collectors from all over the world.

But my favourite eccentric was a gentleman on the Welsh border. He plied us with some very sweet Madeira and then told us how in the war he had been sent to India to look after mules, who provided much of the transport in the mountainous regions. He was a vegetarian and thought he might not get sufficient green stuff out there. So he took hundreds of packets of mustard and cress seeds. At the end of a long, hot day he would take off his wellies, put some seed in them and go to bed. He assured us that come the morning he had a plateful of mustard and cress for his breakfast!

There were one or two people who kept animals in strange places. One man in Bedfordshire had ferrets down his trousers whilst I was talking to him. He said he now only used male ferrets, as the females *were* apt to bite his vital parts. In the same way the rat-catcher of Stockport used to pick out good-looking rats, and instead of killing them had them innoculated by the vet and then kept them in the back garden. He had at least a hundred which he leased out to film producers if they needed rats for a sewer scene or suchlike. There were three running round his neck and chest while he was talking to me. I admit I was terrified. I loathe rats.

One of the attractions of the programme was to try and guess what type of music each participant would choose. It was jolly difficult as a vicar might ask for the Beatles, whereas a roadsweeper might prefer a touch of Beethoven. I was also often surprised by the stories people told me *after* the interview. A dentist said he had wanted to tell the following story but didn't dare. He said an old lady had recently been to see him to have a tooth stopped. He was about to put the drill into her mouth when he had to withdraw it very quickly. 'Do you realise, madam,' he said, 'that your right hand is gripping me in a very vulnerable place?' 'Yes,' replied the old lady softly, 'we're not going to hurt each other, are we?'

Churches and vicars inevitably played a big part in *Down Your Way*. The church was so often the centre of life in the village or town, and the clergy by their profession were usually good talkers. I have never counted how many churches we included in my 733 programmes, but they ranged from all sizes and all ages. For example we went to the newest cathedral in the country at Coventry and in contrast to the tiny church of St Edmunds in the small hamlet of Greensted in Essex. It is the oldest wooden walled church *in the world* and goes back to 845 AD.

When we did a programme from York Minster my final interview was with the Archbishop of York in his palace at Bishopthorpe. After the interview the Archbishop kindly gave me a glass of sherry, and asked me if I would like to hear a story. I said I would be delighted to hear one from an archbishop.

So he told me that when God and Moses were 'negotiating' over the Commandments they went up on to Mount Sinai for six days and six nights. On the seventh morning Moses came down the mountainside through the early morning mist and summoned the multitude. When a large crowd had gathered he said, 'I have two bits of news for you about the new Commandments – one good, one bad. Which would you like first?' 'Give us the good news first, Moses,' shouted back the crowd. 'Right,' he said, 'the good news is that we've got them down to ten.' There were loud cheers from the crowd, and then came a subdued hush as Moses said, 'And now for the bad news – adultery is still in!' Not bad from an archbishop!

Finally there was the time when *I* was asked the question instead of me asking it. Luckily it was not in an interview but as we arrived and knocked on the door of a particularly small house in Kirkby Londsdale. There was our usual little party of the producer, engineer with his recorder and myself. A lady opened the door and must have wondered if she could accommodate us in her small sitting-room. But her question might have been differently phrased. 'Oh, good evening Mr Johnston, how nice to see you. Can you tell me the size of your equipment?!' I was tempted to say, 'That's not a matter which I wish to discuss with a stranger,' but I refrained, though I couldn't help laughing as I replied, 'Oh, it's quite small, our engineer is carrying it in his hands.'

E
for Eton

My father had been to Eton and my two brothers were there when my father died in 1922. It had always been assumed that I would also go there, and although not too well off after my father's death, the family somehow managed to scrape enough together to send me there in 1925.

For the next five years I enjoyed some of the happiest times of my life. Nowadays it is the fashion for some Old Boys to run Eton down and to reveal all the scandals and terrible goings-on that have taken place there. Perhaps I was just one of the lucky ones. Of course in any school things happen which would make the editor of a Sunday newspaper lick his chops. But for me Eton was a place where I made close friends and countless acquaintances among the boys and masters, or 'beaks' as they were known there, and most of these have remained so ever since.

One of the most remarkable things about Eton friendships is that you can meet someone whom you have not seen for years and within a moment you are back on the same wavelengths picking up exactly where you left off.

There is no point in denying that Eton is also a wonderful club. Some people call it the best trade union in the world and I would not argue with that. Certainly it is true that wherever I have been in Great Britain or all over the world I usually run into an Old Etonian and more often than not he has an important job or is in an influential position. So having been to Eton has been extremely useful and has opened countless doors. But perhaps more than anything about Eton I remember the laughter which was never very far away no matter what I was doing.

I joined my second brother Christopher in the house of R. H.

de Montmorency where we shared a room – my eldest brother Michael having left to go to a crammer. 'Monty' was a kind and friendly man who had been an international golfer and had got blues for both golf and cricket when up at Oxford. He was married and had two attractive daughters. The elder, Kathleen, used to wake us up as she returned in the wee small hours from parties in London, often with boyfriends driving an old Bentley with a strap around the bonnet.

The younger daughter Ann was only in her early teens and too young for that sort of thing but was a decorative part of the scene. I had not seen her since 1927 until I met her again as Jim Swanton's bride in 1958.

The actual building, Coleridge House, was in Keats Lane and was an absolute rabbit warren. I am certain that it would never have passed the fire and hygiene regulations of today. For just over forty boys there was exactly one bathroom and each boy was allocated ten minutes on one night only each week under the eagle eye of a KCB (Knight Commander of the Bath). Senior boys took it in turns to do this duty and had to keep a strict check on the time in the bath and the depth of the water. 'Monty' used to call everyone 'little boy' and if he found you in the bath on his nightly round of the house he would say, 'What are you doing, little boy?'

'Having a bath sir.'

'Lucky dog,' Monty would always reply and by God he was right! The only other means of washing, after football for instance, was in a tin bath in one's room which one had to fill and then empty – this was a particularly tricky job.

Each boy had a room to himself where he slept, worked and had tea. This was an admirable idea which gave even the smallest or newest boy a feeling of independence and a chance to shut himself off from the noise and bustle of school life. When I was at Eton there were coal fires in the rooms but you were only allowed a fire on three days a week plus Sunday. You can imagine how cold it was on winter evenings when it wasn't your turn to have a fire.

Boys used to 'mess' with each other for tea, sometimes just two but occasionally as many as four together. The room chosen for tea was the one which had the fire on that day. There was a 'night-watch' who used to go round the rooms in the middle of the night, scraping out the grates and taking away the ashes. She was a great character – a little Scotswoman with a wonderful flow of language which was given full rein when she tripped over some article or trap which we had deliberately set for her. Nowadays the houses have central heating but at least we had our beds made and rooms cleaned by maids – who are of course in very short supply these days.

The rooms were very comfortable with a wicker armchair, a 'burry' or desk, an ottoman, table and chairs and the bed which was pushed up into a recess in the wall during the daytime. As I said Monty used to go round the house each night and visit every boy in his room (or in the bath!) This was a basic part of the Eton education and an admirable idea. It enabled the boy and the housemaster to get to know each other, and to talk over problems of life or work in intimate surroundings. The housemaster could also hand out rockets in a more friendly and effective way than if he had to summon the boy officially to his study.

If you were a lower boy the peace of your room was often shattered by the cry of 'Boy'. All fags had to run to the library which was the sitting-room of the prefects or 'library' as they were called at Eton. The last boy to arrive had to do the job so if you had a room right at the top of the house you got more than your fair share of the work. How long you were a fag depended on what form you had taken on entering the school. I took middle fourth so had five halves' (a 'term' is called a 'half' at Eton) fagging before I became an upper as opposed to a lower boy.

There are many arguments for and against the fagging system, mostly against. On balance, so long as it is not abused and does not interfere with a boy's work, I am still in favour. In my time it certainly did affect one's work. I always had one ear cocked for a 'Boy' while trying to solve some tricky mathematical problem. I believe that nowadays there is a 'close season' during the evening when 'Boy' cannot be called, so that the lower boys can get on with their prep undisturbed.

Another point in favour of the fagging system is that a new boy often arrives with a slightly swollen head after being a prefect or Captain of the XI at his private school. Fagging brings him down to earth and teaches him the idea of service to others. It can help him to understand the point of view of those who provide a similar sort of service in later everyday life, and so treat them with courtesy and sympathy.

At Eton anyway fags took it in turns to do the teas for their 'masters' and so learnt simple cooking, like scrambled eggs. As a result I reckon I am the best scrambler in our family. In his last year or two when it comes to the turn of the fag to be the 'master', he now has a chance to learn how to give orders, to be considerate and not too demanding and above all to be fair. Of course some boys did – and probably still do – abuse these privileges. But they were very rare.

For obvious reasons, a referendum on corporal punishment would almost certainly show an overwhelming majority against. I would agree with this so far as corporal punishment given by the boys themselves is concerned. At Eton both the Captain of the House and Captain of Games had the power to beat but had to get the permission of the housemaster first. This he usually gave without too much investigation into the case and certainly in most cases not hearing the boy's side of the story. Once again the majority of senior boys played fair but there were undoubtedly grave abuses and I am sure that the beatings did the beater far more harm than they did the beaten good.

There were also grossly unfair things called general tannings. We had one once in my house when an unknown boy made some rude drawings on the wall of the lavatory. Nobody would own up and so after due warning the whole house was beaten by the 'library', getting about four strokes each. This naturally caused tremendous resentment and would never be tolerated today. A similar thing happened when I was a member of Pop. This was the Eton Society which consisted of about twenty-five of the senior boys in the school. The reason for the name 'Pop' is probably because although certain boys were *ex officio* members, most of them had to be elected. So, if you were unpopular, you did not get in.

39

There had been a series of fights between Eton boys and town boys in the area of the Arches which carried the railway line from Windsor to Slough. The headmaster, Dr Alington, was determined to stop these fights and warned the whole school to keep away from the Arches in future. One Sunday he ordered a swoop by members of Pop and we surrounded the area and took the names of all the boys found there – at least fifty.

The next day before chapel they were all summoned to the Pop room and beaten by senior members of Pop, although I am sure most had only been out for an innocent Sunday afternoon walk and had never fought with the town boys. Still, they had been warned. One of the victims, now a distinguished merchant banker, did manage to get his own back. The member of Pop who had beaten him was in the sixth form. This form used to walk in a file up the aisle to their seats in the chapel when everyone else was seated. The victim happened to have a seat on the 'knife board' as it was called – the front row of the stalls. As the sixth form walked solemnly by in slow time, he stuck out his foot and tripped up his beater who came an undignified cropper on the stone floor of the aisle!

Another controversial subject is compulsory games. Things have changed a lot now but in my time in the summer everyone on the three half holidays had either to play cricket or row. You were either a dry bob or a wet bob. It was as simple as that. Now you don't have to do either. You can play tennis, squash, golf, walk, swim or just play the guitar as my elder son Barry used to do! In some ways this is an improvement on the old system where a boy who hated cricket (there were and are such people, believe it or not!) was made to play in a badly organised game. The pitch was usually appalling, the scorers fiddled the scores and the umpires gave everyone out so that the game could finish quickly. It really was a farce. William Douglas-Home was one of these forced cricketers. At one time the Captain of the XI could not make a run for the school and the *Eton College Chronicle* reported that he had struck a bad patch. The following week William wrote a letter to the *Chronicle* saying that if the Captain of the XI would come and play on the sort of pitches William's game had to play on, he would strike a few more!

In the winter in the Christmas half everyone had to play the Eton Field Game, a mixture of soccer and rugger and an excellent game to play. The snag was that the only opponents the School XI – called the Field – could play were Old Etonians. The status of a boy in his house was judged by his skill at this game. Until you were good enough to play for your house you had to wear grey flannel knickerbockers to play in. Shorts were not permitted until you got into the House XI. Just imagine trying to run in such archaic clothing! Anyhow I was lucky because at Eton I suddenly discovered I could run fast, something I had never done at my private school. Speed was a very important factor in this particular game, so I quickly earned my shorts in my second year, and my house colours in my third.

Each day when there was not football against one of the other houses, a boy had to do 'time' – take some exercise such as a run, fives, squash, racquets, boxing or beagling. In the Easter half there was a choice of athletics, rugger and soccer to add to this list. I opted for rugger and in the end got into the school XV. But we were always very bad and used to get thrashed by astronomical totals by schools like Rugby, St Paul's, Beaumont and so on. Once again my running stood me in good stead. I was never a great tackler but prided myself on my skill at selling the dummy. Our house became great experts at seven-a-side and won the House Competition in my last year.

I was severely reprimanded after one match when the XV were playing the Welsh Guards from Windsor. They were a tough lot and in great trepidation I once actually fell on the ball in defence. The loose scrum, or ruck as it is called these days, formed round me and I was kicked and trodden on amidst shouts of 'Get off the ball!' From deep down I shouted 'Get off mine first!' which was considered very rude. Not half as rude in a physical sense as a rather fat boy called Burke who used to play in the second row of the scrum and let wind in a series of tremendous detonations. Eventually he had to be dropped from the side as they could get no volunteers to play in the back row of the scrum.

Looking back, the whole system may seem to have placed far too much emphasis on the ability to play games. However, this did ensure that everyone, even those who were no good, did take some form of regular exercise under supervision. Nowadays boys are left very much to their own devices, which at that age, though more pleasant for them is not necessarily a 'good thing'.

A perfect example of someone who loathed games, and of the bad effect they had on him, was Gilbert Harding. He was at a Roman Catholic school, was short-sighted, fat and hated all forms of exercise. He was so bad and made such a nuisance of himself that his headmaster finally excused him all games so long as he went for a walk instead. This infuriated the young cricket master who was a blue just down from Oxford. So when the annual match between the masters and the boys came along he thought he would get his revenge on Gilbert by appointing him as one of the umpires. The masters won the toss, the young blue went in first and hit the boys' bowling all over the field, so that he soon got into the nineties. A bowler bowling from Gilbert's end then got a ball to lift which struck the master high up on his chest. The bowler stifled an appeal for lbw but not before Gilbert had put his finger up signalling that the batsman was out. The master was furious and as he passed Gilbert he said, 'Harding, you were *not* paying attention. I was not out.' 'On the contrary', replied Gilbert with great satisfaction, 'I *was* paying attention and you were *not* out!'

Back to Eton, where my one and only disappointment was my failure to get into the cricket XI. I was still a wicket-keeper and each summer progressed up the scale getting my lower sixpenny, upper sixpenny, lower club and twenty-two – the various colours awarded to the twelve best players in each age group. But in upper sixpenny I blotted my copy book and so only just got my colours.

As usual, I was too frivolous and could not resist the chance of a laugh. I was batting with a boy called Hopetoun at the other end who was rather fat and not too quick over the ground. By some fluke I hit the ball quite a long way and called to him to run. I was pretty fast between the wickets and by the time he was turning to start his second run I had completed two so that we were then running level towards the bowler's end. I soon passed him again so that I had run four as he was halfway through his third. As you can imagine the whole field collapsed with laughter and when the inevitable happened and the ball was returned to the bowler's end no one could work out which batsman was out. All would have been well had not the captain of the XI happened to be watching from a distance and came over to see what all the uproar was about.

To put it mildly he was not too pleased. A similar thing happened in a house match and they all turned to the square-leg umpire for a decision, only to find that it had been his turn to bat and that he was now one of the batsmen concerned!

In my last year a boy called Baerlein who had kept wicket for the school for the last two years decided to stay on for another summer although he was over nineteen years old before the half started. Naturally for a time I felt miserable about the whole thing though everyone was very kind and sympathetic especially our school coach George Hirst, the famous old Yorkshire and England all-rounder. He had a sweet disposition and was loved by all the boys. I used to keep wicket to his bowling and once got a stumping on the leg-side off him much to our mutual satisfaction. Even in those days, aged sixty, he bowled a lively medium pace left arm round the wicket, and swung the ball prodigiously.

Anyway he took me under his wing and at the Eton and Harrow match took me around with him, to the dressing-rooms and even up to the scorer's box at the top of the grandstand. I had one slight compensation for not keeping wicket at the match. Eton had two very fast bowlers, one of whom was particularly wild and inaccurate. Poor Baerlein had a terrible time and actually let thirty-five byes. I would not have been human had I not had a quiet laugh. But I expect I would have let many more. Anyway I captained the Second XI or Twenty-two as it was called and had far more fun than I would have had in the more austere atmosphere of the first.

The Eton and Harrow match was a great occasion and all

the time I was at Eton and for many years afterwards we all used to congregate on Block G (now the Compton Stand) – the open stand to the right of the sight-screen at the nursery end. We barracked unmercifully, shouted ruderies and cracked jokes and it became like a club with everyone returning year after year. So far as we Etonians were concerned the stock jokes were usually about the age of the Harrow players or the number of foreigners or foreign-sounding names in their teams. In these days of race relations I am sure we would be imprisoned for some of the things we used to shout out. But it was all good fun, and some of my best friends have been those same Harrovians about whom we had been so rude.

The only man who ever took the slightest offence was an unsuspecting Harrow father sitting with his son watching the match. While he did so we fastened the end of his immaculate tailcoat to the seat with drawing pins, so that when he rose to leave he found himself attached to the seat. Childish I admit but we had to laugh and so did he in the end.

The great strength of Eton lay in the quality and character of its masters. I may be falling into the old trap but they certainly seemed greater characters then than the masters are today.

By far the wittiest was Tuppy Headlam who ruled over his house with a light rein. He seemed to inspire wit – or an attempt at it – from others. He was called 'the master with a soft "a"' and was the first port of call for many Old Etonians when revisiting the school, for he dispensed drinks or dinner with great generosity. During our time there he was especially friendly with the well-known film actress Anna May Wong. He taught us history and his classroom was in his house, and as he often received telephone calls we all took it in turns to go and answer them for him. One day, just after Anna May had been down to see him, the telephone rang and Martin Gilliat (now the Queen Mother's private secretary) was on telephone duty. As he left the room there was much speculation among us and Tuppy himself as to whether the caller would be Anna May. So there was quite a lot of excitement and then a hush as Gilliat returned.

'Who was it?' asked Tuppy.

'Sorry, sir', said Gilliat without a smile on his face, 'Wong number.'

Another character was Hope-Jones. He had black curly hair, a very loud voice and was a fitness fanatic. A tremendous enthusiast in everything he did, he was a very keen Scoutmaster. One rather cold day he told his Scout troop that he would be the hare and they the hounds. He would have a five minute start leaving a trail behind him and they were to see how soon they could find him. He went off and headed for a fairly deep pond by one of the playing-fields. He jumped into the water and waited for his Scouts to appear. When they did so he disappeared under the surface with just his nose above water so that he could breathe. Although the trail ended rather obviously at the edge of the pond the scouts pretended they could not find him, and searched all round the adjoining fields. Poor Hope-Jones had to stay submerged in the cold water.

One summer holiday he had a bit of bad luck. The headline in our morning paper read, 'Eton master caught bathing in the nude.' Poor chap – he had only gone for an early morning swim on some secluded beach in Cornwall and some nosey parker had sneaked to the police. In those days it was quite something and I believe he was fined for indecent exposure, so you can imagine all the talk when we got back to Eton.

Then there was Sam Slater, a frightening man with a red face and horn-rimmed spectacles. He used to let out the most enormous sneezes during class. This went on for quite a long time until the master in the next-door room could stand it no longer. His name was Lt.-Col. J.D. Hills, later to be headmaster of Bradfield. He commanded the corps and thanks to his habit of somewhat immodestly reminiscing about his wartime experiences, was known as 'the man who won the war'. Anyway he was determined to win this one and instructed everyone in his class to wait for the next sneeze from Slater and then at a signal from him, all were to sneeze as loudly as they could. The effect was magical. When Sam let out his next sneeze he was amazed to hear a deafening chorus of 'ah-ti-shoo's from Hills' classroom. He took the hint and in future sneezed in a more gentlemanly manner.

Mr Crace was a gentle person and looked like Mr Pickwick. We were in his class one day when a messenger brought him a note. He read it and for some reason seemed annoyed. It was from the Treasurer of the Eton mission who asked him if he would please collect from his class in the usual way. It was these last four words which got under his skin and he promptly announced that for the next week he would be pleased if we would give what we could afford to the Eton mission but *not* in the usual way. We were to do it in any way we liked so long as it was not usual.

We thought up all sorts of ideas. We balanced piles of pennies on top of the slightly open door so that when Mr Crace came in they all fell on his mortar board. We arranged to throw coins on to his desk as the school clock struck a particular hour or quarter, so that without warning, possibly while talking to us, a shower of coins would descend on him. If we knew he was likely to refer to a certain book we inserted coins between the pages, or if he was going to use the blackboard we filled the duster with pennies. He loved it and so did we and at the end of the week the Eton mission received a record collection but definitely *not* collected 'in the usual way'.

There were quite a few parsons on the staff. One of them, the Reverend C.O. Bevan was a very pious man as befitted his station. Once a friend of mine named Charles Villiers had been annoying him all morning until in the end 'Cob' Bevan really lost his temper. 'Villiers,' he said in his gruff voice, 'just because I'm a parson you think I can't swear. But I can. Damn you, Villiers, and (a long pause while he plucked up courage) . . . damn you again.' I doubt whether he ever forgave himself.

Quite different was 'Satan' Ford, a very fierce man who was a terror to be up to and who for some reason had a strong nasal American accent. He prefaced most of his remarks with 'Boy' and one of his favourite expressions was, 'Boy, your breath smells like last week's washing.' Charming! He once wise-cracked to a stupid boy, 'Boy, you have as many brains as a snake has hips.' But he came off second-best when he was reprimanding a friend of mine called Jimmy Ford. After a few explosive comments about Jimmy's work 'Satan' said, 'Well boy, what's your beastly name?' 'Ford, sir,' replied Jimmy smartly, with a smile. He knew he had won.

The Provost was M.R. James, a friendly, genial man who wrote all those ghost stories. One of the real treats when one was an older boy was to be asked to supper with him and listen to him reading P.G. Wodehouse out loud until tears of laughter ran down his cheeks.

The headmaster was Dr Cyril Alington, a keen writer of detective stories and later Dean of Durham. He was a distinguished grey-haired figure with an imposing presence, greatly respected by the boys. He was perhaps most famous for his Sunday evening chats from the pulpit. His talk lasted about ten minutes, often less, and there was always complete silence throughout the congregation of five hundred boys, except for the occasional cough.

He always finished with a strong punchline, paused, and then slowly blew out the candles – puff puff. Another pause, then up would come the lights and it was all over. Beautifully staged, and very effective. One always felt like applauding. I remember that in one of his talks he was trying to show how the story of Jesus's trial and crucifixion would not have been sensational news in those days. For Pontius Pilate it was just another job, similar to hundreds he had to deal with. Dr Alington illustrated this by telling the story of a writer who some years later wanted to find out more about the trial of Jesus. So he obtained an interview with Pontius Pilate. 'Jesus of Nazareth,' said Pilate. 'No, I don't remember the name. Who was he?' Puff puff.

Although normally so calm and dignified Dr Alington was slightly taken aback one day when giving communion in the College Chapel. He gave the holy bread to a boy called Danreuther who for some unknown reason put it into his pocket. The Doctor's hoarse stage whisper echoed round the altar steps, 'Consume it here,' and the crisis was over.

One of the doctors at Eton was called Amsler, a tough character who stood no nonsense. It was his job every summer half to issue any 'excused camp' certificates to members of the OTC. Some people disliked the idea of camp, though in fact it was great fun. One summer half there was a bigger queue than usual in his surgery of boys trying to get off. He listened patiently for some time to their feeble excuses, carrying out brief examinations of the more genuine cases. But after an hour or so he lost his temper and his patience. This was bad luck on a boy called Stirling, later to become the Lord Mayor of Westminster. He genuinely had a bad attack of rheumatism, and was bent double as he struggled up to Amsler's desk. Amsler must have thought he was trying to be funny and putting on an act. He interrupted Stirling's 'Please, sir, I've got rheumatism,' with a curt, 'Next man please,' and poor Stirling had to go to camp.

Amsler also used to referee at the school boxing. One year there was only one entrant for the heavyweight division, a large boy called Balmain. This meant that he would have a walk-over and automatically win the cup. But by the regulations if there was no fight there was no prize money which normally went with the cup. So Balmain found another boy in his house called Congreve to whom he offered £1.00 just to enter for the heavyweight division. Congreve had never boxed before but agreed to the proposal when Balmain promised not to hurt him in any way. There was a packed house in the gymnasium when the final bout of the evening was due to start and a surprised 'ooooh' from the spectators when they saw Congreve step into the ring, hardly knowing which corner to go to.

When the bell went the two boxers danced around, bobbing and weaving, but making sure never to get within striking distance of each other. The crowd roared with laughter. But not Dr Amsler. After about a minute he stopped the 'fight' and warned both boxers that if they did not box properly he would stop the contest and declare it null and void. This would of course have meant no cup nor prize money for either boxer. What came over Congreve I don't know, but at the words 'Box on' he rushed at Balmain, swung his right arm and with a tremendous hook of which Dempsey would have been proud knocked the astonished Balmain flat out on the canvas. Pandemonium erupted and the look on Congreve's face when he realised what he had done was worth going miles to see. But it was nothing to the look on Balmain's when he finally came round to find that he had not only lost the cup and the prize money but also the £1.00 he had paid Congreve to enter!

After two years my housemaster Monty retired. Our new man was an Old Wykehamist who years before had made 100 against Eton in the annual match. A red-haired man called A.C. Huson, his face was completely purple as he was said to have one skin less than anyone else. He was a bachelor and a really wonderful person and as near the perfect housemaster as could be. He had a great sense of humour, was kind and understanding and I owe him as big a debt as anyone else in my life. He died ten years after I had left as a result of a strangulated hernia brought on I am sure by a strange habit he had.

In those days the Eton housemasters used to live very well and entertained each other at super dinner parties with only the best wines and beautifully cooked food. Furthermore they always changed for dinner. Immediately after the meal the other housemasters used to return to their houses for their nightly rounds of the boys' rooms. When these were completed they would return to the party for brandy and cigars.

In my last year Huson had been bitten by the keep-fit bug and used to do all sorts of exercises. One of his favourites was to lie on his back and raise his legs up ninety degrees into the air, lower them without touching the ground, up in the air again and so on. Try it and see how many times you can do it before your stomach muscles pack up. You will be lucky if you can do ten. Well Huson used to come to my room in his dinner-jacket straight from one of these dinners, lie down on the floor and do one hundred of these leg exercises. It was a crazy thing to do following a big meal and it is no wonder that he died in the way that he did.

One of his great friends was another red-haired master called Routh who also had a sense of humour and used to snort through his nose every time that he laughed, which was often. His sense of the ridiculous was a great help to William Douglas-Home, when Mr Routh marked one of his history papers we had to do in 'trials' at the end of the half. One question was: 'Write as briefly as you can on one of the following subjects:

1. The future of coal.
2. The decline of the British Empire.
3. Whither Socialism?'

William chose the first question and bearing in mind the instruction to be brief wrote as his answer the one word 'smoke'. To his eternal credit Mr Routh awarded him seven marks out of ten. After all, the answer was both accurate and brief.

It is an unusual thing to be able to say but the food in our house both with Monty and Huson was always excellent. It cost a lot of feed and run a house even in those days. I remember Mr Huson saying that when King George V asked for an extra week's holiday for the boys to celebrate a visit to the school, it was as good as giving £100 to the Huson bank account.

Not all houses were so well fed, especially one on the corner of Keats Lane, which had better be nameless. About six years after I had left one of the boys in this house tried to commit suicide. Luckily he failed, but the housemaster was determined to find out why the boy had tried, and summoned the whole house into the dining-room. He asked if they knew any reason why this should have happened. Was the boy being bullied, was he in financial difficulties, was he worried about his work?

As usual on occasions like this there was a deathly silence. So the housemaster repeated his questions, saying he was determined to get to the bottom of the affair, even if it meant them all staying in and missing their half-holiday.

Thus threatened a boy at the back of the room held up his hand. 'Yes, Ormsby Gore,' said the relieved housemaster, 'what is your theory?' And Ormsby Gore – later Lord Harlech – replied with an innocent air, 'Please sir, could it have been the food?' Collapse of housemaster!

There are also splendid stories told about some of the housemasters' wives, one or two of whom were fairly formidable ladies. One was once at a charity concert given by the local Women's Institute. Somewhat rashly, one of the performers struggled through a recitation of a poem in French. When she had finished to enthusiastic applause the housemaster's wife turned to her neighbour in the front row and in a loud whisper said, 'Beautifully spoken, and how wise not to attempt the French accent!'

Another wife found that her servants were pinching cigarettes from the various boxes in the private side of the house. So she put notices in each one which read, 'Please don't help yourself.' Unfortunately, when the 4 June came along and they had a lot of parents to lunch and tea she forgot to remove the notices before the boxes were handed round to the guests.

It was quite the opposite at the local Eton flower show, when there was often intense rivalry between the various Eton houses as to who had the best displays of fruit. There were baskets of apples, raspberries, gooseberries etc. on display, with the usual cautionary notice stuck in front, 'Please don't touch.' One housemaster's wife feared that a rival's apples were better than hers so she waited for an opportune moment when their owner had left the show tent and placed a notice in front of her rival's apples, 'Please take one.'

Something peculiar to Eton was the office of Dame. Each house had one – they were called M'Dame – and they were a sort of super matron, substitute-mother, state-registered nurse and catering expert all rolled into one. Usually they were even more than that. They became the confidante, comforter and friend of all the boys in the house. They acted as a kind of buffer between the boys and the housemaster and library. They were mobbed, mimicked and laughed at, but at the same time in a funny sort of way were respected and loved. Tea with M'Dame was a regular date each half and there was a saying we used to use about people or things: 'Very good but very old – just like M'Dame's cakes.'

Dames were responsible for the health of all the boys and were expected to deal with emergencies like cuts or injuries at games. In the unmarried houses they did the catering and of course ran the household – the maids, cleaning, linen, etc. To be good they had to be saints and very often were. We had two while I was there, Miss Sealey and Miss Hancock. They both took a great interest in the house and often stood on the touch line in icy weather watching some juniors playing in a house match.

Our Dames also had to deal with the real mothers who varied from the difficult to the impossible with their demands on how 'my boy' should be treated. God bless them both and my grateful thanks and my apologies for the many ways in which I am sure I must have made their lives more difficult.

In this chapter, I have purposely dealt mainly with the lighter side of Eton life. Many others more qualified to do so have written about its ancient traditions and education. All I would humbly like to say is that the system of each boy to his own room, with his own tutor to guide and help him was invaluable and that the traditions and customs helped to create a solid base on which to found one's life. So speaks – a bit pompously I'm afraid – at least one very satisfied Old Etonian.

F
for Family

There is a marvellous card game called Happy Families which I still play with my grandchildren. It has such characters as Mr Clamp the Carpenter, Mr Drug the Doctor, Mr Bull the Butcher, Mr Howler the Singer, Mr Bun the Baker and so on.

We have been very lucky in *our* family where – with the usual few ups and downs – there has been much happiness. I was born in 1912 in The Old Rectory in the small Hertfordshire village of Little Berkhamsted where I joined my mother and father, my sister Anne and my brothers Michael and Christopher. My father worked in the family coffee firm in the City and was also a director of the Midland Bank.

Just before the First World War we moved to a lovely Queen Anne house outside the village of Offley, halfway between Hitchin and Luton. There we spent an uneventful war except for one bomb which was dropped on Hitchin and killed a chicken. We occasionally saw our father when he came home on leave from the Western Front where he was in the Territorials and became a Colonel, winning the DSO and MC.

We had a farm of about 500 acres, so I was brought up among animals. I remember carrying a tiny black piglet up to my mother's bedroom. It was the runt of the litter and the pigman was going to kill it because it was so weak. I used to watch calving, bulls having rings put through their noses, and large farm horses being shod. Two of them, called Boxer and Beauty, pulled the farm wagon and won a prize at the local show.

One of our treats was to stand on the station at Hitchin and watch the Flying Scotsman roar through. It left King's Cross at 10.00 a.m. and passed through Hitchin about twenty-five minutes later. It was a marvellous sight, with steam belching out and the wheels of the train going biddle-de-dum, biddle-de-dum, biddle-de-dum. We also liked visiting the large draper's shop called Spurs, where they had prices like 3s. 11¾d. – whatever that meant. They had one of those little 'overhead' railways along which a ball-like container was despatched to the cashier at the far end of the shop. It held the money and the bill, and as if by magic would suddenly return with the change.

On the farm the two great events were the harvest and the threshing. We used to 'help' with the haymaking, but on one occasion I fell off the top of the haycart and developed periostitis, a very painful bruising of the membrane of the bone. Threshing was especially exciting as an enormous steam engine would arrive hauling the threshing machine and the caravan in which the crew lived while they were with us. This was the time for rat-catching with dogs and sticks. Most of the rats waited at the bottom of the rick until the last moment, and then tried to make a bolt for it.

Sunday was a so-called day of rest but we used to walk one and a half miles to the church and back and try not to giggle during the sermon. If good, we were rewarded with sticky meringues for lunch.

It seems unbelievable today, but for about four years after the war we had a chauffeur, groom, two gardeners, a butler, cook, parlour maid, housemaid and 'tweeny'. We dispensed with the dogcart and had a Fiat Landerlette specially built by the local garage. It went at the terrifying maximum speed of 53 mph.

In addition my father had one of the first Ford Tin Lizzies to take him to the station.

We had a happy four years until September 1922 when my father was sadly drowned whilst we were on holiday in Cornwall. I was aged ten at the time and it meant that I never really knew him well. As I remember him he was kind, quiet and a fairly strict disciplinarian. It's difficult to assess what effect not having a father had on my character. I rather feel that he would have been slightly shocked at my somewhat unusual job with the BBC.

Anyhow we had to sell the beautiful house and farm and

from then on we became rovers with two years at Upwey in Dorset, and four more at Much Marcle in Herefordshire. By then we were all away at boarding schools so they were really only holiday homes. My mother remarried a charming but irascible Irishman called Marcus Scully, chiefly I suspect to help her look after us. We were then 'down' to a cook, a parlour maid with tummy rumbles, a housemaid and a groom turned chauffeur. When cleaning the car he used to hiss through his teeth as he used to do when grooming a horse. He could also tuck his ears in and taught me to do it. I still can, but now only my right ear.

After Herefordshire we moved down to Bude in Cornwall where we stayed until a few years before the Second World War, when my mother and stepfather were divorced. It might seem strange to return to the place where my father had died, but it had always been where we spent our childhood holidays and we loved it. From Bude my mother moved to a charming cottage in the small Buckinghamshire village of Chearsley which was to be her final home.

After the war I was still a bachelor and working in the BBC. On 1 December 1947 my telephone rang and a girl's attractive voice said, 'This is Pauline Tozer. I am working in the photographic section of the BBC and my brother Gordon told me to give you a ring.' I immediately realised who she was, as Gordon Tozer had been my Assistant Technical Adjutant in the Grenadiers from 1942 to 1945.

My normal reaction would have been rather a cool one as I was quite happy leading a bachelor life plus working long and varied hours in the BBC. As a result I had not had much time or inclination for the opposite sex. In fact I learned later from Pauline that Gordon had told her that I would not be interested in her but that I might introduce her to some of my younger colleagues. Certainly at that time most of my friends looked on me as a confirmed bachelor or thought that no woman would ever be brave enough to take me on. But there must have been something in that voice. Anyway I whipped out my diary and asked her to lunch with me two days later.

I went to pick Pauline up at her department in the Old

Langham Hotel and to my delight found that she was a very attractive blonde with blue eyes. We then had lunch in the Bolivar restaurant, later the BBC club. We got on well and laughed a lot, and the next night I took her along to the Chelsea Palace where I was doing a broadcast of a variety show. When I introduced her to Dorothy Squires and Billy Reid, Dorothy asked, 'Are you two engaged?'

We weren't then, but ten days after our first meeting I proposed. Pauline played for time a bit before giving her answer and I don't blame her. However, she finally accepted me on 6 January, just over a month since we had first met. My mother was delighted and the Tozers, though slightly taken aback by the speed of the whole thing, seemed quite happy and gave their approval. I did the old-fashioned thing of asking her father Colonel Billy Tozer for his permission.

I invited myself to lunch with the Colonel in the City and was so nervous that I talked about everything except the engagement. He knew exactly why I had come and was as relieved as I was when after the cheese and biscuits I plucked up courage to introduce the subject. Afterwards he told me that his wife Eileen was waiting for him by the telephone to hear the result of the lunch. They wanted us to get married in June but I pointed out that this might mean me missing the Lord's Test against Australia. So in the end we were married at St Paul's, Knightsbridge on 22 April 1948. As a wedding present the OB Department recorded the whole ceremony and some interviews by Stewart, Wynford and Raymond as we emerged from the church under an archway of microphones.

The first week of our honeymoon we spent at the Grand Hotel, Eastbourne. It was an old haunt of mine from my schooldays at Temple Grove. My parents used to take me there for lunch and we listened to Leslie Jefferies and his Orchestra – the original orchestra from the radio programme *Grand Hotel*, which used to be broadcast from the lounge in the hotel. There was one amusing coincidence. We had shared the cost of the flowers with another couple called Tetley who were being married at St Paul's on the morning of the 22nd. We had never met them though I knew he had been at Sandhurst during the war. When we staggered down to lunch on the first day there was a couple sitting at the next table to ours, and I recognised him. It was the Tetleys!

After a very happy week we flew off to Locarno to stay at a small hotel by the lake for a fortnight. But this was not a success, due to my catching some kind of barber's rash on my face. I could not shave so grew a beard and had to go to a doctor who prescribed a course of injections. These had to be administered twice a day by Pauline in my bottom. Luckily she had been a naval VAD in the war so handled a pretty nifty needle. But it was not exactly romantic, and the injections made me feel very low and dispirited.

Furthermore, in those days we were only allowed £25 of currency each and with the extra cost of the injections on top of the hotel charges we had no money to spend on ourselves. All we did was to sit around the hotel and wait for the 4 p.m. steamer which took us across the lake to a tea-house. We were just able to afford one meringue each day, oozing with cream, an unheard-of luxury in England in 1948.

When we came back to London, we rented a small flat in Bayswater which was singularly devoid of furniture. I had my beard shaved off and returned to work, while Pauline set about finding us a home. I left it entirely to her, with only one stipulation: it must be in St John's Wood, near Lord's.

And so began nearly forty-four years (as I write) of a very happy marriage. Pauline – who likes to be called Polly – has been a tremendous support to me throughout my varied career in broadcasting. She has been remarkably patient at my absences from home, and caring and loving when I return. I hope a bonus for her will have been the great variety of people from the world of entertainment and sport whom she has met. There have also been many trips abroad when I have been covering tours. She has had to suffer all my jokes in private, and listen to my same old stories when she accompanies me to some of the many dinners at which I speak throughout the year. Like all couples we have the occasional little 'local differences' but they never last long and we kiss and make up. Our main difference is that I am the most punctual of people, and she *does* tend to be a little late! But what does that really matter compared with the many years of fun and happiness which we have shared together.

We owe a lot of this to our delightful family, Barry, Clare, Andrew, Ian and Joanna. Except for Joanna, they all have jobs connected with the media. Barry is in radio and presents a weekly programme every Sunday morning for Radio 5. Clare, in addition to looking after her family, does some PR and secretarial work. Andrew is in publishing in a private firm in Shrewsbury and Ian, until the end of 1991, was a general manager in cable television in London. Perhaps wrongly, I sent none of them to a university. I remembered how little work I had done during my three years up at Oxford. So instead I sent three of them abroad to learn about life in Australia and South Africa. The exception was Barry, who went straight into the pop world and worked in the Decca recording studio in West Hampstead.

Our children have been a great joy to us, and except for the usual growing-up problems and worries, there has been only one serious set-back. We remain a united and happy family, augmented by six wonderful grandchildren, three from Clare and three from Andrew. (Barry married in May. The other two are not yet married.) Grandparents have a splendid time. They can just sit back and enjoy the little darlings, and leave everything else to the poor parents.

The one serious set-back was on 28 November 1965. It was to be a very important day in our lives. In the early evening Pauline went into a nursing home to have her baby, and I sat waiting in the hall downstairs. It seemed an awfully long time but at last a nurse came down the stairs to tell me that I had a daughter and that Pauline was fine. But she looked embarrassed and didn't look me straight in the face, then went off before I could ask any questions.

Our family doctor, Dr Cove-Smith, the old rugger inter-national, came down and said that our little daughter was in an incubator and that he wasn't quite happy about her, and would consult a specialist the next day. I went up to see Pauline who was still in the delivery room and had not yet really seen the baby. She seemed blissfully happy at having another daughter, and though I suspected something was wrong I didn't say anything about it to her.

I spent as much of the next day as I could with Pauline but it was a busy time for me, and she was left much on her own without yet seeing the baby. I felt desperately sorry for her. Meanwhile Cove and a paediatric specialist from St Mary's Hospital had examined the baby again, and as a result Cove came in to say that the specialist would like to see Pauline and me alone the next day.

You can imagine how we felt and neither of us slept much. I told our housekeeper Cally what was going on and she was wonderful. She said she didn't mind what the baby was like. She would help to look after her.

The next morning the specialist came to Pauline's room with the baby. He was a charming man, gentle and kind, but did not beat about the bush. The baby, he said, had Down's syndrome but in a milder form called Mosaic. He and Cove had made sure that she was *physically* perfect but she would undoubtedly be backward, and not quite like other normal children. He said she would be pretty, loving and a source of great happiness. (He was right on all three counts.) He pointed out that some parents in our position might *have* to put the baby into a hospital due to their circumstances at home. But he emphasised that a happy home life was the best medicine a child like this could have. Of course we didn't hesitate. Talking it over after he had left we both realised how lucky we had been with our lives and that most of the bad things had passed us by. Now we felt that it was our turn to have a bit of bad luck and that this whole thing would be a challenge to us which we would accept. We promised there and then that we would do everything in our power to make Joanna – as we named her – as near as possible the same as any other child.

One thing was certain, that with Cally, three brothers and a sister, she was not going to lack love and care. Because she was such a rare type Guy's Hospital took a special interest in her, and for the next five years she went regularly to them and Great Ormond Street for blood and development tests and an EEG on her brain. The reports got progressively better, but the doctors never led us to believe that she would ever be completely normal.

Although she was happy and loving Joanna was obviously not always easy to bring up and train, and Pauline and Cally had to exercise a great deal of patience. They also noted down every detail of her progress in walking, talking and so on, and compared this with the rest of the family at her age. The three boys and Clare were wonderful with her. They helped to look after her, bath her and play with her. Except for her big saucer eyes she didn't look *so* different from them. I am sure that her happy home life has helped her enormously and she has certainly added to the happiness and enjoyment of our lives.

I have asked Pauline to add a report on Joanna's subsequent progress. We feel that there must be many other parents in the same position in which we found ourselves. We hope that Joanna's story will be an encouragement to them to overcome what can be very distressing circumstances.

From Pauline:
Because Joanna was a Mosaic it meant that she had a fifty-fifty chance of improvement in all that she did. So we decided to have her educated with normal children, and to mix with them as much as possible. From an early age we treated her exactly as our other children and tried to teach her to count, read 'word cards' and sing nursery rhymes etc. Early on she had some trouble with her tongue which prevented clear speech. She could only manage single words and could not make sentences. Otherwise her health was good except for slight heart murmur.

When she was two and a half years old I started a small nursery group in our church hall with four normal children. Joanna enjoyed being with them but after six months the teacher left and we decided to send her to Frances House, a newly opened nursery school started by parents of a few mentally handicapped under-five-year-olds. Here there was a marvellous lady called Mrs Williams who wrote rhyming couplets about everyday things like 'cleaning my teeth', 'my clock', 'my dog', 'crossing the road' and so on. Our eldest son Barry put music to these and made a small record of the songs. Joanna loved being there but sadly had to leave when she became five years old. Luckily Mrs Williams knew a retired teacher called Miss Vyvian Jenkins and suggested that she might be able to teach Joanna to read and write. This was the best thing that could have happened as Vyvian came to our house twice a week and gave her private tuition. As a result when Joanna went to a Montessori nursery school in a convent in Primrose Hill, she was well ahead of some of her more normal contemporaries. Her handwriting to this day is far better than that of any other member of our family, particularly her father's!

Whilst at this school we discovered that she had diabetes and would have to have insulin injections all her life. We had to learn how to cope with these plus her strict diet. This was very hard for her because all the other children could eat sweets and cakes but she was not allowed to.

About a year later she went to another school which had been started in Bethnal Green by Mrs Wallbank – a pioneer of the idea of integrating normal and handicapped children. She called her new school The Gatehouse Learning Centre and was delighted to welcome Joanna there. It was a fifty minute journey each day from St John's Wood by car and school bus, but it was well worthwhile because Joanna learnt independence and many other skills during her four years there. She made a lot of new friends – some like herself and others able-bodied who helped to look after her.

As she was nearing her teens we thought it would be a good idea for her to go away from home to a suitable boarding school. At home she was beginning to expect to be waited on and to have everything done for her. She was becoming too dependent on us.

After much searching I was again lucky to hear of a PNEU (Parents' National Educational Union) school for fifty girls near Newbury. It was called Flexford House and at the age of thirteen and a half they took her on a trial basis.

It was a great success as Joanna – who has always been gregarious and friendly – mixed with the other girls, five of whom had learning difficulties. She was in classes of her own age, working at her *own* speed – the principle of PNEU. The wonderful headmistress Miss Davison took Joanna under her wing and the staff were constantly surprised at her abilities and enthusiasm for learning all subjects including the piano and particularly dancing.

Unfortunately during her puberty she had many unpleasant experiences due to her diabetes. She was often rushed to hospital in Reading with hypos. At the age of sixteen she left Flexford and another stage in her education was about to begin.

By this time she could read and speak quite clearly and loved learning to count and spell. Whenever we had a car journey we would teach her the 'tables' from one to ten and also practice a few French words. All this made her sound more normal but we had times when she became moody and difficult (like most teenagers!) We had to keep an eye on her the whole time as she was inclined to wander off and get lost. We often had to send out a search party for her, and the St John's Wood police station were very patient with our frequent calls. Once she had been watching a TV advertisement which said 'Dial 999 if you need the police'. She did just that from the telephone in our bedroom. The first we knew of it was when we saw two uniformed policemen coming *down* our stairs with Joanna. When they had answered her call she had let them in on the entryphone. They were very understanding and after giving Joanna a lecture, took her for a drive in their police car with the warning siren going full blast!

In 1984 she went to the Derwen Training College for the disabled at Oswestry. She was a boarder for three years amongst 120 girls and boys aged from sixteen to thirty. Many were physically handicapped, some in wheelchairs, others were mildly mentally handicapped. It was a splendid mix as they all helped each other. They had to be able to learn a trade and there were some excellent workshops to choose from. Dr Kendall and his staff made it a friendly and happy place and they had holidays like other boarding schools. Joanna loved it and chose to learn dressmaking and when she had to leave after the statutory two years she could cut out patterns, use a sewing machine and had made several outfits for herself and a nightie or two for me!

She came back to live with us in St John's Wood and we managed to find a part-time job for her in a West End couturier just off Park Lane. She was naturally treated as a novice and given the job of hemming and tacking customers' skirts. She soon found this boring and difficult to concentrate for hour after hour. So she used to wander off at lunchtime and several times got lost in Mayfair. Or she would go to sleep on the bus and get carried on beyond her stop in Park Lane. (We would put her on the bus in St John's Wood, and the conductor or a kind passenger usually told her when to get off.) On one occasion she got carried right on to Crystal Palace and we had to go and collect her, and on two other occasions we found her in hospital out-patients. We dreaded the telephone ringing!

She stayed for six months but her diabetes began to play up and it seemed best for her to give up the job. (I suspect the kind couturier was secretly relieved!)

Fortunately the Westminster Society for Mentally Handicapped Children and Adults had recently converted Frances House where Joanna had gone as a four-year-old. It was only ten minutes away from us by car and she also learnt to use the bus route to and from St John's Wood. Whilst there she attended the Paddington Further Education College and went on a two-year training course which covered literacy, typing, money skills and even computers. At the Camden Institute she also studied drama which she loves, cooking, music therapy and badminton which she played quite well.

After four years which had involved much travelling from place to place alone on buses, we were suddenly offered a place out of the blue in a new home which was to be opened by the Home Farm Trust in a village near Biggleswade. We had put her name down when she was eleven years old, so it had taken thirteen years to get her in. This is now her permanent home – for life, if all goes well. She shares a house with five boys and three girls and they are looked after by a devoted staff. The Home Farm Trust has another bigger building just nearby where they go each day for various classes in the workshops there. Some also go to local schools for special subjects such as art for which Joanna is showing a real aptitude.

She comes home (by train – forty minutes) whenever she wants. But she likes her new home so much with her own room and new friends that it sometimes takes a bit of persuading to get her to come. Even when she does come to us in St John's Wood she is usually counting the hours until she is due to go back to 'my *real* home'.

At first I felt a bit sad about this but soon realised how lucky we are that she is now finally settled in such happy surroundings.

To sum up. Joanna now leads a near-normal life. She paints, she sews, she plays all games with great enthusiasm and some skill. She is especially expert at card games. She can cook and go shopping alone, though she has to trust the shopkeepers over prices and change. She can travel on buses and trains alone so long as there is someone at either end. She loves music, mostly pop, and dancing. She is a terror in a disco!

Sadly I don't think she will ever be able to concentrate enough to get a regular job, though a few hours a day may be possible.

Diabetes has played a big part in her life. Remarkably since the age of ten she has injected herself twice a day with insulin, and also monitors her own blood-sugar readings. In spite of all temptations she sticks strictly to her diabetic diet and in addition, because those with Down's syndrome tend to put on weight, she avoids all fattening foods.

To make things even more difficult for her she has now had

to have operations on both eyes for cataracts. Touch wood, these seem to have been completely successful.

She will never be able to organise her daily life completely and will always need supervision. But the main point is that she is happy and will be well cared for when both Pauline and I have gone. She enjoys life and what is so nice, people seem to enjoy *her* too.

Finally there is also one person who has made our family life easier and happier. Her name is Ella Callander. She is inevitably nicknamed Cally and has been with us now for thirty-two years. She came when Ian was three in 1960 and saw the arrival of Joanna. She has been with us in our three houses and has devoted herself to looking after us in every way possible.

She started by looking after the children plus cleaning and cooking. She does the ironing, answers the telephone (which hardly ever stops) and helps at every party we ever give. She is a lovely person and I think she enjoys meeting all the many people who come to our home. They certainly enjoy meeting her. She is a marvel. We could not do without her.

G
for Grenadiers

After the invasion of Czechoslovakia it became more and more obvious that war was not only inevitable but imminent, and some of my Eton friends and I thought we must do something to prepare ourselves for it. We had all been in the Corps at school and at one of our lunches in the City decided we should try to get onto the reserve of some regiment. We were unanimous in thinking that if we had to fight we might as well be in the best and most efficient regiment. So we went right to the top and applied to the Grenadier Guards, the senior regiment of the Foot Guards.

My first cousin 'Boy' Browning was then commanding the 2nd Battalion. They had just returned from two years in Egypt and were stationed at Wellington Barracks. 'Boy' was later to become the founder and first Commander of the Airborne Division, and it must have been due to him that I and five or six others were accepted for training by the Grenadiers, and placed on the Officer Cadet Reserve. This involved reporting on one or two evenings a week throughout the summer of 1939 to Wellington Barracks, where we were taught weapon training, basic tactics and regimental history and traditions.

We reported for the first time one evening in May, coming straight from the City in our bowlers, white stiff collars, and dark city suits. We were welcomed in the officers' mess by 'Boy' Browning, who offered us drinks and gave us a short informal talk. This was fine, we thought, as we sipped our drinks and sat in deep comfortable armchairs. A great institution, the Army!

When we had a second round of drinks 'Boy' smilingly suggested that we might like to meet the Regimental Sergeant-Major who he said was waiting for us out on the parade-ground. Innocently we left the comfort of the mess and walked out on to the steps. As soon as we emerged a roar rent the air as the RSM bellowed out to us to get into a double and fall in in front of him. Before we knew what was happening we found ourselves marching up and down the vast parade-ground in double-quick time, being told we were a lazy lot of so-and-sos. About turn, quick march, right turn, mark time, halt. The orders came out like machine-gun fire and we were soon sweating and panting for breath, wondering why on earth we had ever volunteered.

After twenty minutes of utter hell we were dismissed with a 'Good night gentlemen. See you later in the week,' from RSM Tom Garnett – a wonderful man and soldier with whom I was to serve for most of the war. We had experienced Guards discipline at its best – or worst, depending on how you looked at it. We limped back to the mess and sank into our chairs as 'Boy' Browning dispensed some badly needed drinks. We were definitely in a state of shock.

He then gave us an enthralling talk about the Brigade of Guards and the reasons for their fanatical emphasis on discipline in all their training of officers and guardsmen alike. Keith Bryant in his book *Fighting with the Guards* has put it all very succinctly when he details the six basic qualities instilled into every guardsman: cleanliness, smartness, fitness, efficiency, pride and invincibility.

The acceptance of these six qualities demands a tremendous amount from any man but, if achieved, results in the perfect fighting machine – a man who can obey any order without question, no matter how bloody it may seem. Hence the endless and, to the outsider, seemingly pointless, hours of drill. Naturally this automatic acceptance of an order demands an even higher standard for those in command. It becomes absolutely essential that every order is the right one and practicable, something of which I was very conscious when I became an officer later on.

I was filling sandbags outside Westminster Hospital on 3 September when Neville Chamberlain's thin frail voice came over the radio at 11.00 a.m. to announce that we were at war with Germany.

Shattering though the news was, it came in a way as a relief after all the months of tension, and we continued shovelling sand into the sandbags. But we were soon rudely interrupted by the air-raid siren, and were all rushed down into the mortuary for shelter. We reluctantly had to hand it to Hitler for being so much on the ball that within a few minutes of war being declared, his bombers were approaching London. As it turned out, of course, it was only a false alarm but it had given everyone quite a fright.

After a week or so and much badgering of the Grenadier headquarters I was ordered to report for a medical inspection. With a lot of other naked men I had to go through some fairly undignified routines and as a result have always appreciated the old joke about the recruit who started to run as he thought the doctor said 'off' instead of 'cough'. Very painful!

I passed all right but there was one awkward moment when I could not read all the letters on the card with my rather short-sighted right eye. But the doctor must have realised how disappointed I would be if I failed or perhaps they were short of budding officers. Anyway he made it easy for me by opening the fingers of his hand which was covering my left eye, so that I could read all the letters with that eye.

My other friends also passed and in October we reported to the Royal Military College at Sandhurst for a four-month course. It was being turned into an Officer Cadet Training Unit and we were its very first victims. There were lots of people like myself, most of them in their mid-twenties who had come from jobs in the City or one of the professions. It was just like going back to school, but the great thing was that we did not have to think. Everything was organised for us and we were told exactly what to do and soon automatically did it.

After the first shocks of reveille at 6.00 a.m. and long doses of PT and drill, we soon settled down and began to enjoy ourselves. The course was a strange mixture of war and peace. We still each had a room to ourselves with a batman to look after us, and our Company Sergeant-Major – a great character called 'Dusty' Smith – would call us 'Sir' with one corner of his mouth and hand out the most terrible rockets with the other:

'Mr Johnston, SIR, stop being so dozy and get a . . . move on.'
That sort of thing.

It was even funnier with the Regimental Sergeant-Major. We had to call him 'Sir' as well. He used to say, 'I call you sir, and you call me sir. The only difference is that *you* mean it!'

We soon became physically fit and moderately efficient, and unless we were on guard duties were free from midday Saturday to midnight Sunday, which meant a mass exodus to London as soon as the last parade was finished. This led to complete chaos on the first Saturday. We kept our cars in a garage in Camberley and had asked for them to be brought up to the parade-ground by midday Saturday.

We were out on our first route march, and were marching back to be dismissed for our first weekend off. We rounded the bend to go on to the parade-ground, and it looked like a car park at a football match. All the cars were parked in the middle and we had to be called to a sudden halt and dismissed where we were. Our Company Commander was naturally very annoyed and from them on we had to go down to Camberley to collect our cars.

Once again my inability to resist playing jokes got me into slight trouble. We were all out on a TEWT – or Tactical Exercise Without Troops – where the instructors posed various military problems which they asked the cadets to solve.

We had stopped at the top of a hill and looking down at the valley below the instructor turned to me and said, 'Johnston. You and your platoon are defending this ridge. Suddenly at the bottom of the hill you see a troop of German tanks advancing. What steps would you take?' 'Bloody long ones, sir,' I replied and was deservedly 'put in the book' and had to report to the Company Commander next day for a reprimand.

While the 'phoney' was continued in Europe we were gradually being turned into officers. The various Regimental Colonels came down to vet us and check up on our progress, and by February we had all been accepted. Then came the final passing-out parade and finally that day when we put on our officers' uniforms for the first time. The NCOs who had been ordering us around and handing out rockets for the last few months now had to salute us, and I shall always remember the twinkle in Dusty Smith's eye when he 'tore me off' a beauty as I drove away.

It was quite a moment – a Commissioned Officer in the Brigade of Guards. A bit prefabricated perhaps, but at least there was one pip on my shoulder to prove it. I must confess that it was highly embarrassing walking about the West End and having to acknowledge salutes, as well as give them.

We had been granted a few days' leave before joining our regiments and I spent mine seeing all the theatre shows I could. I especially enjoyed the wartime jokes of Tommy Trinder. Take this one: A man walking down Whitehall stopped a passer-by and asked him if he knew which side the War Office was on. 'On ours, I hope,' was the somewhat unhelpful reply.

But my leave was soon up and I was ordered to report to the Training Battalion of the Grenadier Guards at Windsor. . . .

Although we were now officers, life at Windsor was not that different from that at Sandhurst. We were drilled in a special officers' squad by RSM 'Snapper' Robinson, and the Adjutant kept an eagle eye on us as we continued training in weapons, tactics and motor transport.

After a few weeks at Windsor we were considered sufficiently trained to take our turn as one of the junior officers on the guard at Windsor Castle. This involved twenty-four hours in the guardroom up at the Castle and a nightly patrol of all the sentry posts to see that all was well. Since the Royal Family stayed in the Castle a great deal – it was the wartime home of the two Princesses – we at least felt we were doing something practical to help the war effort.

However, I am not sure how effective our methods of guarding really were. In these days of small automatic weapons, hand-grenades or bombs it seemed a bit archaic for a sentry, if he heard footsteps approaching, to call out into the darkness, 'Who goes there?' If there was more than one person the answer would then come back, 'Mr Johnston and others.' The sentry in that case would reply, 'Advance one and be recognised.'

But it does seem to be inviting trouble to order a possible enemy to approach any nearer, even if the sentry has his finger ready on the trigger. There was a hilarious occasion at Sandhurst when an officer cadet was on guard late at night and heard footsteps approaching. Of course he did not know it but they belonged to a new officer instructor with a very long name who had only just arrived.

'Who goes there?' challenged the sentry.

'Blundell-Hollingshead-Blundell,' replied the officer from the darkness.

'Advance one and be recognised,' said the sentry.

We had various training schemes in Windsor Park and also used to guard the polo grounds there against possible parachute landings. I shared one night's vigil with the Duke of Beaufort who was commanding a troop of the Household Cavalry. I often wonder what would have happened had the parachutists landed. By the end of April things were hotting up in France and Belgium and one by one officers from Windsor were being sent out to join fighting battalions out there.

In the first week of May Hitler started his offensive and I was among those told to get the necessary injections at once, collect my full fighting kit and report to Wellington Barracks to await orders to join the 2nd Battalion. It turned out to be quite a long wait which was occupied by guard duties and strengthening various defences in Whitehall. Then I got my orders to leave, and said all my goodbyes. I even proposed to a girl with whom I was friendly. Goodness knows what would have happened if she had said yes. I was in no position to marry anyone, nor was it a very good time to do so. Luckily for both our sakes she had the sense to say no.

Then came a terrible anticlimax. The BEF were in retreat and our 2nd Battalion with everyone else fell back on Dunkirk, from which they miraculously escaped without too much loss, except for all their kit. All my orders were cancelled and after a few days I was sent to Shaftesbury where the Battalion now was. I found everyone exhausted after days of tough fighting and no sleep, and sensed a slight state of shock that the Army had been so hopelessly overrun and beaten in its first encounter with the Germans.

The Battalion had to be re-equipped and my first job was to

help in the distribution of all the stores as they arrived. We were in Monty's 3rd Division, and it was being given priority to be brought up to fighting strength in order to defend the south coast against possible invasion.

It was here for the first time that I came upon a ridiculous custom of the Brigade of Guards, namely that in the officers' mess no one spoke to a newly joined officer except in the course of duty. I gather that in peacetime this could go on for quite a time but in wartime, at least in our Battalion, it lasted for a fortnight. Even friends whom one had known before would avoid one or cut one dead. Then suddenly at the end of the period everyone began to smile and talk and from then on could not have been friendlier. I suppose it was intended to put the new boy in his place and prevent any possibility of him getting a swollen head. But frankly it made all those who took part look not only ridiculous but boorish and bad-mannered and I cannot believe that it did anyone any good.

I wish I had known then the following story which I should have enjoyed telling them. A newly joined officer was ordered to report to his Commanding Officer, who was determined to make him feel welcome and at ease.

'You'll soon settle down with us, I hope,' he said. 'We are a friendly lot and pride ourselves on making everyone feel at home in the mess. For instance, on Mondays we always have a get-together with plenty to drink. We really let our hair down and if anyone gets a bit drunk we turn a blind eye.' 'Excuse me, sir,' said the officer, 'but I'm afraid I don't drink.' 'Don't worry,' said the Colonel, 'there's always Wednesday nights when we invite some of the girls from the WRAC and nurses from the local hospital to a bit of slap and tickle in the mess. Great fun. A bit of sex does no one any harm. You'll enjoy it.' 'Excuse me, sir,' said the new officer again, 'but I don't really approve of that sort of thing.' The Colonel was taken aback, and after a pause said: 'Good gracious. Are you by any chance a queer?' 'Certainly not, sir,' replied the new officer indignantly. 'Pity,' said the Colonel, 'then you won't enjoy Saturday nights either!'

As soon as we had been re-equipped we left Shaftesbury to

take up positions on the beaches near Middleton-on-Sea in Sussex, where I was thrilled to see Charlie Kunz, the pianist with the soft touch, sunbathing in front of his house. But as the danger of invasion receded we moved first to Castle Cary in Somerset and then to Parkstone in Dorset.

To start with I was put in charge of the mortar platoon though I had never seen one fired nor in fact ever fired one in practice as we were conserving our ammunition. For equally good reasons I was given command of the motor-cycle platoon – I had never ridden one in my life! Still I soon learnt and even used to ride up a ramp and 'jump' the machine over some barrels. But I could never manage to start the wretched thing with the kick-starter, and was sometimes left stranded as I desperately tried to do so.

The platoon consisted of about twenty clapped-out second-hand machines which the Army had bought off the general public. On manoeuvres or in action I was meant to lead my platoon riding in a side-car – the sort of machine in which you could see a father taking his wife and two kids to the seaside on a bank holiday.

It was our job, if the invasion came, to proceed down a main road towards the coast until we met the advancing Germans. What was to happen then was not too clear, though I had a pretty shrewd guess! We had no protective armour of any sort and the guardsmen were only armed with rifles slung uncomfortably across their backs. I was even worse off as all I had was a revolver. We had no radio link of any sort, so if we had not been shot up first, all we could have done was to belt back up the road and warn our Battalion. But on our machines we should have been pushed to get there before the Germans.

It's funny now looking back, but rather frightening when you remember that my platoon was to be the advance guard of the crack 3rd Division on which the defence of southern England relied. In spite of Dad's Army I still cannot understand why Hitler never invaded.

We thought Hitler had invaded one night in September. We were playing bridge in the officers' mess when the telephone rang. The duty officer, who happened to be dummy, went to answer it and came back after a few minutes looking white and shaken. He told us it had been Brigade Headquarters who had said: 'Code-word Cromwell' and then rung off. The duty officer had gone to the orderly room, looked up the files and found that Cromwell meant that we were to mobilise the Battalion at once and get ready to move off, as invasion was either imminent or had already taken place.

I wish I could say that we did a Sir Francis Drake and finished our rubber. But in fact we all rushed into action. The Battalion was scattered over a large area and as there was no radio contact, the companies had either to be telephoned or warned by despatch riders, who also had to winkle the guardsmen out from pubs, cinemas and so on. In spite of apparent chaos it all worked quite well and the Battalion was standing by ready to move off in about two hours.

I'm still not clear what really happened that night and whether it was a genuine false alarm or a test of our mobility. Anyhow, as the advance guard, I had been sitting all night in my side-car at the head of the Battalion waiting for the 'off' and as you can imagine I was immensely relieved when we were eventually told to stand down.

In the autumn we moved to Parkstone and it was obvious that my superiors felt I would never make a good fighting solider. From the motor-cycle platoon I was sent on a Motor Transport course at Minehead, with a view to becoming the Transport Officer, although I was not the least technically minded. But I had a bit of luck.

At the end of the course there was to be an exam which I was dreading. On the night before, a friend who had been on the course with me was duty officer, and to his surprise found next day's questions in the in-tray in the Adjutant's room. When he came off duty he rushed round to me with a copy and we hurriedly looked up the answers. As a result I passed with flying colours, although ironically my friend only just passed!

On returning to the Battalion I was congratulated on my report and became the Transport Officer. It was a good job to have. We were left to ourselves, as everyone else knew even less about it than I did. I had a small élite staff of fitters and storemen and was never short of volunteers since we escaped most of the 'bull' and drill parades.

It was about this time that I indulged in my habit of giving people nicknames. In a most unguardsmanlike way I gave people on my staff such names as Honest Joe, Burglar Bill, Gandhi, the Admiral, and even extended it to the officers' mess where the Mess Sergeant became Uncle Tom.

Uncle Tom was a lovely person and looked after us superbly. He had been a cook and made the best chocolate pudding I have ever tasted. I even indoctrinated the regular officers so that in no time one could hear the Commanding Officer saying: 'Another pink gin please, Uncle Tom.' Scarcely credible really when you consider the traditional discipline of the Brigade of Guards. I was especially pleased with my nickname for one of my fellow officers called Neville Berry. He was known as The Hatchet. Got it?

Our Headquarters Company was stationed in an evacuated girls' school and some of the guardsmen slept in one of the old dormitories. They were delighted to find a notice on the wall which read: 'Please ring this bell if a mistress is required during the night'! We had three visits which I remember especially. The first was from Harry Hopkins, President Roosevelt's special envoy who was flying back to America from Hurn Airport after a visit to Winston Churchill. He stayed the night in our mess and breakfasted with us on powdered eggs. He was a quiet, friendly man, who looked pale and sick. He quizzed us about living conditions in Britain, and showed special interest in our families and their reaction to the bombing and blackout, obviously for the benefit of his master.

The next visit was from the Press who descended on us in a public relations exercise organised by the Army. The idea was for them to see how a battalion worked, so when they came to me I decided to give them good value. I gave a lot of pennies to one of my clerks and sent him out to ring my office every few minutes from a call-box. While I was being interviewed by the Press my telephone hardly stopped ringing and as a result I got a jolly good 'press' the next day saying how hard an MT officer had to work.

75

Our most important visitor at Parkstone was Monty – he came to inspect the Battalion. I remember that at lunch he pointedly quizzed our Commanding Officer Lt.-Col. Mike Venables-Llewelyn, on how the weekly five-mile run was going. This was Monty's keep-fit campaign in which everyone in the division from the highest-ranking officers to the lowest other ranks was required to go for a five-mile run once every week. Monty must have asked the question with his tongue in his cheek as Mike had what you might politely call an ample figure and could not have run one mile let alone five. He got away with it but I must admit that not many of us ever did carry out the order.

We used to set out from the mess at a trot looking very businesslike in shorts and gym shoes. But once round the corner out of sight we used to go for a walk round the block and sneak back to the mess through the back door. There was not much danger of being found out. The only risk was that one might run into Mike doing the same thing!

Whilst at Parkstone I had my first experience of a court-martial when one of my staff was due to be tried for being absent without leave.

An accused man was always allowed to pick any officer in the Battalion he wanted to defend him. My chap chose me although he was going to plead guilty on the main charge. But there was a charge of losing some kit which he denied and he also thought I might put in a good word for him and make an impassioned plea for mercy. I accepted the case as I was bound to do, and told the court consisting of a major, captain and second lieutenant that my 'client' was pleading guilty on the first charge but not guilty on the second.

This brought the prosecuting officer – our own Adjutant Neville Wigram – to his feet to read out a list of the kit that was said to be lost. They included small items like a mess tin, knife and fork. When he had finished I thought I would try to show how trivial this charge was against the overall cost of the war and ask for it to be dismissed. So I rose from my seat and advanced towards Neville like Perry Mason, tapped him in the chest and looking straight into his eyes said, 'Captain Wigram

I put it to you . . .' But I got no further and no one ever knew what it was that I was going to put. I am ashamed to say that Neville winked at me as I was talking and I burst out laughing and couldn't say another word. I tried to turn it into a coughing fit, went very red in the face and retreated hurriedly back to my seat, muttering about no further questions.

When I had recovered I did get up to plead for my client, saying what a good chap he was and that there had been extenuating circumstances, taking care not to reveal what they were, as I had not the slightest idea myself. I am afraid he had to pay for his kit. On reflection it does seem rather rough justice that he had to be defended by an officer who knew nothing of military law, court procedure nor how to conduct a case.

In May 1941 I received two bits of news, one bad, one good. The bad news was that No. 35 South Eaton Place, which I had shared before the war with William Douglas-Home, had been wrecked by a landmine which had fallen on the corner of Ebury Street. The Crisps, who had looked after us, were badly shocked but luckily unhurt otherwise. Most of my things were salvaged including a bottle of champagne which, however, I never saw again. A friend who was on leave at the time went round to see how the Crisps were and, spotting the bottle, quite rightly opened it and drank to their lucky escape. The house was impossible to live in again, and for the rest of the war the Crisps looked after a retired colonel in the village of Long Crendon just near to my mother.

From then on, whenever I was on leave in London I used to stay at the Savoy, a suitable base for my twice-daily visits to the theatre. But for the first twenty-four hours I always used to stay in my room overlooking the river and have all my meals in bed. Not only was this a much-needed rest but it was such a treat to be alone and in complete quiet. Some of the worst things in war were the people and the noise, and one was seldom alone, not even in the bathrooms or the loos.

The good news was that a Guards Armoured Division was to be formed and that several battalions were to be mechanised and turned into tank battalions. This meant that all that summer we went on a course to Bovingdon and I found myself being groomed for the job of Technical Adjutant. This involved learning some highly technical matters – which I never really came to understand.

The other battalions all sent people similar to myself and of about the same age. I think the reason for this was that the job of Technical Adjutant was a vital one in a tank battalion. He did not have to be highly technical but needed to be a good organiser and administrator, and able to stand up to the four company commanders, or squadron leaders as they were to become.

So far as the tanks, scout cars and vehicles were concerned the Technical Adjutant's word was law, and if he said a vehicle was not fit for action then the squadron leader could do nothing about it.

I was to remain Technical Adjutant for the next four years until the Guards Armoured Division was disbanded in July 1945. This must be something of a record in wartime when people are usually moved all over the place. But I was happy and I suppose the Battalion must have been too, so it suited us both.

When we became armoured we all had to wear berets and I had to adopt some psychological tactics. I knew what a clot I would look in one, so on the day the berets were issued, I paraded all my staff and said something like this: 'I have called you together so you can see me in my beret. If any of you want to laugh – and I don't blame you if you do – you may laugh now for two minutes. But after that if I ever catch anyone laughing at me he will be put into close arrest for insolence.' It was a bit unorthodox, but they had their laugh, and I never actually caught anyone laughing at me afterwards. So I suppose it can be said to have worked.

I was sent up to the English Electric factory at Stafford to see how our Covenanter and Crusader tanks were made. I was looked after by their new Public Relations Officer, a Mr Attock. They told me an intriguing story about him.

Earlier that year he had been on the short list for the PRO job and he and several others had to appear before a final board. They had been warned that they would have to make a short speech as part of the test, and a great deal would depend on its clarity and delivery. About two minutes before he was due to go before the board Mr Attock dashed off to the loo. While he was spending a penny he decided to take out his false teeth and give them an extra clean so as to give a good impression. Unfortunately he was so nervous that he dropped them down the loo. With now only a minute to go, what would you have done, chum? Remember you had to make a speech which was to be judged on its clarity. I cannot tell you what Mr Attock did. All I can tell you is that he got the job!

There was a well-equipped theatre in Warminister Barracks where Brigade HQ was situated, and Alfred Shaughnessy, the TV scriptwriter, and I put on a few shows. I did my usual cross-talk act, this time with my storeman as my stooge. We also had a first-class tenor, a young Irishman called Tom O'Brien, who really had a superb voice. But in one show his big scene was completely ruined. He was supposed to be a homesick prisoner of war in a realistic prison exercise yard with a strand of barbed wire across the front. This was very difficult to put up as it had to be uncoiled from the side of the stage in a blackout after a sketch. On the night in question Tom took up his position and the pit band struck up the opening bars of 'Shine through my Dreams', a song which normally brought tears to the eyes of the audience and received a tremendous ovation at the end.

But when the curtain rose it was obvious that any tears that night would be tears from laughter. Pinned to the barbed wire was the figure of an officer dressed in mess kit – an unlikely sight in a prison camp. It was in fact one of our own officers Hugh Burge who had been in the audience at the start but had at the last moment volunteered to stand in for an absent stagehand. He had had no time to rehearse but was just told by the stage manager to feed the barbed wire out on to the stage. Unfortunately he got caught in it and could only stand there looking helpless throughout the song. The audience roared their heads off and there were shouts of 'good old Hugh', 'Why are you so stuck up', etc.

The next two years we spent training with our tanks. From

Warminster we went to Norfolk and trained in the battle area which was later used by *Dad's Army* for all the action scenes in their TV series. It was there that we received our first Sherman tanks with which we were later to fight.

General Paget, the Commander-in-Chief, Home Forces came to inspect us and very smart he looked in breeches and highly polished riding boots – but definitely not the correct gear to wear if you intend to inspect a tank. With great difficulty he climbed up on to one of the Shermans and inevitably slipped and slid right down the side of the tank. Highly undignified and very painful.

It was here in Norfolk that the first steps of my BBC career were unknowingly taken.

I was sitting in our mess one day when a great friend in our 1st Battalion, Nigel Baker, telephoned to say he had a chap from the BBC staying in his mess. He was a Canadian called Stewart Macpherson who was attached to them to gain experience as a war reporter ready for when the Second Front came. Nigel asked whether they could come over to dinner and also bring another BBC reporter who was attached to the Irish Guards for the same purpose.

Of course I said yes and we had an hilarious evening, which was not surprising because the second reporter was that effervescent Welshman, Wynford Vaughan-Thomas. I saw a lot of them during the next few weeks and though I did not know it at the time, this chance meeting with these two famous broadcasters was to change my whole life.

From Norfolk we went to Yorkshire and took part in a number of exercises involving many miles in the tanks and nights out in the open even though it was still winter. We bought three white hens which we used to take out with us in a tool-box on top of the cab of the store truck. They laid quite a few eggs and we had plenty of 'fry-ups' in the back of the truck.

Then early in May we moved down the length of England to Hove. There was a big build-up of tension and the whole of southern England was one large and armed camp, full of troops and vehicles getting ready for D-Day, which was obviously fast approaching. We all had the feeling that for some of us this would be the last time we should ever see England and decided to enjoy ourselves while we could.

On 6 June came John Snagge's announcement on the BBC that the invasion had started. From then on we were on permanent stand-by. We reluctantly gave away our three white hens but had two buckets of pickled eggs to take with us in case food was short in France. After the initial landings, bad weather slowed down the build-up of tanks and it was nearly three weeks before we received our orders to move.

One morning the people of Hove woke up to find we had gone, though I suspect the roar and rumbling of our tanks must have disturbed their sleep that night. We moved to near Portsmouth where we loaded our tanks and vehicles on to landing-craft and crossed over to Arromanches in a large convoy. After nearly three years of training and learning to be tank-men we were about to be put to the test. At last we were genuinely at war.

Things got off to a bad start. First some of the guardsmen on our landing-craft mistook the wash-basins sticking out from the wall for something else and used them accordingly, much to the indignation of the sailors. From then on they referred to the guardsmen as 'those pissing pongos'. So much for inter-service relations!

Then we had a calamity with our pickled eggs. We had hung the buckets from the roof of the store truck thinking the landing-craft would deposit it right up the beach. But the weather was still rough and our vehicles had to be unloaded quite a way out to sea. This meant driving down a deep ramp into the water. Our driver did his best but when his front wheel hit the bottom the buckets swung about all over the place and the eggs flew in every direction. We managed to salvage a few from the bottom of the buckets and were soon eating our first fried eggs on French soil in an orchard near Bayeux. This was enclosed farming country known as *bocage* and was quite unsuitable for tanks, which operate best in open country.

There were a few minor actions and skirmishes but everyone became very frustrated at our apparent immobility. We discovered later that Monty was deliberately using us as a sitting target to draw the fire and attention of as much of the German army as possible. This was to enable the Americans under Patton to break out from the west right across France and so trap the German 7th Army in the famous Falaise Gap.

It was not much fun just sitting there being shelled every day, but even that was better than the Division's first big battle on 18 July. This was a bloody and chaotic affair fought for much of the time in clouds of black dust churned up by our tanks. The first I saw of my very first battle was hordes of bombers going over us at dawn as we lay in the fields waiting to advance.

There were two thousand of them and they were meant to soften up the opposition with their blanket bombing. It looked as if they had succeeded because as we advanced slowly through the dust thousands of bedraggled German prisoners passed us marching disconsolately back to our prisoner-of-war camps. But we were soon to meet tough opposition from some strategically placed Tiger tanks which with their big guns knocked out nine of our tanks. Most of them blew up and we suffered the inevitable casualties, many through burning. For us this was our first taste of real war and it was not much fun.

I am not going to attempt to give you a round-by-round commentary on what we did from then on. I was only the Technical Adjutant and although from my own point of view I was often too damn close I was not one of those actually fighting the battles in the tanks. They are the people best qualified to tell the tale. But I am never likely to forget those hot summer days from June to October.

The heat and the dust, the flattened cornfields, the 'liberated' villages which were just piles of rubble, the refugees, the stench of dead cows, our first shelling, real fear, the first casualties, friends wounded or killed, men with whom one had laughed and joked the evening before, lying burnt beside their knocked-out tank. No, war is *not* fun, though as years go by, one tends to remember only the good things. The changes are so sudden. One moment boredom or laughter, the next, action and death. So it was with us.

From the frustrations of Normandy with the Americans

getting all the headlines and glory, we were suddenly given the green light to 'go'. We made a mad dash across France and Belgium and actually advanced 395 miles in seven days, with a final spurt of ninety-three miles in one day on 3 September to liberate Brussels. It was exhilarating and thrilling and our good old Sherman tanks performed wonders as they tore up miles and miles of French and Belgian roads with hardly a breakdown.

The scenes of welcome and enthusiasm were unforgettable and the cheering crowds in the towns and the villages often held up our progress as they thrust flowers, fruit and eggs onto the passing vehicles. Better still, the pretty mademoiselles showered kisses on anyone they could reach – even the Technical Adjutant. But it was not roses all the way. Parts of the country were still held by the retreating Germans and hard fighting took place here and there. After passing through one cheering village with the pavements lined with women and children, and gay flags and bunting, we rounded the corner and came upon one of our tanks knocked out, with two of its crew lying dead beside it. So all along the route as we raced towards Brussels, joy and sorrow went hand in hand.

Brussels really went wild as our tanks roared into the city late in the evening of 3 September. Everyone was delirious, the hospitality was fantastic and there was no sleep for anyone that night. Unfortunately for us it was short-lived as we left the next afternoon following hard on the heels of the Germans. They had left Brussels by one end as we entered it at the other and so had had no time to blow up bridges or burn important papers.

More important from our point of view was a secret store full of Krug vintage champagne to which a friendly Belgian led us. It had been left by the Germans and we distributed a bottle apiece to the tanks there and then, and put the rest onto one of our petrol lorries, which for the next few weeks went up to the tanks at night with the petrol convoy, but carried bottles instead of jerry cans.

A fortnight later our tanks made another dash – this time across Holland – to capture Nijmegen Bridge. The idea was to link up with the airborne forces who had 'dropped' at Arnhem across the River Waal. As we approached the town of Nijmegen we were met by the officer commanding all the airborne troops some of whom, like himself, had glided in on our side of the Waal.

It was my cousin 'Boy' Browning – now Lieutenant-General. It was a dramatic moment for him as he greeted his old 2nd Battalion which he had commanded in its infantry days just before the war. After a desperate struggle a troop of our tanks under the present Lord Carrington captured the huge Nijmegen Bridge, but alas the planned link-up with Arnhem never took place. If this was a history of war I would try to explain why, but luckily it isn't. But had the plan succeeded the war would probably have been over by Christmas.

As it was we had a cold and unpleasant winter digging our tanks out of mud and snow. It was not until the end of March that we finally crossed the Rhine and fought our way up through Germany. Although it was obvious that the war was nearing its end the Germans on our front, many of them from the navy, put up a fanatical resistance and we suffered many casualties in the last few weeks. It was a terrible time for the men in our tanks. They knew that either victory or death was just around the corner but which would it be? For some sadly, as I've said, it was death.

On the lighter side, I actually captured three German prisoners all off my own bat. At about 5.00 p.m. one evening I was going up in my scout car to some tanks of ours in a burning village which a squadron had just taken. It was nearly dark and we were travelling very slowly when all of a sudden three grey figures rose up out of a ditch and ran towards my scout car. I had visions of hand-grenades and quickly pulled down my armoured hatch.

There were loud bangings on the side of the car and I peeped out through the visor at the side. To my relief I saw six arms in the air and heard voices shouting, 'Kamerad!' Quickly I stuck my head out of the hatch and became every inch a true Grenadier!

With signs, I ordered the Germans to clamber onto the car

1a The Boat Race,
1989, before the start.
(*L to r*) Tom Boswell,
Tom Sutton, B.J.,
Caroline Elliott
(Producer).

1b B.J. as Junior Office
Boy in the family coffee
business, 1934.

2a *Down Your Way* in Sutton Coldfield.
B.J. with twelve-year-old Helen Feltrup, one of
his youngest 'victims' and a brilliant violinist.

2b (*Below left*) B.J. in 'Pop' at Eton, 1931.

2c (*Below right*) B.J. with friend in the full 'Pop' dress – white tie,
carnation, coloured waistcoat, sponge-bag trousers.

3a The Johnston clan taken in the garden of our home in St John's Wood on 15 December 1991. (*L to r, standing*) Andrew, David Oldridge (son-in-law), Joanna, Barry, Ian; (*l to r, sitting*) Gilly (daughter-in-law) with Georgia, Pauline, B.J., Clare with Sophie; (*front row*) Emily, Nicholas, Harry, Rupert.

3b (*Below left*) 2nd Lieutenant Johnston on joining the Grenadier Guards, February 1940.

3c (*Below right*) Technical Adjutant Johnston with TQMS Cross (*left*) and Sergeant Reed, 1944.

4a B.J. getting fit before a Test match under the direction of England cricket trainer Bernard Thomas.

4b 'Let's Go Somewhere', 1951. B.J. disguised as a Channel swimmer treads water as Sam Rockett feeds him with grapes.

5 'Let's Go Somewhere', 1949. B.J. attempting to stand up
on a horse at Harringay Circus.

6 'Let's Go Somewhere', 1950. B.J. laughs hysterically
after being hypnotised by David Stewart.

7 'Let's Go Somewhere', 1950. B.J. plays a street piano outside the stage door of the Victoria Palace as he and Bud Flanagan sing 'Underneath the Arches'.

8 The famous Long Room at Lord's.

and we bore them back in triumph to Battalion Headquarters where I was treated as a bit of a hero until I owned up to what had really happened.

By the last week in April the Division was on the outskirts of Bremen and Hamburg, and they fell to us on 26 April and 2 May respectively. The next day General Sir Brian Horrocks, our 30 Corps Commander, paid us a visit and seemed far less enthusiastic than usual. He suggested to our Commanding Officer that we should take things quietly for a day or two and not attempt to advance any further. He said he wanted to review the situation. But of course as he told us afterwards he knew that the armistice was about to be signed any day, and he wished to avoid any unnecessary loss of life in the last few hours of the war. Still, at the time, I must admit that we thought he was getting senile and losing his drive.

We actually heard the good news on the radio on 5 May and it was amazing how calmly everyone took it. Peace. We just could not believe it. So far as I remember I went and sat on the loo out of relief. We had a few celebrations in the Mess tent that night and I had a few drinks with my own boys. But the greatest treat was not having to 'stand to' at dawn for the first time since arriving in Europe. Reveille was actually put back to 7 a.m. What luxury!

As soon as the war was over we had been told that we were going to be turned back into the infantry. This meant saying goodbye to our tanks, which we did in a giant parade in front of Monty on Rotenburg airfield on 9 June. In true Guards fashion the tank crews cleaned, painted and polished their tanks and burnished their guns.

Over 300 tanks were formed up in one long line and they dipped their guns in salute as Monty stepped out of his aeroplane. He then made an extremely complimentary speech – '... I want to say here and now that in the sphere of armoured warfare you have set a standard that it would be difficult for those that come after to reach. ... You have achieved great results. ... You will long be remembered for your prowess in armoured warfare.' Not bad coming from Monty. It made our three years of training all seem worthwhile.

I ceased to be Technical Adjutant after what must be a record four years and was promoted to be a major in command of the HQ Company, with special responsibility for welfare. We soon set about preparing a revue which we called *The Eyes Have It* (the insignia of the Guards Armoured Division had been an ever-open eye).

We staged the revue in a well-equipped theatre in Bad Godesberg where it played to packed houses for a week. We then spent much of the remainder of the summer touring with it round all the units of the Division. It was quite an ambitious production with a pit orchestra, professional sets and lighting. We even imported two girls from Brussels.

I am afraid many of the jokes would not pass the BBC censors even with today's liberated outlook. Two samples: A man and girl riding a tandem cycle came to the bottom of a hill. Said the man, 'Get off. We are going to push it up here.' Replied the girl, 'Suits me but what shall we do with the bike?' Or, a honeymoon couple were having a very late breakfast in their hotel bedroom. The bride rang the bell and ordered bacon and eggs for two and lettuce for one. 'What's the lettuce for?' asked the groom. 'I want to see if you also *eat* like a rabbit,' said the bride. See what I mean?

The autumn became a series of leaving parties as wartime-only officers and men were gradually being demobbed. In November it was my turn and Hugh Burge (of the barbed wire) and I gave a big party in the *schloss*, with band, cabaret and lashings of champagne.

And so I returned to England, drew my blue pinstripe demob suit from Olympia, and went down to my mother's cottage to sort myself out and decide exactly what I was going to do with my future.

H
for Health

Good health may not ensure happiness, but it certainly helps. Bad health may not ensure unhappiness, but it usually does. One definite exception is my daughter Joanna. She is now twenty-six, has a fairly mild form of Down's syndrome and for nineteen years has been diabetic. A happier person it would be hard to find.

I myself (touch wood) have been immensely lucky. I have no real secret ingredient for my good health except, perhaps, luck. I do not smoke; I drink only champagne or white wine; I try to walk at least a short distance each day; and I am frequently laughing, which I am told is good for you.

In forty-seven years of broadcasting I have never had to miss a single day through illness. On two occasions when I had operations two *planned* broadcasts had to be postponed. But I never failed to turn up after a broadcast had been advertised in the *Radio Times* – that includes nearly 1,350 days of Test cricket over forty-six summers, and 733 programmes of *Down Your Way* over fifteen consecutive years. Obviously there were times when I didn't feel 100 per cent, but only once did I nearly have to stop a broadcast because I was unwell. This was in Northern Ireland where we recorded one *Down Your Way* programme on the first day, and halfway through recording a second programme the next day I got the most terrible pain somewhere in the left side of my stomach. It was agony and as I learnt later was a stone passing through my urinary duct. My interviewees were very kind and sympathetic and gave me various pills to kill the pain. These were semi-successful and I was able to finish the three remaining interviews. My producer dropped me at the airport in Belfast, still clutching my side and looking utterly miserable. But amazingly as I sat there waiting for the plane the pain suddenly stopped. I went straight to my doctor on arriving home, and he diagnosed what had happened.

The same thing occurred in the middle of the night to my son-in-law when we were all staying at a hotel in Shropshire for my son Andrew's wedding. My daughter woke me up and said her husband David was rolling about on the floor in agony. We quickly telephoned for an ambulance, but by then I remembered that I had once been told of a possible cure. So I made him sip a glass of boiling water and miraculously before the ambulance had arrived, his pain had gone. It's not a bad tip if it ever happens to you.

As a boy I had the usual chickenpox and measles but luckily avoiding whooping cough and mumps. I have always been particularly apprehensive of catching the latter after being told at Eton about a housemaster called Mr Sladden. We were told that when he had mumps his testicles swelled up to the size of coconuts! However I did suffer quite a few set-backs *before* the war. When aged six I fell off the top of a hay cart and fell heavily on my left leg. I was in great pain and the doctor said it was something called periostitis – the bruising of the membrane of my shin-bone. At this time X-rays were just being developed and my leg was X-rayed at a medical function before a lot of doctors who had never seen an X-ray before.

My next mishap was in Brazil during the carnival in February 1938, the hottest and stickiest month of the year. I had been joining in the revelry when I gradually felt a numbness in my legs and arms, and I began to lose the use of them. I was helped back to my hotel and by then was semi-paralysed. It was terrifying. Luckily there was a first-class Brazilian doctor who knew exactly what was wrong. It was a sort of beriberi called acute peripheral neuritis. He told me it was something brought on by too much gin or by childbirth! The first *could* have been the cause, but definitely not the second! He went on to say that it was probably due to a deficiency of vitamin B, and he suspected that I had not been eating sufficient vegetables. He was right. Anyhow the wife of one of our firm had been a doctor and she was an absolute saint. She took me into her house and nursed me for nearly six weeks. Each day I was injected twice in the bottom with vitamin B, fed on raw vegetables – including lots of tomatoes which I have hated ever since, and also had daily massages and sunbathing. You can imagine my relief one day when I found I could wriggle my big toe and gave a shout of joy.

I gradually got better and was put on a boat back to England where I spent six months recuperating. Gentle exercise but no games, no drink, lots of sleep and not too much excitement. It enabled me to watch a lot of cricket including the second Test at Lord's where Hammond made a brilliant 240.

It had all been rather a shock, and ever since then I have tried to eat plenty of green vegetables and fruit (except tomatoes) and have also cut out gin. My dislike of tomatoes brought quite a funny sequel. About forty years later I was doing a *Down Your Way* in Banbury where Heinz have a large factory. During the interview I said to one of the directors how much I enjoyed the Heinz tomato soup. 'Why, especially?' he asked. 'Oh,' I said, 'because it *doesn't* taste of tomatoes which I hate.' He nearly had a fit and wanted to cut the recording. But to me, at least, it *is* true – it tastes nothing like tomatoes.

My next health mishap was in 1941 after the 2nd Battalion Grenadier Guards had become armoured. This involved a lot of lifting of heavy things like tracks or wheels and I got a hernia. I was operated on in a hospital in Salisbury and was away from duty for about six weeks. This recalled the old joke about the man recuperating from a hernia – he went to Hernia Bay, stayed at a Truss House Hotel and had a rupturuous time!

At about the same time I suffered severe damage to my nose when my scout car pitched into an old shell hole on Salisbury Plain and I was flung forward and smashed my face against the armour plating. There were no seat belts in a scout car. Our Medical Officer cleaned me up and did a great job of stitching it but I still have the scar to prove it.

Nothing more happened until 1956 when I had to have another hernia operation – on the other side. There was a strange coincidence about this. My doctor, the old England rugger international, R. Cove-Smith, sent me to a surgeon in Harley Street. He examined me, and paid particular attention to the faint scar on my right side. He asked me who had done the operation.

'Oh,' I said, 'some army surgeon at Salisbury who came from the London Hospital.'

'Yes,' he said, 'it's not a bad job. I must have been in good form that day. I'll try to match it on the other side!' Believe it or not, he had been the surgeon in Salisbury.

Like everyone else I suffer from general aches and pains sometimes in the shoulder, or the various trigger spots. Over thirty years ago I suffered with what was called a 'cold shoulder', with shooting pains down my right arm. On someone's advice I bought one of those copper bracelets and have worn one ever since on my right wrist. Believe it or not, the pain soon went away and has so far never returned. For the trigger spots I use a cream called Balmosa which works like magic and dissolves any of the 'screws' in a day or two.

Four years ago I had to have another hernia operation on my right side but otherwise have – as I write – remained unscathed.

I realise how lucky I have been when I have seen so many great games players and athletes limping around with sticks with either knee or hip trouble. The late Marquess of Exeter (Lord Burghley the Olympic hurdler) was completely crippled, as were W. Wakefield and R. Cove-Smith, the famous duo in the England pack, sharing over sixty caps between them. Cricketers like Bob Wyatt and Gubby Allen had countless hip operations, and the knee brigade include Denis Compton, J. J. Warr, Bob Willis, Mike Procter and Ted Dexter. It's doubly sad to see such great performers suffering where lesser mortals go free.

I

for *In Town Tonight*

In January 1946 I joined the BBC's Outside Broadcast Department, mostly covering theatres and music-halls. At that time, and right into the mid-fifties, *In Town Tonight*, with its famous 'Knightsbridge March' signature tune, was BBC Radio's flagship programme. It had the amazing listening figures of 20,000,000 or more every Saturday night until, with the opening of the Sutton Coldfield (1950) and Holme Moss (1952) transmitters, BBC TV was able to cover most of the country. Then for a year or two *In Town Tonight* was broadcast simultaneously on both TV and radio, being produced in Lime Grove instead of Broadcasting House.

It was a live programme and anyone who was 'anyone' who was in London that night was invited to take part. Indeed many agents of the stars begged for their clients to be included. It was a great shop window for all visiting personalities from anywhere in the world, not just from the world of entertainment but for businessmen, sportsmen and politicians as well.

In addition to the important and well-known guests the programme also contained ordinary people from all walks of life who had a good story to tell of some adventure or achievement.

Unbelievably today, every interview was fully scripted even including 'good evening' or 'thank you'. There was also a complete run-through earlier in the evening. As a result, however interesting the person interviewed might be, unless they could read a script cleverly it all sounded stilted, flat and unexciting. No unexpected or off-the-cuff remarks were allowed. The script had to be strictly adhered to and so it never really sounded like a casual conversation which is what a good interview should be.

There was a panic one Saturday night when Danny Kaye –

a bit of an eccentric – was the star guest, due to come on last. It was the turn of Lord Rootes, the car manufacturer, to be interviewed by the presenter John Ellison. Danny Kaye left the control room where he was waiting and went into the studios. As a joke (?) he snatched Lord Rootes' script and flung the pages all over the studio as if throwing confetti. Lord Rootes was plainly shaken but a secretary dashed in with a script and so saved the day.

In addition to the half dozen or so interviews in the programme there had for some time been an extra ingredient – a live outside broadcast of about three and a half minutes.

It started with Michael Standing's *Standing on the Corner*, when he used to interview passers-by and incidentally got some pretty fruity answers! This was followed by *Man in the Street* featuring Harold Warrender and later Stewart Macpherson. This in turn became *On the Job* where John Ellison interviewed anyone who might be working on a Saturday night – newspaper seller, barman, bus conductor etc. These were unscripted but were inevitably restricted to words without any action.

In the spring of 1948 John was promoted to studio interviewer, and the producer Peter Duncan asked me to take over from John. Throughout the spring and summer I accordingly interviewed a number of people for *On the Job* including, I remember, a wheel tapper at Waterloo station. I tried to find out why he tapped the wheels of a train but, although he had been doing it most of his working life, he did not know the answer! I expect you have noticed that there are no wheel tappers today. I found it all rather tame and too similar to what was happening in the studio. Peter Duncan thought the same and asked my boss Lobby (Seymour de Lotbinière) and me whether it would be possible to do something with more movement and excitement and even with the occasional bit of humour – in complete contrast to the scripted interviews in the studio. So we decided to revive a feature called *Let's Go Somewhere* which John Snagge had done in the thirties.

Let's Go Somewhere was to start in October and we immediately set about thinking up some ideas. Little did I think then that I would do 150 of these broadcasts, and that except for the summer break which *In Town Tonight* always took, Saturday nights would not be my own for the next four years.

I could never had done the series without the help and skill of our enginners in OBs. Spud Moody, a dynamic little grey-haired man, was to be my 'Svengali'. He was responsible for many of the ideas, and worked out how they could be done technically. This was not always easy if I was riding a horse round a circus ring or being rescued from the sea by a helicopter. Without his cheerful support I could never have gone on week after week. People of course sent in ideas but many of them were impossible to do and others I just did not fancy. Like the listener who suggested that I jump off Nelson's Column with an open umbrella as a parachute!

The spot was always live, not recorded, and lasted from three and a half to four minutes. This meant that each Saturday became a 'first night' and one either got it right or wrong. There could be no retakes. As a result we had our failures and, I hope, our successes. But it was always hit-or-miss. I had no producer to help me and I even had to carry and keep an eye on my own stopwatch, no matter what I was doing. My team just consisted of myself and our engineer Nogs Newman, who, with occasional relief from a colleague, Oggie Lomas, gave up all his Saturday nights. He never complained and remained cheerful, wet or fine, failure or success. I owe these backroom boys a deep debt of gratitude for all their skill and loyalty. But like me they seemed to enjoy it. It was a challenge with plenty of variety and the skills required by both engineers and commentator in order to produce a good broadcast were really what broadcasting is all about.

I won't bore you with a complete list of all the things I did during the course of our show, but will select a few from each category – exciting, funnies, musical, theatrical and so on.

The very first came from the Chamber of Horrors in Madame Tussauds. There was a story going about that they would pay £100 to anyone who would spend the night there alone. It was rumoured that one or two people had tried and had gone off their heads. We checked with Tussauds' Public Relations Officer Reg Edds who denied the story completely. He added that no member of the public had in fact ever been there alone after the section closed at 7.00 p.m. He offered to let me be the first person to do this and that after *In Town Tonight* I could stay on until 11.00 p.m. for a later broadcast but definitely *not* all night.

I was secretly very relieved at this and we agreed to do *Let's Go Somewhere* at about 7.30 p.m. and then a later broadcast before the Home Service closed down at 11.00 p.m. Just before 7.00 p.m. I went, somewhat apprehensively, down the twisty stone staircase into the Chamber of Horrors, and through the iron gate which clanged shut behind me. Nogs had left a microphone and a pair of headphones by a chair under the only light in the Chamber – a very dim bulb rather like those in a wartime railway carriage. The leads from the mike disappeared through the iron gate, and were my only link with the outside world.

Reg had had the chair placed in front of a group of murderers consisting of Crippen, Smith of the 'brides in the bath', and Mahon the Eastbourne trunk murderer. These figures were tremendously likelike and were dressed in the actual clothes they had worn when alive – Madame Tussauds used to buy them off the widows. In addition to all the murderers, there were instruments of torture like the rack, a guillotine and the actual bath used by Smith. Definitely not a place for the squeamish. I had brought the evening paper with me and while waiting sat down to read the football results. I had the uncanny feeling that Crippen was looking over my shoulder to see how Arsenal had got on.

Then I tried walking round the dark Chamber but it was too eerie and I felt that all the staring eyes of the figures were following me around. So I hurried back to my chair and something soft brushed against my head – it was the noose of a hangman's rope! Even worse when I sat down, there was a low rumbling noise and all the figures began to sway slightly. It shook me for a moment but then I remembered we were directly over the Bakerloo line and that this must be the trains passing by underneath.

I was in quite a state by the time I put on my headphones to get my cue from John Ellison, and my voice was unusually shaky as I greeted listeners for my first *Let's Go Somewhere*. I described the Chamber to them and tried to give a picture of what it was like down there alone in the semi-darkness with all those terrible people. I said goodbye with great reluctance when my time was up, as it was the last time I would be speaking to anyone for the next three and a half hours. Home Service were to come back before they closed down to check up if I was still sane.

I must say it seemed a very long wait. Pauline had provided me with some food but when I took my first bite at an apple it echoed round and round the Chamber. I did not dare walk round again so just sat and got colder and stiffer. And for those of you who, like me, are interested in that sort of thing, I can reveal that there was a bucket available should the call of nature make it necessary. But in fact it wasn't. Anyway I was extremely relieved when Home Service called me up just before 11.00 p.m. and Reg Edds unlocked the iron gate to let me out. It was not an experience I want to go through again, and although I think I just managed to keep my sanity, I have never been down there since.

As a boy I had often read thrillers in which the hero was trapped on the railway, and had to lie down between the rails and let the express roar over him. He always emerged none the worse for the experience, so we thought we would try in in real life.

Southern Region (SR) gave me permission to do the broadcast from a stretch of line about a mile out of Victoria Station. It was not as dangerous as it sounds, as at that spot there was a deepish pit between the lines where it was possible to crouch as the trains roared by overhead. We ran out the microphone cable under the lines but had to be very careful as they were of course electrified and my heart was in my mouth each step I took over one. A man from the SR and myself took up our position in the pit and it was hoped to time the broadcast to coincide with the arrival of the Golden Arrow. Unfortunately it was late and when they cued over to me I had to make do with an electric train. It was quite a frightening sight as it thundered towards me in the dark, sparks flying everywhere. When it got about thirty yards away I ducked down and I must say got a terrible shaking as it sped over me. It made quite an exciting broadcast with my build-up of the approaching train and the sound effects when it finally arrived.

The SR man told me to stay where I was as the Golden Arrow was now due on the same line and when it had passed we should have more time to negotiate the live rails in the dark. It was jolly lucky we were not on the air when the Golden Arrow did eventually come – as when it passed over me someone was washing their hands – at least I hope they were! I got absolutely soused and my subsequent language would not have enhanced my BBC career had it gone out over the air.

One Christmas I went to the circus at Harringay Arena and tried my hand at riding bareback (the horse not me!) round the ring during a performance before a packed audience. This involved some rather tricky technical arrangements as I was suspended on the end of a pulley so that if I fell off I would be landed gently into the middle of the ring. The idea was to canter round once or twice in the normal position, then try kneeling and finally standing up.

I just managed the kneeling part but as soon as I tried to stand up lost my balance and was swung across the ring. I breathlessly described my efforts into the microphone tied across my chest. But for good fun I had added one extra ingredient. One of the clowns lent me his 'quick-release' trousers and as I felt myself falling I pulled a tape and the trousers fell down to my ankles as I landed with a plop in the middle of the ring. The audience had been told that I was broadcasting in *In Town Tonight* and the sight of 'the man from Auntie' with no trousers brought the house down.

There was a sequel to this. A few weeks later a friend of mine went to the same circus when my clown friend came on disguised as a member of the audience to try his hand at riding the horse. He always did this at the end after everyone else had tried, and in fact I had filled his spot. He did what I had done, though of course far more skilfully and at the end down came his trousers. Two people sitting behind my friend said: 'What a shame. He must have been listening to *In Town Tonight* and he has pinched Brian Johnston's idea.'

Something rather more frightening was when we decided to see how effective a police or guard dog could be in chasing and catching a criminal. A broadcaster called Trevor Hill owned an Alsatian called Rustler who was trained to do almost anything and had in fact played himself in a TV series *Riders of the Range*. I was given a special coat with heavy padding on the left arm and was assured that Rustler had been trained to go for this, and no other part of me. For the broadcast I got Pauline to walk across the BBC cricket ground and I crept up behind her and snatched her bag, and ran off. As rehearsed, she let out a piercing scream and Trevor was soon on the scene with Rustler on a lead. After hearing Pauline's explanation of what had happened he released Rustler and ordered him to 'get' me. By this time I had gone about eighty yards and was quite out of breath trying to talk and run at the same time.

I could hear Rustler padding up behind me and it reminded me of the *Hound of the Baskervilles*, as he got closer and closer. When he reached me he leaped through the air and seized me by my padded left arm, and his weight knocked me to the ground. I could just feel his teeth through the padding, but as soon as I was down he let go and stood on guard wagging his tail as he waited for Trevor to arrive. But when I tried to get up and escape he bared his teeth and seized me once again. So I thought it wiser to lie still until Trevor arrived and put him on his lead. It had been an impressive performance and I hope acted as a deterrent to any potential bag-snatcher who happened to be listening – especially as they would not have the benefit of the padded arm.

I was several times challenged to be the target for a knife-throwing act but always refused, making the excuse that there was bound to be an element of risk of serious injury and that it would not be fair to Pauline. Actually of course I was scared stiff at the prospect. I reckoned that even knife-throwers are human and can make mistakes, just as a great batsman is clean bowled or an expert shot misses the bull's-eye.

But I did accept a similar challenge and looking back, I was a fool even to do that. There was a darts champion called Joe Hitchcock who in his spare time used to visit pubs and give demonstrations of nail-throwing in aid of charity. He had a stooge who stood sideways about ten feet away and Joe would then throw six-inch nails with specially sharpened points. The stooge would start with a cigarette in his mouth. Joe would knock this out with a nail. The cigarette was then replaced with a matchstick, with the same result. The stooge then turned his back on Joe and stuck a cigarette in each ear and whizz would come the nails and knock them out – usually but not always first throw. Then the stooge would again stand sideways, fling his head back and balance a penny on the end of his nose. This time Joe took one or two 'sighters' but always just above the penny not under, as otherwise the nail would have gone slap through the stooge's nose.

Then, as if that were not enough, came the climax. The penny was replaced by a pin of all things, and once again Joe knocked that off. I felt an awful coward but all I would agree to Joe doing was the cigarette stuck in the mouth and ears. Even so I was frightened and let the listeners hear the pounding of my heart as I held my mike over it. It was a horrid moment waiting for those nails realising that the slightest mistake and one of my eardrums could be punctured. He missed once or twice – deliberately I am sure to build up the tension – and each time the nails whizzed by my head. That was a broadcast I did not enjoy. About two years later I had another challenge from Joe. He said he was now doing the act blindfolded. You can guess what my answer was!

Equally frightening was riding pillion on a motor bike through a wall of empty beer barrels. This was a stunt done by a character called Mad Johnny Davies. He also used to ride through burning hoops or even through a sheet of glass. He did this stripped to the waist and afterwards had to pluck bits of glass splinters out of his body. I decided to play safe and chose the barrels as being the least dangerous. But in all these stunts I always made sure first of the skill and safety record of those with whom I was working. In the same way that Joe Hitchcock's stooge was apparently unharmed, Johnny Davies was still in one piece.

So I strapped a mike to my chest, got on the pillion and prepared to take a 200 yards' run at the barrels which were piled high in a pyramid fifteen feet high. We were on a large recreation ground and it was a bit greasy from rain. But we soon got up speed and by the time we reached the barrels were going at a good fifty m.p.h. I really was scared at what lay ahead but I tried to keep talking as we roared across the ground. I must confess that I was hugging Johnny as if he had been my girlfriend. I had worked it out that I would be the third thing to hit the barrels, first the front wheel of the bike, then Johnny, then me.

There was a terrific bang as we hit the barrels, piles of debris shot into the air and the bike slithered and skidded all over the place. But Johnny managed to keep it upright and we came to a welcome halt. Apart from the impact as the bike struck the barrels I had not felt anything except a few bits of barrel landing on my head. But it's not a way I would like to earn my living.

Another test of my nerves was when I lay on a table on the ice rink at the Empress Hall and was jumped over by a speed skater. Once again I made sure he was an expert but even so the flash of the skates as they passed inches over my body were a fairly forbidding sight. Some years later on TV I was jumped over by four horses as I sat drinking a cup of tea at an army trestle table. This was during a rehearsal for a military tattoo and I think that I preferred the skates to those hooves.

At the start of the series we had been asked to get some movement into the programme and we did our best to carry out our brief. I piloted a light aircraft, drove a steam train, launched a lifeboat, rode on the Big Dipper, and tried to keep talking as I was hurled round and round the Rotor at the Olympia sideshows. I also challenged the Brighton police to catch me in my car after doing a smash-and-grab and needless to say I lost.

One of the coldest jobs was when I went out in a boat five miles off Folkestone with Sam Rockett the channel swimmer. We wanted to see what it was like for a swimmer to be fed while in the water. I trod water by the boat as Sam leant out and fed me with nuts, dates and grapes and gave me orange juice to drink. This I understand was the staple diet for such occasions but I found it almost impossible to talk and eat and avoid swallowing oceans of sea water. It was also freezing cold so far out and I was frozen and exhausted when lifted back into the boat. I had only been in the water for about five minutes. Channel swimmers stay in for fourteen hours or more. Rather them than me.

One of the most painful things I did was to try out the ejector seat which pilots use to escape from the cockpits of jet planes. In the old days a pilot could clamber over the side and drop with his parachute. But now the jets go so fast that if a pilot stuck his head out it would be like hitting it against a brick wall at 500 m.p.h. So now he slides back the canopy of his cockpit and pulls a small canvas screen over his face. This fires two charges which eject the seat at great speed, sixty feet into the air clear of the plane. The seat has its own little parachute which opens and gives the pilot time to get out of the seat, drop off and open his own individual parachute.

The purpose of the screen over the face is to prevent burning and blast on the face when it meets the air at speed. It also pulls the head and neck down. Otherwise they might be thrown back and the neck possibly broken. The seat was invented by Sir Martin Baker and is made at a factory at Denham where they have a test seat which shoots sixty feet up a vertical tower and is halted when it reaches the top. I broadcast from this seat and had a nasty few seconds before pulling the face screen down. I shot up into the night. The acceleration was phenomenal and I had no time to say a word before I reached the top. It is a wonderful invention and has saved hundreds of lives all over the world. The only snag from my point of view was that I had a terrible pain up my backside for a few days, as a result of the tremendous boost when the charges went off. I wonder if other people who have ejected have experienced the same thing.

Just before Christmas 1950 we did the first ever live broadcast from the actual face of a coalmine. It was at Snowdown Colliery in Kent, one of the deepest mines in the country. We went down over 3,000 feet in a cage at what seemed a terrifice pace. I believe it was forty m.p.h. but we got the impression of greater speed as we shot down through the hot, dust-laden air which blew up the shaft. At the bottom we walked a few hundred yards and then travelled over a mile in a paddy – the miners' name for an underground truck. Finally we had to crawl on our hands and knees along the coal face, only three feet high. I broadcast, half kneeling, half lying, in a temperature of 90°F, trying to hew some coal with a pick. It was back-aching and nearly impossible and I only managed to loosen a few measly lumps. I was only at the face for half an hour and down the mine altogether for about two hours, but it seemed a lifetime to me. I felt trapped, shut in and completely at the mercy of nature.

I couldn't help thinking of the 3,000 feet which lay between me and the surface. It seemed that the only things which prevented the coal above from crushing us were the wooden pit props. These have been replaced in some pits I believe by aluminium props. But the miners told me that they preferred wood as they could tell by their creaks when danger was near.

After this experience, I have always believed that miners were entitled to a specially high wage. I certainly won't take any criticism of them from people who have not been down a mine, as they can have no idea what the job is like. The long journey to the coal face, working in cramped conditions for hours on end, the dust and the heat. No smoking, no telephoning girlfriends, no popping out to get a haircut or a breath of fresh air. Plus of course the ever-present sense of danger.

At the end of a long and monotonous day there is the journey out of the heat into the cold above and the task of cleaning up before going home. Whatever our jobs, most of us are lucky just to be able to breathe fresh air. It does not smell so good 3,000 feet below the earth.

Two of our broadcasts brought Piccadilly Circus to a complete standstill, one intentionally, the other not. The first was on a date many Londoners will remember – 2 April 1949. This was the night that all the signs and neon lights came on again in Piccadilly Circus, after nearly ten years of darkness. By arrangement with the authorities and the police it was timed to coincide with *In Town Tonight*.

I was on a balcony overlooking the huge crowd below and they could hear all that was happening through a public-address system. In the broadcast I interviewed Hubert Gregg who during the war had written a song so many of us sang – 'I'm going to get lit up when the lights go up in London.' Then Zoe Gail, the girl who had made the song famous in the show at the Prince of Wales Theatre, came out on to the balcony, dressed in top hat, white tie and tails. A spotlight was on her and the crowd cheered and wolf-whistled as she shouted, 'Abracadabra – Lights up,' and pressed a switch. As if by magic up came all the lights and Zoe then sang the song to the crowds below who all joined in. It was quite a moving moment after ten long years and I expect many people did get lit up in London that night.

The other occasion was the one which became known in the BBC as 'the Piccadilly incident' and which for some reason – probably shortage of news – caused quite a sensation in Fleet Street. At least five Sunday papers had columns about it and the *People* went so far as to splash across their front page in one-inch type: BBC STUNT STARTS A GIRL STAMPEDE IN PICCADILLY. Headlines in other papers included, 'Cruel Hoax', and 'Broadcast in worst possible taste'. With the coming of television and the sort of things that are now broadcast there would have been no fuss at all if it had happened today.

Our idea was to discover whether people ever read the agony columns in the newspapers and if so whether they act on them. The editor of the *Evening News* was a friend of mine so I swore him to secrecy and asked him to insert the following in his personal column in all the editions on Friday: 'Well set-up young gentleman with honourable intentions invites young ladies seeking adventure to meet him in the steps of the Criterion Restaurant, Lower Regent Street 7.15 p.m. Saturday, 19 May. Identified by red carnation and blue-and-white spotted scarf. Password "How's your uncle?"' and their reactions might have made a jolly good broadcast.

On the Saturday I was doing a TV commentary at Lord's

and then dashed off by taxi down to Piccadilly Circus. As we approached the bottom of Regent Street we made very slow progress. There was a traffic jam ahead and large crowds were milling around. I paid off the taxi and fought my way through to the front entrance of the Criterion and once inside rushed round to the swing doors in Lower Regent Street. My heart sank. The street was packed solid, with a row of policemen with arms linked trying to prevent the crowd from pushing up the steps. No traffic could possibly get through and the police told me later that there were four or five thousand in the crowd. There were hundreds of girls and middle-aged ladies, some pretty, some not, and never say that modern youth is not opportunist – dotted among the crowd were several young men sporting blue-and-white spotted scarfs and red carnations.

I kept out of sight until John Ellison cued over to me and then I hurriedly explained to the listeners that there would be complete chaos and told them why. I then stepped out through the swing doors and hundreds of voices greeted me with 'How's your uncle?'

Amidst all the uproar and noise I managed to talk to some of the girls as they rushed up the steps past the police barrier, but I doubt if the listeners heard much. Most of the girls said that they had read the advertisement or had had it pointed out by friends and had come along to see what the adventure would be. None of them seemed disappointed that I was neither well set up (whatever that means) nor young, and they appeared to be enjoying themselves. I found no one who had known that it was a BBC stunt beforehand, though once I had come out on the steps with a microphone many in the crowd recognised me from the TV and realised what was up.

The police as usual were wonderful but a somewhat annoyed inspector told me to ask the crowd to disperse as quickly as possible after my interview. This I did, thanking them all for coming and apologising if they thought they had been cheated. They shouted goodbye and I grabbed some of those I had interviewed and took them with me inside the Criterion for a drink. I certainly needed one.

After the adverse reaction of the Sunday critics, the weeklies had time for reflection and were kinder to me. One went so far as to say, 'Praise to Variety boss Michael Standing for ignoring stuffy criticism of Brian Johnston's Blind Date episode for Saturday's *In Town Tonight*. The stunt was original and it had a purpose – to see what response the "agonies" get. Let us defend the right of the BBC to be free.' Michael's department ran *In Town Tonight* and he and Lobby were wonderful in the way they supported me in spite of some pressure from above. They took the view that the BBC were always being criticised for being stuffy and stuck-up, and having no new ideas. Now as soon as they tried something original and made an effort to get away from the 'Auntie' image, the critics were still complaining. One man who did *not* complain was my friend the editor. He now knew that his readers did read the personal column.

I have said that the police were wonderful. They were at the time, but our good relations were nearly wrecked on the Monday morning. I had a long discussion with Lobby about the broadcast, and he supported me 100 per cent, with one slight reservation. He thought we should have asked the permission of the police beforehand. I agreed with him but pointed out that had we done so they would not have given it. A few minutes after I had left Lobby's room his telephone rang and the conversation went something like this.

Voice: This is Inspector —— of —— police station speaking. I am ringing about the affair in Piccadilly Circus on Saturday night.

Lobby: Quite good, Brian, but not quite good enough. That's not the sort of voice a police inspector would use.

Voice: What do you mean? This *is* Inspector—— speaking.

Lobby: I don't believe it. It's you, Brian, so please ring off. I'm busy.

Voice: Well, if you *don't* believe me ring this police station at REG—— and check.

Lobby: (*with a sigh*) All right, I will.

He did and it was of course the real Inspector, who was naturally very annoyed by now. Lobby calmed him down and tactfully explained that I had this strange habit of ringing people up pretending to be someone else. The Inspector, though obviously puzzled at such goings-on in the BBC, was mollified and said they would take no further action in the matter. But he extracted a promise from Lobby that in future, for any similar type of broadcast, we would always get their permission first. So I got away with it – just.

One broadcast which I hope did some good was when I became a blood donor (for the first time). In those days people knew very little about it except from that very funny broadcast by Tony Hancock. As a result everyone – including myself – was a bit scared of giving their blood. But while on the air I was able to describe the actual insertion of the needle and blood running off into the bottle. Except for a slight wince when the needle went into the vein, I hope I made it all sound as easy and painless as it undoubtedly is, and possibly secured some badly needed recruits for the Blood Transfusion Service.

But I certainly did not help the medical profession when I was hypnotised on the air. Some thought it one of the funniest things they had heard on the radio, others were shocked and frightened. We originally got the idea from Cicely Courtneidge's famous record in which she accidentally inhales some laughing gas and becomes hysterical with laughter. We thought I might be given some of this gas to see what happened. But we discovered that laughing gas is the same as that used by dentists which when administered in a certain way can produce laughter. So we discarded that idea, as it might make people lose confidence in their dentists if they felt they made fools of themselves when under gas. So we then thought of hypnotism.

We had read how stage hypnotists could put a whole audience to sleep or make them all cry or laugh. Here surely was something which would give us our laughter on the radio and at the same time prove whether this kind of hypnotism was genuine or not. We got in touch with an ex-RAF officer called David Stewart who was practising as a professional hypnotist, both privately and with stage shows. He had been badly shot up in the leg during the War, and while lying in pain in hospital had found he could hypnotise himself into believing there was no pain. So successful was he that the surgeons were actually able to perform a lengthy operation on his leg without even a local anaesthetic.

David came to visit me in my office, an impressive-looking man with flashing eyes, big black bushy eyebrows, and a handlebar moustache. I told him what we wanted and asked him to try and see if he could make me laugh. I had three of my colleagues in the room with me as witnesses to prove it was all genuine, because I made it quite plain to him that this broadcast was not going to be faked. If he did not hypnotise me into laughter then I would say so on the air and would not laugh. As I have said, we wanted to see whether this type of hypnotism worked in addition to getting the laughs.

His technique was fascinating. There were none of the staring eyes and pointed fingers that one had always heard about. Quite the opposite. The first thing he did was to ask me if I was willing to be hypnotised. He explained that no one who was *not* willing could be hypnotised against his will. A comforting thought, which I for one had not known before.

He then started to 'work' on me. He sat me in a chair and told me to relax completely and close my eyes. For about five minutes he then kept up a continuous drone of talk in a quiet monotonous voice which somehow gave me complete confidence. He seemed to ooze kindness and understanding. I felt myself trusting him completely.

I began to find myself breathing slowly and more heavily while in the background I could hear: '... you're relaxed completely, you're feeling tired and sleepy, you've got no worries, in a few moments you will do just as I tell you, but you will be quite happy to do it, just relax, don't worry, you're feeling fine. You've got a tingling sensation running up your legs and arms. ...' And so it went on in this soft, soothing voice, and I felt a tingling in my arms and legs. He gradually began to make me do various physical things such as getting up out of the chair and falling back completely stiff into his arms.

Or again he said my arms would slowly leave my sides and rise very gradually until they met above my head. I could hear him telling me all these things, and just felt I wanted to do

—

them. I made no effort to get out of the chair, nor to raise my arms above my head. They seemed to float ever so slowly upwards. My witnesses told me afterwards that they could hardly see them moving, they went so slowly. After another five minutes he tried to get me to go back to my childhood and speak and write as I did then. This was not very successful, so I was told afterwards. He then started on the laughter. He made me relax in the chair again and began to drone again: 'You're just going to hear the funniest thing you've heard in your life. When you hear it you will laugh and laugh as you've never laughed before. You won't be able to stop until I snap my fingers and tell you to. Listen, this is very, very funny. Just picture a policeman directing the traffic in bathing trunks and a policeman's helmet. Nothing else. It is very funny. . . .'

About here I began to feel my stomach muscles move, and my whole body began to shake like a jelly. A chuckle which seemed to come from the depth of my stomach crept up and up until it reached my mouth and grew into a laugh. A steady cackle at first, getting quicker and shriller, ending up in a peal of high-pitched laughter. All this I learnt afterwards from my friends who were watching. All I knew was that I was laughing.

Suddenly I heard him say, 'I am now going to snap my fingers and when I do so you will stop laughing. Before I snap my fingers I am going to try a little pre-hypnosis. When you come round you will be quite normal. You will feel fine and talk quite naturally to me. I will then point to Vic Moody who is standing in a corner and when you look at him you will go straight off into your laughter again.'

He snapped his fingers and said, 'Stop laughing now, it's no longer funny' and my cackles slowly stopped like a gramophone running down. I sat there still with my eyes closed but quite quiet and composed. He said to me, 'Before you open your eyes I just want to say this – no one, not even myself, can ever hypnotise you again unless you yourself wish it. Now open your eyes.'

I had heard all he said, and felt compelled to open my eyes. I looked in front of me and saw the amazed look on my colleagues' faces. I talked normally to David, who asked me how I was and whether I felt any ill effects. I said 'no' truthfully, because I was feeling fine. He said, 'Just look behind you.' I did so, and there in the corner was Vic Moody. I remember pointing my finger at him and going off into shrieks of laughter again until David stopped me by another snap of the fingers.

And so our experiment ended. It had obviously been a success. I had laughed, and hypnotism had worked. There could be no question of a fake – no one could pretend to laugh like that for such a long stretch. I give you my word it was genuine. I just could not help myself. And so we decided to put it on the air. David explained to me that as he had already 'worked' on me, so long as I was willing again, he would now only have to walk into a room and he could get me laughing in under one minute. We took one important precaution. His voice at the moment of hypnotising me must not be heard on the air. It might affect those listening, and some lonely people sitting alone in their rooms might be sent off into peals of laughter, with no David Stewart there to snap his fingers at the end.

So at the beginning of *In Town Tonight* they came over to me in one of our offices and I told the listeners what was going to happen. They then went back to the studio for another short interview, during which time David hypnotised me into the early state of complete relaxation and semi-coma.

At the end of the studio interview, they cued back to Henry Riddell, who was in the office with a microphone and he was able to tell listeners what David had done and then let them hear David actually making me laugh. It went just the same as it had in the original experiment, except this time when I came round I pointed my finger and laughed at Henry Riddell. Rather bad luck on him in front of millions of listeners. They must have begun to think he really looked funny. And so the broadcast ended as they faded out to the sound of my laughter.

The next two days were pretty hectic. As I have said, the reaction was fairly well divided between those who had thought it very funny, and those who had found it frankly horrifying. I listened to the recordings and was inclined to agree with the latter. The laughter sounded terrifying, at times even maniacal, as someone put it in a letter: 'It was as if your soul had gone into another world.' We kept the item in the repeat of *In Town Tonight*, but cut down the laughter.

We had proved to a lot of sceptical people that hypnotism worked, but we had also brought pain to others. Inadvertently, too, we may have frightened people away from hypnotism as a new force in the medical world, especially in its growing use in cases of childbirth. We had chosen laughter because we thought it would be funny and also became almost anything else could be faked. If David had made me do something like standing on my head, or reciting Shakespeare, the listener would have had no proof that I was hypnotised. I could have pretended to be by just doing the things he told me. But in all the many letters which we received for and against the broadcast, not one suggested that I was 'putting on' the laughter, for it was too hysterical for that. And so although we had done what we had set out to do, had we been able to listen to it on a recording beforehand, I feel sure we would never have put it out on the air. As soon as I heard it I swore that I would never be hypnotised again.

Later I achieved something which I would never have believed possible. I played a street piano in a side street near the Victoria Palace and, wait for it, I actually sang 'Underneath the Arches' with Bud Flanagan. When I had first heard Bud and Ches (Allen) sing it together in the early thirties, little did I think I would ever have the honour of actually taking Ches's place. But Bud was a real friend of mine, and to help in my spot, came out of the Victoria Palace, placed his hand on my shoulder and sang just as beautifully as if he were appearing in a Royal Variety Performance. What a lovely man he was. This really was one of the greatest moments in my broadcasting life.

I actually earned some money from one of my musical broadcasts, when I sang disguised as a tramp in the Strand. I had always felt sorry for street musicians and singers and wondered what they felt like – ashamed, embarrassed, or scornful of those who either slipped them the odd penny or sixpence or pretended not to notice them as they passed by.

I put on a dirty old macintosh and hat and the oldest pair of trousers and shoes that I could find. I dirtied my face and my hands and with a microphone hidden under my scarf shuffled out into the street from under an archway where I had been waiting. I carried a small tin with some matchboxes on it and started to sing 'Tipperary' in a very shaky voice. It was extremely embarrassing singing in a public street – you try it sometime and see how you feel. I had to force myself to do it and tried not to look at the various passers-by, most of whom were trying to avoid me. However, in my three and a half minutes I did collect nearly a shilling, though twopence of this was given by one of our engineers *pour encourager les autres*.

He also threw in a halfpenny at the end as a signal that my time was up, as a tramp would obviously not have a stopwatch. I was immensely relieved when it was all over and ever since then if I pass one of these singers I always try to give something – however small. I know exactly how they are feeling.

I had always wanted to test out the theory that if you suck a lemon in front of a brass band they will dry up. So one Saturday I went on stage at the Aldephi Theatre and by prearrangement interrupted Jimmy Edwards in the middle of his trombone act. I challenged him to play as I sucked. I had a very juicy lemon and as he started to play I began to suck it right in front of his face. For about half a minute he struggled bravely but what had started as *presto agitato* rapidly became *andante*. He got slower and slower and began to drool at the mouth. In the end he was just pushing the rod of his trombone backwards and forwards, and all that came out were a few phut phuts of air. He gave up and burst out laughing. He claims it had nothing to do with the lemon but that it was the sight of my face, coupled with the laughter from the audience. So I never really discovered for certain whether my theory was right or wrong.

I had always been an admirer of the way Peter Pan and the fairies in pantomimes flew unconcernedly about the stage. I was therefore delighted when I was invited to be a member of the Flying Ballet during a performance of the Ice Pantomime at the Empress Hall. I was disguised as a fantastic-looking bird, with feather wings and a large yellow beak and so on. They fastened a belt round my middle onto which were attached two very thin wires hanging down from the roof. They had to be small to be invisible to the audience but I was assured they would bear the weight of a twenty-two-stone man, so I decided to take the risk. There were six other 'birds' in the ballet and as the orchestra struck up we were hoisted into the air high above the glistening black ice fifty feet below. I did not know the steps of the ballet or whatever they are called in the air – but I flapped my wings and then held them spread out as if swooping like a bird. It was terrifying looking down at the upturned faces of the audience and realising that I was only being suspended by the two thin wires. That ice looked horribly hard. After being swung three times up and down the length of the arena I was slowly lowered on to the ice. I can understand birds enjoying flying through the air. It was a very pleasant sensation. But they don't have to worry about two thin bits of wire. And I never did discover how they knew the wires would take up to a twenty-two-stone man. Had they tried a twenty-three-stoner and had the wires broken? If so, that's one job I would not like – a flying-ballet-wire tester.

One of the most uproarious and chaotic of the broadcasts was when I was shaved and shampooed by the Crazy Gang during their show *Together Again* at the Victoria Palace. They had a barber's-shop sketch and I took the place of the man who twice nightly was given the full treatment. They lent me some old clothes, a macintosh, and a wig and all I had to do was to sit in the chair and try to keep talking into the microphone. As soon as I sat down they pulled off the wig and poured bottles of coloured shampoo all over my real hair and face – green, yellow, red, any colour you can think of. They had an enormous brush, dipped it into some white lather and 'shaved' me. The lather went into my mouth and up my nose and as I tried to talk they stuffed the brush into my mouth. They were having the time of their lives, and so were the audience. Teddy Knox and Jimmy Nervo were the chief culprits, and I finished up on the floor as they poured water down my trousers and tickled me on the tummy.

It must have sounded chaotic to listeners at home. All they could have heard was my screams and the roars from the audience. But it was surprising how many people told me afterwards how much they had enjoyed it. That's one of the great things about radio. It encourages the use of one's imagination. I took over an hour to clean up and get all the colours out of my hair and skin. As I left the theatre one man came up and shook me by the hand. It was the actor who normally sat in the chair – I had spared him the ordeal for at least one performance.

The Crazy Gang were wonderful people, always friendly and cheerful and would go to any lengths to make a successful joke. At one time Jack Hylton used to leave his best suit in one of their dressing-rooms so that when he came up from a day at the races, he could change into something more suitable for the theatre. The Gang hired a tailor to come in each day and take about an eighth of an inch off the bottom of his trousers and then sew it up again. For the first few times Jack did not seem to notice anything but after a bit he began to let out his braces and could not understand why the trousers were creeping higher and higher up his legs. In the end his braces would not let out any further and he became suspicious, and finally found out. But showman that he was, he appreciated the trouble that they had taken to produce a laugh.

One of the most unusual places from which I broadcast was from inside a letter-box at Oxford. It was Christmastime and the idea was to see how people were helping the Post Office by writing clearly, putting the town in block letters, and sticking on the right stamp when posting their Christmas cards.

We went to Oxford as this was the only box the Post Office could find large enough to contain me. I crouched inside with my microphone and as the letters and cards dropped in I reported on the things that had been done right or wrong. All went well but as usual I was tempted and went a little too far. No one had any idea that I was inside so to finish I put my hand up to the slit through which the letters are posted and when a lady came up to post her card I put my hand out and took the letter. There was a loud scream and I gather she nearly fainted. You can hardly blame her. You don't expect to see a hand emerging from a letter-box to grip your letter. It was a rotten trick to play.

One date in 1950 was too good to miss. The first of April happened to fall on a Saturday so, although one is not supposed to operate after 12 noon, we decided to make an April Fool of John Ellison. I told him that I was going to do street interviews that night about 1 April. Secretly we had tried out various impersonators to see if they could copy my voice.

Funnily enough, only one of them could, and he got my rather stupid giggle off to perfection. It was Peter Sellers. On that night I hid in the studio and John, quite unsuspicious, cued over to Peter, thinking it was me. Peter did perfectly and I must say sounded just like me. After a few hilarious interviews he pretended he was feeling ill and that the crowd was pressing against him, so cued suddenly back to John in the studio. Peter Duncan in the control panel signalled John in the studio to take over. John, quite nonplussed, said, 'We're sorry Brian is obviously not feeling too well, so we will go on to the next item.' (He told me afterwards that he thought I was drunk!) As he said that I crept from behind a screen, went up behind him, tapped him on the shoulder and said, 'April Fool.' He turned round and looked amazed, but was decent enough to admit that we had caught him fair and square.

One day late in 1950 I was sitting at my desk thinking out future stunts when I suddenly realised that I must be nearing my 100th 'performance'. I checked up and found that all being well I would reach it on Saturday 24 February. I puzzled my brain as to how best I could celebrate it. I thought of one or two sensational things I might do, but discarded them pretty quickly. I did not want it to be my 100th-and-last *Let's Go Somewhere*. So I hit on another idea.

Why not get Peter Duncan to allow me to do something I had always wanted to do on the air but which I would obviously never do in the ordinary course of broadcasting? In fact as a birthday treat I asked for 'the freedom of the air' to do what I wanted. It was not an outrageous request, and Peter agreed to it straight away. For three and a half minutes on 24 February I could try and be a cross-talk comedian! I was lucky with my straight man. Ever since I had shared an office with John Ellison we used to try out gag routines, many of them picked up in music-halls where we used to go for *Round the Halls*. So we arranged that we would do the 'act' in front of the *In Town Tonight* audience in the studio.

We spent days preparing a suitable script, and some of my most treasured gags had to go – victims of the blue pencil. But this time I was censoring myself, and however good the gag, if it was at all 'blue' I would not let myself be influenced by myself. It was out! Finally the script was ready – all taken from my file and as you can imagine as old and corny a collection of jokes as were ever heard on the BBC – and that is saying something! Our only hope was that they were so old that the younger generation of listeners might never have heard of them. We also decided to sing (rather à la Flanagan and Allen) the usual treacly sentimental song with which so many comics finish their acts.

We rehearsed for days as we wanted the act to go with real punch and speed – we could not afford to dawdle with some of those jokes! We eventually managed to get it off slickly enough, and the studio audience were very kind and laughed quite loud and often. And – an unheard-of thing in the somewhat austere atmosphere of the *In Town Tonight* studio – they even applauded at the end of the act. So I had my birthday wish and I think I got away with it.

There was an amusing sequel. On the following Monday a well-known radio comic was walking up Shaftesbury Avenue when he was stopped by the 'funny' man of a radio cross-talk act. The conversation went as follows: 'I say, Ted, did you hear Brian Johnston in *In Town Tonight* on Saturday? He pinched all the gags from my act and I don't know what to do now. I've got Henry Hall's *Guest Night* tomorrow.'

And we thought the gags were old and corny! So that you can judge for yourself, here is the script as we did it that night. I hope you have not heard them all before, and that you get at least one laugh out of it.

J.E. Ladies and gentlemen, tonight I am going to give you a serious monologue entitled 'The Orphan's Return' –
'Twas a dark cold night in December

114

And the snow was falling fast,
Little Nell lay in the gutter –
And the rich folk by her passed.
You may ask me . . .

B.J. I say, I say!

J.E. Yes, yes, what is it?

B.J. I've just seen forty men under one umbrella, and not one of them got wet.

J.E. Forty men under one umbrella and not one of them got wet – it must have been a very large umbrella!

B.J. Certainly not, it wasn't raining.

J.E. (*Indignant and exasperated*) What d'you mean by coming on here and interrupting me while I'm reciting – now go away. I'm sorry, ladies and gentlemen, I'll begin again – 'Twas a . . .

B.J. It's in all the papers tonight.

J.E. What is?

B.J. Fish and chips. We don't want London Bridge any longer.

J.E. Why not?

B.J. It's long enough already. D'you know who's in the navy?

J.E. No, who?

B.J. Sailors. I've got a goat with no nose.

J.E. Really? How does it smell?

B.J. Terrible.

J.E. I don't want to know about that. Will you go away!

B.J. I've got a letter here. If I post it tonight, do you think it will get to Glasgow by Wednesday?

J.E. My dear fellow, of course it will.

B.J. Well, I bet it won't.

J.E. How's that?

B.J. It's addressed to Shoreditch.

J.E. It seems to me you're next door to a blithering idiot.

B.J. Well move over and give me a chance. By the way, I nearly saw your brother the other day.

J.E. How do you mean, you nearly saw my brother?

B.J. Well, isn't your brother a policeman?

J.E. That's quite correct – he is a policeman.

B.J. Isn't he PC 49?

J.E. That's quite right – he is PC 49.

B.J. Well, I met PC 48.

J.E. You met PC 48 . . . Well, you may think you're very very clever, but let me tell you I've got a brother who even though he was on the dole, always managed to live above his income.

B.J. That's impossible, he couldn't be on the dole and live above his income.

J.E. Oh, yes he did. He had a flat over the Labour Exchange. By the way, what's your brother doing these days?

B.J. Nothing!

J.E. Nothing? I thought he applied for that job as producer of *In Town Tonight*?

B.J. Yes, he got the job. They call him Button B, you know.

J.E. Button B, why on earth do they call him that?

B.J. Well he's always pressed for money.

J.E. Well, I must say I don't know what your wife thinks about all this.

B.J. That reminds me, here's a letter from her.

J.E. (*Reading letter*) But there's nothing written on it.

B.J. No, we're not on speaking terms. Not that it matters, I've just got six months for rocking her to sleep.

J.E. You can't get six months for rocking your wife to sleep.

B.J. Oh yes I can, you should have seen the size of the rock.

J.E. I'm sick of this, let's go into this restaurant and get something to eat. Waiter, do you serve lobsters here?

B.J. Yes, sir – sit down, we serve anybody.

J.E. I see you've got frogs' legs.

B.J. Yes, sir – it's the walking about that does it.

J.E. How long will the spaghetti be?

B.J. I don't know, sir, we never measure it.

J.E. I think I'll have some soup.

B.J. Right, sir – here it is.

J.E. I say, waiter, there's a fly in my soup.

B.J. All right, sir, don't shout – all the others will want one.

J.E. Have you got any eggs?

B.J. Yes, sir.

—

J.E. Are they fresh?

B.J. Don't ask me, sir, I only lay the tables.

J.E. Oh, this is hopeless. I think I'll have a drink. What do you suggest?

B.J. I'd have a mother-in-law, sir.

J.E. Mother-in-law, what's that?

B.J. Stout and bitter. Terrible weather, isn't it, sir?

J.E. Yes, terrible.

B.J. I call it Madam Butterfly weather, sir.

J.E. Madam Butterfly weather?

B.J. Yes, sir, one fine day. But cheer up – just around the corner may be sunshine for you . . .

Brian Johnston and John Ellison into song
Just around the corner may be sunshine for you,
Just around the corner skies above may be blue –
Even tho' it's dark and cloudy
Mister Sun will soon say 'How-dy'
Just around the corner from you –
We'll see you later,
Just around the corner from you.

I did my final *Let's Go Somewhere* on 17 May 1952 when I was winched out of a boat in the Solent by a Royal Naval helicopter. It was not an easy operation as the back-stream from the chopper blew the boat backwards and forwards. But of course in the safe and skilful hands of the Royal Navy it was perfectly safe and an everyday job for them. It was, however, with a sense of relief that I was safely pulled aboard the hovering helicopter and was able to say a final goodbye to the listeners of *Let's Go Somewhere*.

I would not like to be so immodest as to say I went out at the top but I was determined to stop before everyone began to get bored with me. During the next few years people often asked me why I had stopped and could I not do some more. If I had continued they might have begun to ask why I didn't stop. As it was I was able to declare the innings closed with a final score of 150 not out.

J
for Jokes

Jokes have played a large part in my life – far *too* large a part I
suspect. I must have been a pretty intolerable schoolboy, always
trying to be funny. At my private school I was called 'the voice'
and my early reports were spattered with the word 'buffoon',
much to the chagrin of my mother and stepfather. I'm afraid
that I haven't improved with the years and my friend William
Douglas-Home compares me to a batsman who, when served
up with a half volley, tries to hit every one for four. Only about
one in six ever reaches the boundary which is a vast improvement on the success rate of my jokes. But at least I do try, and
when the easy chance comes up, I have a go.

Just what is a joke? The Concise Oxford Dictionary describes
it as 'A thing said or done to excite laughter – witticism – jest –
ridiculous thing . . .' There are so many different types of jokes
– puns, riddles, one-liners, cross-talk, patter routines by comedians and of course stories. These also come in different
categories based on a true happening, clean, dirty, *double
entendre*, shaggy dog and so on. It has always fascinated me how
a story starts, and who thinks of it first. The risqué topical
stories reputedly come from the stock exchange and are passed
from broker to broker. These brokers then go home to all parts
of the country and tell the story to their friends. Hence the
amazing speed with which stories spread so quickly. But it still
doesn't answer who first made up the story.

It was the same at school where a story told in the morning
would probably be round the school by the evening. I remember
the first story I made up and I'm not particularly proud of it!
It was about a motorist driving up the old A1 and he came to a
town which he thought was Baldock, but he wasn't sure. So he
drove slowly past a pedestrian who was wearing a bowler hat

and shouted out to him 'Baldock?' The man shouted back to him, 'As a matter of fact I am. But how the hell did you know that I was a doctor?' This quickly led to another of the same ilk. A motorist in America wanted to know the way to Chicago. As he was passing a man walking along the road he shouted 'Chicago?' 'Of course it doesn't, otherwise I wouldn't be walking!' I doubt if either of these stories spread around, but they got a laugh or a groan at the time.

A groan is the best reward you can get for a good pun which has to be quick and spontaneous, and is seldom repeatable. Mine are no exception, but I will risk repeating the sort of puns I have perpetrated with cricketers' names. Colley of Australia became Melon. Pandit of India, One Armed, and Sharma of India, Snake. Mansoor of Pakistan was Eddie Gray, and Rodney Marsh of Australia, Much Binding, because he bound his fingers with tape – hence Much Binding on the Marsh.

By far the biggest source of jokes were the music-halls in the thirties to sixties. Since then radio and TV have been a poor substitute, and anyway several million listeners and viewers will have heard the joke. In the old days of music-hall the comedians could go round the variety circuit for years using the same jokes. What is so interesting is that it didn't seem to matter if you heard a comedian repeating the same old jokes. In fact with Max Miller if he didn't tell one or two of his more fruity ones that you knew, you felt cheated.

This proves that however good a joke may be, its success depends on timing and delivery – or the way you tell 'em, as Frank Carson so often points out. There's another important thing to remember about telling a joke. Try not to say, 'Have you heard this one?' Wait for a suitable time in a conversation, and make sure everyone is listening. There's nothing worse that interrupting someone's conversation just to tell your joke. And do your best to make it personal as if it had happened to you or one of your friends. That is certainly one of the secrets of after-dinner speaking. A good comic can stand up and deliver a rapid series of one-liners, often with no connection with each other. He can get away with it. But in a speech there must be a reason for telling the story or the joke and if possible tell it as if it has actually happened. Don't start off with 'Someone told me a good story the other day', or 'Have you heard the one about . . .?'

One of my jokes *could* have got me into trouble. It was soon after the announcement of the engagement between Prince Charles and Lady Diana. They were up at Balmoral with the rest of the Royal Family and had agreed to meet all the Press for photographs. A friend of mine was one of the press secretaries at Buckingham Palace and was suddenly detailed to arrange the press conference. He caught an afternoon plane up to Aberdeen and arrived at Balmoral, slightly flustered, some time after 8.00 p.m. He was told by a footman that the Royal Family had already started dinner, and he was to join them. Quite an awe-inspiring experience! Anyhow they made him welcome and he was asked to sit at the Queen's end of the table. Opposite him was Prince Andrew who had obviously just read one of my books. I think it was *It's a Funny Game*. He was talking to the Queen and said he had enjoyed one or two of my stories. He proceeded to tell her and the rest of the table a perfectly harmless one. They all laughed politely so he embarked on another which my friend immediately recognised as completely unsuitable for the Queen. It was the one about the girl and her chihuahua dog. He plucked up courage and interrupted Prince Andrew, politely suggesting that he shouldn't go on with the story. So I was saved from the Tower!

Life to me would be dull without jokes, good or bad, and here is a list under different categories of some of my own favourites – just one or two stories under each heading.

Animals

A lady got onto a bus with an alligator on a lead.

'That's a nice-looking alligator,' said the conductor, 'taking him to the zoo?'

'No,' replied the lady, 'we went to the zoo yesterday. Today we are going to Madame Tussauds.'

*

A man went into a pub with a newt on his shoulder. The barman said in surprise, 'Did you know that you have a newt on your shoulder?'

'Yes,' said the man, 'it belongs to me.'

'What do you call it?' asked the barman.

'Tiny,' said the man.

'Why Tiny?'

'Oh,' said the man, 'because it's my newt'!

Business

Caller on the telephone: 'Can I speak to the Chairman please?'

Secretary: 'No. I'm sorry. He's not here this afternoon.'

Caller: 'Doesn't he work in the afternoons then?'

Secretary: 'Oh no. It's the *mornings* he doesn't work. He doesn't *come in* in the afternoon.'

Manager to office boy: 'Johnston. You're late. You *should* have been here at 9.30.'

Office boy: 'Why sir? What happened?'

Children

A mother took her seven-year-old son to the doctor who asked what was wrong with him.

'Oh,' said his mother, 'Johnny thinks he is a hen and can't stop clucking.'

'How long has this been going on?' asked the doctor.

'For about four years, doctor.'

'Why didn't you bring him to me before then?'

'Well, candidly doctor, we needed the eggs.'

Another small boy accidently swallowed a five-pound note. His mother rang up the doctor in a panic.

'What shall I do?' she asked anxiously.

'Oh, give him a strong dose of castor oil, and give me a ring if there's no change in the morning,' said the doctor.

Cricket

A man whose wife was expecting a baby telephoned the hospital to see what the news was. By mistake he dialled the local cricket ground. When he asked for the latest position the reply came back: 'There are seven already, and the last two are ducks.'

In a village match the batsman came in with only one pad on his right leg. The bowler pointed out to him that he had only one pad. 'Yes, I know, but we've only got three pads between us.'

'But you've got it on your right leg,' said the bowler.

'Yes, but I thought I would be batting at the other end,' replied the batsman.

In a village match the visiting bowler appealed to the local umpire for lbw. The umpire hesitated, then called out to his friend who was batting, 'Get your legs out of the way, Joe, I've got to make a decision and I can't see the wicket.'

Doctors

A woman went to her doctor with a bad cough. He examined her throat and said, 'Yes, it looks a bit sore. Do you get a tickle in the morning?'

'I used to, doctor, but not now. They've changed the milkman.'

A well-known drinker went to his doctor and complained that he was not feeling well. His doctor examined him and then said, 'I can't find anything organically wrong with you. It must be the drink.'

'Okay, doctor,' said the man, 'I'll come back when you are sober'!

Drink

At a temperance meeting about the dangers of drink the lecturer took two glasses and filled one with water and one with whisky. He then took some worms and put them in the water. They swam around and looked perfectly well and happy. He then got some other worms and put them into the glass of whisky. They immediately shrivelled up and sank to the bottom of the glass obviously dead.

The lecturer held up the glass of whisky and asked a man in the front row, 'And what conclusion do you draw from that, sir?'

The man replied without hesitation, 'If you've got worms, drink whisky!'

An after-dinner speaker had made what he thought was a pretty good speech. When he sat down a man who had obviously had too much to drink came up and shouted, 'That was the most boring speech I have ever heard – an awful lot of balls.' The chairman of the dinner rushed up and dragged the drunken man away. 'I'm sorry,' he said to the speaker, 'I didn't hear what he said, but pay no attention to him. When drunk he only repeats what everybody else is saying.'

Football

A small boy got lost at a football match, and told a policeman that he'd lost his dad. The policeman was sympathetic and started looking around for a likely person. 'What's he like?' he asked the boy, who quickly replied, 'Beer and women.'

*

A centipede was playing for a team of insects, but he came on the field half an hour late. It had taken him longer than he thought to put on his boots.

Golf

Jimmy Tarbuck had a friend who told him that he had a little white poodle who accompanied him on all his rounds of golf.

'He's wonderful,' the friend told Jimmy. 'If I do a good drive, or sink a long putt, he gets up on his hind legs and applauds me with his front paws.'

'Ah,' said Jimmy, 'But what happens if you go into a bunker or miss an easy putt?'

'Oh, he turns somersaults,' said his friend.

'How many?' asked Jimmy.

'Depends how hard I kick him up the arse!' was the reply.

I knew a man whose friends called him a Second World War golfer – out in 39, back in 45. He was very superstitious and always wore two pairs of socks – in case he got a hole in one.

Horses

A vicar was driving his bishop around his parish in a pony cart, when the pony let off a rather rude noise.

'Sorry about that, Bishop,' said the Vicar.

'Don't worry,' said the bishop, 'if you hadn't apologised I'd have thought it was the pony.'

A horse was grazing in a field next to the village cricket ground. The local team was one short so the captain asked the horse if he would play. He agreed, batted last, and hit a brilliant fifty, hoofing the ball all round the ground.

When the village fielded, none of the bowlers could get the visitors out. So the captain approached the horse, who had been galloping round the boundary, and asked him if he'd like to bowl.

'Don't be stupid,' said the horse, 'whoever heard of a horse who could bowl?'

An Irishman driving a horsebox arrived at the racecourse. A stable-boy opened the door. 'There's no horse in here, Paddy.'

'No,' said Paddy, 'I know. I only bring the non-runners.'

Irish

Two Irishmen were sitting on an iceberg in the North Atlantic. One of them suddenly shouted, 'Look Paddy, we're saved. Here comes the Titanic'!

At the end of a gruelling three weeks an Irishman won the famous bicycle race, the Tour de France. When it was time for the presentation ceremony, they couldn't find him anywhere. Someone then discovered that he'd set off to do a lap of honour.

Law

A judge was about to sentence a prisoner who had been found guilty. 'Anything you want to say, my man?'

'No, m'lord. Bugger all.'

The judge was a bit deaf so called down to his clerk, 'What did he say?'

'Bugger all,' replied the clerk.

'Oh no,' said the judge, 'he definitely said something. I saw him move his lips.'

A well-known judge lost his thumb in an accident and from then on was always called Mr Justice Fingers.

'Remember, you are on oath,' the judge told the third party in a divorce case.

'Have you ever slept with this woman?'
'Not a wink, m'lord,' was the answer.

Mothers-in-Law

A husband was infuriated by his mother-in-law's habit of always saying 'I know, I know' whenever he told her anything. So early one morning when she was staying with his wife and him, he went down and met the milkman when he drove up in his cart. He offered the surprised milkman £10 if he could borrow his horse for half an hour. All he needed was for the milkman to unharness the horse, bring it into the house, lead it up the stairs, put it in the bath and leave it there. The milkman, tempted by the money, rather reluctantly agreed but asked what it was all about. 'Well,' said the husband, 'when she gets up my mother-in-law will go into the bathroom, and when she sees the horse will rush out screaming, 'Help, help. You'll never guess what I've found. There's a horse in the bath.' I shall then just sit reading my newspaper and say, 'I know, I know.'

Old Age

'When you get old three things happen to you,' an old man warned his son. 'The first thing is you lose your memory . . . and I cannot remember what the other two are.'

An elderly man and his son went into a chemist and the son ordered seven condoms. 'That's rather a lot. What do you want all those for?' asked the father.

'Quite easy, Dad. Monday, Tuesday, Wednesday, Thursday, Friday, Saturday, Sunday.'

'Oh, in that case,' said the father, 'I'll have a dozen.'

'You've got to be joking, Dad. What do you need a dozen for?'

'Quite easy, son, January, February, March, April etc.'

*

An elderly couple decided to celebrate their diamond wedding by going to stay in the same hotel, same bedroom, and same bed where they had spent their honeymoon sixty years before.

As they lay in bed the wife fondled her husband and as she stroked him all over whispered, 'Darling, do you remember how ardent and romantic you were on our first night? You bit me in the neck, on my shoulders and then my breasts.' At that the husband leapt out of bed and dashed into the bathroom. 'What's happened, what are you doing?' shouted his wife. 'Fetching my teeth,' he called back.

School

A young boy arrived late at school one morning. 'Why are you late, Johnny?' asked the teacher.

'I'm sorry, Miss, but I had to get my own breakfast.'

'Very well, Johnny, now settle down. We are doing geography and here is a map of India and Pakistan. Can you tell me where the Pakistan border is?'

'Yes, miss. He's in bed with my mum. That's why I had to get my own breakfast.'

A pretty young schoolteacher in a miniskirt bent down to pick up a piece of chalk off the ground. A small boy started to giggle. 'What are you laughing at, Tommy?'

'Oh, Teacher,' he sniggered. 'I saw your garters.'

'Well go and stand in the corner for an hour,' she snapped.

At that a boy sitting in the front row picked up his satchel, put on his cap and started to leave the room.

'Where are you going, Charlie?'

'Well, Miss, if Tommy got one hour in the corner for what *he* saw, after what *I* saw, my schooldays are over.'

The Sea

A whale was swimming in the Atlantic when he came across his friend the squid. 'How are you, Squid?' he asked.

'Not at all well. I'm feeling very ill.'

'All right, then, why not come for a ride on my back? I'm going to see my friend the octopus.'

So the squid jumped on to the whale and after a short time they met the octopus.

'Hello, Whale, how are you?' he shouted.

'I'm fine thanks,' said the whale. 'I've brought you that sick squid I owe you.'

A man was walking along a beach and saw a girl shouting for help being slowly washed out to sea. So he threw her a cake of soap. When asked why, he said, 'To wash her back, of course.'

Sex

A young innocent bridegroom was very nervous before his honeymoon. He had never made love to a girl before and asked his best man for advice. 'Don't worry,' said the best man. 'Once in bed you'll soon find out what's what.' So on the first night the bridegroom lay alongside his bride and started to stroke her body. He started with her face and got lower and lower. Suddenly he asked her, 'What's that?' 'What's what?' she replied. 'Ah,' he sighed with relief, 'that's it.'

A businessman missed his last train home and had to catch the milk train which got him home at 4.00 a.m. When he entered his house all the lights were on and his wife was standing in the hall in her nightie.

'Oh, thank goodness you've come back, darling. We've had a burglar.'

'Did he get anything?'

'Yes, I'm afraid he did. In the dark I thought it was you!'

The Services

A commanding officer was addressing his battalion before they set sail for Egypt. He was stressing the dangers of contracting venereal disease. 'Why spoil your health and future life for just ten minutes? Any questions?'

'Yes, sir,' said a young soldier, 'how do you make it last for ten minutes?'

At a regimental dinner soon after the war one officer said to the other, 'How nice to see you old man. How are you?'

'Oh, I'm all right but feeling very frustrated. I haven't made love to a woman since 1946.'

'Well, I shouldn't worry too much if I were you,' said his friend looking at his watch. 'It's only 20.30 now.'

Shaggy Dog

A man went into a pub and said to the landlord, 'I have got a unique white mouse here. He can play the piano.'

The landlord roared with laughter. 'Come off it,' he said, 'tell me the other one.'

'Well I'll prove it to you,' said the man, and sat his white mouse down on the stool of the pub piano. It then proceeded to play a number of the classics and various tunes from musicals. The landlord was amazed and gave the man £50 for the mouse. Next day the same man came in with another white mouse. 'What does this one do?' asked the landlord suspiciously.

'Oh, this one can sing, and to prove it ask the pianist mouse to play any song and this mouse will sing it.'

So the landlord asked for 'I Can't Give You Anything But Love', and the mouse sang it in a high treble.

'Remarkable,' said the landlord. 'My customers will love it. Here's another £50.'

The next day the man came in again. 'What have you got this time?' asked the landlord. 'Have you a mouse who can dance?'

'No,' said the man, 'I've got nothing today. It's merely that my conscience is pricking me. You know I said that the second mouse could sing? Well, it can't. The first mouse is a ventriloquist!'

*

A man looked out of his window one morning and to his surprise saw a gorilla in one of his trees. But he didn't panic. He went straight to the Yellow Pages, looked up Gorilla-Catcher and dialled the number. The gorilla-catcher answered and when told what had happened said, 'No problem. I'll be round in twenty minutes.' Sure enough he arrived in a van from which he took a ladder, a pair of handcuffs, a shotgun and a bull-terrier.

'What are all these things for?' the man asked the gorilla-catcher.

'It's quite easy,' he explained. 'I take the ladder, put it against the tree, climb up and then shake the tree. The gorilla will then fall to the ground. At that moment I want you to release the bull-terrier who is trained to bite people in a very painful place. The gorilla, knowing this, will cross his hands over his private parts to protect himself. You must then run forward with the handcuffs and put them on the gorilla's crossed hands.'

'That's fine,' said the man, 'I understand all that. But you haven't mentioned the shotgun. What is that for?'

'Sorry,' said the gorilla-catcher, 'I should have told you. Sometimes when I shake the tree *I* fall down instead of the gorilla. In that case get the shotgun and shoot the bull-terrier.'

Shops

A woman went into a butcher's shop and complained about a sausage she had bought there last week. 'It was dreadful. It had meat at one end, and bread at the other.'

'I'm sorry, madam,' said the butcher. 'In these hard times, it's very difficult to make both ends meet.'

A man walked into a pet shop and said he wanted to buy a wasp. 'I'm sorry, sir,' said the pet shop owner. 'We don't sell wasps.'

'Well,' complained the customer, 'you've got one in the window.'

Stage

One Saturday night in a crowded music-hall a large, rather elderly lady soprano was doing her best to sing a light operatic piece, amidst boos and cat-calls from the rather drunken largely male audience. They hooted and clapped as she gallantly tried to carry on. A grey-haired man in the front row then stood up and faced the rowdy audience. 'Shut up and be quiet,' he shouted, 'let's give the poor old bitch a chance.' The noise temporarily subsided and the singer said to the man, 'Thank you very much sir. Thank goodness there's one *gentleman* amongst you.'

Transport

A lady was driving up the middle lane of the M1 with her hands through the wheel knitting as she sped along at about fifty m.p.h. Suddenly she became aware of flashing lights and a police siren, and noticed a police car drawing alongside her. One of the policemen unwound his window and shouted to her, 'Pull over.' She shouted back, 'No, a pair of socks.'

A small girl used to bite her nails, and to try to stop it her mother said to her, 'If you go on biting your nails you'll get fat with a big tummy.' The next day they got on to a bus and her mother pointed to a fat man of about twenty stone and said, 'You'll get like him if you go on biting your nails.' At the next stop a blonde lady got on, obviously in an advanced state of pregnancy. The little girl kept staring at her until the blonde couldn't stand it any more. 'Why are you looking at me like that? Do you know me?' 'No,' replied the little girl, 'but I know what you've been up to!'

Zoo

A husband and wife visited the zoo, and the wife got too close to the gorilla's cage. He seized her in his arms and started to kiss her. 'Help, help,' the wife cried out to her husband. 'The gorilla is trying to make love to me. What shall I do?'

'Tell him you've got a headache as you always do to me,' said the unsympathetic husband.

K
for Knowledge

It's said that a little knowledge is a dangerous thing. I'm not sure if I agree. But I am absolutely certain that a *lot* of knowledge, if not dangerous, can be highly embarrassing. The trouble is that the knowledge is there somewhere in the brain but the older you get, the more difficult it becomes to turn on the tap to let it out.

In my career at the BBC I have amassed a tremendous amount of information, facts and figures. I have been the chairman of a number of quizzes – *Treble Chance*, *Sporting Chance*, *Trivia Test Match* and so on. I have interviewed thousands of people in programmes like *Let's Go Somewhere*, *Today*, View from the Boundary on *Test Match Special*, *Stage Door Johnners*, numerous sports programmes and of course *Down Your Way*. I have asked goodness knows how many questions, and all the answers add to my store of knowledge. So after forty-six years of asking questions I should be one of the best-informed persons in the land. But I am not, and because people expect you to know all the answers, it is embarrassing.

Take *Down Your Way* where I interviewed about 5,000 people all over the country. If someone mentions a place I can usually remember two out of the six people I talked to, and quote one or two facts about their town or village. But the other four people often remain a blank, plus the information which they gave me about their jobs, hobbies or historical facts. I do, however, remember some of the interesting derivations, of sayings or phrases which have originated all over the country, and here are just a few of them.

Eyam, Derbyshire

This village was nearly wiped out by the bubonic plague which often started with a sneeze. It became customary to say 'Bless you' to the sneezer, praying that God would save him or her from the plague. I still say 'Bless you' when somebody sneezes (especially Trevor Bailey in the commentary box, where he often produces eight sneezes on the trot).

In a museum in Eyam I found a silver ring called Richard III's Ring, which he gave to his mistress. It has a piece of wood set into it which is said to have come from the Cross. People who were sick or infirm would get his permission to touch it, hence the expression 'touch wood'.

Newcastle Emlyn, Wales

In an old water mill we discovered a machine like a mangle – two wooden rollers turned by hand. The corn was fed through these rollers, and separated into different sizes. If the man turned the rollers too fast the friction of the wood would make the rollers catch fire. It was an American machine called a Temse after the maker's name. If a worker was idle and turned the rollers slowly they used to say, 'He'll never set the Temse on fire.' I had always thought that saying was something to do with the River Thames.

Lampeter, Wales

We were shown some seventeenth-century love spoons. They were made of light wood with two or three little cavities containing tiny marbles which indicated the number of children the bridegroom hoped to have. Hence the word 'spoon' or 'spooning' to describe a 'demonstratively fond lover', or wooing in a 'silly sentimental amorous way'.

Newmarket, Suffolk

During a visit to the Jockey Club we learnt the origins of two popular phrases, 'on the mat' and 'the game's not worth the candle'.

In the old days at a stewards' enquiry the stewards would sit at a horseshoe-shaped table. In the open space in front of them would be placed a mat, on which the trainer or jockey being interviewed would have to stand. So if anyone did anything wrong they were told, 'You'll be on the mat.'

In the card-room all the tables had slots at each corner into which the players used to put their candles which they had brought with them. If they lost heavily at cards they would say, 'The game's not worth the candle.'

Doncaster, Yorkshire

In the beautiful Mansion House two silver goblets were on display. They had handles on either side and were known as Whistling Cups. When the drinker had drained his cup there was a little whistle at the bottom of the cup to summon the waiter to refill it. From this came the phrase 'to wet your whistle'.

Nantwich, Cheshire

Nantwich was a major centre of salt mining. The labourers were paid in salt, not money, so they were said to be 'worth their salt' – or not, as the case might be.

Coventry, Warwickshire

During the Civil War Coventry was a strong parliamentary centre. Royalist prisoners who were sent there were totally ignored. The people refused to speak to them and were generally unpleasant. This explains 'sent to Coventry' at school when everyone would cut you dead.

Ulverston, Lancashire

Ulverston was the birthplace of Stan Laurel of Laurel and Hardy. It was also the place where the Quakers got their name. A twenty-four-year-old preacher, George Fox, was had up before the local judge and told him, 'You should all quake in fear of the Lord.' 'Oh,' said the judge, 'you would have us all quakers, would you?' And the name stuck.

Melton Mowbray, Leicestershire

The Marquis of Waterford had a party one night and he and his guests all became merry with drink. They armed themselves with pots of red paint and brushes, and starting at the toll-gate worked their way through Melton. They daubed everything with red paint, including a night watchman who naturally was not too pleased. He reported them to the police and they were put in gaol. So after that a noisy party celebrating in the streets was said to be 'painting the town red'.

Also in Melton there was a famous tailor called Pink who made all the hunting clothes for the gentry. This is the reason why the wearer of a red hunting jacket is often said to be wearing '*pink*'.

Toppesfield, Essex

Ted Wilson and his son Chris were wheelwrights. They told us that they used to saw the wood over a saw-pit, using a long saw with a handle at each end. One man used to stand at the top of the pit, the other down in the pit itself. This meant he had to push upwards – far harder work. In addition he would get all the sawdust in his eyes. For some reason these sawmen were called dogs, so you got the 'top dog' and the 'under dog'.

Stockton-on-Tees, Co. Durham

We found a very old church somewhat circular in shape. It was very small and there were no seats so everyone had to stand. Anyone feeling faint or who was elderly or infirm got first choice of standing 'with their backs to the wall'.

I also picked up many odd bits of historical information as for example at Hastings where I was reliably informed that Harold was not shot in the eye at the Battle of Hastings. An arrow stuck in his head but he pulled it out. He was killed later in the battle in armed combat.

This rather spoils the story told about when Harold was desperately short of men and sent out his officers to recruit some new archers. One of his officers returned at the end of the day with just one recruit. 'He's the only one I can find. But he's not much good. He's so inaccurate with his bow and arrow that he will probably shoot some poor bugger on our side in the eye.'

When in Tavistock in Devonshire we were surprised to learn that it was the birthplace of that great seafarer, Francis Drake. I had always been told that he was knighted by Queen Elizabeth at Greenwich when he returned from his circumnavigation of the world. The Queen certainly went to meet him and for some reason was accompanied by the French and Spanish Ambassadors. As Drake landed the Queen turned to the French Ambassador and said, 'Have you got a sword?' 'Yes, Your Majesty', he replied. 'Well, *you* dub him,' she said. And he did!

We were always coming across places which claimed to be the first. Two good examples were Colne in Lancashire, and Whitstable in Kent. The former claimed to have had the first public cinema, the first fish-and-chip shop, and the first and only surviving pair of wheeled stocks in the country.

Whitstable went better still with *eight* firsts. The first divers in the world who salvaged the wreck of the *Royal George* in May 1826. In 1830 the first steam-drawn passenger train went into service a few months before the Liverpool-to-Manchester line was opened. The first passenger tickets were issued and the harbour was the first in the world to be served by a railway. The first steamboat to sail to Australia – the eighty-one-ton vessel *William IV* – set out from Whitstable, skippered by a Whitstable man. The town also claims the world's first sea cadets founded by Henry Barton in 1854. And the final claim – in 1920 Whitstable built the first council houses in the world. Phew! How's that for knowledge?

Perhaps the most fascinating things we found out about on our journeys round Great Britain were the ancient ceremonies and annual celebrations going back hundreds of years.

The traditions are carried on with great respect for the past and mark the most important day in each place's calendar. Here are a few examples.

Abbotsbury, Dorset

The GARLAND DAY on 13 May when the children from the village carry garlands of flowers from house to house.

Abbots Bromley, Staffordshire

The HORN DANCE on the Monday following the Sunday after 4 September. Its origins are Anglo-Saxon and it is performed by twelve dancers and musicians on the road wearing Tudor costume. Six men balance reindeer antlers on their shoulders and a seventh rides a hobby-horse. There's a fool with a pig's bladder, a boy with a bow and arrow, accompanied by a young girl. The dance is played by an accordionist and a boy with a triangle.

138

Haxey, Humberside

The HAXEY HOOD GAME every year on 6 January. Neither war nor weather has forced the game to be cancelled in its 700-year-old history. It is basically a terrific scrummage in the mud, containing anything from thirty to a hundred people. They are fighting for a 'sway' hood made from a cylinder of leather twenty-four inches long. There's a Lord, the inevitable fool and a team of Boggans led by the Chief Boggan. They take on all comers and the game ends when the hood and the scrummage reach one of three pubs in the area. Not recommended if you don't like getting your shoes or boots dirty.

Helston, Cornwall

The ancient Flurry Dance on 8 May each year – FLORA DAY. There is a succession of dances through the streets starting at 7 a.m. and going on for about twelve hours. The high point is at the first stroke of midday when the Principal Dance begins with everyone dressed as if for a royal garden party, the men in grey toppers and tails, and the ladies in gorgeous hats and dresses. I expect everyone knows the famous tune which accompanies the dancers – the 'Floral Dance', in recent years made even more famous (or infamous!) by a recording by Terry Wogan.

Hungerford, Berkshire

The HOCKTIDE CEREMONY on the second Tuesday after Easter. It goes back to 1350 when John of Gaunt gave commoners rights to ninety-nine houses in the town. On Hocktide Day the commoners gather for their Hocktide Court: two Tithemen are sent out by the constable to visit all the ninety-nine houses. At each house they are given money (it used to be a penny) and a certain amount of 'sustenance'. In return they give the ladies a kiss. The Tithemen carry a pole decorated with a nosegay, at

139

the top of which is an orange sitting on a spike in a little copper cup.

When the Tithemen return there is a formal lunch. Newcomers to this lunch are called 'Colts', and afterwards they are literally shod by the local blacksmith who hammers a horse's nail into the heel of each Colt's shoe.

Knutsford, Cheshire

ROYAL MAY DAY celebrations, called Royal by permission of the Prince of Wales in 1887 when he was staying in nearby Tatton Park in order to cut the first sod in the construction of the Manchester Ship Canal. He was delighted with the celebrations which make Knutsford the only place in the world where the streets and pavements are ceremonially decorated with coloured sand. This is done by the Sandman and the tradition goes back to King Canute who got sand in his sandals when fording a river. He sat on a rock and shook out the sand. As he did so a young couple passed by and he wished them much happiness and as many children as there were grains of sand in his sandals!

The Sandman starts out at 5.00 a.m. and writes messages in coloured sand outside certain homes, especially those of young marrieds. The Sandman told us that in thirty years he had never known a couple split up after he had left a message outside their house.

Whitby, Yorkshire

PLANTING THE PENNY HEDGE takes place every Ascension Eve, and originated in Norman times. The Hermit of Eskdaleside was set upon by the Norman soldiers and suffered fatal injuries. Before he died he imposed on them and their successors a penance. It was that a hedge built of branches and twigs should be built in Whitby harbour on the Eve of Ascension at 9.00 in the morning. If they failed to build a hedge or if the hedge failed to stand three tides they would forfeit their land to the Abbot of Whitby. This custom still takes place today and at the end of the ceremony an ancient horn is sounded and the bailiff of the Manor of Filing delivers the rebuke: 'Out on ye, out on ye' – the words of the hermit of Eskdaleside at the time of his death.

Whitstable, Kent

The HOODEN HORSE was an old Kentish custom that used to be performed by farmers on 21 December each year. The Hooden Horse was a type of hobby-horse made of a horse's head on a pole with a long cloak behind it. It had sea shells down its nose, little bits of holly between its ears and a jaw that worked with a clicking noise. The farmers visited houses singing and collecting money for their Christmas feast. The Hooden Horse was accompanied by several characters – the Rider, a man who would lead it with a whip and a man dressed as a woman and known as Molly who walked behind the Horse with a besom broom. Nowadays the Hooden Horse has been taken up by the East Kent Morris Dancers who use it at Christmastime and also at the end of hop picking.

As the umpire on the quiz show *Trivia Test Match* I also picked up a lot of knowledge from the questions set by Peter Hickey and Malcolm Williamson. Most of it was trivia but nevertheless amusing and informative. How many of the following facts did you know?

- The most popular sport in American nudist camps is volleyball.
- When Elgar took his three dogs for a drive in his car he made them wear goggles.
- The novelist Anthony Trollope invented the pillar-box.
- Professor Arthur Lintgen can identify classical records by looking at the grooves.
- To hypnotise a frog you rub its belly.
- Amy McPherson was buried with a telephone in her coffin so that she could contact the living world.

- George II died by falling off the loo. It was officially announced that he had fallen off the throne.
- In a hurdle race you can knock down every hurdle and still win.
- The Eiffel Tower is six inches taller in summer than in winter.
- The inventor Reuben Tice died trying to invent a machine to take the wrinkles out of prunes. It exploded.
- Johnny Weismuller's famous Tarzan call was recorded and consisted of a scream of a soprano C and a hyena's howl – all played backwards.
- Tibetans have long nails on their little fingers so that they can clean out their noses more efficiently.
- There are as many as 2,500,000 spiders in one acre of an English field.
- The world record for sitting in a bathful of cooked spaghetti is thirty-six hours.
- The Glenturret Distillery cat, Towser, had killed 25,716 mice up to 1988 – a world record.
- There are six offences for which the death penalty still stands in the UK: treason, piracy with violence, sex attack on certain members of the Royal Family, killing the Lord Chancellor or any High Court Judge, levying war against the Sovereign and intending the death or bodily harm of the Sovereign.
- The first time a penguin sees a human being it falls over backwards.
- The last item shown on British television before the Second World War began was a Mickey Mouse cartoon. The screen then went blank without any closing announcement. It remained blank until the war ended.
- In 1439 in England kissing was made illegal – to stop the spread of disease.
- The philosopher Jeremy Bentham had a most unusual pet – a teapot. A wag said that he used to have a toast rack – but it died!

And finally two sporting facts:
- In 1935 the Cup Final at Wembley was stopped by fog. Fog was the name of the referee.
- A soccer team won a cup-tie 4–0, yet never scored a goal. Never was the name of their centre forward.

L
for Lord's

When we got married in 1948 my wife Pauline asked me where I wanted to live. 'As near to Lord's as possible,' I replied. I must say she didn't do too badly. Within a few months we were installed in a house in Cavendish Avenue – about eighty yards from the Nursery End of Lord's. It was from here that whenever I went to have a net at Lord's I would walk down the road already padded up with bat in hand – much to the surprise of the locals.

Forty-four years later we are still in St John's Wood, though not so close to Lord's. To walk from Cavendish Avenue it took me two minutes, from Hamilton Terrace eight and a half minutes, and now from Boundary Road sixteen minutes on a good day (I'm older and it's further).

So Lord's has been a very special part of my life – almost a second home. Not just in the summer when, apart from commentating on Tests and other big matches, I often slip in for an hour or two to watch whatever cricket is going on, sitting in the sunshine in the Mound or Grandstand; but in the winter I also go there to visit the library or the shop, or to the cricket school where I can try to spot the stars of the future.

I first heard of Lord's when I realised that it was the ground on which my boyhood hero, Patsy Hendren, played. I didn't go there until 1926 for my first Eton and Harrow match. It was a great social occasion in those days, with crowds of up to 10,000 parading round the ground during the intervals. All the men and boys were in top hats and tails, sporting carnations or cornflowers. The ladies showed off their new hats and dresses and much entertaining took place on the various coaches encircling the ground.

I soon collecting a coterie of friends who met every year in the 'free' seats at the top of Block G – on the right of the sight-screen, now the Compton Stand. I'm afraid we made an awful noise barracking or shouting support for our particular school. On one occasion a messenger came over from the Pavilion on behalf of Plum Warner, asking the 'young gentlemen' to make less noise. I was later told that due to my misbehaviour my election to MCC during the war was put back a year or two.

It was all harmless fun and we had regular visitors such as Frank Mann and two sons, and an Old Harrovian, Gerald du Maurier, who came to hear our dreadful jokes. For instance, if a well-dressed, pompous-looking man arrived we would shout, 'There's a message here from Moss Bros. They say can you return your morning suit to them by 6.00 tonight, as it's needed for a wedding in the morning.' Or, even worse, we would sit behind someone and pin their tails to the seat with drawing pins so that they couldn't get up. All this went on for almost ten years or so after the war and we even had a 'Block G' Eton v Harrow match at Hurlingham each summer.

Alas, as a wicket-keeper I never got my XI at Eton so never played in the Lord's match. But in my last year, as compensation, I was allowed into the hallowed Pavilion and spent most of the match in the Eton dressing-room eating the cherries which Lord Harris always sent in a large basket every year. I was also given my first tour of Lord's by our coach, George Hirst, a lovely man with a twinkle in his eye and a kind heart. We even went up to the scorer's box over the Grandstand scoreboard, something I have never done again.

Apart from the Eton and Harrow matches I also attended the Easter Classes from 1927 to 1930. I was coached in wicket-keeping by Fred Price of Middlesex and England. In 1937 he caught seven catches in one innings against Yorkshire at Lord's! He was having a drink in the Tavern afterwards when an excited lady rushed up to him and said, 'Oh, Mr Price, when you held your seventh catch I was so thrilled that I nearly fell over the balcony.' 'Well, madam,' replied Fred, 'on my form today I would probably have caught you too.'

Things were different in those days, compared to the marvellous facilities available today. When it rained we had to practise on matting pitches under the Grand and Mount stands, and the schoolmaster who ran the classes on behalf of the MCC was dressed in a blue pinstripe suit and wore a bowler hat.

I shall always remember Tuesday 1 July 1930. It was the fourth and last day of the Second Test v Australia and some of us were allowed up to Lord's for lunch in one of the Tavern boxes. That afternoon we watched Percy Chapman and Gubby Allen attacking the Australian bowling, with Chapman making 121, including four giant sixes off Clarrie Grimmett. Chapman was eventually caught out behind the stumps by Bertie Oldfield. He told our cricket master that he only got out because he had 'a bloody big bluebottle in my eye'! Australia needed 72 to win and there was some excitement when they lost 3 wickets for 22, including – much to our disappointment – Don Bradman, who was brilliantly caught by Chapman low down in the gulley. He only made 1, but at least we had caught a glimpse of this magical figure in the baggy green cap.

Except for the Varsity match each year I saw little cricket at Lord's at that time, but I was lucky enough to see an eighteen-year-old called Compton make a brilliant 87 against Northants in only his second match for Middlesex. I also saw him play a match-saving 76 not out against Australia in England's second innings of the 1938 Test. And I was privileged to see Wally Hammond's 240 in the first innings, one of the greatest Test innings I ever saw. He slaughtered poor Fleetwood-Smith with some merciless driving.

The next year, 1939, provided a sensation in the Eton and Harrow match. Harrow won the title for the first time since 1908! Those Etonians present thought it was an unhappy omen, and it meant that war was now inevitable. How right we were!

I paid my next visit to Lord's in 1946 when I did my first Test commentary against India. Later that year Ronnie Aird kindly asked me to become a member of the Cross Arrows, a club for the members of the Lord's staff. In those days they played their September matches on the main ground. I played for them twice and had the thrill of changing in the Middlesex dressing-room, walking for the first time through the famous

Long Room, and out on to the field through the little white gate – a path trodden by countless great cricketers of the past.

In one of the matches played on the edge of the square by the Grandstand, I kept wicket to a chirpy sixteen-year-old off-spinner from Kentish Town. I remember that he had very long hair and that Plum Warner told him to get it cut. Imagine that happening today! It was my first introduction to Freddie Titmus and I have always been proud that I actually made a leg-side stumping off him.

Since then Lord's has played a big part in my commentating career, with county matches, cup finals and Test matches both on television and radio. At the start we had to sit out in the open on the small balcony outside the Committee dining-room. We had no cover and used the stone parapet as our table. We often got very wet, with dear old Roy Webber's scoresheets becoming unreadable after being spattered by rain. When the Warner Stand was built both television and radio were moved into boxes there. Radio has since moved back to the Pavilion into our own spacious box on the top balcony above the visitor's dressing-room, from which we have a superb view of the ground.

This is not a chronicle of Test matches at Lord's but undoubtedly the most exciting one was in 1963 against the West Indies, when Colin Cowdrey emerged with his left arm in plaster to join David Allen with 9 wickets down, 2 balls to go, and 6 runs needed for victory. With Wes Hall bowling at his fastest in poor light, David successfully played the 2 balls and it was an honourable draw. Colin did not have to bat, but had he had to do so he intended to bat as a left-hander, using only his right hand.

This exciting finish produced a unique television occasion. The last over was due to start just before 6.00 p.m., and we were ordered to leave Lord's and hand back to Alexandra Palace for the BBC News. It was a terrible thing to have to do and we were all furious and frustrated. But luckily the controller of television was then Kenneth Adam, who was a mad-keen cricketer. He was, of course, viewing and was equally horrified at what had happened. Television was about to miss what could be one of the most exciting Test match finishes ever, and he immediately rang the newsroom and told them to go straight to Lord's at once. The poor newsreader had just begun to read some item about President Kennedy when he received his instructions in his earplug. He stopped in his tracks and hastily said, 'We are now going straight back to Lord's' just in time for what I think was the second ball of the last over.

At the beginning of this match Jim Swanton and I were commentators and we were told that they were electing a new Pope in Rome. Thousands of people were assembled in St Peter's Square awaiting the white puff of smoke which always comes from the Vatican chimney to announce that a new Pope has been elected. We were advised that as soon as this happened BBC TV would immediately leave Lord's and go straight over to Rome to find out who the new Pope was. While commentating and waiting for this call to Rome I suddenly noticed that the old Tavern chimney had caught fire and black smoke was belching out. We immediately switched our cameras on to it, and I was able to say. 'There you are. Jim Swanton has been elected Pope!' He was delighted.

We always tried to have fun with our cameras and on one occasion I spotted J. J. Warr sitting in the Grandstand with his fiancée, Valerie. I couldn't resist saying, 'Warr and piece'.

Another time was when the Lord's Taverners were playing an Old England XI one Sunday. Our cameras were showing Norman Wisdom playing the fool as he batted, falling about all over the place, and causing tremendous laughter among the large crowd. An MCC member had fallen asleep but suddenly woke up and saw Norman's antics. After a few seconds he turned to his neighbour and said, 'I don't know how good a cricketer that chap is, but he'd make a bloody fine comedian.'

I've only made one of my many gaffes at Lord's. It happened in 1969 when Alan Ward, playing in his first Test, was bowling very fast from the Pavilion end to Glenn Turner of New Zealand. Off the fifth ball of one of his overs Glenn was struck a terrible blow in the box. He collapsed in the crease, writhing in pain. The camera panned in on him and I had to waffle away as he lay there. After about two minutes he slowly got up. I reported,

'Someone is handing him his bat, and although he looks rather pale and shaky, he's pluckily going to continue batting. One ball left!'

In May 1987 I decided, after fifteen years and 732 programmes, to give up my BBC radio programme *Down Your Way*. I was given the choice of where I wanted to go for my last broadcast and without hesitation I chose Lord's. MCC did me proud and it was one of the happiest days of my life. On arrival I noticed that the Grandstand scoreboard had put up a total of 733, the highest score ever recorded on it. The previous highest had been 729 made by Australia in 1930. At that time they had no figure 7 and had to hang out a tin plate with 7 on it in front of the 29.

I always interviewed six people on the programme and my 'victims' at Lord's that day included the President, Colin Cowdrey; the Secretary, Lt.-Col. John Stephenson; the Curator, Stephen Green; the Groundsman, Mick Hunt; and Nancy Doyle, who had presided over the best table on the county circuit for twenty-eight years. In addition to looking after all the players and officials, she caters for the Committee's lunches and for the more modest needs of our commentary box. Each morning during a match we get coffee and biscuits, with a special packet of two brown-bread-and-meat sandwiches for me. For the sixth 'victim' to represent all the great players who had played at Lord's, I chose Denis Compton. So it was a fair representation of all that Lord's means.

MCC gave a lunch in honour of the programme and presented me with an MCC mug. It was a perfect day with only one slight snag. Both the President and Denis chose 'My Way' for their piece of music. But Colin kindly gave way and selected 'Underneath the Arches', which, by coincidence, is the only tune I can now play on the piano.

In the summer of 1989 – sixty-three years after my first visit in 1926 – I commented on my fifty-second Test at Lord's, far more than at any other ground. During these years I have made so many friends at Lord's – the Secretariat, the players, the Pavilion attendants, the gatesman and the groundstaff. They have always made me welcome. Imagine, therefore, my delight when towards the end of the summer I received a letter from the President, Field Marshal Lord Bramall, saying that I had been elected by the Committee to be an honorary life member of Lord's.

My cup overflowed at such an honour.

M
for Music-Hall

Variety is the spice of life – or rather it was. Television has a lot to answer for. It killed off music-hall in this country. I first became addicted to variety when I came to live in London in 1934. Right up to the war, except when I was away in Brazil, I would go at least once a week, mostly to the Palladium, Holborn Empire, Victoria Palace or Chelsea Palace. Then after the war I fell on my feet when I joined the BBC. I was given the job of producing and introducing *Round the Halls* every Tuesday night at 8.30 p.m. on the Light programme.

This was a live broadcast direct from the stage of one of the dozens of music-halls which existed in Greater London and in the big cities around the country. It was my job to find a theatre with a strong bill, and then to choose three acts suitable for broadcasting. This meant negotiations with agents such as Lew and Leslie Grade, who in spite of touring round the various halls every night, were always in their offices by 7.30 a.m. The theatres liked having the broadcasts because it meant good publicity for the remaining four days of the week. On the whole customers, except perhaps on Fridays and Saturdays, did not bother to book in advance. They just turned up.

On the Monday I would go down to the theatre in the early afternoon and meet the artists who had been chosen and who had agreed to appear. The patter comedians were not always so keen as it meant giving away their 'material' over the air. But a 'visual' comedian like Norman Wisdom loved it, as the listeners would hear gales of laughter and so would want to go along to see what it was all about. The tricky part was to get the timing right as we had to begin at 8.30 p.m. and finish exactly by 9.00 p.m. Singers and musical acts were easy. One could time their three numbers and allow for applause between the songs, and as they took their bows at the end. But comedy was a different matter. One had to judge how much laughter to allow for after each routine or joke. Some comedians – knowing thousands of listeners could not see them – put in extra bits of visual business and 'milked' the laughter they were getting.

But it was fun to try to get it right. One of the secrets if you were ending with a comedian who finished with a song, was to time the song and then give him a red light as a signal to start singing. There was also the tricky business of censorship, which often meant having to ask a comic to take out a particularly blue or dirty joke. They often protested that these were their biggest laughs but usually agreed to cut them out. Today it would be easy – almost anything goes. But in the forties and fifties BBC censorship was ridiculously strict. Over the air comedians were not meant to make jokes about sex, religion, politics or people's infirmities, nor, of course, were they allowed to make any innuendos. Even mother-in-law jokes were frowned on as they might embarrass a family sitting at home with Ma-in-law present. So the poor comics had precious little left to make jokes about! It's difficult to believe it now but I was given a rocket for passing the following:

'Have you seen the PT mistress?'

'Oh yes. She's stripped for gym.'

'Lucky Jim.'

Of course sometimes they would slip in a joke which I had asked them not to. As the broadcast was live, there was nothing that I could do about it. As when a 'drunk' comic took a drink out of a jug on the table, and spat it out with the words, 'I'll kill that bloody cat!'

These variety artists were fabulous people to meet. They were warm and friendly and I was always made welcome in their dressing-rooms. For the first time I met and made friends with stars like Arthur Askey, Tommy Trinder, Flanagan and Allen, Ted Ray, Hutch, Terry Thomas, Jimmy Edwards and so on. In one broadcast from the Kingston Empire I introduced two then unknowns appearing in a bill presented by Jack Payne – Frankie Howerd and Max Bygraves.

I was never as keen on Old-Tyme Music-Hall with its

chairman and his gavel, as I was on the variety of the thirties to sixties. I always enjoyed the thrill of seeing the number of the next act coming into the frame at the side of the stage. The format of most bills was usually the same – two halves of about an hour each with twelve acts or so.

No. 1. The overture by the pit orchestra. The conductors were usually great characters. They had to be in order to deal with so many artists with different types of acts – and temperament. It was fun to watch at rehearsals as each artist produced their band parts for the orchestra to try to decipher.

2. Could be a troop of dancing girls, acrobats or Chinese tumblers.

3. The first comedy spot, an unenviable position on a first house on a Monday before the usual sparse audience.

4. Time for some sort of music, a xylophonist, pianist, mouth-organ or ukulele.

5. The second comedy spot, usually No. 3 in the billing.

6. To close the first half and the No. 2 on the billing. If the No. 1 was a comedian then this would be a lady singer or vice versa (e.g. Vera Lynn/Max Miller or Jimmy James/Gracie Fields).

7. The second half began with a lively noisy overture to entice the audience away from the bars and back to their seats.

8. Possibly a specialist act such as a juggler, ventriloquist or impressionist with the accent on comedy.

9. A dancing spot with two step dancers, or adagio dancers.

10. Comedy – either a double act, songs at the piano or plain knockabout comedy.

11. Possibly an animal act with dogs, chimps or doves. This was safest if the star to follow was a comedian, performing in front of the cloth. But if the final act was a singer who needed a drawing-room scene with grand piano and standard lamp, then the manager had to make sure that the animal performers were house-trained!

12. The star of the show – followed by 'God Save the King' (or Queen) which was *always* played at the end of every show, even in the humblest music-halls.

And they did vary in comfort, décor and audience, and in the days before the dangers of smoking was realised they were usually smokey and too warm. However in Collins's Music-Hall in Islington it was so cold that I once saw the pianist in the pit wearing mittens and an overcoat. At another – the King's Theatre, Southsea – there was a notice in every dressing-room warning artists to hang their shoes up on the nails provided on the walls, otherwise they might be eaten by rats!

It would be nice to think it possible to recreate *regular* music-hall again. Various attempts *have* been made to resuscitate it, notably at the Hackney Empire, one of London's outposts from which we used to broadcast *Round the Halls*.

However the cost today of producing ten acts plus an orchestra would be prohibitive. It would of course be possible to reduce the number of acts and in the fifties this was taking place. Artists like Max Miller would put on their own bill doing the whole of one half of the show. Sometimes Max would do the first half so that he could catch an earlier train to Brighton.

On an occasion like that he would probably do about fifty minutes – a long time for a comedian. But if he was the top of a normal bill his time would be about eighteen minutes – leaving the customer hungry for more.

Of course the modern equivalent of Max Miller – Ken Dodd – thinks nothing of doing an act for well over an hour, or more if they let him. But with two houses, discipline on timing has to be strict. On many occasions he has kept the second house customers outside in the cold, or if it was the second house, caused many of them to miss their last train home. He is not popular with the management when he does this, as it involves heavy overtime payments to the orchestra. In fact when he had his show at the London Palladium in 1990, I noticed that he kept looking at his watch, and the curtain actually rang down on time.

There was one artist in the thirties who rivalled him for

longevity on stage. He often had either to be dragged off, or have the curtain rung down on his act. He was a crazy-looking, long-haired, excitable French Canadian called Herschell Henlere who sang, joked and played the piano magnificently. He used to say, 'And now we'll have some jizz' and he would switch from some classical number to some old-time jazz number. In contrast to him was the soft rhythm of Charlie Kunz. I broadcast him several times and he always did exactly eighteen minutes – his act divided into three parts of three numbers in each. He didn't speak, breathed heavily and had his back in a brace. But what a fantastically light touch.

One final thought about timing. If you appeared on the Moss Empire's circuit you kept exactly to your time – or else! The powerful booker was one Cissie Williams and if you transgressed by running overtime, you were never booked again. No excuses.

You probably realise that my main delights at the music-halls were the comedians. I could write a book about their different styles and techniques, and what made them funny. I have always preferred the spoken comedy to the visual, and have never really enjoyed clowns. To give you some idea of my favourites I have made up two variety bills with the accent on comedy, and on pp. 157–8 I have listed all those artists whom I have met and whom I broadcast in the days of *Round the Halls*. You will see from the list of comics that I could produce many more bills which I would guarantee to make you laugh. It was easier for them in the old days when they could cover the music-halls all over Great Britain using the same act and basically the same material year after year. For aficionados of variety, see if you agree with my two selected bills from artists whom I have seen or broadcast. Sit back in your seat in the stalls and watch for the numbers as they come up in the frame.

FIRST BILL

1	Sydney Caplan and Orchestra
	Overture
2	Wilson, Keppel and Betty

3	Billy Bennett
4	Western Bros.
5	Nellie Wallace
6	Jimmy James
7	Gracie Fields

★★★★★

8	Orchestra
9	Teddy Brown (xylophone)
10	Tommy Cooper
11	Hutch
12	Flanagan and Allen

SECOND BILL

1	Orchestra
	Overture
2	Nicholas Bros.
3	Eddie Gray
4	Charlie Kunz
5	Tommy Trinder
6	Vera Lynn
7	Sid Field

★★★★★

8	Orchestra
9	Murray and Mooney
10	Layton and Johnstone
11	Florence Desmond
12	Donald Peers
13	Max Miller

As a frustrated comic and a music-hall buff I was naturally delighted to appear on the stages of the Palladium, Victoria Palace and the Adelphi. It was all part of my four-minute live spot *Let's Go Somewhere*. At the London Palladium I broadcast from the hind legs of a donkey in Tommy Trinder's pantomime. At the Victoria Palace I twice took part in a Crazy Gang sketch, the first time as the victim in the barber's chair (see p. 111) and the second when they dressed me up in a jumper with some massive false boobs, and I joined them in their sketch as the ladies selling violets by the statue of Eros in Piccadilly Circus.

In addition to the music-halls in the thirties, I used to haunt the Café de Paris to watch their famous cabaret. I made friends with the head waiter who used to allow me to sit in the gallery for a supper of scrambled eggs and a jug of lager, for which he charged me a nominal £1.00 instead of the pricey supper charge.

I saw stars like Sophie Tucker (with Ted Shapiro at the piano), Florence Desmond, Noël Coward, Billy Bennett, Dougie Byng, Beatrice Lillie and so on. It was always a dramatic moment when the lights were dimmed, and the spotlights picked out the star as she or he walked majestically down the staircase on to the dais in front of the band.

On one occasion I saw a hero of mine, Schnozzle Durante, passing my table. We had similar noses and a lot of my friends called me Schnozzle. I couldn't resist getting up and pointing to my nose. 'It's a bigger one than yours, Mr Durante,' I said. He looked at me and said, 'It's the moick of distinction – the moick of distinction.' I loved his act sitting, singing at the piano and cracking jokes like this one after he'd sung a particularly high note. 'I got that note from Bing Crosby – and oh boy *was* he glad to get rid of it!'

Variety artists with whom I have either broadcast or performed on TV or radio in my capacity as commentator, presenter, interviewer or performer are listed over the page:

Double Acts or with Company	Flanagan and Allen	Naughton and Gold
	Sid Field and Jerry Desmonde	Caryll and Mundy
	Jewell and Warriss	Clapham and Dwyer
	Elsie and Doris Waters	Nat Mills and Bobbie
	Mike and Bernie Winters	Arthur Lucan and Kitty McShane
	Murray and Mooney	Revnell and West
	Collinson and Dean	Jimmy James and Company
	Bennett and Williams	Will Hay and Company
	Nervo and Knox	The Western Brothers

Impressionists	Florence Demond	Peter Cavanagh
	Peter Sellers	Peter Goodwright
	Bransby Williams	Joyce Grenfell
	Jack Watson	Jack Train

Musical Acts	Charlie Kunz	Peggy Cochrane
	Nat Gonella	Rawicz and Landauer
	Teddy Brown	Joe Henderson
	Herschell Henlere	Semprini
	Ivor Moreton and Dave Kaye	Winifrid Attwell
		Turner Layton

Singers	Binnie Hale	Bob and Alf Pearson
	Jessie Mathews	Flotsam and Jetsam
	Anne Shelton	Monte Rey
	Elizabeth Welch	Cavan O'Connor
	G. H. Elliott	Talbot O'Farrell
	Donald Peers	Peter Dawson
	Vanessa Lee	Phyllis Robins
	Vera Lynn	The Beverley Sisters
	Hutch	Dorothy Squires

Ventriloquists	Saveen and Daisy May	Ray Allen and Lord Charles
	Peter Brough and Archie Andrews	

Singing or Instrumental Comedians	Gracie Fields	Max Bygraves
	Harry Secombe	Albert Whelan
	Douglas Byng	Dickie Henderson
	Forsythe, Seaman and Farrell	Jimmy Edwards
		Max and Harry Nesbitt
	George Formby	Reg Varney
	Two Leslies	Tessie O'Shea
	Randolph Sutton	Ronald Frankau
	Nellie Wallace	Stanley Holloway
	Roy Castle	Libby Morris
	Stanelli	Joan Turner

Comedians and Comediennes	Cicely Courtneidge	Will Fyffe
	Jack Hulbert	Eric Sykes
	Tommy Trinder	Cardew Robinson
	Tommy Cooper	Bernard Miles
	Arthur Askey	Billy Russell
	Claude Dampier	Dickie Murdoch
	Vic Oliver	Nosmo King
	Billy Danvers	Harry Tate Junior
	Ted Ray	Dickie Hearne
	Suzette Tarri	Norman Evans
	Bruce Forsythe	Jimmy Wheeler
	Benny Hill	Max Wall
	Bob Monkhouse	Wee Georgie Wood
	Norman Wisdom	Nat Jackley
	Roy Hudd	Johnny Dennis
	Ken Dodd	Lupino Lane
	Jimmy Tarbuck	Frankie Howerd
	Michael Bentine	Gillie Potter
	Sonnie Hale	Dick Henderson Senior
	Chic Henderson	Tony Hancock
	Harry Worth	Jack Warner
	Scott Saunders	Beryl Reid
	Cyril Fletcher	Leslie Crowther
	Dave Willis	Arthur English
	Sandy Powell	Max Adrian
	Terry Thomas	Bill Pertwee
	Naunton Wayne	Russ Abbott
	Eddie Gray	Richard Stilgoe
	Charlie Chester	Clarkson Rose

158

N
for Newspapers

In *Who's Who* I have listed newspapers as one of my hobbies. I would like to qualify that slightly, and insert the word 'some' in front of newspapers. Like a lot of people I enjoy a bit of gossip – but only up to a point. There is a limit and there are about four tabloids which usually exceed it. The sad thing is that it obviously boosts their sales, and we as readers are as guilty as they are. It's only when something is written about oneself or a close friend that one realises how inaccurate they can be, and how deliberately dishonest and untruthful. There is no limit to what they will invent in order to get a good story. A perfect example happened to me a year ago.

When I was seventy my godson, Graham Cowdrey, sent me a cricket protector or 'box' as cricketers call it. It was dedicated to his 'aged godfather' with some rude comment about it not having too much to protect these days! Eight years later the *Express* somehow got hold of this story and added that my wife Pauline had whispered, 'It's too small anyway – the *box* I mean!' Quite untrue. She never said any such thing to anyone. But it was good for a laugh.

Most papers provide great value and entertainment, especially if you have as many interests as I have – politics, theatre, people, TV and radio and sport of all kind. Plus a vital extra bonus – the crossword. I always find it difficult to know where to start but it's usually in this order:

1. Quick glance at the headlines on the front page.
2. Sporting pages. This takes a long time in the summer.
3. Theatre, TV and radio, especially reviews.
4. General news including a column such as Peterborough in the *Telegraph*, and the gossip of Nigel Dempster in the

Daily Mail. I also enjoy all the political sketchbooks about the previous day's proceedings in the House of Commons.

5. If I have the time, I try to read the letters in *The Times* which are often revealing and amusing.

6. I try to avoid the obituary columns as the older you get, the more depressing they become. I also don't look at the births as most of my friends are now incapable of having babies. But I do check the birthdays so that I can send a belated card, or ring up a friend.

There are two good obituary stories. The first one is credited to the veteran actor A. E. Matthews. He is accredited with saying that 'each morning my wife brings me a cup of tea and *The Times*. I drink the tea, then look in the obituary column. If I'm not in it, I get up.' The other one concerned the late Lord Desborough. Lord *Bess*borough died and the next day *The Times* published an obituary of Lord *Des*borough. He read it at breakfast and then rang up *The Times* and asked to speak to the Obituary Editor. The editor came on the line: 'Who is speaking, please?' he asked. 'It's Lord Desborough here.' There was a few seconds silence, and the editor asked in a trembling voice, 'From *where* are you speaking?'!

7. Finally I turn to the crossword puzzle. On trains I have a bash at *The Times*, but it's far too difficult for me. I have a friend Humphrey Fisher who can do it in about ten minutes without writing in a single word. I also knew someone who used to complete the crossword in the morning on his way to work. Sometimes for a joke he would buy another copy and on the train home in the evening ostentatiously turn to the crossword and fill it in in about two minutes. An impressive performance for those in the carriage who didn't know him.

Normally I try to do the *Daily Telegraph* which I can usually manage to finish about two days out of the six. They obviously have two or even three different composers, and there's one special one on whose wavelength I seem to be – he likes anagrams and plays on words. The others I admit are sometimes beyond me, and even when I look at the solution the next day I don't get it!

My favourite story about crosswords is a bit naughty I'm afraid. It's about the bishop sitting in a corner of a crowded railway carriage trying to do the crossword. He was obviously struggling and looking rather embarrassed. After a lot of head shaking he asked the others in the carriage, 'Can any of you tell me a four-letter word with a female connection ending in –UNT?' A bright young man in the opposite corner said, 'What about aunt, sir?' 'Ah,' said the bishop, looking mightily relieved, 'thank you very much. Has anyone got a rubber?'

Sports coverage is more plentiful and extensive than in the old days but its character in all but the top four papers has changed. It has degenerated into overemphasis on incidents and bad behaviour *on* the field, or prying journalists into *off*-the-field activities. All this is at the expense of reporting what has actually happened during the game or sport. On cricket tours these days some papers send two reporters, one to report the cricket, the other to nose around for a 'story'. This results in many of our players being portrayed as drunkards, adulterers or whatever. When I went on my ten tours for the BBC I and my companions in the press concentrated solely on the game. It was not our job to comment on private behaviour unless of course it concerned the reputation of the team. A cynic might say we didn't sneak on them because they might have sneaked on us. (I'm only joking!)

In spite of or perhaps because of the vastly increased time devoted to politics on both TV and radio, the newspapers too give the political news much space. Unlike TV or radio they don't hide their feelings and quite openly support either the government or the opposition. Naturally Labour says that this gives an unfair advantage to the Conservatives who have, I suppose, the support of at least seventy-five per cent of the Press. Whether this influences the way people vote I'm not sure. The voting public are more intelligent than they are sometimes given credit for. They have the unbiased presentation of TV and radio as a guide, plus a fairly common suspicion of the veracity of most newspapers.

I find the show-business coverage fascinating to read and follow as many of the theatrical and media critics as possible. Again it's difficult to assess how much influence they have on their readers. In New York it's accepted that a bad review by one of the butchers of Broadway will kill a production instantly. In England this is not always so – the best examples being *Charley Girl* and *Les Misérables*. Both got terrible notices but enjoyed runs of five years or more. Good advance publicity, and good connections with the coach trade can help enormously overcome a bad start. In the end, however, it is word of mouth that wins the day and in spite of a few exceptions I think most shows – irrespective of the critics' comments – get the success or otherwise which they deserve.

As regards TV and radio, with the exception of a review of a new series, it seems illogical that viewers and listeners seem to like to read about a show which they have seen the night before.

Presenters, commentators and reporters are frequently accused of gaffes – e.g. Colemanballs in *Private Eye* – but newspapers tend to escape criticism of their misprints. I have two special favourites. During a drive round London Queen Mary was reported as having *pissed* over Westminster Bridge. An article about Sir Francis Chichester said of him: '. . . Sir Francis Chichester, the great yachtsman, who with his twenty-four-foot cutter *circumcised* the world!'

Those were misprints. But what I suspect was a deliberate headline occurred in the *Oxford Mail* in 1932.

It was the time of the gold crisis and the National Government. As a result money was short (when is it ever not?) and the various colleges decided as an economy measure to cancel their commemoration balls which normally take place at the end of the summer term. For one edition only the *Oxford Mail* came out with the headline: 'UNPRECEDENTED EVENT. UNDER-GRADUATES SCRATCH BALLS'! I cannot believe that this was not spotted before going to press.

One London evening paper also came up wth a splendid

headline about a police search for a girl: 'SHEPHERD'S BUSH COMBED FOR MISSING GIRL'!

In spite of some of the things which I have said, I think we are lucky to have such a varied number of national newspapers. There is something for everyone but if you don't like them you don't have to buy them.

O
for Oxford

When I came towards the end of my time at Eton, I still had
no idea what I wanted to do with my life. There was our family
coffee business as a possibility but it didn't seem too exciting to
me. Strangely I had no wish to go to university, although many
of my friends were going to do so.

Luckily I had a sensible housemaster – Mr Huson – who
gradually persuaded me to try and get into Oxford. My father
had been to New College, and my brother Christopher was
there at that moment. In those days the colleges used to
encourage the family connection. (They don't now!) Mr Huson
pointed out that three years as an undergraduate would give
me time to sort myself out and decide what career I wished to
follow. He assured me that I would have three wonderful years,
and that I would learn how to deal with sex and drink, and
how to mix with people from all walks of life – a contrast to
Eton. His logic persuaded me and thanks to an indulgent
examiner at New College, I managed to pass the entrance
exam. My family connection undoubtedly stood me in good
stead.

New College had an excellent mix of undergraduates. There
were a lot of brainy Wykehamists, about twenty not-so-clever
Etonians and Rhodes Scholars from America, Australia,
Canada and New Zealand. It was quite a tough life in those
days. Everyone had their own bedroom and sitting-room up a
rather draughty staircase. There was no running water and no
central heating, but each staircase shared a scout who did
everything for one. He brought a jug of hot water, and looked
after the coal fire. He also would bring breakfast or lunch to
your room. I used to share breakfast with three other chaps,
and we took it in turns to use each others' rooms.

So far so good. But if you wanted a bath you had to go outside and walk across the quadrangle in your dressing-gown in all weathers. Why we didn't catch pneumonia I will never know.

We normally dined out in one of the many clubs but we were required to eat in college so many times a term. Our gang used to sit at one long refectory table and I'm ashamed to say behaved disgracefully. There were straw mats on the tables and we used to hurl these through the air at the top table, where the dons and their distinguished guests were quietly sipping their port. The Dean would come down in a justifiable rage but we all denied it was us, and pretended to be involved in serious conversation. There was little he could do except make sure that in future there would be no mats on the table.

Dean Henderson was a charming man who for some reason spoke in a broken German accent. He *could* be tough and dish out punishments such as 'gating' for a number of days, which was the equivalent of being confined to barracks. As a last resort he could ask the Warden to send the culprit down perhaps for a week or two, or even a term.

He was quite a psychologist in the way he dealt with rowdy parties. I remember once that some drunken visitors from another college began to throw stones at the windows in the quadrangle. The Dean was summoned and swiftly summed up the situation. They were not *his* undergraduates and he was heavily outnumbered. So he picked up a stone and said, 'Let's just break one more window and then all go home to bed.' So saying he flung his stone, there was a tinkling of glass and the threatening crowd melted slowly away, apparently quite happy.

He was a bit old-fashioned in his outlook, as we found on one occasion when we were summoned to his room. We had been out in a friend's new car and when testing it at about seventy m.p.h. (very fast in those days) were stopped by a police trap who reported us to the college. Knowing his views we decided to say that we had been travelling at no more than thirty m.p.h. When we told him this he stepped back startled, and a low whistle escaped his lips. 'Ach,' he said gutturally, 'if you must travel at such a speed you must expect to get into trouble.' He promptly gated us for a few days. Goodness knows what would have happened if we had admitted to our real speed.

The dons were a delightful lot. The warden was H. A. L. Fisher, a brilliant historian who for a short time had been Minister of Education in Lloyd George's Cabinet. Whenever he could he would say, 'When I was in the Cabinet. . . .' He amused a group of French visitors when he tried it in French. 'Quand j'étais dans le Cabinet. . . .' (In French, cabinet means water closet!)

There was an unfortunate Chaplain called Lightfoot who used to have his leg pulled unmercifully by the undergraduates. He told how one day they had gone too far. 'They crucified me with croquet hoops.' They had indeed laid him out on the lawn and pinned his arms and legs with the hoops so that he couldn't move.

Each of us had our own tutor and as I read history I was allotted to a Mr Wickham Legge who snorted whenever he laughed, which he did frequently. *We* laughed too when he was telling us about the bad fevers which Henry VIII used to suffer. 'Personally,' he said, 'whenever I have a fever, I toss off everything within reach.'

I'm afraid I didn't work too hard. I attended lectures or tutorials in the mornings, and played some sort of sport every afternoon. In the summer I played cricket almost every day and captained the college for two years. (In my second year David Townsend was the nominated Captain, but as he was playing for the University, he asked me to take his place.)

In the winter I played rugger and was even selected to play in 'Cuppers', which was the Inter-College Knockout Competition and was extremely rough and tough. I did manage to achieve something which I am sure is quite unique in the history of the game. I scored a try in a macintosh! Someone had tackled me and my shorts were ripped off. I stood on the touchline whilst a friend went off to the pavilion to get me another pair. A kind person seeing me shivering said, 'You had better put on my macintosh to cover your confusion whilst you are waiting!' The ball came down the three-quarter line and when it reached the left wing I shouted to him, 'Outside you' and without looking he passed me the ball and I ran on to touch down between the posts. The referee should have stopped me as I hadn't got his permission to return to the field, but he was laughing so much that he couldn't blow his whistle!

Clubs played a large part in Oxford life and I belonged to three. My first was the Gridiron or Grid which was open to anybody but moderately exclusive. Then there was Vincents which is a famous sporting club, most of the members being blues at some game or other, plus of course rowing and athletics. My third club was the Bullingdon which was unashamedly upper crust. It was small and exclusive and had a tiny dining-room with one long table. The food was definitely 'schoolboy', the favourite dish being scrambled eggs. Most of the members were Old Etonians and very horsey. I got in partly because I was an Old Etonian, but also because of a practical joke a friend of mine and I played on the horsey set.

Four of them lived in digs in the High and had lots of horses and hunted with the Bicester or the University Drag several times a week. We asked whether we could see them to get advice on what to do about our horses which we wished to stable in Oxford so that we could hunt. We asked whether we should bring our grooms, and how many horses we would need, bearing in mind we would want to ride in all the point-to-points during the Lent term. They took it all very seriously and welcomed us into the horsey set. Of course we really had no horses or grooms, but left them convinced that we had. They were so nice to us that we felt rather guilty, and made sure within a day or two that they knew they had had their legs pulled.

Little did I think then that two years later I would actually ride in a point-to-point or 'grind' as they called it at Oxford. I think it was William Douglas-Home's idea, which was very brave of him as he had never hunted and hardly ever ridden. I at least had hunted as a boy. Anyway we hired two horses and went for one or two practice rides though we never dared to see if our horses could jump.

William had a steady old black horse called Nero. Mine was a nice-looking bay called Tip Top, and was said to be the half-brother of April the Fifth who had won the Derby in the previous year. We entered for the New College Member's Race and got more and more frightened as the day approached.

There were only eight runners and some of my 'friends' went round the bookies making bets on Tip Top in very loud voices, so to my horror I started as third favourite. We were both left at the start but gave chase after the others. Tip Top's ears were pricked and he raced away obviously enjoying himself. He could have stopped whenever he wanted. I just sat there hoping for the best but his racing blood stood him in good stead and he jumped beautifully. We actually came in fifth and why I didn't fall off I don't know. Prior to the race I had been an advocate of the 'forward seat' but after the first jump I was leaning so far back that my head nearly hit his hindquarters. My friends cheered me loudly as I rode into the unsaddling enclosure but there were some mild boos from those who had been fooled into backing me.

Poor William, not surprisingly, didn't get very far on Nero. He scrambled through the first fence but Nero refused at the second. I can't say I blame him and I think William was very relieved.

One of the features of the Oxford point-to-points was a tipster called Captain Dean, though I doubt if he had ever been in the services. He actually tipped me to win on some of the cards which he sold. But he was always careful to tip every horse in the race so that at least some of his customers were bound to be satisfied. He had some wonderful patter. 'There are jockeys here today who couldn't ride in a railway carriage unless the door was locked,' or 'They've sent a horse from Leicester here today. It's so thin that it reminds me of Napoleon in exile – they couldn't have St Helena horse!'

One Sunday evening I earned my first money ever. There was a concert in New College chapel so I collected some pictures off the walls of some of my friends' rooms. I placed them against the wall outside the porter's lodge in Queen's Lane, past which the concertgoers would have to come. I dressed up with a fake moustache in an old macintosh and dirty cap, and sat on the pavement alongside the pictures. When the concertgoers walked by I begged in a whining voice saying I had a wife and five children to keep. I had arranged for one or two of my friends to drop some silver coins osentatiously into my tin murmuring things like, 'Poor fellow', 'Very sad case', 'What a shame', 'A most deserving cause', etc. The concertgoers were thus encouraged to drop their coins – mostly a few pennies – into my tin, and in the end I collected about five bob.

I had to leave rather hurriedly when my spies warned me that the proctors had been called and were on their way with their two bowler-hatted 'bulldogs'. I gathered up my pictures and fled.

We formed a club called The Allsorts and played cricket, rugger and soccer against schools and various clubs in the city, including a team of waiters from the hotels. We always lined up before the kick off and one of us would dress up as a VIP and shake hands with the two teams. Our matches were regularly reported in the *Oxford Mail*.

As you may have gathered I had a wonderful time at Oxford. Looking back I feel ashamed at the small amount of work which I did. Even in my last term when I should have been preparing for my final exams, I still played cricket four times a week. On the other two days I went to a crammer who filled me with some essential facts which I ought to have known about the various periods of history. He told me, no matter what the questions were, to bring these facts into my answers. This I did and just managed to get a third in history. Nothing to be proud of, I fear. But I *did* enjoy myself and made a lot of friends with whom I have kept up to this day. Also one night at a dinner in Brasenose College I drank far too much port, and have never touched a drop since, which has saved me a lot of money.

P
for Prep School

In 1921 at the age of eight and three quarters I joined my brothers Michael and Christopher at Temple Grove School at Eastbourne and became Johnston Min. 'TG' was then said to be the oldest prep school in the country and was situated very near to the Saffrons cricket ground.

There were two other schools alongside us, one of them being St Cyrpians which we called Kippers. For some reason we were deadly enemies. Perhaps it was because of their noisy bugle band whose wrong notes came floating over the wall which separated us. By the time I arrived we did not even play them at any game. Rumour had it that during one cricket match whilst they were batting their cricket master, who was one of the umpires, stuck the bails on to the stumps with glue. The result was that however fast our bowlers bowled, the bails never fell off when the ball hit the stumps. An unlikely tale!

Looking back, Temple Grove was a pretty tough school. There was the usual amount of bullying and a ghastly initiation ceremony for new boys. When it was wet, and so there were no games, the senior boys would organise a 'concert' in which all new boys had to perform – singing, reciting or whatever they could do. The senior boy would stand over the poor performer with a heavy book which he would bring down with a thud on the victim's head if he dried up or failed to do some sort of turn. It was a terrifying experience but even in those days I used to tell bad jokes so, by making them laugh, I got off lighter than most.

The discipline was very strict, possibly due to the extraordinary masters and their methods of teaching. The Headmaster was the Rev. H. W. Waterfield who beat the worst offenders with a thick short cane which looked like a rhinoceros whip. I was once given two of the best and my goodness it hurt, but in other ways he was a kindly man. He had had one eye knocked out when he was playing squash. For some reason he was nicknamed 'Bug' and the standard jokes was:

'Bug has got a glass eye.'

'Really – how do you know?'

'Oh, it came out in the conversation!'

Mrs 'Bug' had an enormous bottom and walked (possibly because of arthritis) bent right forward nearly parallel to the ground. We really only saw her on the last night of the term when she would come up and supervise our baths and ensure that we went home clean behind the ears.

The highlight of a boy's career at the school was the 'leaving pi jaw'. This was meant to complete his sex education, but poor old Bug got terribly embarrassed and spoke a lot of gobbledy-gook. We were warned by old boys that one of his questions required a firm 'no'. It was: 'Do things happen at night?' Sure enough he asked each one of us, but we had not the slightest idea what he was getting at. However, much to his relief we all said 'no', except for one boy called Monck-Mason. He acciden-tally said 'yes' and we all waited with bated breath. But all Bug did was to put his head in his hands and cry out, 'O Mason, Mason,' without offering any advice or explanation.

The climax of the pi jaw came when Bug asked, 'Do you know where babies come from?' I quite honestly said, 'No sir.' 'Well,' he said, 'if you have shared a bath with your sister you will know that women have a hole in front. That's where babies come from!' I remembered seeing my sister's navel and for some time afterwards thought that was the one he meant!

Several of the other masters believed in physical punishment. Mr Fritch used to knock boys about the head with his knuckles. We called it a 'fiddler fotch' and it was very painful. Mr Bellamy had a round ebony ruler with which he too used to hit boys on the head. I am not sure how many boys suffered in later life from brain damage, but it's a wonder we all survived. Mr Taylor kept a cane under his desk which he would use occasionally in class, until a boy called Corrie bravely snatched it from him, and broke it across his knee. There was nothing that Taylor could do about it as, of course, he was not meant to beat boys.

The games master was fairly normal, as was a nice old man who taught copperplate writing which he wrote beautifully. His name was Bill Wigg and he kept his spectacles in a Three Nuns tobacco tin.

There was also an ex-Chief Petty Officer called Creese who used to teach us rifle shooting, and take us in drill and PT. We actually won the Ashburton Cup for Preparatory Schools' Rifle Shooting one year, so he must have been a good instructor. He was also responsible for punishments awarded by the Head-master. One of these was to run round a cobbled quad with arms above the head holding an iron dumbbell in each hand. It was good old-fashioned naval discipline and very unpleasant in freezing weather (no gloves allowed).

The domestic staff were equally strange. There was little old Miss King whose feet pointed to ten and two on the clock, and for some reason she smelt of Secotine. Matron was a large cheerful burly woman with a formidable bosom and a club foot. Through her I had my first introduction to the wireless as she had a small cat's-whisker set. She used to allow me to listen and I still remember the voice of Stainless Stephen with his 'semicolon', 'comma' or 'full stop' after each of his jokes.

Matron was called Putty Allen and she 'did' me in a kindly way during my last term. We used to slip out of school and buy some very mild cigarettes called BDV. We used to smoke them behind the fives courts purely out of bravado because none of us really enjoyed them. One day in her room I saw her ostentatiously light up a BDV cigarette. I went down to my playbox where I kept my cigarettes, and sure enough they had all gone. She had obviously pinched them knowing there was nothing I could do about it. But she never reported me to Bug.

It was not surprising so soon after the war that the food was pretty awful and that there was not enough of it. We seemed to be permanently hungry and used to augment our meals with biscuits sent by our parents, and especially with Marmite. It was then in a white jar and pronounced 'Mar*meat*' and all my family have enjoyed it ever since.

I hope I have not been too hard on the school. For the most part I enjoyed my time there, especially the cricket where I kept wicket for the school for two years. I also saw my first first-class cricket at the Saffrons in Eastbourne where each year we watched H. D. G. Leveson-Gower's XI against Oxford and Cambridge. It is still a beautiful ground and I saw many great players between 1921 and 1925.

Two years before I got into the First XI there was a star batsman who regularly made hundreds for Temple Grove against the other schools. This made him especially popular because whenever he did so, the whole school was excused prep. Had he not lost both his legs in an air crash before the war, I feel sure he would have played for England, not only at cricket, but also as a brilliant fly-half at rugger. His name was Douglas Bader, who later became the famous wartime fighter pilot and Group Captain with DSO and DFC.

To sum up, I suspect that we were quite well taught. At one time it was thought that I might get a scholarship at Eton which would certainly have helped my family with the fees. I went up to Eton with Bug to take the exam but failed dismally. In the end I had to take the common entrance and only just passed that!

Q

for Questions

Why? does the taxi you hail at night always seem to be going home in the wrong direction?

Why? are books published at £13.99 and £14.99 etc? What's wrong with £14.00 and £15.00?

Why? do newsreaders on TV press what appears to be a computer button at the end of reading the news?

Why? has cranberry sauce taken over from bread sauce as one of the trimmings with turkey?

Why? are bank dispensers usually closed or out of order at weekends when the banks are closed?

Why? do restaurant or buffet cars on trains have to close down half an hour – or sometimes earlier – before the train is due to arrive? They say it is in order to do the accounts. Could this not be done at the journey's end for the convenience of passengers, *not* the catering staff?

Why? when you buy an electric toy or gadget is there usually no battery with it?

Why? do so many people wear tight jeans? They must be so uncomfortable – and how do they get their feet through the narrow hole at the bottom?

Why? in so many restaurants does the wine waiter arrive with, and pour out, a bottle of Perrier Water, presupposing everyone wants it and not one of the many British varieties? Have Perrier got better salesmen?

Why? are the telephones at theatre box offices seemingly permanently engaged?

Why? do banks implore you to have an overdraft or to take out a loan when times are good, and then hound you – with threats – for repayment as soon as the economy is depressed? Wasn't it their fault to start with by increasing a false demand for money and thus fuelling inflation?

Why? in these days of man going to the moon, satellites, fax, computers etc. is it still so difficult (or impossible if you have fingers like mine) to wire a 3-pin, 13-amp plug?

Why? do top entertainment artists get paid such vast sums? (£10,000 plus per week in the theatre or £10,000 plus to present a quiz show on TV.) Furthermore it means that the smaller artists in the shows get comparatively badly paid. There also have to be smaller choruses, orchestras and casts.

Why? are the 'quality' Sunday papers impossible to handle and read properly because they have so many supplements?

Why? is it legal to buy cigarettes, food, sweets etc. on a Sunday, but illegal to buy a Bible?

Why? does the coffee shop in the TV soap opera *Neighbours* never have more than two other customers besides the main characters? How does Harold make it pay?

Why? do most modern TV or radio news reporters drop their voices at the end of each phrase or sentence?

Why? on a motorway do speed restrictions come on *miles* before the accident or road repairs? As there is nothing in sight motorists pay little or no attention.

Why? is the last Christmas card dropped through your letter-box on Christmas Eve always from the *one* person you have forgotten?

Why? does my *evening* paper arrive *before* lunch?

Why? does the eye of a needle have to be so small?

Why? do most theatres now not serve tea beforehand or during intervals? Usually there is only coffee.

Why? when you have been waiting twenty minutes for a bus, does a convoy of three of the number you want arrive together? Or, even worse, when you've just arrived at the bus-stop, do you see three of your buses disappearing in the distance?

Why? do shops buy in *special* stocks for what are supposed to be sales of goods *already in the shops*?

Why? on motorways, is there a queue on the outside lane whilst the middle and inside lanes are often comparatively empty?

Why? if a car comes close up behind you flashing its headlights on a motorway is it always a Vauxhall Cavalier?

Why? when waiting in one of the queues at a railway station booking office, or at a post office, does *your* queue always contain a lady who has to rummage in her handbag to find her purse or Access card?

Why? is a wrong number never engaged?

Some questions which I *can* answer:

Why? did a man who lived on the fifty-fifth floor of a skyscraper always get out of the lift at the forty-fifth floor?
A. Because he was a dwarf and could not reach the fifty-fifth-floor button.

Why? if the *answer* you *heard* was '9 W', what was the question?
A. Mr Wagner, is your name spelt with a V?

Why? are policemen so strong?
A. Because they can hold the traffic up with one hand.

What? has got six eyes and can't see?
A. Three blind mice

Why? do squirrels swim on their backs?
A. To keep their nuts dry.

What? is the similarity between a debutante and a man with his flies undone?
A. They both have coming-out balls.

What? do you call a Frenchman who is shot out of a cannon?
A. Napoleon Blownaparte.

What? lies shivering at the bottom of the sea?
A. A nervous wreck.

If? a fly flying to China passed a flea flying to London, what would the time be in China as they passed each other?
A. Fly past flea.

What? is worse than a giraffe with a sore throat?
    A. A centipede with chilblains.
How? do porcupines make love?
    A. Very carefully.
How? do you get down off an elephant?
    A. You don't. You get it from a swan.

R
for Religion

I suppose that everyone from time to time asks themselves, 'Do I really believe in God? Is there really an afterlife?' I know I do and I never come up with very satisfactory answers.

Can there possibly be just one 'person' who is and has been there from the start, the Father of all mankind, and responsible and caring for them all? You only have to think of all the terrible things that happen in this world – wars, famines, earthquakes and other such disasters – to wonder how anyone who loves and cares can allow them all to happen.

And yet there is the miracle of the human body with the intricate mechanism of the brain which produces sight, hearing, speech, movement and memory. To say nothing of the complicated workings of the heart – rather like the carburettor on a car. Someone *must* be responsible.

Without God where is the incentive and inspiration to live a good life? What is the purpose of life? I call myself a Christian and try in my everyday life to thank God for my blessings, or pray for my sick, poor or bereaved friends. I am not a regular churchgoer though I think of myself as part of St John's Wood Church. All my children have been christened there, and they all went regularly to Sunday school. Now that they have flown the nest, Pauline and I possibly only go to church twice or three times a year – always at Easter and Christmas. I sometimes feel that the Church pays too much attention to worship as opposed to saying thanks. I think that some of the fulsome praise in the prayers is overdone, and must be embarrassing to our Lord for whom humility is so important.

I find the afterlife an impossible thing to imagine or to genuinely believe in, though I persuade myself that there must be some light at the end of life's tunnel. But I do not find it easy to conceive what it might be.

I lay great store on kindness. My judgement of people is largely based on whether I think they are kind to their fellow human beings, especially to the old and to children, and not least to animals. My practical Christianity is based on the character in Charles Kingsley's *Water Babies* – Mrs Do as You Would be Done by. It is a wonderful target to aim at, and if only everyone in the world could do as they would be done by, our problems would be largely solved. It is certainly worth trying to think before saying or doing something to someone, 'How would I like to be treated like that?' Much of the terrible cruelty inflicted on others would disappear immediately.

I am obviously not a very satisfactory Christian. I make feeble excuses for not going to church more often. I say like so many others that at school we had an unnecessary surfeit of services. At my prep school there were prayers and a short service every evening, plus of course two services on Sunday. At Eton it was even worse – chapel every morning and twice on Sundays, and prayers *every* night in one's house after supper. But enough of excuses. If God were to write my end of term report I'm sure he would say, 'Could have done better.'

As with most things in life I have always found plenty to laugh about in religion. At Eton we had five masters who were clergymen and there was a rhyme about them:

> Chaffey, Channon, Chitty, Chute
> All went to heaven in a parachute
> Who should they see when they got to heaven
> But none other than old 'COB' Bevan

The latter was Rev. C. O. Bevan who disliked swearing (see p. 46 for an amusing story about him).

When we lived in Much Marcle we had a splendid vicar called Mr Duncan. He was quite good at the organ and one year took a sabbatical up the Congo. He took with him one of those small piano keyboards with just the notes but nothing else. It was meant to keep his fingers supple, and he surprised and amused the natives as he sat there playing without any sound coming out. To start with they thought that they had all gone deaf.

Mr Duncan once asked in his parish magazine for anyone who wished him to attend any function to book him as early as possible 'as my evening services are now much in demand'. A parishioner is also said to have gone up to him after he had been at Much Marcle a short time. 'Until you came here, Vicar,' she said, 'we didn't know what real sin was!'

During the war I greatly admired the padres who were attached to our battalion. They were immensely brave in action and were an essential link between the Commanding Officer and the ordinary Guardsmen with their personal and domestic problems. It must also have been difficult for them to reconcile their consciences, since they were part of an establishment whose sole purpose was to kill other people. It has also often occurred to me how difficult it must be for God to decide whom to support in a war, seeing that both sides pray to him fervently for his help. On the other hand I suppose the last world war was easier for him, as it was so obviously a fight against evil.

There was, however, one padre to whom we took temporary objection. When we were officer cadets at Sandhurst in October 1939, there was the usual church parade every Sunday. One week in his sermon the padre complained that the congregation was not putting enough money into the collection plates, and rather forcibly urged us to be more generous in future.

The next Sunday we all took to chapel as many coppers as we could get into our trouser pockets. When the NCOs came round with the plates we poured out our coins and the plates were soon overflowing into the aisles. More plates had to be fetched and tremendous chaos followed up at the altar where the padre was waiting with one large master gold plate to receive the contents from the small plates. He was then meant to raise it above his head and make the sign of the cross with it. But this time it was so heavy that he couldn't lift it and we reckoned that it was game, set and match to us!

Cricket has had many connections with the Church, especially at village level, where the vicar was often an essential

9 The 733rd and last *Down Your Way*, recorded at Lord's, May 1987.
B.J. interviewing the Head Groundsman, Mick Hunt.

10a Harry Secombe and B.J. sing a cricketing duet
in *Highway* on ITV, 1988.

10b B.J. tackles the *Daily Telegraph* crossword
on the beach at Nidri on the island of Lefkos, 1989.

11a Oxford, 1934. B.J. on Tip Top takes the last jump in the
New College Grind, finishing fifth. Not a bad seat!

11b Temple Grove First XI, 1921, with wicket-keeper Johnston
on left of row on chairs.

12a The *Trivia Test Match*
team before recording in the
pavilion at Eggington Cricket
Club, June 1991. (*L to r*) Tim
Rice, Paul Merton, B.J.,
Willie Rushton, Alfred
Marks.

12b The Hirsel, Coldstream,
1933. B.J. dressed up as a
mad deaf parson to pull the
leg of an aunt of William
Douglas-Home.

13 Daughter Joanna watches master golfer B.J. about to sink
an impossible putt on the last hole of the Isle of Purbeck Golf Club.

14a The *Test Match Special* team in the commentary box at Headingley, 1977.
(*L to r, standing*) Alan McGilvray, Freddie Trueman, Christopher Martin-Jenkins;
(*l to r, sitting*) John Arlott, Bill Frindall, B.J.

14b The *Test Match Special* team, 1991. (*L to r*) Bill Frindall, Christopher
Martin-Jenkins, Don Mosey, Freddie Trueman, Tony Cozier, B.J., Trevor
Bailey, Jonathan Agnew, Vic Marks, Peter Baxter, Mike Selvey.

15a Lord Home of the Hirsel in B.J.'s *This is your Life*, 1982.

15b A waffle of commentators at an Outside Broadcasts party, 1987.
(*L to r*) B.J., Stewart Macpherson, Godfrey Talbot, Rex Alston,
Raymond Baxter, Wynford Vaughan-Thomas.

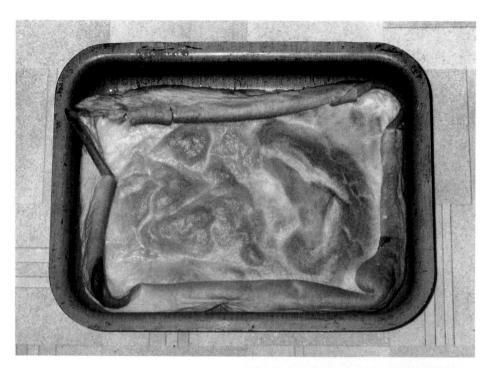

16a The Yorkshire pudding
has risen to perfection – crisp
round the edges, soft in the
middle.

16b To prove how non-U
I am. My gnome singing his
signature tune 'Show Me the
Way to Go Gnome'.

member of the team. I can think of quite a few who played first class cricket:

A bishop	the Rt. Rev. David Sheppard
Three canons	Canon J. H. Parsons
	Canon F. D. R. Browne (Tishy)
	Canon F. H. Gillingham

There was also the Rev. E. T. Killick of Cambridge, Middlesex and England, a fine opening bat who died on the cricket field when playing in a diocesan match. And from Hampshire Father R. P. H. Utley, a master at Ampleforth in Yorkshire. On one occasion Kenneth Parkinson – later President of Yorkshire – was batting against him and off Utley's first two very fast balls was credited with two fours down to fine-leg. Actually they had hit his wooden leg, not his bat, but as the umpire heard the ball hit wood he signalled runs instead of leg byes!

I have purposely left to the last a very dear friend of mine – and of everyone in the cricket world – Canon Hugh Pickles. For years he was the vicar at Blewbury in Oxfordshire and listeners to *Test Match Special* will often have heard me refer to the 'Rev.' He attended every Lord's Test match, telling his parishioners that he was going on a pilgrimage to 'Lourdes'. He was a great supporter of Worcestershire and himself was a splendid bowler who played for his village and the Oxford Clergy.

He was a great character and had a famous dog which used to sit by the altar steps as he gave communion. He once mistakenly booked a christening on the same day as a needle village match. He is said to have been batting when the church clock struck the time for the christening. He hurriedly 'retired hurt' and with his pads still on under his surplice, christened the baby and returned to the field to continue his innings.

He would also try to choose hymns to coincide with the latest Test score so that the board might read something like this:

316

7

58

He was a kind, humorous man who is sadly missed by his many friends.

During Test matches in this country and abroad John Woodcock and I would often go to evensong in a small parish church. On one occasion I went with Jim Swanton to a very high church evensong in Harrogate. When we came to the Creed, Jim, as was his habit I discovered later, genuflected. I thought he had slipped and tried to help him up, much to his annoyance.

I have already mentioned David Sheppard, the Bishop of Liverpool. Soon after he was ordained he went on tour to Australia with Ted Dexter's team. On Sunday evenings he used to preach in the cathedrals of the big cities, and drew packed houses, many travelling in from the outback just to hear him.

In Adelaide Colin Cowdrey, John Woodcock and I went to hear him in St Peter's Cathedral, and decided to have a sweep on the length of his sermon. We opted for something between twenty to twenty-five minutes, and we got very excited when he went over the twenty mark. At one point he paused and we thought he had finished, so passed our money to Colin who was the winner. But after a long pause (did he suspect what we were up to?) he said, 'Just one more thing before I finish. . . .' and went on for another five minutes. So we got our money back off Colin and as none of us was right we called off the bets. Disgraceful behaviour by the Vice-Captain of MCC, the *Times* and BBC cricket correspondents.

David was also the butt of one of the best jokes on the tour. He batted well and made a fine hundred at Melbourne. But he had been out of first-class cricket for two years preparing for his priesthood, and as a result his fielding had got a bit rusty. He had always been a good catcher, but on the tour dropped more than a few catches. A young English couple had recently emigrated to Australia and since their arrival had had a baby boy. 'Great,' said the husband who was a keen cricketer, 'we'll ask David Sheppard to christen him.' 'Not likely,' replied the wife, 'he'd only drop him!'

There are of course many stories about the Church, some I hope are true!

There were these two bishops sitting in front of the fire at the Athenaeum Club. They were up in London for one of those synods at Church House and were discussing the subject for the next day. It was a difficult one for bishops – premarital sex. They were discussing how they would deal with it.

'For instance,' said one, 'I never slept with *my* wife before I married her. Did you?'

The other one thought for a moment.

'I can't remember,' he said, 'what was her maiden name?'

On the same tack a young man about to be married the next day asked the vicar, who was going to marry him, 'Do you object to premarital sex?'

'No,' said the vicar, 'so long as it doesn't keep the guests waiting.'

There was another bishop who had a bad reputation in his diocese for preaching long and boring sermons. He used to visit a different parish every Sunday and preach the same old sermon, so his reputation had spread. One Sunday he arrived at a small village church and was greeted by the vicar, who led him into the church. To the bishop's considerable horror and annoyance there were only three people in the church – the vicar's wife and their two children. The bishop was very angry.

Didn't you warn the parishioners that I was coming, Vicar?'

'I certainly did *not*, Bishop,' replied the vicar. 'But I'm jolly well going to find out who did!'

There was another occasion when two men were having coffee in a café in Canterbury. One of them spotted in the far corner a man with fluffy grey hair and spectacles.

'Look,' he said to his companion, 'that's the Archbishop of Canterbury.'

'Of course it isn't,' said the other.

'Like a bet on it?'

The first man agreed and said he would go over and check, and if he was wrong he would pay his friend a fiver. He walked across the café, had a few words with the grey-haired man and came back looking rather glum.

'What did he say?'

'Oh, he told me to mind my own b-----y business and to f--- off.'

'What a pity. Now we shall never know whether it was the Archbishop or not.'

A bishop was presenting prizes at a girls' school, and got tired of murmuring the same words of congratulations. So he thought that he would ask the next girl about her future career. A pretty blonde came up, and as he handed her the prize he whispered to her, 'What are you doing when you leave school, my dear?'

'Oh Bishop,' she said, 'I *was* going back home to have tea with mum. But I can easily cancel that!'

During one winter an historic cricket match was arranged to be played the following summer at Lord's between the Protestants and Roman Catholics. There was naturally intense rivalry between the two and the Archbishop of Canterbury was determined to win. So he summoned David Sheppard, appointed him Captain and gave him special leave to scour the country to find the best possible team from all the clergy throughout Great Britain. He also told David that he had decided to give Ken Barrington a crash course and ordain him in time for the match so that would be qualified to play.

He kept his secret until the big day, when Barrington duly arrived at Lord's in a white dog-collar. The Archbishop himself could not get to Lord's till teatime, so at lunch rang up and asked to speak to his Captain.

'How are we doing, David?' he asked anxiously.

'Not very well I'm afraid Your Grace. At lunch we are 50 for 6, of which I was lucky enough to score 37.'

'But what about the Rev. Ken Barrington. How has he got on?' asked the disappointed Archbishop.

'I'm sorry to say, Your Grace, he was out first ball for 0. He was yorked by a young priest who was bowling at tremendous pace from the Nursery End.'

'Oh,' said the Archbishop. 'This is dreadful. What was the young priest's name?'

'Father Fred Trueman, Your Grace,' replied David.

To finish off with a joke: A man once bought a pair of budgerigars but was disappointed when after a few months there were no eggs. So he went back to the pet shop and asked the owner whether there was any way of checking if in fact the budgies *were* male and female, and if so, was it possible to tell which was which.

'Yes,' said the owner. 'Get up at 3.00 one morning, creep downstairs into the sitting-room and take the cover off the cage. If they are making love, the one on top will be the cock. I suggest that you then tie a piece of white ribbon round his neck so that you will know him in the future.'

The man did as the pet shop owner suggested and sure enough at 3.00 a.m. the two budgies were making love. So he tied a piece of white ribbon round the neck of the one on top.

Next morning the vicar called and went into the sitting-room. The cock budgie seeing the vicar's white collar piped up. 'So he caught you at it too, did he?'

S
for Sport

I have always liked to consider myself a sportsman. I was brought up on the maxim, 'Go on. Be a sport.' I regarded this as a challenge and interpreted it as meaning, 'Have a go. Have fun.' This I have always tried to do in all sports, although I have never been particularly good at any of them – just average.

Over my lifetime the nature of sport has changed a lot, especially with professionals, but to some extent with amateurs too. In most cases the standards of performance have increased considerably. People run and swim faster, they jump longer and higher. They serve faster at tennis, and go round golf courses in fewer strokes. In athletics and cricket, records are continually broken. Some of this improvement is due to better playing equipment, better tracks and better training methods. I asked Roger Bannister why, after his record in beating the four-minute mile at Iffley Road, he had collapsed into the arms of waiting officials. Nowadays they do far better times, and yet have the energy and breath to do a lap of honour, waving to the crowds. Roger answered, 'Quite simply – I wasn't fit!' I wonder what he would have done with modern training methods and the time to train. As it was he had to fit in his running between his studies.

This is the reason for much of the improvement. The professional has more time, and is supported by sponsorship in all sports. Everyone is more competitive. Winning – and the money that goes with it – has become more important. The next best thing is not to lose. In fact in cricket players tend to make sure that they cannot lose, before they try to win.

The disappearance of the amateur has done away with much of the fun and the sporting spirit. In its place in most games there is an unacceptable standard of behaviour and sportsmanship. In soccer there is even something acknowledged as 'a professional foul'! I must quickly absolve golfers from this criticism. However much the tension they usually behave impeccably.

In defence of the professionals there is undoubtedly more tension and publicity due to television and radio coverage. The case of 'Gazza' last year, ending in that sad spectacle in the Cup Final, is a perfect example of how too much hype can ruin a player's career.

One of the big changes in sport is the way it has generally been brutalised, and become more reliant on strength than on style and technique. If your side has the heavier pack, you are more likely to win at rugby football. The heavier crew usually wins the boat race. If you have the fastest serve at lawn tennis you stand a better chance of winning and in cricket, sadly, the team with the fastest bowlers wins most of the Tests.

Two interesting facts emerge which I cannot explain. Swimmers swim faster, though the water has not changed, and horses don't run faster, at any rate over long distances. The record for the Derby was made by Mahmoud in 1936, and has never been equalled since.

I hope that I don't sound too critical, and I must emphasise that most of my strictures apply to professional sport. A lot of the old standards of sportsmanship still apply in amateur sport where ordinary people play for fun and relaxation. Winning is still important, but not at any price.

I have had a go actively at most sports, but follow them *all* in the media. Cricket of course has been my first love, and from my early days at my preparatory school I have always kept wicket. I'm not quite sure why. Probably because I thought that the hard ball would not hurt so much if I wore gloves. Anyway I was in the First XI at my prep school, but at Eton I only captained the Second XI or 'Twenty-two' as it was called.

At Oxford I played not only for my college but for many other clubs like I'Zingari, the Butterflies, the Oxford University Authentics and most of all for the Eton Ramblers. I had many happy and often hilarious games for them, some of them in what was called 'country house cricket'. This meant that we all stayed together in a large house with its own ground and needless to say much fun was had by all. We also went on tours, one regular one being in Cheshire.

Looking back I am ashamed at some of the things I did. Once when playing against the Staff College at Camberley a Major with a bristling moustache was batting. John Warner, son of Sir Pelham, and a leg-spinner, tossed a ball high up in the air. The Major stretched right forward to play it and missed. I saw that he had almost overbalanced, so after taking the ball, I leant forward and pushed him gently in the back. He fell forward lifting his hind leg as he did so. I promptly whipped off the bails and appealed for a stumping. I hasten to add that we quickly withdrew the appeal and apologised. But naturally he was not too pleased.

Nor was the Colonel playing for Liverpool against the Ramblers at Aigburth. When he came in I politely wished him good afternoon. After a few balls I put on a false moustache without him seeing, and the next time he turned round he got quite a shock. A few overs later I slipped on a pair of dark glasses with a false nose attached, and he began to think that he was seeing things, and soon got out.

I met him twenty years or so later when he was on the Committee of Lancashire. I told him that I used to tour with the Eton Ramblers before the war. He scowled and said that on one occasion when he was playing against them, a young whippersnapper keeping wicket had put on a false moustache and a false nose. 'What a bloody stupid thing to do,' I said, and hurriedly changed the subject.

After the war I played for MCC and BBC and in a large number of charity games. In those days there was no Sunday league so all the England Test cricketers and the visiting teams were available to play. So for about twenty years after the war I kept wicket to some of the world's greatest bowlers, Lindwall, Miller, Bedser, Trueman, Worrell, Laker, Benaud etc. I began to think that I was getting quite good behind the timbers but one day I was brought down to earth with a bump.

I was playing in a charity match at the Dragon School at Oxford. Richie Benaud was bowling a mixture of his googly, top-spinner, flipper and leg-break. Crouching behind the stumps I 'read' them all though most of them went for four byes! However when the last man came in, Richie bowled him a terrific leg-break. The batsman went down the pitch, missed the ball by miles, and as the ball came into my gloves I whipped off the bails with all my old speed (or so I thought). The umpire gave him out – a great moment for me stumping someone off the Australian Captain. I was looking rather pleased with myself as I walked back to the pavilion. The bursar of the school, Mickey Jones, came up to me and said, 'Jolly well stumped.' 'Thanks very much,' I replied modestly. 'Oh, yes,' he said, 'there's just one more thing. I'd like to congratulate you on the sporting way you tried to give him time to get back!' I gave up wicket-keeping from that moment. I can take a hint.

I played a great deal of lawn tennis as a boy and used to copy some of the old Indian colonels who lived near us. They never drove a ball, they cut it with a sort of chop shot. Quite effective if not particularly stylish. I also used to favour the lob, hitting the ball high into the air. At Bude where we lived the tennis club was right on the edge of the cliffs, and on certain days a howling gale would blow in from the sea. It was doing this during a tournament in which I was playing, and actually won, to the disgust of everyone there. I simply lobbed every ball high into the wind towards the sea. It was then blown back and bounced so high in our court that my opponents had to run onto the next court to play it. I wasn't too popular!

I never played soccer seriously, and only played in various scratch games. I remember one which we played on the beach in South Africa when the media played Mike Smith's team. I was defending when Bob Barber came running through the middle and I stuck out a foot and promptly broke his toe – or so it seemed. Luckily it was only badly bruised although he had to miss a game but was luckily fit for the Test.

I have told how I scored a try at rugby football when wearing a macintosh. Although not a great player I could run quite fast and was an expert at selling the dummy. I wasn't too keen on tackling but somehow got away with it.

Mixed hockey was equally rough and dangerous which we

used to play in the holidays. There's something about a hockey stick which inspires ladies to perform deeds of the utmost ferocity. They were quite ruthless and didn't seem to mind where they hit you.

I wish I had had more time to play golf. I was taught as a boy in Bude by the same professional who had taught the famous Joyce Wethered. He had far more luck with her!

Actually I didn't play again for about another forty years, when I took it up on holiday in Swanage. I have never had an official handicap and only play with very close friends who tolerate my eccentric play, especially my persistent slice over extra cover. I have, however, a philosophy about golf which has cheered me up considerably after my many defeats. I possibly play two or three *good* shots during a round. My friends, who play so much better, probably play two or three *bad* shots. But in the bar at the end of the game I only remember with pleasure my good shots, whilst my opponents worry about those bad mistakes which they made.

There was the golfer who normally drove 250 yards or more. But gradually over a number of weeks he began to find that he was hitting the ball fewer and fewer yards, down to 220, 200, 150 and finally he could only just manage 100 yards. He decided to go to his doctor who told him to go behind a screen and take his clothes off. There followed a very close examination after which the doctor told him to put his clothes on and sit down at the desk. 'I have two bits of news for you,' the doctor said, 'one bad, one good.' 'Let's have the bad news first,' said the golfer nervously. 'I'm sorry to tell you that you are changing into a woman.' The golfer gasped and said hoarsely, 'Give me the good news, quick.' 'Well the good news is that from now on you will be able to drive off the ladies' tees,' said the doctor with a cheerful smile.

And here is a warning to any golfer who is playing at a club where he has never played before. A man had a good game with three friends on a strange course. Afterwards he told them to go and have a drink on him, but he couldn't join them as he had to rush off for a business meeting after a quick shower. So he had his shower and was about to step out to get a towel when to his horror he heard ladies' voices. He peeped out through the curtain and saw two elderly ladies, and a smashing blonde. Obviously, not knowing the geography of the clubhouse he had gone by mistake to the ladies locker room. What was he to do? He *had* to go to his appointment. He decided to make a dash for it, covering his face with his flannel. He parted the curtains and ran past the two old ladies. One of them looked down at him and said, 'I wonder who that is. It's certainly not *my* husband.' Her companion also had a quick look. 'He's also certainly not mine,' she said. By this time he was passing the gorgeous blonde. She looked down and said, 'And I can assure you he's not any member of this club either.'

For several years after I joined the BBC I used to play squash with my friend John Ellison in the squash court at Lord's. John had had a flying accident before the war, and one side of his face was paralysed, so that he couldn't blink his eye. He was up the court and looked round to see me playing a ball off the back wall. Unfortunately I gave it a real crack and it hit him in the eye, which he was not able to close. The result, as you can imagine, was very painful and he dropped his racket and clasped the injured eye. Geoffrey Peck had been watching us, so I shouted to him to run to the bar and get a double brandy. Poor John was groaning with pain when Geoffrey returned a few minutes later carrying a large tumbler of brandy. Geoffrey took one look at John, was horrified by the appearance of his eye, and quickly swigged the brandy himself!

Poor John's eye was badly scarred and he had to wear glasses for the rest of his life. I never played squash again. I couldn't face it.

I had a go at other sports at Oxford including my ride in a point-to-point, a spot of not very serious rowing and an attempt to play real tennis, which I found complicated and very tiring on the wrist.

It's perhaps surprising that I have not done commentary on any game except for cricket. Geoffrey Peck and I were given a trial in 1946 at a mid-week game Queen's Park Rangers were playing at Loftus Road. I knew little about the teams but noticed a headline in the previous Sunday's paper describing a

QPR match on the Saturday. Their centre forward scored three goals and the headline read: '3-GOAL McGIBBON!' So when we arrived at the ground we looked for the number 9 on the back of the QPR centre forward and gave him the full treatment. 'There goes 3-goal McGibbon – a typical dribble, you can spot that long raking stride of his, obviusly an England prospect etc. etc. . . .'

It wasn't until we left the ground that we read in the evening papers that McGibbon had withdrawn unfit at the last moment and we had been describing his substitute! Neither of us ever became a soccer commentator.

I only know one soccer story which was told me by Joe Hulme the old Arsenal right wing, and a very fast runner he was too. He told me that before the war Arsenal were playing in Italy in a 'friendly' game. Arsenal's left half was called Wilf Copping who was a very tough robust player, with a devastating, sliding tackle.

As soon as the game started he tackled an Italian player, cutting his legs from underneath him with a crashing tackle. The Italian referee rushed up and wagged his finger at Copping. 'No more of that please. This is a friendly game.'

A few minutes later Copping did the same thing again. Up came the referee, wagging his finger even more rapidly. 'If you do that again, I shall send you off. No more dirty play please.'

About ten minutes later Copping did it again. As he saw the referee coming towards him he muttered, 'Oh, bugger off.' The referee put away the red card he was about to show as he sent Copping off. 'That is good,' he said. 'You apologise. I will not send you off.'

As you will have read I *did* commentate on the Boat Race, and for a short period in 1947 and 1948 actually attempted to describe showjumping with its double oxers and open ditches. But in general I played various games, and only commentated on one – cricket.

T
For *Test Match Special*

My transfer from TV to *Test Match Special* (TMS) in 1970 was the start of what have been some of the happiest years of my life. *TMS* is a rather unique institution. There is nothing like it in any of the other countries who broadcast cricket. The BBC itself has called it a 'new art form'. This I have always felt is rather overdoing it, but it is certainly a different type of commentary from anything that has been done before.

I have to admit that it's during the last twenty-one years that it has gradually taken on its present form, and I must bear some of the responsibility for this. In view of the success of *TMS* this may sound boastful although in fact there is, I'm sure, a section of our listeners who disapprove of our way of broadcasting. Luckily for us, they are a minority, but we do realise that they would probably prefer the old straightforward method of commentary without all the funnies and the buses, pigeons and cakes. They obviously have a case, but from the wonderful reaction which we get from so many listeners we feel that we are doing what the majority enjoy. It is gratifying that wherever one goes – and especially when I travelled round the country for fifteen years in *Down Your Way* – people come up to say thank you (of course I realise that people who *don't* like you don't bother to come up or don't even write).

It always amazes me that so many people say, 'You won't guess what I do – I *watch* the TV, and *listen* to TMS.' This is really completely illogical because if a TV commentator were to speak as much as we have to, he would get a shoal of letters telling him to put a sock in it. But I know one of the reasons why viewers do so. TV has become full of super technology – eight cameras (when we started in 1946 we were lucky to have three), instant playbacks, cameras in the stumps, everything on the screen computerised, and so on. It is a technical exercise of pure, cool efficiency and has thereby lost some of the human touch. The commentary is matched to it – cool, very efficient, with the emphasis on the technique of the game from knowledgeable ex-Test players. Radio, without all these visual aids, just has to do something different and try to be friendly and human.

Our commentary is founded on the original concept of providing the listener with an accurate, colourful and lively description of a day's cricket, bearing in mind that cricket *can* be dull and therefore needs the occasional injection of colour and fun.

Our approach is quite simple. Five or six of us go to a Test match for just the same reasons as other spectators – except that we luckily don't have to pay! We go to have fun and enjoy ourselves, and even have the odd glass of something. Our aim is to behave *naturally* as a party of friends would. *Never miss a ball* but if one of us has received an interesting letter or been told a funny story then we share it with the listeners. The word *naturally* is important. It means – to be ourselves in front of the microphone. If there *are* strengths in *TMS*, they are the complete contrasts in personality to all the commentators and summarisers. We are totally different in voice, background and character, and often in opinions too. Yet one of the surprising things is that over a span of forty-six summers I have never had a quarrel nor seen one *in* the box on either TV or radio. I suppose it's due to our mutual love of cricket, and the fact that we all believe that cricket should be fun. It is something to savour and enjoy.

The conditions under which we work are not ideal, being often too cramped, too crowded and too hot. One would expect this to make us all niggly and touchy but somehow we never seem to mind.

The boxes are far better than they used to be. In the past we would often sit out on the Pavilion roof under a rather flimsy tarpaulin, or have to climb sixty feet up a precarious piece of scaffolding. (At Old Trafford the sight of Jim Swanton and Roy Webber scaling the ladder used to attract large crowds!)

Trent Bridge is the best sited, slung below the Pavilion balcony right behind the bowler's arm, and about twenty feet above the ground. Our box at the Oval is comfortable and also well placed behind the bowler although it is possibly a shade too high. So too is our spacious box at Lord's on the balcony above the visitors' dressing-room. But in spite of looking over mid-off and not directly behind, we have a magnificent view of the ground.

Headingley is long and narrow and is situated under the roof of the Rugby League stand. We get a good view of the wicket but no sight of the sky, which makes it a rather gloomy place in which to work.

Edgbaston is well situated but very small with room for only two of us to sit at the microphones plus of course the 'bearded wonder' Bill Frindall, who inevitably takes up a lot of space with his score-sheets, stopwatches, reference books, minicomputer and so on.

Ideally there should be room for four to sit in a row – the commentator, the summariser, Bill Frindall and any visitor to the box whom we want to interview.

Our worst box used to be at Old Trafford alongside the scoreboard at the Stretford end but now we are situated high up on top of the hospitality boxes in a new stand and get a splendid view of the game.

I suppose one of the features of our *TMS* boxes is their complete informality. Sometimes journalists spend a day with us to write a 'behind the scenes' story. I know that they are all surprised by the apparently casual way in which we behave. They comment on the lack of tension and strain, and the many asides, jokes and leg-pulls which take place throughout a long hot day. But behind all this apparent casualness there is an innate sense of discipline without which the whole structure would collapse. We are all experienced broadcasters for whom the microphone no longer holds any terror. There are certain basic rules such as microphone technique, timing and punctuality when it's one's turn to take over or to hand over to somebody else after our twenty-minute stint.

Any success we have in this mixture of professionalism and

easy-going behaviour is largely due to our friendly producer Peter Baxter. He rides us all on a light rein but can be tough when necessary as for instance when we go slightly over the top or get an attack of the giggles. (Luckily he is a great giggler himself!)

We get asked a lot of questions about *TMS* so perhaps I should clear up one or two points.

Cakes

We *do* get sent a lot of cakes, sometimes up to four a day. It all started about fifteen years ago when some kind lady sent me a chocolate cake for my birthday, which usually coincides with the Lord's Test. I, perhaps unwisely, thanked her *over the air* and after that they began to come in a steady stream – mostly chocolate but other special recipes as well. We of course eat some ourselves, give some to the TV commentators, to our hard-working engineers and to the many visitors who come every day to our box. Any leftovers we send to old people's homes or childrens' hospitals.

It is extraordinary the trouble that people go to in order to decorate the cakes, generally with a cricket motif. One was a beautiful replica in coloured icing of a famous picture in the Lord's museum. It was such a work of art that I took it home and kept it in our freezer for three years. When people came to our house, instead of showing them pictures on the wall, we took them to look in the freezer.

Letters

During a season we get hundreds and hundreds of letters. Those with an s.a.e. or of a personal nature I take home and answer myself. Some we answer over the air either when rain stops play or during our lunchtime session on the last day of each Test, when three of us reply to as many as we can get through. The remainder are ultimately acknowledged by the BBC which

I can appreciate is not very satisfactory if you have asked a question.

You can imagine the chaos in the box with all the letters being opened and parcels undone. That is why we implore people *not* to send valuable photos, autographs or old newspaper cuttings through the post. They can so easily be lost and it's an extra responsibility if the sender wants them returned.

The contents of the letters are varied and fascinating, and a large percentage come from women. We are asked questions about the laws, sent details of some special cricketing feat or offered suggestions for improving the over-rate, ways of dealing with short-pitched bowling or criticism of the selectors.

We value especially the number of young boys and girls who write. It's good to know that we have so many young listeners who are keen on cricket. They also send us some pretty awful jokes! One was: Ask Fred what animal he would like to be if he was standing naked in a snowstorm. Answer: A little otter! Or a recent one last summer: 'Why didn't the skeleton go to the ball?' Answer: 'Because he had no body to go with.' If it is raining very hard I sometimes risk repeating them on the air!

Nicknames

I tend to give people nicknames or add 'ers' to their names e.g. Jenkers, Aggers etc. The Bearded Wonder for Bill Frindall was easy. He *is* bearded and he *is* a wonder with all his statistics. Tony Lewis became ARL because when Peter Baxter puts up a list for our commentary periods it looks like this:

11.00 – 11.20	BJ
11.20 – 11.40	ARL
11.40 – 12.00	NO

Thus 'NO' was for Neville Oliver the Australian commentator in 1989. He obviously became The Doctor.

The Alderman was the nickname given to Don Mosey after a quiz in Lancaster where he was the producer and was helping to entertain us in the Mayor's parlour. He looked very alder-manic in those surroundings, and it has stuck ever since.

Trevor Bailey is called The Boil because when he used to play football for Leytonstone the cockney crowd used to shout out, 'Come on B*oiley*'.

Henry Blofeld is inevitably Blowers and we missed him a lot last summer. People wrote in and asked where all the buses, pigeons and helicopters had gone. The answer is that he took them to another broadcasting organisation who paid him far more than the BBC! I still think his classic was once at Headingley when he said, 'I can see a butterfly walking across the pitch, and what's more it's got a limp!'

I sometimes call Fred Trueman 'Sir Frederick', which led to an amusing incident – at least I thought it was funny. I had just written a book and sent copies to my *TMS* colleagues. I wrote in Fred's, 'To Sir Frederick, with happy memories of days in the box.' I asked my publisher to send them off and a secretary innocently posted Fred's copy addressed to Sir Fred-erick Trueman. One morning the postman ran up the path waving the parcel and shouting, 'You've got it at last, Fred.' I dread to think what Fred said at the time, but he did tell Peter Baxter later in polite terms, 'That Johnners is a right one.'

One feature of *TMS* which I enjoy doing is the Saturday lunchtime interview spot called *A View from the Boundary*. It's great fun to do and we ask well-known people who love cricket to come and spend the day in the box with us. They need not be players, though some still do play. Their only qualification has to be a love of cricket, and we just carry on a conversation for twenty-five minutes or so during the luncheon interval. On pp. 203–4 there is a list of those who have taken part and it is further proof of the close affinity which the arts – especially actors, have with cricket.

My brown-and-white co-respondent shoes

I have worn brown-and-white shoes at every Test match on which I have commentated since the first Test against Australia at Edgbaston in 1961. It came about this way. I had always coveted a pair of these shoes since I first saw them in the musical comedies of the twenties and thirties. For some reason all the stars wore them, Leslie Henson, Stanley Lupino, Jack Buchanan, Bobby Howes and Jack Hulbert. Somehow I had never had the courage to buy a pair.

However in April 1961 I flew out to Port Said with a TV crew to meet the liner in which Richie Benaud and his Australian team were travelling to England. The idea was that we would join the liner for two days on its voyage to Malta, from where we could fly back after interviews and shots of the team at deck games or just relaxing in the sun.

We had to wait at Port Said and it was pelting with rain. So to get some shelter we went into a shoe shop and had to pretend that we wanted to buy something. Luckily to my surprise there were a pair of brown-and-white shoes on one of the shoe racks. I told the Egyptian shopkeeper that I would like to try one on and amazingly it fitted me perfectly. To pull his leg I said, 'Thanks very much – I'll buy that one', which made him very excited, explaining that I would have to buy the other one as well. Which of course I did.

When I got home I decided that I would always wear them at Test matches, fooling myself that they would bring England luck. In the 190 Tests on which I have commentated since 1961 England have won sixty-two, lost forty-eight and drawn eighty. So I suppose on balance my shoes *have* been lucky for England!

Incidentally the original pair eventually wore out and recently fetched £40 in a charity auction. The pair I wear now were handmade especially for me by Barker's of Earls Barton and will see me out.

Leg-Pulls and giggles

I have mentioned that we do have a lot of leg-pulls in the box which often result in helpless giggling. All rather schoolboyish I'm afraid, but that's me.

Two of the funniest were perpetrated against Alan McGilvray

(see p. 261 and 268). One of my first was against another overseas commentator – Tony Cozier.

During the first Test match at Queen's Park, Trinidad, on Colin Cowdrey's tour of 1967–68, rain stopped play for some time. Tony wanted to go across the ground to the press box, and I said I would 'man' the commentary box, so as to keep the studio advised about the state of the weather. It was still raining slightly when I saw Tony returning across the field about half an hour later. As he came up the steps into the commentary box I pretended that I was speaking to listeners on the air. As he entered the box I said, 'Well, those are the up-to-date statistics of the MCC team to the nearest decimal point, and you know all their ages, dates of their birthdays and their exact batting and bowling figures. Ah, I see Tony Cozier has just come into the box so I'll ask him to give you exactly the same information about the West Indies players. Tony . . .' I have rarely seen a greater look of horror on anyone's face. He sat down at the microphone and began to stammer, making frantic signals to the scorer to hand him a copy of *Wisden*. To gain time he said, 'Well Brian, I'll try to tell listeners in a moment, but perhaps you'd like to hear something about the state of the pitch, which I have just passed on my way back.'

'No, sorry, Tony,' I said, 'we've just talked about it whilst you have been away. All we want – and straight away please – is the information about the West Indies statistics.' At this point I just could not go on, he looked so miserable and desperate.

'Well, Tony, if you can't give us the details I suppose we had better return to the studio. So goodbye from us all here.' There was a hush for a few seconds, broken only by Tony's heavy breathing. Then I told him that we had *not* been on the air. It took him quite a few minutes to recover, and looking back I realise that it really was rather a dirty trick to play on anyone, and I am always on the lookout for someone trying it on me! Anyway, Tony has, I hope, long since forgiven me, and we always look forward to welcoming him to the box whenever the West Indies visit this country.

We often try this sort of leg-pull on unsuspecting commentators who come into the box, not knowing that we have gone back to the studio and therefore are not on the air. We ask them to give some impossible figures or statistics and then watch the horror on their faces as they realise they haven't the foggiest idea what to answer.

All very cruel, as was our leg-pull on Henry Blofeld one day at Lord's. It was pelting with rain after lunch and we were obviously in for a long afternoon of conversation and discussion. We all settled down in front of our microphones, and it was Blower's turn to start. It was about the time that Kerry Packer had entered the cricket arena. Blowers didn't approve of him and got really stuck into him, speaking very fast and looking straight ahead. He went on for about four minutes, completely ignoring us. So, without him noticing, we crept silently out of the box.

He went on regardless so we got Peter Baxter to go in and put a piece of paper in front of him which read, 'Well done. Keep going till half past six.' Blowers read it as he talked and then looked around the box to find nobody there to support him. He looked shaken and it taught him a lesson not to ignore his colleagues!

One of the worst giggling fits occurred at the Oval during the fifth Test against the West Indies in 1991. Jonathan Agnew and I were doing a summary duet at the close of play on the Friday night. We got to where Ian Botham had been out hit wicket. He had in fact overbalanced when attempting and missing a hook, and did the splits over the stumps removing a bail as he did so.

Jonathan was explaining all this and finished up by saying, '. . . he knocked off a bail, he just couldn't quite get his leg over!' This was too much for me. Botham of all people! I tried valiantly to go on with the summary in a very quaky voice, as everyone in the box was in fits of laughter. Gradually I lost all control, and murmuring 'For goodness' sake, stop it, Aggers,' I went into complete hysterics. In the true tradition of 'the show must go on' I continued to try and read the score-sheet, giving details of Lawrence's innings. Interspersed with moments of wheezing and complete silence I reported in a high pitched giggle that he had hit a four over the wicket-keeper's head. I tried to say this twice, in between convulsions. I just managed to describe how Tufnell was out before giving the bowling analysis, after which I gradually regained control. It really was a terrible feeling knowing that millions of people were listening to me completely out of control. It seemed to go on for ever, but in fact lasted only ninety seconds.

Everyone I met during the next few days seemed to have heard it – it was even selected for *Pick of the Week*! I had countless letters and telephone calls. One of the latter was from Ronnie Corbett who said his wife Ann was driving up the M1 and had to draw in and stop in the breakdown lane. Another listener wrote to say it had caused a ten-minute hold-up at the entrance to the Dartford Tunnel. He was roaring with laughter himself and had to stop and noticed lots of other drivers doing the same thing as they too howled with laughter. This was not very popular with those drivers who were *not* listening to *TMS* and so hadn't the faintest idea what was going on, and reacted by all blowing their horns.

I have a cassette of this ninety seconds, and occasionally I listen to it and go off into a fit of giggles. I defy anyone not to.

To sum up my feelings about *TMS* I have often worried that I have spent much of my working life describing a piece of wood hitting a round piece of leather. But I hope the following story will illustrate why I think it has been so worthwhile.

At Headingley in 1981 Fred Trueman and I were discussing our two dogs. He had a giant old English sheepdog called William, and in contrast we had a little Yorkshire terrier called Mini. I told him I was a bit worried about her as Pauline was on holiday in Jersey, Cally was also away and I was at the Test match. So for the first time ever we had to put Mini into one of those dog hotels for a fortnight. I told Fred what an awful thing it is to leave a dog like that. The look of complete misery in her eyes had made me feel guilty. She must have thought that she was being left there forever, and that we would never come back to collect her.

I thought no more about it and went on with the commentary. About an hour later there was a knock on the commentary door and outside was a man with a dozen red carnations. Inside was a little note which read, 'It's all right. All well here. I know you are coming back for me. Love and licks from Mini.'

I must say I nearly blubbed. It was such a sweet and kind thing to do. I discovered later it was a friendly florist in Hounslow who had heard me and promptly rung up a florist in

Leeds. I really was touched and it made me feel what a close and friendly contact we have with our large family of listeners.

Views from The Boundary

1980
Ted Moult
Ben Travers
Jack Fingleton
Richard Gordon
Ian Carmichael

1981
Ian Sproat
John Alderton
Billy Wright
Tim Rice
Leslie Thomas

1982
Brian Rix
Bill Tidy
Patrick Moore
Henry Kelly
Peter Tinniswood
Robin Bailey
Ian Wallace

1983
Richard Stilgoe
Peter Skellern
Jimmy Armfield
Michael Bentine
Dusty Hare

1984
Alan Curtis
Robin Bailey
Michael Charlton
Bill Beaumont
Derek Nimmo
Barry Norman

1985
Roy Hattersley
Benny Green
Michael Craig
Leslie Crowther
Rory Bremner
James Prior

1986
Bernard Cribbins
John Cleese
Tim Brooke-Taylor
Julian Bream
Miles Kington
William Rushton

1987
Sir Bernard Lovell
Christopher Lee
Michael Parkinson
Barry John
William Franklyn
HRH The Duke of
Edinburgh

1988
Michael Jayston
Robert Powell
Gary Lineker
Bill Pertwee
John Ebdon

1989
Peter Scudamore
David Essex
David English
John Kettley
Jack Buckner
Max Jaffa

1990	Eric Idle	**1991**	David Tomlinson
	George Shearing		Lord Runcie
	Neal Foulds		Max Boyce
	John Major		Graham Taylor
	Vic Lewis		Peter O'Toole
	Harold Pinter		Robin Askwith

At the end of the 1991 season, the future of ball-by-ball commentary was in some doubt. The broadcasting bill decreed that the BBC's medium wave on Radio 3 on which *TMS* broadcast should be made available for a new commercial station. At first the BBC considered putting *TMS* on Radio 5, where it would have had to share air time with all the other sports but happily, due largely to the vocal and written support of thousands of loyal listeners, the BBC relented. From 1992 *TMS* will continue to broadcast ball-by-ball commentaries on all One-day Internationals and Test matches on Radio 3 FM. It does mean that for thirty-seven days of the summer music lovers will be robbed of their *daytime* music but I hope that they will not grudge cricket lovers their few hours of pleasure!

Finally, I would like to place on record a debt of thanks to my old friend Ian Orr-Ewing, but for whom I doubt if I would ever have been a cricket commentator.

In March 1946 my telephone rang and it was Ian on the line (we had been friends at Oxford). He was now Head of Sport at BBC TV and explained that they were going to televise the two Tests against India at Lord's and the Oval. He knew I could play cricket a bit, that I had quite a good knowledge of the game, and that I would have no difficulty in talking all day! Would I like to have a shot at being a TV commentator?

How lucky could I be, and you can guess my answer. As a result I commentated on all Tests on TV in this country up to 1970, when I went over to radio. I expect there are some listeners who wish Ian had never called me, but I, somewhat naturally, just wanted to say 'thank you'.

U

– or Non-U

What *is* Non-U? Everyone will come up with their own particular answers. This is mostly my own personal list based on so many things which I have experienced during my lifetime: the way I was brought up, at my schools and university, in business, in the Grenadier Guards, at cricket and in the whole world of entertainment since I joined the BBC in 1946. Some will appear old-fashioned, some perhaps snobbish, others just unimportant or merely trivial. I am grateful to some of my friends who have supplied me with *their* ideas of what is non-U. Nancy Mitford also wrote the definitive book on the subject, *Noblesse Oblige*. I have never read it, but I am sure that she must have originated the whole idea. Many of her definitions have been handed down to posterity and have been generally accepted by everybody as 'U'. For this we must all be grateful to her.

Non-U

To – take a bitch on heat to a meet of foxhounds
  – light a cigarette before the royal toast (unless Princess Margaret is present when lighting-up time is *before* the starters!)
  – say 'a *double* whisky' when asked if you would like a drink
  – pick your nose in public and flick the bogey away
  – say 'serviette' instead of 'napkin'
  – button up the bottom button of your waistcoat
  – wear an Old Etonian tie – especially if you were not at Eton!
  – sit or talk through the national anthem
  – keep the telly on when a visitor enters the room

- drink a cup of tea with your little finger cocked
- argue with or show dissent to an umpire
- allow your dog to cock its leg (or worse) on someone's gatepost
- tip a porter or a waiter in a gentleman's club
- ask your guest whether he or she would like *another* drink
- show your white waistcoat below the sides of your evening tail coat
- wear brown shoes with a blue suit
- say 'cheers' when drinking
- eat a slice of toast or bread without cutting it in half first
- rest your knife and fork against your plate with the handles on the table
- fail to ring up or write to your hostess after a stay or a party
- send a dirty postcard *not enclosed* in an envelope
- pronounce golf 'goalf'
- walk on the *inside* of a lady on the pavement
- drink soup through the tip of the spoon instead of from the side
- have a garden gnome (we have one!)
- put your decorations after your name on a letterhead
- outstay your welcome at a lunch or dinner party
- smoke a pipe in other people's houses
- leave an empty loo roll on the roller
- do your host's crossword puzzle unless he has asked for help
- say 'white please' instead of 'with milk' when asked how you like your coffee
- read a book or newspaper in the bathroom when staying with someone – others may need the bath
- leave your hairpiece or false teeth in the bathroom when a guest is in the house
- smoke a cigar with the band on
- say 'pardon' when you cannot hear what has been said
- say 'ta' instead of 'thank you'
- wear a grey top hat at a funeral or memorial service
- tuck your handkerchief inside the cuff of your coat

206

– comment on your hostess's dress (My wife did it once when we arrived for dinner with a friend. When our hostess opened the door of her flat, my wife said, 'Oh, I'm sorry, I thought we were changing for dinner.' 'I have done so,' replied our hostess icily.)
– pass the port anticlockwise at the table
– say 'sweat' instead of 'perspire'
– break wind in public. (A man did so once at a dinner party, and his host said, 'How dare you break wind in front of my wife.' His guest replied, 'I'm sorry, I didn't know it was her turn!')
– say 'the cruet' instead of 'the pepper and salt'
– call the midday meal 'dinner'
– say 'perfume' instead of 'scent'
– *take* a bath instead of to *have* a bath
– call the sitting-room a lounge
– call the knave a jack at cards
– cover the spare loo roll with a woolly hat
– sign 'sincerely' or 'faithfully yours' instead of 'yours sincerely' or 'yours faithfully'
– wear, if you are a man, a gold ring other than on the *little* finger
– put the milk in the cup *first* when pouring out tea
– pot your opponent's ball at billiards
– call the lavatory or loo a 'toilet', and lavatory paper 'toilet paper'
– go 'horse-riding' instead of 'riding'
– call an Earl an Earl – he is always referred to as Lord —
– if you wish to put Esq. after a man's name it is perfectly right to do so, but *never* put *Mr* John Smith, Esq.

V
for VIPs

I have been lucky to have known, met or interviewed many important people in all walks of life – from royalty to those in politics, business, entertainment and sport. It would be imposs- ible to write about them all or even a fraction of them. So I hope the others won't be offended if I pick out eight Prime Ministers, a Prince, a Field Marshal and two personal friends who both merit being called VIPs.

Winston Churchill

One night in the mid-thirties I went to the Palladium with a friend who afterwards took me to Pratt's in St James's Street. This is a very exclusive private dining club formed, I believe, by one of the Dukes of Devonshire. It's one of those places with a long table, where members who drop in sit anywhere they like. The food, so far as I remember, was what is now called schoolboy food – simple but delicious.

Anyhow we had just sat down to supper when in came the 'great man' alone, and joined us at the table. We were the only other people there. My host was a well known man-about-town Old Etonian called 'Buns' Cartwright. At one time he had been Private Secretary and speech writer for the Earl of Birkenhead. In fact I believe that one or two of Birkenhead's witticisms can be attributed to him. Because of this contact with the political world, Buns knew Churchill and we were soon chatting away. At this time Churchill was in the political wilderness, warning the nation of the danger of Germany and crying out for the National Government to rearm. He was keen to know the reaction of ordinary people to what he was doing and it was a fascinating hour. I was completely spellbound by the magnetism of his personality.

I next met him in 1944 when he visited the Guards Armoured Division in Yorkshire. He insisted on going out on the moors in one of our Sherman tanks. He was an amazing sight looking out of the Tank Commander's turret, wearing that extraordinary half bowler, half top hat which he wore so often on his journeys round the country. He was walking with a stick in those days and he took it into the tank with him. As the Sherman ploughed its way across the rough countryside, he leant over and tapped the driver, just below him, with his stick. 'Faster, faster,' he cried. It was lucky that the driver was wearing a helmet, not a beret!

Anthony Eden

At one time I used to have a regular weekly feature in the *Today* programme. It was called 'Many Happy Returns' and was a short recorded interview with someone whose birthday was in that particular week. I wrote to a number of famous people, politicians, sportsmen, actors, film and TV personalities. Many of them accepted and one was Anthony Eden just after he had resigned as Prime Minister. He was having severe stomach trouble at the time, but kindly invited me down to his delightful house in Pewsey in Wiltshire.

I remember that we had roast pheasant for lunch and afterwards sat in the garden to do the interview. I usually asked the same sort of questions:

> Do you enjoy birthdays?
> Does getting older worry you?
> How will you spend your birthday?
> What about presents?
> What are you doing now or in the near future?
> If you had a birthday wish, what would it be?

Sir Anthony may not have been one of our greatest Prime Ministers, saddled as he was by Suez and ill health, but he was certainly the most courteous, charming man and was kindness itself to an unknown broadcaster. I wish I could remember what his birthday wish was, but at the time he seemed obsessed with his herd of pedigree cows. So I suspect it was to live in peace in the country with his lovely wife, his farm and his memories.

Harold Macmillan

I wasn't so lucky with my invitation to Harold Macmillan who wrote a polite refusal in his own hand, begging to be excused. However I was to meet him twice later on, both occasions to do with the Grenadier Guards, with whom he had served with distinction in the First World War. In 1985 the Grenadiers asked me if I would interview him on tape for their museum at Wellington Barracks. He had agreed to be interviewed at 2.30 p.m. at his publishing offices just off the Strand. We were warned that he would be lunching at the Turf Club before he joined us. We set up two microphones in the boardroom, and waited, and waited and waited. Various secretaries telephoned the Turf Club from time to time to check on his progress. He was evidently enjoying himself with some old friends and did not intend to be hurried. He was then aged ninety-one and we began to worry whether he would be too tired to do the interview. At about 4.00 p.m. he entered the room, with his stooping, shuffling walk and hooded eyes.

We were introduced to him whilst a secretary reminded him what it was all about. I had met him once before at a Grenadier gathering, but I doubt if he recognised me. As soon as he sat down, he spotted the microphone, and waved it away with his hands. 'We don't want that thing,' he said. It was gently explained to him that it was essential for it to be there if we were to record his voice.

I had done my homework, my brief being to get him to reminisce about his time with the Grenadier Guards during the Great War. I put the first question to him and it was like turning on a tap. With just a few prompts he spoke non-stop for over half an hour. It was a superb mixture of dramatic facts, humour and comment. We were all spellbound, and since he died just over a year later, it must have been one of the last recordings of his voice. His memories of the battles, the trenches, of his being wounded and his convalescence never faltered. It was a remarkable performance similar to those interviews he used to do on television.

It was a well-known fact that when he was Prime Minister his chief relaxation was reading Trollope. He told us that in the war he always carried a Trollope book in his uniform pocket. On the occasion when he was wounded he lay in a shell-hole in No Man's Land quietly reading Trollope whilst waiting to be rescued. His rescue came with the arrival of the Regimental Sergeant-Major who climbed down into the shell-hole and in true Grenadier fashion gave a terrific salute and said, 'Permission to rescue you, sir!'

He also told us of the occasion when he and his fellow officers were in a dugout right up in the front line. Their Commanding Officer disapproved of officers drinking, but they had managed to smuggle two bottles of port up into the dugout. They were enjoying drinking them when they heard a shout from the Sergeant-Major, 'Stand by for the Commanding Officer.' They just had time to take two lighted candles and stick them into each of the bottles, pretending they were using the bottles as candlesticks.

They leapt to attention and saluted as the Commanding Officer came in and looked around the dugout. After a short chat he left to continue his inspection of the lines with a 'Well done, good night and good luck,' to the young officers.

Six months later Macmillan was on leave in London. One day in the Guards Club he spotted the Commanding Officer and with some diffidence went up to him and asked if he would like a drink. 'Thank you, Macmillan, I would.' 'Glass of port, sir?' asked the young Macmillan. 'No, thank you,' said the CO giving Macmillan a steely look, 'it might taste of wax!'

Sir Alec Douglas-Home

If Anthony Eden was the most charming Prime Minister, Alec
Home was certainly one of the nicest. I was lucky to meet him
in the thirties when I went to stay with my friend William
Douglas-Home at the family home in the Hirsel, Coldstream,
and Douglas Castle in Lanarkshire. Alec was then MP for
Lanark, and Parliamentary Private Secretary to Neville Chamberlain. William and I went to one of his political meetings on
Lanark racecourse. Sir John Simon, the Foreign Secretary, was
the speaker and was talking about Hitler and the Nazis. 'Who
knows where it will all end?' he asked. I felt that if he, the
Foreign Secretary didn't know, it wasn't much good asking us!

William and I shared a house in South Eaton Place. One day
in 1938 Alec dashed round to say he had to go off to Munich
suddenly with Mr Chamberlain, and could we lend him a shirt.
We duly obliged and went down to Heston to see them off in
what looked like (and probably was) a very small and rickety
plane. We were there to welcome them back when Chamberlain
waved his piece of paper signed by Hitler and proclaiming 'It's
peace in our time.'

Alec is a true countryman with shooting and fishing playing
an important part in his life. But so does flower arranging and
bird life – a most unlikely Prime Minister. He was superb on
foreign affairs and not too good at economics. He really did use
matchsticks to do his sums! But he was a shrewd delegator and
acted more as Chairman of a company, leaving the experts in
each department to get on with their jobs.

After eleven months at Number Ten he only just lost the
General Election to Harold Wilson by four seats. Had he been
more photogenic on TV I feel he would almost certainly have
won. With his late wife Elizabeth he made Number Ten a
happy family place. Sadly he had to make an undignified exit
from the back door as Wilson entered in the front. It was typical
of him not to try to cling on to the leadership of the Conservative
Party after his defeat, and equally typical to be quite happy to
serve as Foreign Secretary under his successor Edward Heath.

Edward Heath

I formed a very high opinion of Edward Heath in 1971 when he gave a reception at No. 10 in honour of Ray Illingworth's victorious MCC team. At the end of the tour I had written the words of a victory song which we put to the music of an old music-hall song called 'Show me your winkle tonight'. Decca kindly recorded the team singing this Ashes Song, with band-leader Vic Lewis collecting all the top session musicians to accompany us. The tune was good but the words were pretty dreadful and we never reached the top 1000. However at the party I left a copy of the record for Mr Heath, and a few days later received a letter from him in which he wrote: 'I enjoyed listening to it and congratulate you on your musical and literary skills!' I only wish the public had thought the same – our royalties reached the princely sum of £53.86!

I have met Mr Heath on several occasions at various functions, and he has always been friendly, with those shoulders shrugging up and down at the odd joke although he obviously finds it difficult to communicate with people on an everyday basis, and seems shy and withdrawn. But when he gets up to speak he becomes a different person and is confident and witty. It's an amazing transformation.

Margaret Thatcher

Although I have met Denis Thatcher on a number of sporting events, and he has been a welcome visitor to our commentary box, I have only met Margaret Thatcher once and then our conversation was brief. 'Good evening,' she said. 'Good evening, Prime Minister,' I replied. The occasion was a charity reception on 1 November 1990 at No. 10, which she and Mr Thatcher were hosting for the Lord's Taverners, as part of their ruby celebrations. It was a thoroughly enjoyable evening and a remarkable one.

Pauline and I arrived at 6.35 p.m. and were duly received by the Prime Minister and Denis. She looked radiant and completely relaxed. As I've said it was a brief encounter. She has a handshake which I have only previously experienced at a captain's cocktail party on board a large cruise ship. It steers the guest on his or her way past the shaker with a strong push towards the other guests who had already been received. It eliminates the chance of even the briefest conversation, and with so many hundreds to welcome, it is an understandable ploy.

Mrs Thatcher stayed for over an hour and was vivacious and friendly, mingling with the guests before standing on a chair and making a rousing speech. She left at about 7.50 p.m. to the applause of the guests for a real *tour de force*.

The remarkable thing about the evening was that at 6.00 p.m. Sir Geoffrey Howe had called unexpectedly at Number Ten, and stayed for half an hour, during which time he tendered his resignation from the cabinet. He left at 6.30 p.m. in which time Mrs Thatcher must have had an inkling that this was the beginning of the end and that her long stint as Prime Minister might be near its end. And yet, there she was, five minutes after he left, receiving her guests as if nothing had happened. It was a truly remarkable performance, and to make it even more so, when she left at 7.50 p.m. she must have gone upstairs and composed her letter to Sir Geoffrey which was shown on the 9.00 news.

We only learnt of this hidden drama when we left No. 10 at about 8.00 p.m. to be met by a battery of TV cameras and lights. An interviewer asked me how the Prime Minister had reacted to Sir Geoffrey's resignation, and I told him that no one at the reception knew that he had resigned.

I must confess that I had always been a great admirer and supporter of Mrs Thatcher. After that evening at No. 10 I was even more so, and to think that four weeks later she was no longer Prime Minister.

John Major

During the last three summers John Major – usually accom-panied by Robert Atkins, now the Sports Minister – has been a regular visitor to the *TMS* commentary box. He usually stays about half an hour and displays a keen knowledge of cricket, its history, techniques and records. He chats away to all and sundry probing the experts with searching questions whilst enjoying the odd piece of cake or cup or glass of something. His outstanding characteristic is his friendliness and he has that wonderful gift of making you feel that you are the *one* person he wants to meet. He also did us the honour of being our guest on my Saturday lunchtime interview spot, *A View from the Boundary*.

Brought up in Brixton, he has always been a keen Surrey supporter and until he had an accident was quite a good bowler himself. His niceness is now legendary. But here's further proof. In those exciting five days before the election between him, Mr Hurd and Mr Heseltine, I sent him a postcard to Number Eleven wishing him luck. I told him that I hoped he would be promoted from Number Eleven and would soon be batting at Number Ten. Incredibly, on the morning of the election itself, I received a letter of thanks from him with a PS in his own handwriting bemoaning England's performance in the 1st Test at Brisbane.

Sir Robert Menzies

In recent times there have been several English Prime Ministers who have loved cricket besides John Major. Stanley Baldwin, Clement Attlee, Alec Douglas-Home, for example, but perhaps an even greater fanatic than any of these was Sir Robert Menzies of Australia. He seemed to find time to attend all the Test matches in Australia and to speak at many cricket dinners which he did *par excellence*. He used to love pulling Freddie Trueman's leg and in one speech ruminated on what Fred was saying as he muttered to himself as he walked back to his mark. Possibly some Greek iambics, he suggested.

He used to arrange his conferences over here to coincide with the Lord's Test, and even then had a television installed in the back of his car so that he could follow the game on his journeys round London.

I interviewed him once for a TV programme and he was most helpful and friendly. He used to listen to Alan McGilvray and myself and told us that we both talked too fast. 'You should follow the example of Clive Harburg,' he said, mentioning a commentator in Queensland, '*he* knows the value of the pause.' He certainly did, because often in his commentaries he would say, '. . . He bowls and the ball goes through to the keeper.' He would then wait for the next ball without saying another word. It's an interesting technique, especially in these days of the fast bowlers walking back thirty yards or so.

Willie Whitelaw

One cabinet minister whom I know well is Willie Whitelaw. Willie and I were both in the Guards Armoured Division. Probably because neither of us was a bit technical, we were both made Technical Adjutants in our respective battalions. We went on a tank course to Bovingdon and he and I and a distinguished grey-haired barrister called Gerald Upjohn formed a small syndicate. At our passing-out test we had to dismantle, then reassemble, a tank engine. We had been warned that the stripping down was easy enough but that the putting back together was a far harder task. People who had done the test previously had always been left with some surplus nuts and bolts and what's more the examining officer Major Hoad knew all about this. Sure enough, it happened to us and Willie and I looked around for somewhere to hide our surplus. When he wasn't looking we slipped the nuts and bolts into Upjohn's overalls' pocket.

When Major Hoad came round he inspected our engine and congratulated us on our handiwork. He then said, 'Just as a matter of course, gentlemen, I always ask officers to turn out their pockets to see if they have any nuts and bolts left over.' Willie and I turned out our pockets with looks of innocence on our faces. Major Hoad then asked an indignant Upjohn to turn out *his* pockets. 'Of course, I haven't got anything to hide – it's quite ridiculous,' he said, as he turned out his pocket and a shower of nuts and bolts fell to the ground. Even Major Hoad had to roar with laughter but 'Daddy' Upjohn was furious and never forgave us.

Peter Carrington

Peter Carrington, another cabinet minister whom I know well, was in the 2nd Battalion Grenadier Guards with me. He was a regular who had joined before the war and was already a Captain when I joined. He was affectionately known as 'The Small Peer' and was a most amusing companion and a first-class soldier. It was his troop of tanks who actually drove onto and captured Nijmegen Bridge, in spite of what you saw in the film *A Bridge Too Far*. In the film Robert Redford, as an American officer, was shown walking across the bridge *towards* our tanks, shouting to them that it was quite safe to advance as the Americans had already captured the bridge! When I protested to the producer Dickie Attenborough about this travesty he said that he had had to pay Redford an enormous fee to take part in the film, and so had to give him an important part of the action.

I had first met Peter in the early thirties when I used to play cricket for his father's team at Bridestowe in Devon. Their house and the team were called Millaton. There was a delightfully picturesque but small ground with a thatched pavilion. The rather elderly team was made up of parsons, doctors, solicitors and one or two young chaps on holiday, or on vacation from a university like myself. One of the parsons was called Arundel and was so old that he had to keep wicket because he couldn't run around in the field. He was the original Ancient Mariner – 'he stoppeth one in three.' It was such a small ground that they had to make boundary byes worth only 2 runs instead of 4, otherwise the visitors might have won just with extras. He was very keen on cricket and at the end of every prayer in church would say 'Over' instead of 'Amen'.

After the war I met Peter in Australia when he was the British High Commissioner. He was tremendously popular with

217

the Australians, and it's no secret that they would have liked to have him back as their Governor-General. Unfortunately he had to think of his family and went into the City. He told me of the time when Harold Macmillan was Prime Minister and came out on a visit to Australia. He was at the height of his popularity and wherever he went groups of British immigrants would gather round the house or hotel where he was staying. He would invariably gave them a lordly wave of the hand and say, 'I bring you greetings from the old country.' They loved it. He got into the habit of doing this even when travelling in a car. Peter said that one day they were motoring in the outback, a long way from any town, where there were just large acres of scrub. Whilst he and Macmillan were deep in conversation, the Prime Minister would automatically wave his hand, and murmur, 'I bring you greetings from the old country,' even though it was only to the odd kangaroo, wombat or koala bear.

It was of course Peter who gave the classic reply when he was asked who would succeed Mrs Thatcher if she was run over by a bus. 'It wouldn't dare,' he replied.

The Duke of Edinburgh

My first meeting with the Duke was rather sudden and dramatic. In his capacity as Twelfth Man and Patron of the Lord's Taverners, he was attending the annual ball at Grosvenor House in the fifties. Those were the days when, as the cabaret, the Lord's Taverners challenged the world's best at any sport, the contest taking place on the ballroom floor. In this particular year the sport was athletics and I was representing the Lord's Taverners in the three-legged race. I was in the centre with Macdonald Hobley on one side, Peter Haigh on the other. As we were racing across the slippery dance floor we slipped and landed with a crash. As I had both my arms round the necks of the other two, I couldn't break my fall and landed heavily on my left shoulder right in front of the Duke's table. I was in great pain but of course put on a brave smile when he asked me how I was. I was given a painkiller and it was later diagnosed as a dislocated shoulder. It took months to get better and I don't recommend it to anyone.

In 1977 I did the unforgivable and interviewed him as he was walking in the Queen's walkabout from St Paul's to the Guildhall after the thanksgiving service. For some reason I was allowed to follow about ten yards behind the Queen and the Lord Mayor with a small mobile transmitter. She stopped frequently to talk to the huge crowd and to accept gifts of flowers. Prince Philip was left a long way behind and I could hear roars of laughter as he chatted up the girls in the crowd.

As we reached Guildhall he realised that he ought to catch up with the Queen, and came past me at a fair pace. Carried away by the excitement of it all I forgot entirely about protocol, and went up to him with my microphone and asked him if he was enjoying himself. He naturally looked slightly taken aback, but smilingly shouted above the noise of the crowd, 'I can't hear myself think!'

Later I interviewed him in his study at Buckingham Palace. The first time was for *Down Your Way* when we were covering the National Playing Fields Association of which he is President. Once again I inadvertently broke protocol. His secretary asked me to sit on a sofa and went off to fetch the Duke. After introductions he showed the Duke to a chair on the opposite side of the room. Rather nervously I had to explain that we would have to sit a bit closer as we only had one microphone. Muttering something about Auntie's antique equipment, he came and sat beside me on the sofa. The interview then went well except that we were so close that our knees touched from time to time – definitely not the done thing with royalty but he didn't seem to mind.

The second occasion was for my Saturday interview spot on *Test Match Special*, the only time we have ever recorded it. We had learnt our lesson, and this time took *two* microphones. I can't resist quoting his answer to the final question which I put to him: 'Is there anything about modern cricket which you would like changed?' I had expected a whole list of changes in the laws and playing conditions, but all he said was, 'I only wish that sometimes their trousers fitted a bit better'!

Field Marshal Viscount Montgomery

I had quite a few dealings with Monty. In 1940 as General Officer Commanding 3rd Division he came to inspect our battalion at Parkstone in Dorset. I was by then the Transport Officer and I had prepared a tremendous display for him – an engine being craned out of a truck, mechanics lying under jacked-up vehicles, motor cycles being tested – the lot. I saluted and offered to show him our work. He wasn't in the least bit interested and completely ignored our display; instead he walked straight over to a line of our three-ton trucks. He asked each driver to switch on his sidelights and to my horror – and to his obvious delight – not a single light came on. He asked one of the guardsmen why they weren't working. (I'm sure he already knew the answer.) The guardsman explained that all drivers kept the bulbs of their sidelights in their pockets otherwise they got pinched.

Monty had obviously been tipped off about this habit and triumphantly asked what would happen if there was a sudden emergency and the driver couldn't be found. There would be a vehicle without lights.

I timidly explained to him that the vehicles wouldn't start without the drivers anyway as they were all instructed to immobilise their trucks by removing the rotor arms which they also kept in their pockets. I thought that made it about fifteen all but he had made his point.

We used to broadcast the El Alamein Reunion every year from the Royal Albert Hall. It was always done live so the timing had to be spot on and I soon realised why Monty always got such a good press. He would personally instruct everyone taking part to do exactly what the BBC asked. He would then say to me, 'How long have you allowed for my speech?' 'Oh, about twelve minutes, sir,' I would say. 'You shall have it,' he replied. And we did. He knew the value of PR and good publicity.

I also interviewed him in one of his caravans parked in the garden of his Old Mill House near Alton in Hampshire. I found it strange that he should have a portrait on the wall of his old rival Field Marshal Rommel and said so. 'Fine soldier,' Monty said, 'admired him – the 8th Army gave him a bloody nose'!

A remarkable man, Monty, who undoubtedly thought highly of his own ability. Surprisingly he also thought highly of the Guards Armoured Division and its Commander, General Allan Adair. He came to our farewell parade in Germany when the Guards changed back into infantry. Over 300 tanks were on parade and dipped their seventeen-pounder guns in salute as they slowly drove past Monty on the saluting base. They then drove off over a hill completely out of sight forever. The large arena was temporarily empty until, to the sound of a Guards band, marching infantry came over the hill from where the tanks had gone. It was a dramatic moment and a symbol of the Guards resuming their natural role as infantry.

W

for The Wood (St John's)

I had always wanted to live in St John's Wood near Lord's and in 1948 we moved into a house in Cavendish Avenue where we stayed for nineteen years. All our five children were born while we were there and it got too small. It was a friendly road. Paul McCartney, our most famous resident, lived just opposite and there was usually a queue of Beatles fans waiting outside his gate. They did not often see him because he used to live a night life, getting up at 11 p.m. His butler used to exercise his dog during the daytime. Everyone seemed to know each other and in Coronation year we had a stupendous street party with donkey races, tables down the middle and a piano. We weren't short of musicians because there was pianist Dame Myra Hess and Joan Cross the singer.

We moved about a quarter of a mile away to Hamilton Terrace, one of the longest, broadest and most tree-lined roads in London. Here we had a four-storey house with a big garden to house our large family, a nephew, two friends and our housekeeper Cally and her two teenage children. She had come to us at Cavendish Avenue and, as I write, has been with us for thirty-two years. A dear friend and very much part of the family.

Hamilton Terrace, with its big Georgian and Victorian houses, was full of good neighbours. Our house belonged to the Harrow Estate though Harrow School got none of our rent. It all went towards the upkeep of Harrow Road which was bad luck on the school. In the mid-sixteenth century John Lyon had left some land to the Governors of Harrow School, with the proviso that the profits and rents should go towards repairing the highway between the school and the City of London.

After sixteen happy years the large house became very

expensive to maintain, and most of our family had left the nest, so we moved to our present smaller house in the aptly named Boundary Road. The inevitable happened. Two of our family drifted back, and others wanted to stay, so we had to build a loft conversion and put the old kitchen into the garage. Again we are very lucky to have a lovely garden facing south. Pauline is the green-fingered grower, whilst I am the destroyer with the occasional mow, clip or dehead.

I would never want to live anywhere else in London except St John's Wood. It got its name from part of the Middlesex forest which in the thirteenth century was given to the Knights Hospitaller of St John of Jerusalem by the then Lord of the Manor. It was then thickly wooded and full of stags, wild boars and bulls. It was later used as a hunting ground by Henry VIII and Queen Elizabeth I.

By the beginning of the eighteenth century much of the forest had been cleared for cultivation, and there were two large farms with sheep and cattle grazing on the pastures. One of these farms was on what is now Lord's Cricket Ground. It had a duck pond which some people say is still one of the causes of the drainage problems of the ground.

The Wood gradually became residential from the start of the nineteenth century, and attracted rich city merchants and the gentry who found it convenient to have a villa a few miles away where they could house their mistresses. It also attracted, and always has done to this day, artists, musicians, politicians and many theatrical people. As an example of this I have included at the end of this chapter a list of some of the famous people who have made their homes in St John's Wood.

There are many stories about their goings-on. My favourite concerns Sir Thomas Beecham who lived on the corner of Circus Road and Elm Tree Road. His doctor, later Lord Hunt, told me that one evening about 7.00 p.m. Beecham rang him at his home. 'Come at once,' he demanded, 'it's urgent.' So Dr Hunt leaped into his car and found Beecham in his black homburg hat and evening dress standing impatiently on the corner. He greeted Dr Hunt with, 'I can't get a taxi. Drive me straight to the Albert Hall. I'm late for a concert!'

Because it was once a forest, one of the main attractions of the Wood is its broad tree-lined roads and avenues, which in the spring provide a perfect picture of various coloured blossoms. If you are lucky enough to own a house you will almost certainly have a fair-sized garden, which for me is a must if you have to live in London.

Geographically it is well placed, high up and with plenty of clean air. By car you can get to Piccadilly in fifteen minutes, to Marble Arch in ten, the A40 in ten, the M1 in fifteen and London Airport in thirty-five – door-to-door. There is also the Jubilee Line from St John's Wood station to take you as far south as Charing Cross plus plenty of buses to take you north or south.

Naturally it has changed considerably in the last fifty years or so – often for the worst. The High Street no longer has the cobbler, draper, family grocer, ironmonger etc. but is now lined with gift shops, boutiques, restaurants, estate agents and absurdly expensive chocolate shops. Many of the old characters have gone but there are still pockets of small shops tucked away behind roads like Abercorn Place.

There are now three large hospitals, two synagogues and three private schools including the American school. There's also the large Quinton Kynaston Comprehensive School. The St John's Wood Barracks is the home of the King's Troop Royal Horse Artillery. If you are up early or live nearby, you can hear the sound (rare in London these days) of the clip-clop of horses' hooves as they ride out for their morning exercise, leaving some valuable manure behind them for the keen gardeners.

There are legions of good, well-patronised pubs, several art galleries and recording studios – including the famous Abbey Road where the Beatles made their records. This is still a shrine for Beatles lovers.

Inevitably there are many new luxury flats in the main roads, but the side roads and avenues have so far been protected from these thanks largely to the St John's Wood Preservation Society, of which I have the honour to be President.

At the Lord's roundabout there is the modern Hilton Hotel

overlooking the ground, and the white St John's Wood church where my children and grandchildren have been christened, and my daughter married. It plays a big part in the community life of the Wood.

The vicar when we arrived was Noel Perry-Gore. One day he was listening to my commentary on television and bet his children half a crown that he could make me mention the church in my commentary. He rushed round to the vestry and although it was just before lunch, rang the church bell. Sure enough I interrupted my commentary with, 'That's the bell from St John's Wood church. I wonder why it is being rung at this time of the day?'

Other pleasant amenities include the Regent's Canal running through on its way to Regent's Park, which is our usual place for a Sunday walk. It also houses the Open-Air Theatre but there is no cinema in the Wood. For cheap shopping there is the Church Street market every Saturday and nearby in Lisson Grove the best fish-and-chip shop in London.

The Wood still enjoys a village atmosphere and the natives (I'm one now) are extremely friendly. It is rare to pass anyone without a greeting, and we have a successful Neighbourhood Watch with everyone prepared to help each other. Unlike in Mayfair or south of the Park, you can walk about in any old clothes round the tree-lined avenues, or further afield to Regent's Park and Hampstead Heath. There is no excuse not to take exercise even if it's only round to Lord's in the winter to visit the library there or the indoor school to watch the nets and try to spot the stars of the future.

I am, I suppose, fairly recognisable after all these years, and I must end with something which happened to me about two years ago. I had gone to our local cleaners and there was a relief behind the counter – our usual lady was on holiday. 'Could you please clean these trousers for me?' I asked the unknown lady.

'Certainly Mr Johnston,' she replied.

'That's very clever of you to know me,' I told her.

'Oh,' she said, 'I recognised your voice before you even spoke!'

I can't think of a nicer place to live than at St John's Wood.

Past and present residents
in St John's Wood

Artists

Oswald Birley
'Blondin' (*Tight-Rope Walker over Niagara Falls*)
Simon Elwes
Edward Halliday
Dame Laura Knight

Edwin Landseer
Phil May
Bernard Partridge
Michael Noakes
William Reid-Dick

Musicians and Singers

Janet Baker
Thomas Beecham
Benjamin Britten
Clara Butt
Joan Cross
Hamilton Harty
Myra Hess
Max Jaffa
Joe Loss
Paul McCartney

Mantovani
Denis Martin
Olivia Newton-John
Peter Pears
Roger Quillter
Mark Raphael
George Solti
Victor Silvester
Solomon
Maggie Teyte

Poets

Louis MacNeice
Caradoc Prichard

Stephen Spender

Politicians

Leo Abse
Beverly Baxter
Clement Freud
Lord Lambton

John Platts-Mills
Lord Shinwell
Derek Walker-Smith
Woodrow Wyatt

Royalty

HRH Prince Arthur of Connaught

Earl of Harewood

Sportsmen

Ronne Aird
Gubby Allen
Jack Bailey
Donald Carr
Lord Cobham
R. Cove-Smith
Billy Griffith
Patsy Hendren

Colin Ingleby-Mackenzie
Frank Lee
Harry Lee
Gary Lineker
R. W. V. Robins
E. W. Swanton
J. J. Warr

226

Theatre/Films
TV/Radio/
Writers

Henry Ainley
Oscar Asche
Sir Squire Bancroft
Alan Bates
Dick Bentley
Sheila Bernette
Joyce Carey
Harry Corbett
Adrienne Corrie
Leslie Crowther
Jerry Desmonde
William Fairchild
Gracie Fields
Bruce Forsythe
J. L. Garvin
Binnie Hale
Cedric Hardwicke
Charles Hengler
Leslie Henson
Gladys Henson
Martita Hunt
Eric Idle
Isabel Jeans
Jerome K. Jerome

Douglas Jerrold
Peter Jones
Mirian Karlin
Lily Langtry
Edna May
Mary Malcolm
Austin Melford
Bernard Miles
Bob Monkhouse
Owen Nares
Anna Neagle
Sean O'Casey
Des O'Connor
Sir Arthur Pinero
Archie Pitt
Stephen Potter
Peter Pratt
Lee Remick
Mrs Siddons
Marie Tempest
Barry Took
Austin Trevor
Herbert Wilcox
Sir Charles Wyndham

X
for Ex-Commentators

X gives me the opportunity to pay tribute to some of my old colleagues in the commentary box. Ex means that they have either retired or, sadly, died. I have had to leave some out because of space and have restricted myself to those with whom I worked most closely, Henry Longhurst being the only exception.

Wynford Vaughan-Thomas

Wynford died in February 1987, aged seventy-eight. Right up to his death he was his old ebullient and effervescent self, and still riding round Wales on a horse, although he had had to give up his favourite hobby of climbing.

He was probably the most gifted of all commentators, with a wide variety of talents and an immense knowledge of practically everything, as demonstrated in many quiz and general knowledge games. His talents were awe-inspiring. The words just flowed from his mouth with the lilting inflections of a true Welshman. He was a highly entertaining raconteur and his travels abroad both in war and peace had given him a vast supply of material. With a retentive memory, a sense of humour and the ability and wit to gild the lily, he made the most of his material and could keep a roomful of people spellbound for hours. He was a musician and played the piano like a professional. He was a draughtsman who could illustrate his own writings and a connoisseur of wines and food in almost every country in the world. His knowledge of history and geography would have put any schoolmaster to shame. A remarkable, rather small, grey-haired, rotund man, who in spite of a penchant for good living kept himself so fit that he was able to enjoy climbing mountains.

As a commentator he had an encyclopedic vocabulary and the gift of description, and was really the last of the old-fashioned 'Lobby men'. He joined the BBC in 1934 and since commentating on King George VI's Coronation, had performed at all subsequent major events, including royal tours. His bubbling enthusiasm brought every occasion to life, and if it may sometimes have run away with him, it enabled him to portray everything in a better light. With Wynford there was no such thing as a boring broadcast.

He was one of the BBC's star war correspondents, and made an epic recording in a bomber flying over Berlin during an air raid in 1941. He covered the Anzio landings in Italy and whether by intent or mistake was the first ashore from his particular landing-craft. There followed his hilarious adventures with the Americans both in Italy and the south of France, and finally the crossing of the Rhine. This ended with his famous broadcast from the desk of Lord Haw-Haw in Hamburg, on which were an empty gin bottle and a copy of his last script, left by the fleeing traitor. A most satisfying climax to a war correspondent's wartime service to be able to broadcast through Lord Haw-Haw's actual microphone using those chilling words we had heard so often during the last five years, 'Geermany calling. Geermany calling' – even though there was the suspicion of a Welsh accent.

It was Wynford who gave me my test when I was being considered for a job in Outside Broadcasts at the end of 1945. He was doing interviews one Saturday night outside the Monseigneur Newsreel Theatre at Marble Arch. When he had finished his programme he gave me a short lesson in the art of interviewing. Get to 'know' the person you are about to interview and gain their confidence – if you have the time. Never ask a question to which the person can only answer yes or no. Although you should always have a next question ready, listen to the answer to your last one; there may be a completely different question to ask as a result of that answer. Be courteous and friendly and don't hector but if the answer is evasive or inconclusive, press on politely until you get something definite. Finally – and most important – remember you are only the link between the listeners and the person being interviewed. They want to hear him or her, so keep your own opinions to yourself, your questions as short as possible, and don't swamp your victim with your own personality.

This was excellent advice of which many modern interviewers might well take heed. Anyhow, when Wynford had finished I recorded my interviews with passers-by, asking them what they thought of the butter ration. Well, if you ask silly questions . . . But although I wasn't very good, Wynford reported to Lobby that at least I kept talking and did not dry up. So I'm afraid you have to blame Wynford if you have been listening to me for the last forty-six years.

As one so prone to 'gaffes' myself, I cannot resist recounting Wynford's most famous mistake, which happened when he was the commentator for television at the launching of the *Ark Royal* at Birkenhead by the Queen Mother. The producer, Ray Lakeland, had told Wynford beforehand, 'Don't talk while the Queen Mother is breaking the bottle of champagne on the bows of the ship. Keep quiet as the *Ark Royal* glides slowly down the slipway. Wait until she actually hits the water and then start talking to your heart's content.'

All went according to plan. Number One Camera showed the Queen Mother making her short speech and breaking the bottle. Number Two Camera showed the ship as it gradually moved, and Number Three had shots of the cheering crowds. Ray punched all these up in turn so that they came on to the screens of the viewers at home. Then just before the *Ark Royal* reached the water he noticed Number One camera had got a marvellous picture of the Queen Mother smiling in that charming way she has. Ray was so enchanted that he forgot all that he had told Wynford and immediately pressed the button which filled the viewers' screens with the Queen Mother; this unfortunately coincided with the exact moment that the *Ark Royal* hit the water. Wynford was watching this and not his television screen, and remembering his instructions began to talk, 'There she is,' he said, 'the huge vast bulk of her!'

John Snagge

John was one of the most versatile of all broadcasters and certainly the longest-standing, broadcasting from 1924 to 1980. He joined the BBC as Assistant Director of BBC Stoke-on-Trent – a lofty title, but he actually had to do all the bits and pieces, including announcing. He became an announcer at Savoy Hill in 1928 in the days when they all had to put on dinner-jackets to read the news. They also used to have a pianola in the studio, which the announcer was responsible for playing to fill in occasional interludes. One day John was off duty in the rest room when he heard strangled noises coming from the studio. He rushed in to find that the tie of one of his colleagues had caught in the pianola roll, and he was gradually being pulled into the pianola and strangled to death.

In John's early days at Stoke he was a conspicuous figure in his Oxford Bags, unexpected gear for an Old Wykehamist and son of a judge. But when he came to London the standard of dress was higher and if anyone's shoes were down at heel the offender was sent out immediately to get them mended.

John will always be famous all over the world for his commentaries on the Oxford and Cambridge Boat Race. He did his first commentary in 1931 and was the main commentator on the race for the next fifty years.

Some people thought that the Boat Race would be no more when John retired in 1980, aged seventy-five. Indeed, in 1981 it took four commentators to replace him. For fifty years his voice had told the world about it and he must have been one of the few people alive who had never heard the Boat Race commentary. His great strength was his complete knowledge of all things to do with rowing. He had known all the world's great oarsmen over the period and knew all the inside talk and gossip. Every year he used to dine with both crews in the last week before the race and he presented them with a George IV golden sovereign dated 1829 – the first year of the race – for them to toss with. He was remarkably impartial, never letting his Oxonian background influence his commentary, either in the many years when Oxford were generally the losers or in the last decade when they have been on top. Unlike so many of us other commentators, he never got overexcited, keeping his cool even in the most dramatic moments, though he did make the odd gaffe. In 1949, in a desperately close race, he said, 'It's a very close race and I can't see who is in the lead – it's either Oxford or Cambridge'! And he once said of an Australian blue: 'He's the only overseas blue rowing in both boats'!

The Boat Race, Henley Regatta and Olympic Games, which John covered throughout his career, were actually only a small part of his broadcasting life. He joined OBs in 1933 and covered almost every sport either as commentator or reporter. In addition he did a variety of what can be called stunts in a programme called *Let's Go Somewhere*. (This title was 'pinched' by a certain B. Johnston for his live four-minute spot in *In Town Tonight*, 1948–1952.) He also commentated on a number of events such as the Aldershot Tattoo when, on seeing the Royal Car arrive escorted by a military policeman on a motor bike, he said, 'Here comes Queen Mary and her motor cycle.'

During the war John moved over to become Presentation Director, and in addition to being an announcer once again, was in charge of all the others. His rich, deep voice, unlike any other, was so easily recognisable that it was ideal for wartime. It gave a feeling of trust, confidence and credibility, and soon earned him the sobriquet of 'The Voice of London'. Perhaps his most famous wartime broadcast was the announcement of the Normandy landings on D-Day. I remember hearing it in Hove where the Guards Armoured Division was waiting with its tanks. But in addition to D-Day he also announced VE Day, VJ Day and the deaths of King George VI and Queen Mary.

His job as Head of Presentation meant that he had little time for commentary but in 1953 he was the radio commentator in Westminster Abbey, against strong opposition from Richard Dimbleby who covered the Coronation on television.

In 1954 he was told by the Director-General, 'Don't make any announcements without my personal permission. Your voice is so associated with important announcements that as soon as you come on, people will assume Winston Churchill has died.'

His career came full circle when in the last few years before he finally gave up broadcasting, he did a series for Radio London called *John Snagge's London*. He recorded over a hundred of these in which he met people, tried out their jobs or visited interesting and historic places.

John is as friendly a person as he sounds, with a fund of BBC stories going right back to 1924 and the days of Sir John Reith. My own favourite, perhaps naturally, is the occasion when he was reading out the cricket scores, and said, 'Yorkshire 232 all out – Hutton ill. I'm sorry – Hutton one hundred and eleven'!

Another one occurred in 1939 when the King and Queen were paying a visit to Canada, crossing the Atlantic in HMS *Vanguard* – John was the commentator at the quayside and the broadcast was scheduled to last for twenty minutes. John had done his homework and while the tugs were fussing around the big ship, he described the scene, the crowds, the Royal Marines band, the bunting and details of the *Vanguard* and the programme of the tour in Canada. Unfortunately the tugs were having some difficulty and the twenty minutes soon became thirty. John was running out of material from all his notes, so for the umpteenth time said the King and Queen were waving from the bridge. Then he noticed that the Queen whispered something to the King and immediately left the bridge. 'Ah,' said John, 'the Queen has now left the bridge and gone below for some reason or other.' He then got stuck for something to say and after a few moments added in desperation, '. . . and now I can see water coming through the side of the ship.'

Raymond Glendenning

In the thirties Teddy Wakelam was the first of the multi-sport commentators with his rugby, soccer, tennis and cricket. The war produced two more, Raymond Glendenning and Rex Alston.

Raymond came to London from the BBC in Northern Ireland in the early 1940s and found the world of sport wide open to his talents. Because of shortage of staff, he took on anything and by the end of the war numbered racing, soccer, boxing and tennis as his top sports. Because of Rex he did not do athletics, but was used in the 1948 Olympic Games for the showjumping, and also covered the Greyhound Derby and other races. In fact he was once strictly timed at 176 words in thirty seconds during one race, and over 300 words in a full minute.

He had a rich, plummy, mellow voice and had remarkable powers of description, (managing even to describe our exit from the church when Pauline and I were married and OBs gave us a recording of the ceremony). He had a wonderful memory for facts and figures on any sport but of course he could never devote enough time to any one of them. As a result, the boxing public were apt to think that he knew more about racing; or the soccer world thought he should concentrate on boxing. It is in fact an impossible task to be the number one expert on such a diversity of sports. For instance, to be a racing commentator you must live racing, go to all the meetings, get to know all the racing personalities well. But Raymond could not do this, so had what was called a 'race-reader', who would stand alongside him feeding him with facts and the position of the horses during the race. This was made possible by the invention of the 'lip-mike', which the commentator held right up to his mouth so that nothing except his voice could be heard by the listener. But you can imagine how difficult it made his job, trying to speak and listen at the same time. The race-readers were full-time racing journalists and one of these was Claude Harrison, followed for a short time by Peter O'Sullevan. The BBC did not try to hide what they were doing, and the race-reader was given his credit over the air.

In boxing, Raymond had the help of W. Barrington-Dalby – an ex-referee who knew the sport backwards. He summed up for fifty seconds or so between the rounds, but then of course Raymond was left on his own to describe the actual fighting. There was a tremendous furore when Raymond was accused of favouring and shouting home Sugar Ray Robinson in the fight which was in fact won in the end by Randolph Turpin.

Raymond was an easily distinguishable and much carica-tured figure. With his horn-rimmed spectacles, his handlebar moustache and his somewhat ample figure he looked in fact not unlike Billy Bunter with a moustache. He was a gregarious person, a great mixer, and greeted by everyone wherever he went. He enjoyed his drink and would recommend a swig of honey in whisky to maintain stamina and the voice during a broadcast. He could speak at a remarkable speed and his voice at the end of a race, or when a goal was scored, reached an incredible crescendo.

It was lucky that he was a good improviser and a bit of an actor, because on several occasions during the war, he had to commentate on games or races which he could not see. The point was that the BBC was monitored by the Germans, so no commentator could ever mention anything about the weather. For the same reason no broadcast could ever be cancelled because of bad weather; if conditions were too bad, then no commentary took place. There was no explanation to the listener of why not – except perhaps that famous 'technical hitch'.

Certainly on one occasion at Cheltenham, Raymond had to invent what was happening while the horses were 'out in the country', only picking them up as they came through the fog in the home straight. Luckily it was not television and he was able to readjust the position of the horses, having been careful to avoid any falls during his fictitious account. There was also fog at Elland Road on Boxing Day 1942, so Raymond could only see one side of the pitch, and had to make up what was happening on the other side to coincide with the reactions of the crowd on that side. Not easy!

Raymond's silver tongue let him down seriously only once when during the Grand National he remarked, '. . . and now coming to the rider jump there's a waterless horse out in front!' Raymond gradually faded away in the sixties but for twenty years he had been the BBC's outstanding personality among the sports commentators and the big sporting events were never quite the same without him.

Richard Dimbleby

In the seventy-odd years of broadcasting one person stands out head and shoulders above all the rest – that supreme broadcaster Richard Dimbleby. That is a sweeping statement and perhaps can only be truly appreciated by those who were watching television in the fifties and early sixties. For nearly twenty years Richard was the voice of the nation, much loved and respected by every class of listener and viewer. He was arguably the best-known face in Britain and when he died at the early age of fifty-two in December 1965, both the BBC and ITV interrupted programmes to announce his death – ITV beating the BBC to it!

During the closing stages of his long illness he received thousands of cards and letters. Presents poured into St Thomas's Hospital, including six bottles of champagne sent personally by the Queen. The Dean of Westminster offered the Abbey for his memorial service, and it was packed with a congregation of VIPs, his colleagues and friends, and hundreds of ordinary people who had never known him personally. The Queen and Queen Mother were both represented and remarkably the service was televised live by the BBC. I can't imagine the BBC honouring a commentator in such a way today! He was sometimes unkindly accused of being obsequious to the Monarchy and too Establishment-minded. Because he was so often broadcasting on important occasions some people who did not know him also thought that he was pompous. He was unashamedly a royalist and a patriot and had high principles about good manners which probably all came across in his commentaries, but pompous, never! He had an impish sense of humour with a distinctive chuckle, and could always see the funny side of things. I once went with him as co-driver to report the Monte Carlo Rally and we enjoyed a full ten days of fun and laughter.

He was large, fat and jolly and a wonderful mixer with everyone whom he met, or with whom he worked. OB engineers are the best judges of a commentator's character. They work with him at close quarters and see him under strain when things go wrong. They share the triumphs and disasters. I never heard a single word against Richard from any of the television or radio engineers. When he died it seemed like a personal loss to thousands who had never known him other than through his broadcasts. For them the BBC would never be the same again. Nor, in a way, was it.

He began, like so many broadcasters, as a journalist. In 1936, aged twenty-three, he joined the BBC as their first News Observer. His very first commentary was from Heston Aerodrome, when he described Neville Chamberlain's return from Munich, and we heard Chamberlain's famous 'Out of this nettle danger, we pluck this flower safety.' Later, when war broke out, he became the BBC's first War Correspondent. He came into prominence with his reports from the Middle East Desert War. Then when the Second Front started in Europe he broadcast from anywhere the action took him. From the beaches on D-Day, from Belsen with the first broadcast account of its horrors and from Hitler's armchair in the Chancellery, where he was the first Allied reporter to see the terrible bomb damage. The memory of Belsen was to live with him for the rest of his life.

Back home after the war he became disillusioned with the BBC administrators, who he thought did not fully appreciate his wartime broadcasts. So he resigned from the staff and became a freelance. First of all he was to continue to make his name on radio with programmes like *Down Your Way* (he presented 300) and *Twenty Questions*. But television was gradually awakening from its enforced wartime sleep and Richard began to devote most of his time to it. Programmes like *Panorama* made him a well-known face, while his voice – rather like Terry Wogan's today – was in constant demand for every type of commentary, other than sport: King George VI's funeral, the Coronation, royal visits overseas, Princess Margaret's wedding, Trooping the Colour, openings of Parliament, the first cross-Channel television broadcast, Churchill's funeral and a lot more.

His voice was quiet and friendly and I never heard it raised in excitement. He had such a command of the language and such a quick mind to match it, that his producer on so many royal occasions and other big events, Antony Craxton, has said that he never once heard Richard say 'er'. There are not many of us who could boast that! His timing and his judgement of when to speak or keep quiet on television was impeccable. Television does not require 'waffle'. It needs short, crisp sentences to match the picture. But no matter how perfect the delivery, and the composition of the sentences, the success of a commentator also depends on his material and the information he is able to give.

This was one of Richard's great strengths. More than almost anyone else at the time – or since – he devoted hours to intense research and preparation before any broadcast. He knew that to sound authoritative he had to know all the facts, and he made sure that he did. He used a number of small white cards with everything he might need to know neatly typed on them in note form. By the end of a broadcast he might not have used more than ten or twenty of them. But they were there – just in case. At Princess Margaret's wedding, when she was nearly an hour late arriving at Tower Bridge to leave for her honeymoon on the Royal Yacht, no one would have known that anything was wrong. From the notes which he had prepared Richard was able to give the viewer a potted history of the Tower, the River Thames, Tower Bridge, the wharfs, the river police and the Royal Yacht itself.

Richard, although he could wax indignant at some official pomposity or administrative blunder, never really lost his temper. But he did have one piece of bad luck which caused him to hit the headlines. It was during the Queen's visit to Berlin and BBC Television was there to broadcast this historic event. There were a lot of technical problems with the lines which meant that the broadcast started six minutes late. Richard started off and was going splendidly when a message came through from London that they were not receiving the broadcast. They said they were getting neither sound nor vision. Dick Francis, the producer, said to Richard through his headphones, 'Hold everything. We're not on the air. London isn't getting us.' Richard was naturally exasperated after giving of his best.

'Jesus wept,' he said, not thinking he was on the air. But for some reason, in spite of the messages to the contrary, London had been receiving the broadcast perfectly and Richard's words had gone into every home in Great Britain. The BBC had to issue an apology as every paper headlined the story. Most were highly critical but the *Daily Mirror* probably summed up best the feelings of the average viewer. 'So he is human after all,' was their comment.

In addition to our Monte Carlo trip together I was lucky to work with Richard on a number of important television broadcasts. He handed over direct to me at the King's funeral when he was in St James's Street and I was at Hyde Park Corner. When the Queen and Prince Philip returned from the Australian tour in 1954 he was at Westminster Bridge, and I was halfway down Whitehall. On other occasions such as the Coronation and Princess Margaret's wedding I was stationed along the routes listening in my headphones to Richard's usual impeccable performance from Westminster Abbey.

The broadcast of the return of the Queen and Prince Philip did not go quite according to plan, although as a result some people said to me the next day, 'You were very good. Your commentary was one of the best you have ever done, and nearly matched that of Richard Dimbleby.' High praise indeed! But read on . . .

The Royal Party were due to sail up to Tower Bridge in the Royal Yacht and then travel in a launch to Westminster Bridge. Here they were to get into an open carriage for the drive back to Buckingham Palace. Television's Outside Broadcasts were due to cover the journey from Westminster Bridge with Richard at Westminster Pier, myself halfway down Whitehall and Berkeley Smith at Buckingham Palace. At our conference beforehand it was decided that Richard should deal with the arrival and reception at Westminster Pier. I was to cover the journey down from Whitehall giving details of the horses, the carriage and the Household Cavalry escorts. Berkeley Smith was to describe the arrival at Buckingham Palace.

On the day it was foggy and the river was shrouded in mist. When the broadcast started I heard in my headphones Richard identifying all the people assembled to welcome the Queen. There was the Queen Mother, Princess Margaret, various ministers, a Lord Lieutenant, a mayor, plus the Guard of

Honour of the Queen's Company 1st Battalion Grenadier Guards. Richard was doing his job superbly as usual, but did keep mentioning that the Royal Launch was still not in sight, no doubt delayed by the fog. Soon even Richard began to run out of material and obviously a bit desperate, he began to poach on my preserve. He described and gave details of the open carriage, and named all the horses which had been given to the Queen by the Queen of Holland. When there was still no sight of the launch he went on to talk about the escort of the Household Cavalry, naming the officers, describing the uniforms and adding bits of regimental history of the Blues and Life Guards.

At last the Royal Launch came into sight and he was able to give his commentary on the various presentations to the Queen. When the Queen and Prince Philip stepped into the carriage I heard him cue over to me as arranged.

I remember saying something like, 'Yes, the carriage is just turning out of Westminster Square into Whitehall . . .' After that I said nothing as it made its way through the cheering crowds lining Whitehall. When I saw in my monitor that it had gone through Trafalgar Square and passed under Admiralty Arch into the Mall I said, 'And as the Queen and Prince Philip reach their home straight after their long journey, over to Berkeley Smith at Buckingham Palace.'

In other words, I really said nothing because there was nothing to say. So unintentionally I gave a lesson in the art of television commentary, which is never to say anything unless it adds to the picture. No wonder people said that I was good!

However, there was one way in which I could never match Richard and that was in cars. He had a succession of Rolls-Royces – always the latest model and, what is more, he was the first person in Great Britain to have a telephone in his car. He even beat Lew Grade! He often took his car on his various jobs in Europe, and it always caused quite a stir as the BBC commentator drove up in a Rolls.

For the last five years of his life Richard had cancer and was often in great pain when he broadcast. He frequently went straight to the microphone for a commentary after enduring painful treatment at St Thomas's. His courage was magnificent and he never complained, in fact he seemed to drive himself harder and harder with a work schedule that would have shattered most fit men. When it was obvious in the summer of 1965 that he was not going to be cured, some of us tried to see whether he could be knighted before he died. No television or radio performer (as opposed to actors, film stars, authors, dancers, musicians) had ever been so honoured, although Directors-General, controllers and chief engineers had received knighthoods.

How right and proper it would have been if Richard could have been the first knighted commentator, but it was not to be. Through Lobby we tried Buckingham Palace and Number Ten but to no avail and Richard died in December much loved and mourned by the people of Great Britain. They had lost their voice at the BBC. We, his colleagues, had lost a friend and the greatest broadcaster there has ever been.

Henry Longhurst

If I had to pick out my favourite commentator on any sport – an invidious task – I think I would pick Henry Longhurst. Like John Arlott on cricket and Dan Maskell on lawn tennis, he indelibly imprinted his personality and individual style on golf. It is significant that all three specialised in one sport on which they were an authority, not only on the skill and laws of the game, but even more perhaps on its history, traditions and personalities.

Commentary on cricket and lawn tennis had been broadcast on television and radio before the war. In golf there were some brilliant reports and comments by that great writer, Bernard Darwin. There were also a few attempts at describing the play, including one by Henry himself on the British Amateur Championships in 1935. After the war golf was a virtual newcomer, however – especially to television, whereas now, thanks to the pioneer work done by Henry, it has become one of the top television sports.

Henry had many achievements during his varied life. He captained the Cambridge University golf team to victory in 1931. During the war for a short time he became a Member of Parliament. He wrote 1,000 consecutive pieces for the *Sunday Times* as their gold correspondent for forty-five years. In 1965 he became the first Briton to work regularly for the American networks. He was awarded the CBE and in 1969 was given the Journalist of the Year Special Award. But perhaps the honour he valued most of all was when he was made an Honorary Life Member of the Royal and Ancient in 1977. Although a very sick man at the time he insisted on going up to St Andrews for the presentation.

What was his secret? His style was ideally suited to television. More than any television commentator that I have ever known, he knew by instinct when to talk and when to keep quiet. Someone quite rightly once described 'his brilliant flashes of silence'.

His gruff, confidential voice, his slow delivery, his wit and the ability to produce the apt phrase on the spur of the moment, were just what the viewer wanted. He became the friend of us all and the kind critic and friend of all the competitive golfers. He knew their difficulties and could appreciate all their tensions – especially when putting. He himself gave up golf because he got the putter's 'twitch'. 'Once you've had 'em, you've got 'em,' he once said. With a whispered comment he could make the viewer at home in his armchair feel that he was actually about to putt.

It was a tribute to Henry's style that he was as popular in the United States as in Great Britain. The golf commentator's job is not easy. He has to speak against a background of silence, so that his every word is like dropping a pebble on to a still pond. Rugby, racing and soccer commentators can all get away with the slight fluff or not-so-perfect English, against the noise of the crowd. But in golf, lawn tennis, snooker and, of course, cricket, a mistake seems to be magnified by the backdrop of silence.

Henry was as near perfect as any commentator could be, even towards the end when he was sadly struggling against ill health. He was humble but at the same time a great deflater of pomposity. He died aged sixty-nine and in his last year made a typical comment, 'Three under-fours – not a bad score in the circumstances.' When ill health finally forced him to retire from work, he wrote, 'Now it is time to lay down my pen and alas the microphone too, and to reflect in whatever time may be left how uncommonly lucky I have been.'

What a lovely thing to have been able to write at the end of a successful and happy life. As one of his obituaries remarked about his CBE – he was a Commentator Beyond Excellence.

Robert Hudson

Robert has officially retired but I would not be at all surprised if he is resurrected to take part in some future national occasion.

Of all the leading commentators since the war the must unsung and least known to the public must surely be Robert Hudson. This is largely due to his quiet, unobtrusive and retiring personality. He is, in fact, one of the very few commentators who is not an extrovert. At the same time he is probably the most conscientious, and puts most of us to shame with his meticulous preparation and research before any programme in which he is taking part. He is essentially the broadcasters' commentator. We know all the difficulties he has to overcome and so appreciate his great skill. To the listeners, however, he makes it all sound too easy.

After leaving the army as a Major in the Royal Artillery he did his first cricket broadcast in 1947 for television, and for radio in 1948. His career has mostly been with radio and he has mainly commentated on cricket, rugby and ceremonials. He has had two spells as an administrator, first up in North Region, as it was then, and later when he succeeded Charles Max-Muller as Head of OBs in London.

His commentaries on cricket and rugby were hard to fault for accuracy of description, and he made sure that his knowledge of the laws and details of the players' careers was complete. In cricket, for instance, whereas most of us rely on the brains of

Bill Frindall in the box, Robert always had his own little black book full of the records of all the players in the match. Most of us stroll casually into the box half an hour or so before the start but Robert would be there at least an hour beforehand, concentrating on the job ahead.

I always had the feeling that it was quite a strain for him until the first ball was bowled. After that he was a different person and sounded confident and efficient, giving a completely accurate account of what was happening. Although in private life he has a good sense of humour, it did not often come through in his broadcasts, so he lacked some of the colour of someone like John Arlott.

Before I joined *Test Match Special* in 1970, Robert had become Head of OBs and given up regular commentary. It was in fact entirely due to him that I was invited to join the *Test Match Special* team when I was dropped by television. Since he had left the commentary box I did not work a lot with him, which is perhaps just as well. I doubt whether he would have wholly approved of all the fun and games which we enjoy in the box today.

In addition to sponging his face before a broadcast, he was also a tremendous fiddler while commentating. He used his hands the whole time to pick up pencils, rubbers or bits of paper. In those days Bill Frindall used to secure his score-sheets to wooden boards with large rubber bands and these were special favourites of Robert, who used to pull them out and stretch them to their utmost limit. During one Test he had just finished describing a particularly exciting over, during which he had been fiddling away with one of the rubber bands. As Freddie Brown started his between-over comments Robert fiddled once too often, and one of the bands came off the board. As if catapulted, it shot across the box and hit Freddie a stinging blow in the left ear. Freddie let out a yelp but, after a nervous glance over his shoulder, continued talking, not sure whether he had been stung by a wasp or struck by a poisoned dart.

In spite of his great concentration Robert did make one amusing gaffe, during the England v New Zealand Test at

Lord's in 1969. The two teams were, as usual, being presented to the Queen in front of the Pavilion during the tea interval. 'It's obviously a great occasion for all the players,' Robert said. 'It's a moment they will always forget.'

One rather unusual feature about Robert was that at the end of the day he tended to fade away, and due to his shyness seldom mixed or talked with the players. In one way this is not a bad thing, as it is easier to criticise someone you don't know personally. But it also meant that the players hardly knew Robert and often used to ask, 'Who was that giving that excellent commentary?'

I have dealt with Robert as a cricket commentator but he was equally admired and respected by rugby enthusiasts. He is, however, best known as radio's number one ceremonial commentator. He has covered all the big royal occasions and until he decided to give up in 1981, had broadcast twenty-five Trooping the Colour parades. The drill is always the same each year but somehow, by diligently talking to as many as possible of those taking part, Robert managed to make his commentary sound different. As for the royal occasions, his research and meticulous timing put him into the Dimbleby class. He is always cool, calm and confident.

E. W. Swanton

Jim Swanton is a big man in both senses of the word. He has a strong personality, holds high principles and likes to get his own way (which he usually does). Some people who don't know him think he is pompous and so, I suppose, do his many friends, which is why we enjoy pulling his leg. On tours Jim had a habit of staying with Governor-Generals or dining with Prime Ministers and High Commissioners. I expect that he himself would admit that he was a wee bit of a snob. Anyhow, the thought prompted a now famous remark about him: 'Jim is such a snob that he won't travel in the same car as his chauffeur'!

Cricket has been his life and in addition to broadcasting he has written or edited about twenty books and been cricket correspondent of the *Evening Standard* in the thirties, and of the *Daily Telegraph* from 1946 to 1975. So far as I am concerned he wrote and said all the right things about cricket, and he made sure that he was given plenty of space to air his views. He also ensured that none of his copy could be sub-edited without reference to him. How his press colleagues envied him this unique journalistic licence! He was forthright in all he wrote and his often unfavourable comparison of modern cricket with that of the past did not always endear him to modern cricketers.

He began his radio broadcasting with some reports in 1934, followed by commentary on the 1938 and 1939 Tests in England. But his big chance came in the winter of 1938/9. He became the first commentator to be specifically booked by the BBC for an overseas tour – South Africa v England in South Africa. He started off with a commentator's dream when he was able to describe a hat trick by Tom Goddard in the first Test at Johannesburg.

During the war he was captured by the Japanese at Singapore and was a prisoner of war in Siam from 1942 to 1945 but in 1946 he took up where he had left off as a member of the radio commentary team with Rex Alston and John Arlott. Jim had played cricket for Middlesex against the universities before the war, so with his deep, rich, authoritative voice, was well qualified for the job. He was also a cricket historian with a thorough knowledge of all the developments of the game and its players. Between us we evolved a form of TV commentary, trying hard not to speak more than necessary. Our styles were very different. Jim was factual, serious, analytical and critical, myself almost certainly too jokey, and too uncritical. I was also always eager to find extra ingredients to the actual play. To me a cricket match does not consist solely of what is taking place out in the middle. There is so much else which is part and parcel of the game – a member asleep, a bored blonde reading a book or some small boys playing a game of their own, oblivious of the cricket they are supposed to be watching. This meant close cooperation with our producers, Peter Dimmock and Barrie Edgar in the early days, and then Antony Craxton, Ray Lakeland, Phil Lewis and Nick Hunter. With a good producer, the camera can capture so much of the 'atmosphere' of a game, and I still believe that it gives better entertainment to the viewer than just sticking to bat and ball.

In addition to commentary, Jim used to do close-of-play summaries and both on television and radio these were better than anyone else's, so good was his analysis and reading of a day's play. On television he would sometimes stop and snap his fingers and ask someone moving behind the camera to keep still. It takes a bit of guts to do this, and also breaks the train of thought, but he always seemed able to pick up where he had left off. I only once saw him flummoxed. When he finished his summary he used to remove his field-glasses from around his neck, and place them on the table in front of him. He would then give the close-of-play score and say goodbye. He did this once at a Test at Trent Bridge when they had the giant electric scoreboard. 'Well that's it then,' said Jim. 'A fine day's play – one I shall always remember. Let me just give you the close-of-play score.' So saying, he looked up at the scoreboard, only to find that it had been switched off, and there was nothing on it! As so often happens, Jim could not remember the exact score, so there was a lot of snapping of fingers, while an assistant hurriedly wrote it down on a piece of paper for him.

As I've said, he was an ideal subject for leg-pulls. In 1964 for some reason Jim had a chauffeur to drive him around. He was doing the television commentary with us at Trent Bridge, which was packed. At about 12.00 noon Denis Compton went to the man on the public-address system and asked him to read out a note which we had written up in the box. Between overs the crowd heard, 'If Mr E. W. Swanton is listening will he please go to the back of the pavilion, where his chauffeur has left the engine of his car running.' Quite untrue of course, but I've never heard such a roar of laughter from a cricket crowd.

One other leg-pull took place a year earlier at Canterbury when we were televising the August Bank Holiday match. Colin Cowdrey, who had broken his left wrist in the Lord's Test, was one of our commentary team, and before play started we arranged everything with that arch leg-puller Peter Richardson, then Captain of Kent. We knew that he would be batting and

247

so told him that we would wave a handkerchief from our scaffolding when Jim was commentating. We had also embroiled Bill Copson, the umpire, in the plot.

When Jim had been commentating for an over or so, we waved the handkerchief. As soon as he saw the signal Peter went and had an earnest mid-wicket conversation with his partner, looking up at our commentary box. They then went and had a word with Bill Copson. He began to walk towards our scaffolding and Antony Craxton, our Producer, said to Jim in his headphones, 'What's going on, Jim? Comment please on the mid-wicket conference, and what Bill Copson is doing.'

'Ah,' said Jim, 'obviously some small boys by our commentary position are playing about and putting the batsmen off. Quite rightly Bill Copson is coming to sort things out.' By then Bill had got about twenty yards from us, stopped and, cupping his hands to his mouth, shouted so that all the crowd (and television viewers) could hear, 'Will you please stop that booming noise up there in the commentary box. It's putting off the batsmen. Please stop it at once.'

Colin Cowdrey, just to rub it in, shouted back to Copson, 'Sorry, Bill, we couldn't quite hear. Will you repeat that please?' Copson did so, and once again we heard a cricket crowd roaring with laughter. Jim of course soon realised that his leg had been well and truly pulled, and said that Peter Richardson must be up to one of his silly tricks, and that we should get on with the game.

As you may have gathered, we had many happy days in the television commentary box, and in spite of our irreverence, I know that Jim too enjoyed his time in the box with us.

Rex Alston

The majority of sports commentators have played or participated at some level or other in the sport on which they commentate. Some, like Harold Abrahams, Richie Benaud, Jim Laker, Nigel Starmer-Smith and Cliff Morgan, have been of international class. I must emphasise here, by the way, that I am talking about commentators, not summarisers.

One non-international (but better qualified than most) was Rex Alston. He won an athletics blue at Cambridge and ran in the sprints as second string to Harold Abrahams. From 1924 to 1941 he was a master at Bedford School, and while there captained Bedford at rugby football and also played for Rosslyn Park and the East Midlands. In cricket he captained Bedfordshire in the Minor Counties Championship. Not surprisingly, his three main sports were cricket, rugby and athletics, to which he added lawn tennis.

Already you will have a clue to his character – a schoolmaster for seventeen years with obvious powers of leadership. He joined the BBC in 1942 and became a freelance when he reached retiring age in 1961. While on the staff he was the office organiser and commentary-box leader in all four sports. He was precise, meticulous, fair, unbiased and demanding of a high standard of behaviour on the field, the track, the court and in the commentary box itself. He could at times sound like a schoolmaster, gently reproving any lapse in standards of play or behaviour, but he was a friendly, gregarious person and the commentary box was always a happy place when he was in command.

In my opinion, of the four sports, he was best at athletics, closely followed by rugby. At cricket he was – as we all were – slightly overshadowed by John Arlott. He was prone to slight mishaps and had more difficulties than most with the commentator's five-letter nightmare – 'balls'. At Canterbury once he described the scene during the tea interval: '. . . the band playing, the tents with their club flags, the famous lime tree, people picnicking round the ground, whilst on the field hundreds of small boys are playing with their balls.'

At Wimbledon during a ladies' singles match there was a slight delay and Rex said, 'Louise Brough cannot serve at the moment as she has not got any balls.' I myself was guilty on one occasion of saying, 'Play has ended here at Southampton, but they play till 7.00 up at Edgbaston, so over there now for some more balls from Rex Alston.'

Like all of us, Rex made quite a few general gaffes. He once cued over to, 'Your next commentator, old John Arlott at Trafford.' One for which he cannot be blamed was in Australia, when he said, 'Lindwall has now finished his over, goes to the umpire, takes his sweater and strides off.' What Rex did not know was that in colloquial Australian, 'strides' are trousers.

Perhaps his most memorable statement was made at Lord's in 1962 during the MCC v Pakistan match. Pakistan's touring team included a player call Afaq Hussain, a name to strike terror into any commentator. On arrival at Lord's we all rushed to look at the score-card to check whether Afaq was playing. To the immense relief of us all, he had not been selected. However, I thought I would stir things up a bit, so left the television commentary box and went next door to find Rex in the radio box.

'Jolly lucky,' I said, 'that this chap Afaq isn't playing, isn't it?'

'Don't say that name, please,' replied Rex. 'I shall only get it into my head.'

'I quite understand,' I said. 'I'm as relieved as you are that he's not playing.' As I went out of the box I deliberately muttered, 'Afaq, Afaq, Afaq.'

Late in the afternoon MCC were about 200 for 6 with Barry Knight of Essex playing a useful innings. Burki, the Pakistan captain, threw the ball to a new bowler and Rex was heard to say, 'There's going to be a change of bowling. We are going to see Afaq to Knight at the nursery end.' When he realised what he had said and how his remark might be misconstrued, Rex held his head in his hands and said, 'What am I saying? He's not even playing!'

Peter West

Peter retired surprisingly early in 1986 and lives a quiet country life tending his garden in Gloucestershire. I should think that he could justifiably claim to have commentated more hours on television since the war than any other commentator. He has certainly been a jack of all sports, partly because the producers knew he would never let them down. He quickly learnt all the intricacies of television commentary and presentation and is the complete TV professional. Of the major sports on television he has covered cricket, rugby, tennis, hockey, rowing and field events in six Olympics. In addition he has been chairman and presenter of at least twenty games or quizzes on television and radio, including fifteen years of presenting *Come Dancing*. As if this were not enough he has written and edited books and magazines about cricket and till 1983 was the rugby correspondent of *The Times*, and did rugby commentary for radio. He also found time to be an active chairman of a public relations firm with strong sporting contacts.

All this is proof of his versatility and capacity for hard work – something we seem to find in most commentators. But, as with Raymond Glendenning, versatility had certain disadvantages. Because he did cricket, tennis and *Come Dancing*, rugby supporters, for example, were apt to think he could not know much about their game. Peter's answer to this would be that the producers had faith in him or they would not have continued to employ him. And, throughout his broadcasting life, working always as a freelance, he was always in full employment as a commentator – which certainly has not been the case with every freelance.

Peter is a very friendly person with a good sense of humour and much of our happiness in the box was due to him. These characteristics stood him in good stead, and in cricket he became the presenter and interviewer as opposed to commentator.

He came into cricket by pure chance. He once telephoned some copy for C. B. Fry who took a liking to him and admired his efficiency, and recommended him to the BBC. He went to the Royal Military College at Sandhurst and served in the war with the Duke of Wellington's Regiment. We was a good gamesplayer, especially at cricket, but a bad back prevented him from playing seriously, except in our many charity matches. As a commentator at cricket he combined his knowledge of the game with quick assessment, and was not afraid to give his opinion with some force. But because he knew all the players so well, he was always a kind critic and enjoyed and engineered quite a few of our pranks in the box.

Peter did not escape the occasional unlucky choice of words. Once, when commentating at tennis, he remarked, 'Miss Stove seems to be going off the boil.'

John Arlott

John Arlott did more to spread the gospel of cricket than any other man alive. For thirty-four years his rich, gruff, Hampshire burr spanned the world. He took cricket into palaces, mansions, cottages, crofts, mud huts and, for all I know, igloos. He rightly became the voice of cricket and was more imitated than any other commentator. Although he started his working life as a clerk in a mental hospital, followed by nine years in the police where he rose to Detective-Sergeant, he was basically a poet. He could do naturally what we lesser mortals had to work at – paint pictures with words. The sound of his voice alone conjured up visions of white flannels on green grass, and the smell of bat oil and new-mown grass. His powers of description with the ever-apt phrase enabled the listener to 'see' the scene he was describing. He always tried to imagine that he was talking to a blind person and coloured his commentary accordingly. A perfect example of this was the way he once described the run-up to the wicket of the Pakistani Asif Masood. (Bill Frindall says I once called him Massive Ahsood!) He used to run with knees bent and John portrayed him with the words, 'He reminds me of Groucho Marx chasing a pretty waitress.'

One of the classic commentaries of all time was his hilarious description of the Lord's ground staff removing the covers off the square at Lord's. They took at least twenty minutes and John never missed a trick, covering every detail of what was going on. He also gave a very fine word picture of the streaker at Lord's in 1975. I know if I had been doing it I should have gone too far – 'two balls going down the pitch at the same time' – that sort of thing. But John struck exactly the right note.

He had the enviable gift of being able to produce the apt witty comment on the spur of the moment. When he was with the MCC in South Africa the MCC Captain, George Mann, was clean bowled by the slow-left-arm South African bowler 'Tufty' Mann. It was an unplayable ball, pitching on the leg stump and taking the off-bail. Without a moment's hesitation John said, 'Mann's inhumanity to Mann'!

He had always adored cricket and with his retentive memory soon became one of the great cricket historians. How good he was as a player I am never quite sure. He did travel round with the Hampshire team before the war, and once at Worcester actually fielded as twelfth man for them in a county match. He was also a great listener and throughout his career cultivated the company of the county cricketers all over England – wherever he was commentating. He was not afraid to ask, and so learned much about the technique and skills of the game.

He also made many friends among the first-class cricketers, and which had a happy result when they elected him President of the Cricketers' Association. This was a tribute and an honour and it was an office he continued to hold until his sad death last December.

We all have to have our piece of luck and his chance came in 1946 when India was touring England – the first tourists since the war. After leaving the police John had become a poetry producer for the Far Eastern Service and they selected him to follow the Indians round the country, in order to send nightly reports on the matches back to India. It was soon obvious that cricket had made a find and Lobby chose him to commentate along with Rex Alston and Jim Swanton. From then until he retired he was a member of the radio commentary team at every Test played in this country.

He was a home-lover and very much a family man so he did not tour with MCC as much as Rex Alston or, later on, myself, Christopher Martin-Jenkins and Don Mosey. In fact he paid just one visit each to the three main cricketing countries, Australia, South Africa and the West Indies.

He was an emotional, kind and compassionate man, not ashamed to cry if he was affected that way – and incidentally he had more than his fair share of personal tragedy. He was also witty, much enjoyed conversation and could tell a funny story very well. This he usually did before play started and after he had recovered from his exertions of climbing up to the commentary box. He always arrived hopelessly out of breath and more often than not mopping his brow with his handkerchief. He loathed the heat and several of us have suffered rheumatic pains in the back through his insistence on having the commentary-box door open, so as to produce a through draught.

His commentary was in the Lobby mould, describing the action until the ball was dead and then adding a piece of 'colour' until the next ball was bowled. In the same way that Neville Cardus had largely created the characters of those old Yorkshire and Lancashire professionals, so John built up the physical appearance of the cricketers — 'deep-chested', 'raw-boned', 'broad-shouldered' were frequent adjectives. He would be fascinated by trousers too tight or shirts billowing in the breeze. The umpires in their funny hats and caps were easy game for him. He never restricted himself to just the cricket, however; like me, he saw a game of cricket as something more than whether the ball was doing this or that. He would comment on the action going on all round the ground with a slight penchant for the pigeons feeding in the outfield. It was wonderful stuff and brought the cricket match alive.

Of course broadcasting cricket was only part of his life, albeit a very important part. He was a man of many talents and an expert on books, wine, aquatints and glass. To visit his home was like going to a very hospitable museum. His cricket library was one of the largest and best private collections in the world and in addition to cricket he had valuable first editions on other subjects.

Besides being such an expert collector, John was a prolific writer, whether reporting cricket or commentating on wine for the *Guardian* or writing on average one or two books every year. It was also the accolade for any book on cricket to have a foreword by John Arlott. He must have written hundreds. It always amazed me how he could maintain this output and still find the time and energy to commentate. For many years he did the full stint of commentating and then at close of play went off

254

to write his piece for the *Guardian*, but in the last five years or so he used to do only three commentary periods, finishing by 3.00 p.m. so that he could go off to the press box to write. This would be enough for most men, but on Sundays he shared the BBC2 television commentary with Jim Laker on the John Player League. This would often mean travelling a hundred miles or more from the Test match, and having to be back fresh for *Test Match Special* on Monday. One thing he told me once surprised me. He always took the first stint on BBC2 from 2.00 to 3.00 p.m, then he would do the first stint after tea, from about 4.30 to 5.30 p.m. and then go home or back to wherever the Test match was. This meant that he had never actually seen the finish of any of the John Player matches on which he had been commentating.

At the beginning of the 1980 season John announced that it was to be his last as a Test match commentator – remember that he had commentated on every Test played in England from 1946 onwards. He explained, 'I'm going while people are still asking me why I'm going rather than thinking, "Why doesn't he go?"' A salutary lesson for all of us – especially for me at my time of life! In other words, although he didn't say so, he was going out at the top. The result was a series of dinners and presentations which went on non-stop throughout the summer – everyone wanted to give him a farewell dinner and they did! How he stood up to it I don't know but somehow he arrived fit and well for what would be his last day – the fifth day of the Centenary Test at Lord's.

Some unwise radio reporter tried to interview him as he arrived, puffing as usual, at the top of the stairs. Whilst he opened the morning session there were cameramen perched in dangerous positions filming him through the window of the commentary box. There were film lights inside the box, and rows of champagne bottles sent by admirers. It was a unique day for a unique person. We couldn't really believe it all in the box – after 2.50 p.m. there would be no more John Arlott on *Test Match Special*. He got through the morning session in his usual good form, in between opening cables and letters, and celebrating in the way he knew best. We were all dreading his final twenty-minute stint, which was due to start at 2.30 p.m.

We all gathered in the box – it was packed – no one wanted to miss this historic moment in broadcasting history. The clock moved up towards 2.50 and as he started what was to be his last over, we all expected him to begin a series of thank-yous and farewells to the listeners. No such thing happened. He finished the over without one single mention of his departure and then when the last ball had been bowled, calmly said, 'And after Trevor Bailey it will be Christopher Martin-Jenkins.' There was a second or two's silence and then we all stood up and clapped. John got up and slowly left the box as Alan Curtis announced to the crowd over the public address system, 'Ladies and Gentlemen! John Arlott has just completed what will be his last ever Test match commentary for the BBC.' The reaction was wonderful. The crowd applauded, the Australians and the two England batsmen turned round and clapped, and the members on the top balcony applauded and clapped John on the back as he threaded his way through them to disappear from sight. It was a dramatic and heart-rending display by the cricket world at the headquarters of cricket saying goodbye to an old friend who had been their favourite commentator for thirty-four years. What a triumph and what an exit. John's timing, as ever, had been impeccable. As a final accolade, at the end of the season MCC made him an Honorary Life Member. No cricketer could wish for better than that.

John retired to Alderney and died on 14 December 1991. Strangely, except for one day at Old Trafford in 1989 to open the Neville Cardus stand, he never went back to a Test match, although he listened to *TMS* and I suspect mildly disapproved of some of our antics in the box. Our commentaries are the worse without his wit, unique style and voice.

Peter Jones

Sadly, Peter collapsed in the BBC launch whilst he was doing the radio commentary on the 1990 Boat Race. He died soon afterwards while still in the prime of his broadcasting life.

How versatile Welsh broadcasters are – Wynford Vaughan-

Thomas, Cliff Morgan, Alun Williams and of course Peter himself. Put a microphone in their hands and they will talk and commentate about anything. It's not just the gift of the gab. They seem to have a natural exuberance and enthusiasm, and words stream out of their mouths like a waterfall. Long, beautiful words too. I honestly don't know where they find them. If anyone was, then Peter was the Roget's Thesaurus of broadcasting. He had a pleasant, lilting voice to go with it too, which he often dropped on the last word of a sentence.

He came into broadcasting late in life and like a few of us had that necessary little bit of luck which was to change his way of living. He got a blue for soccer at Cambridge in 1951 and 1952, and his Captain was Peter May, who surprisingly captained Cambridge at soccer but not at cricket. Peter (Jones) also played as an amateur for Swansea under the captaincy of the legendary John Charles. After Cambridge he went to Bradfield where he was Master in Charge of Soccer. Living nearby and playing for Reading at the time was Maurice Edelston, and Peter arranged for him to go and coach the boys at Bradfield. They became great friends and one day when Maurice was doing a soccer commentary for BBC Radio at Southampton, he took Peter along with him. After the match they had a drink in a pub with Tony Smith, the BBC producer from Bristol who was in charge of the broadcast and during the conversation Peter mentioned that he would love to have a shot at commentary one day. Tony promptly replied that he wanted a report from a match at Aldershot the following Saturday, and would Peter like to do it. Peter leapt at the chance and did a satisfactory job with his report. So much so that Angus Mackay, then in charge of Radio Sports News, heard it and offered Peter a job in the Sports Department. So Peter left Bradfield after thirteen years as a schoolmaster and became a broadcaster. Like myself, he happened to meet someone at the right time and took advantage of his luck. He was soon to make his mark, because Angus chose him to succeed Eamonn Andrews as the introducer of *Sports Report*, and Peter did this for five years, learning his trade as a soccer commentator at the same time.

He soon found that soccer commentary is not as easy as the

commentators make it sound. The ball is constantly changing direction, up field, down field, and across from touch-line to touch-line. On its way it is passed from player to player. I remember Raymond Glendenning telling me that on average he could only mention one pass in three, unless his commentary was to become a list of players' names. And of course in those days there were the great players such as Matthews, James, Finney, Shackleton, Logie who tried to beat their man by controlled dribbling. Nowadays the players – no doubt because they are fitter – run all over the place and get rid of the ball to someone else as soon as they receive it. How seldom does one see a player trying to pass his opponent with a dribble or a dummy. This means that there are far more passes in modern football and it is quite impossible for the commentator to cover them all. Peter had therefore evolved what I call 'thinking aloud' commentary. When play was in mid-field and there was little likelihood of a goal, he would muse over what tactics the team was trying, what was going on in a certain player's mind, how the game would affect either of the team's position in the table, how the manager was feeling, and so on. He would do this for a few moments and then pick up the play again as one of the goals was threatened. Other commentators now do the same, and the soccer commentary is far less descriptive of actual play than it was. Were individual skills to be revived to the standards of say twenty or thirty years ago, then there would be something other than just passes to describe.

Peter had many roles other than soccer commentator. He became radio's number one for the big occasion, be it a jubilee procession, a wedding or a London Marathon. He was, I would say, happier outside than covering a service or ceremony indoors. He had one favourite expression which you could bet he would use at least once in any big radio broadcast. He loved to describe a person or people as 'walking tall', which he physically did himself. He was tall and good-looking, with wavy hair and bags of charm. He was always debonair and smartly dressed and was in the international class as a chatter-up of the opposite sex! In addition to presenting sporting programmes such as *Sport on 2* and *Sports Report*, he had been chairman of innumerable quiz shows like *Sporting Chance*, *Treble Chance* or *Brain of Sport*. He also commentated on other sports including rowing and, of course, swimming where he shone at many Olympic or Commonwealth Games, one of them producing the following classic phrase: 'Welcome to the Olympic pool where an enthusiastic crowd are cheering the exciting races which are taking place. I've never seen such excitement. It's the pool that sets them alight!' Good old Peter. We miss him.

Alan McGilvray

One or two older readers may remember someone called Jack Smith, the whispering baritone. He used to sing songs like 'Baby Face' and 'Miss Annabelle Lee' very softly at the piano during the twenties and thirties. For nearly fifty years the Australian Alan McGilvray – from now on 'McGillers' – was the whispering commentator. His style was utterly unique. He spoke right up against the microphone so confidentially and so quietly that even if you were sitting next to him, you could not hear what he was saying. It was a very effective method as it gave the air of intimacy making the listener at home think himself the one person to whom Alan was talking. His commentary flowed freely at about the same level, his voice rarely generating excitement. His description of play was completely factual and he had always been wary of following the English style of 'colourful' commentary.

I would say he was the most unbiased commentator I have ever heard. He liked to enjoy cricket, no matter who was winning, and had very high principles as to the conduct of players and the spirit in which the game was played. He was a fine reader of the tactics and cricketing skills and was well qualified to give his judgement. In addition to the experience gained during his fifty years of commentary, he also captained New South Wales in the Sheffield Shield in 1934–36. He succeeded Don Bradman as Captain and had people like Bill O'Reilly and Jack Fingleton under his command, he himself being a useful fast medium bowler.

One other unusual feature of his commentary was that he looked through his binoculars while commentating, the field-glasses resting on the top of the microphone, his elbows on the desk in front of him. I find this a very difficult thing to do; BBC commentators rarely do it and then only for the odd ball or two. The trouble is that although you get a fine close-up of the batsman and stumps, if the ball is hit anywhere, it goes out of your vision. It is then very difficult to take down the binoculars, and pick up where the ball has gone.

McGillers did his first cricket commentary in 1934, and so is by far and away the longest-serving and most experienced commentator. He broadcast his 200th Test at Melbourne in 1980, and received a tremendous ovation from the crowd when this fact was recorded on the giant scoreboard. He first came here to represent the Australian Broadcasting Commission in 1948 and has been here many times since. But his first Test broadcasts were done from an Australian studio when they were covering the 1934 and 1938 Test series in England with 'synthetic' commentary. McGillers and others would sit in front of a studio microphone and be fed with cables sent direct from England describing each ball, where it had gone, how many runs scored or how a wicket had fallen. There were certain code signs so that they were able to say, as the cable describing the second ball of an over was thrust in front of them, 'Bradman has cut that one down to third man – Leyland fields and returns over the top of the stumps to Les Ames, while they trot through for an easy single.' After some experience they could pick that up easily enough from the cable. But the difficult part was when the next cable was delayed for some reason, and to fill in they had to make up 'drinks coming out', 'a dog running across the pitch', and so on. It was all backed up by sound effects of applause, cheers or gasps for a missed catch or near thing.

I gather it all sounded very realistic and they were even still prepared to use the method in 1948, if the actual commentary being relayed from the grounds became too difficult to follow due to atmospheric interference. (In those days there was no Commonwealth cable laid to take the broadcasts.) It must, have been a tremendous strain on the commentators, though, having to improvise off the cuff, using only their knowledge of the game and their imagination.

It must all have been good training for McGillers, who stands head and shoulders above any other Australian radio commentator. With the Sheffield Shield competition, and a regular visit each year from one of the cricketing countries, he got plenty of practice. He did a little television but basically stuck faithfully to radio. I always remember a conversation he and I had with that great cricket enthusiast, Sir Robert Menzies. I have said that McGillers's commentary flows along more or less non-stop. So, I suppose, does mine. Anyway, Sir Robert told us that he enjoyed our commentaries but that he preferred so-and-so up in Brisbane, 'because he knows the value of the pause'. McGillers and I understood what he was getting at, but I'm afraid it did not have much effect on our style.

I had got to know McGillers well on his visits to Great Britain, but as I did television exclusively until the mid-sixties, I had never worked with him until I went to Australia in 1958 for my three months' 'grace leave' with ABC. He was kindness itself in the box and a great help to me in my first attempts to give the score in the Australian way. We have since enjoyed twenty-five years of friendship in the commentary boxes of Australia, South Africa and England.

There was an occasion at Edgbaston in 1975 when he indvertently reduced the box to complete silence for nearly twenty seconds, except for the sound of suppressed giggles. We were desperately trying to fill in time during a long period when a thunderstorm had stopped play. We were talking about the Chappell brothers and in particular the youngest one, Trevor. He had done the double in the Central Lancashire league the previous season, but we were not sure how much first-class cricket he had played for South Australia. 'Well,' I said, 'let's ask someone who should know the answer. He is sitting at the back of the box – Alan McGilvray. Alan, what about it?' I turned round and there indeed was Alan at the back of the box – but fast asleep. Everyone began to laugh and I had to make a quick decision. Should I let Alan down by saying that he was asleep, or should I pretend that he had left the box? I chose the latter, although there was no real reason why he should not have been asleep – he was not on duty at the time. Anyway, I quickly said, 'I'm so sorry, but Alan must have just slipped out of the box. He was here a moment ago.'

Unfortunately, Alan's subconscious mind heard his name and with a snort he suddenly woke up and said loudly, 'What's that? Does someone want me? What do you want to know?' By then that rotter Don Mosey had rushed from the box with his handkerchief stuffed into his mouth, and I was left alone with Trevor Bailey, who was having quiet hysterics to my right. It was too much for me and I began to laugh uncontrollably. There was no way in which I could speak. I covered up the microphone with my hand and for once there was complete silence from *Test Match Special*, except for some strange wheezing noises. After what seemed eternity I apologised to the listeners and decided to come clean and explain what happened. I must say Alan took it remarkably well but it took several minutes before we were able to return to normal.

McGillers is about five months younger than me, and will certainly be remembered as the longest-serving commentator, universally respected by his colleagues as the real professional, and with a large number of appreciative friends both in Australia and England. I am sure that listeners everywhere would universally award him the supreme accolade of 'The man who always gave the score' – something I think we could all learn from him.

Y

for Yorkshire Pudding etc.

I'm a plain eater. I like nursery or schoolboy food. None of this *nouvelle cuisine* with its stupid little helpings and a mixture of vegetables in a dish the size of a saucer. My wife says this makes me difficult to cater for – I can't see why. All I dislike are the extra ingredients which clever cooks think that they have to add to every dish. I happen to dislike tomatoes and it is practically impossible to buy a sandwich without tomato in it. Why does roast lamb need garlic? Why do they put onion rings on smoked salmon?

Basic English food is so good. Roast beef or lamb, steak-and-kidney pudding or pie, bangers and mash, fish and chips, scrambled eggs, any roast bird or game with lots of bread sauce. Yet on most menus roast turkey is nowadays served only with *cranberry* sauce. In one hotel I asked the waiter if I could have some bread sauce. 'I'll ask the chef,' he said and went away. When he came back he said 'The chef says he hasn't got any.' I exploded at this. 'Of course he hasn't *got* any. He has to make it.'

It's the same with my great favourite – Yorkshire pudding. My wife makes the best I've ever eaten and so she should – she's a Yorkshire girl. She gets if just right – crisp round the edges and soft in the centre, and in a flat pan. In hotels they serve it up to look like a miniature cottage loaf and it's always far too hard. I got a shock once at a hotel in Yorkshire of all places. At dinner one night I chose the roast beef but there was no YP. 'Oh no, sir,' said the waiter, 'we don't serve it in the evenings.'

I am particularly fond of Irish stew and stewed rabbit, but they must be served with dumplings. Shellfish are out but I like all the normal fish like whiting, cod, haddock or plaice. Plus of course salmon or halibut if we are feeling rich. Honestly, based on the above, I don't see why I am said to be a fussy eater – at least so far as the main courses go. I'm a bit difficult I admit about starters. No avocado, prawns, mussels, oysters. Just melon, grapefruit or smoked salmon.

I'm good on all vegetables except for artichokes, swedes and parsnips. My special favourites are good old cabbage and runner beans (but not those round worm-like French beans). I also like cauliflower and Brussels sprouts but they *must* be well cooked and not hard as they always are in restaurants.

As for puddings I must be the easiest person ever. I love them all. Roly poly, treacle sponge and tart, spotted dog, bread-and-butter pudding, banana fritters, pancakes, apple, plum or gooseberry pies (I prefer them cold with cream). Fruit salads, summer pudding, strawberries, raspberries, peaches – all fruit goes down a treat. Of course for the sake of my figure very few of the above ever 'go down' but I *do* like them.

I often get asked to send my favourite recipe for some book being written for charity. Here it is – guards' pudding – which in its finished state looks just like a Christmas pudding but is delightfully light and fluffy to eat.

For four to six people

6 oz fresh white breadcrumbs
6 oz chopped shredded suet or butter
4 oz brown or sand sugar
3 tblspns strawberry jam
2 small eggs
1 level tspn bicarbonate of soda
Pinch of salt

Mix dry ingredients together. Add jam and egg beaten up with bicarbonate of soda. Mix thoroughly and then turn into a well-greased mould which should be a little more than three parts full. Steam for three hours.

For the Sauce (very important)
1 whole egg

1 egg yolk
1 ½oz castor sugar
2 lge tblspns orange juice

Place ingredients in a bowl and then place this bowl in another bowl of very hot water. Whisk until thick and frothy. Serve immediately or, if not, whisk for one minute before serving.

I'm sure that you will find it delicious and it's ideal for a very special dinner party.

PS One curious thing that I find with my food is the importance which I attach to the ingredients extra to the main course. What would roast beef be without Yorkshire pudding, roast lamb without mint sauce, roast chicken or turkey without bread sauce, Irish stew without dumplings, roast pheasant or grouse without breadcrumbs, pancakes without lemon, strawberries and raspberries without cream, smoked salmon without thin bread and butter, plum pudding without brandy sauce, cheese without celery, soup without croutons, salmon without mayonnaise, sausages or cold ham without mustard or boiled eggs without salt?

I'm sure you can all add a few more of your own.

Z

for Zany

From time to time in my life certain zany things have happened which still make me laugh when I think of them today. I feel a bit ashamed when I recall them because most of them seem to be at the expense of some innocent person who becomes the object of our laughter. It's true I suppose that a lot of laughter has an element of cruelty in it.

For example there was an occasion when I was only aged about seven. A favourite aunt came to stay and my mother asked an old friend to come for tea to meet my aunt for the first time. My brothers and I told our aunt that the lady visitor was stone deaf and from the moment when they were introduced she would have to shout.

We waited anxiously for the front-door bell to ring and as soon as it did, we rushed to meet the visitor before our mother could greet her. We quickly told her that we had a very deaf aunt staying with us, and that she would have to shout at the top of her voice to make our aunt hear. For some reason she believed us and you can imagine the result. As soon as our mother introduced them to each other they both began to shout, and I'm afraid we became quite hysterical with laughter. It was quite a few seconds before they realised something was wrong. Our mother, though finding it difficult *not* to laugh, was not too pleased!

During one summer holiday at Bude we were sitting by the outdoor sea-water pool. It was built snugly into the cliffs and the salty water was grey and murky. A man, wearing a rubber swimming cap and goggles, stood on the edge of the pool at what happened to be the shallow end where young children bathed. He obviously did not realise this since he couldn't see the bottom of the pool through the murky water. He looked around, then held his nose, bent his knees and took a terrific leap into the air assuming he would be going down into at least six feet of water. Instead his legs crumpled up beneath him as his feet hit the bottom only about a foot deep. With a yelp of pain he lay spluttering in the water as everyone around collapsed with laughter.

In Cornwall there was a small hunt called the Tetcott which hunted in rather boggy country where the jumps were banks rather than fences. The followers were mostly local farmers plus a small number of retired army officers who mostly lived in Bude. One of these was my stepfather, Colonel Scully, and another a retired Brigadier-General called Van Renen. He had a white bristling moustache and talked at the top of his voice. In contrast to the farmers who mostly wore cloth caps and tweed coats, the General and my stepfather were regarded as true hunting gentlemen with top hats, pink coats and white breeches. They were sitting on their horses chatting away about the army whilst the hounds were 'drawing' a covert. Unknowingly, alas, they were on a particularly boggy piece of ground and as they talked their horses slowly began to sink into the mud as if they were on quicksand. It looked just as if they were slowly descending in a lift.

The General and my stepfather were so intent on their conversation that they did not realise what was happening until they felt the mud oozing over their boots. By then it was too late and their whole legs disappeared into the mud which was by then right up to the saddle. Luckily at that point the horses struck firm ground. In their pink coats and white breeches the two riders gingerly dismounted into the mud which came well up to their waists. As they waded out I fear that once again there was universal laughter at someone's mishap.

One spring I was the commentator at an outside broadcast of the reopening of the Hythe and Dymchurch Miniature Railway. The Mayor of New Romney performed the opening ceremony, and was then asked to go for a ride in the first train. He got into a special open carriage at the end of the train. The guard waved his flag, blew his whistle and the train slowly drew out of the station. The Mayor took off his tricorn hat and started to wave goodbye to the crowd. But he soon stopped when he saw that he was not leaving the station with the rest of the train. They had forgotten to attach his carriage to the one in front!

There have been many moments both in *Down Your Way* and *Test Match Special* which I recall with special amusement. There was the well-known incident of Alan McGilvray and the chocolate cake which happened during the Lord's Test Match one year when someone had sent me a cake for my birthday (it usually falls during the Test). I had cut the cake into slices and placed it beside me as I commentated. One or two of the commentators had already helped themselves to a slice when McGillers came into the box. As I commentated I pointed to the cake and he nodded and took a slice. He was putting it into his mouth as I said, '. . . that one goes off the outside edge of the bat and drops just in front of second slip.' Seeing that McGillers was now munching the cake I quickly added '. . . and I'll ask Alan McGilvray if he thought it was a catch.' He tried to speak but only succeeded in blowing out crumbs all over the box resulting in gales of laughter from everyone. He has never really forgiven me, and from then on refused to accept anything which I offered him!

There were one or two occasions on *Down Your Way* when either I or the person I was interviewing got a fit of giggles and we had to stop the recording. The trouble was when I caught their eye. In fact if I suspected them of being a giggler I would take care *not* to look them in the face when I asked my questions.

The worst case was at the 'book town' of Hay-on-Wye in Herefordshire when I was talking to a rather eccentric character called Richard Booth. He lived in an old castle and had declared UDI and Hay-on-Wye a free zone with ambassadors to various European countries.

He had turned Hay into a town of books and at that time had six second-hand bookshops with over fifteen miles of shelving and over 2,000,000 books. People came from all over the world because they knew that they would find hundreds of titles on their favourite subject be it gardening, bridge, cricket or astronomy.

At the end of our conversation I asked him to choose a piece of music and unfortunately caught his eye. He started to laugh and so did I and our producer and engineer. Through his sobs he tried to ask for *The Golden Years* by David Bowie. Try as he could he only managed to splutter and was unable to get a coherent word out. Of course we had to stop the recording and try again. Each time I put my question, trying to suppress my laughter and each time he too broke down. After about six attempts we decided to have a short break and then tried again. We failed several times more but finally with me turning my back on him, he just managed to blurt out his request.

Years later we broadcast these 'out-takes' in a programme produced by Michael Craig called *It's a Funny Business*. Jimmy Tarbuck told me that he was driving his car when he heard it and had to pull in at the side of the road as he was laughing so much, which proves how infectious laughter can be.

As I've said, comedy can often be cruel with laughter provoked by an accident happening to somebody else. During an Old Trafford Test match some of us were staying in a small hotel in Lymm. It was kept by a great character and cricket enthusiast Roger Allen. One of his special attractions was a trolley in the dining-room at breakfast which carried at least twenty pots of different types of marmalade.

One evening Roy Webber and I had been out to dinner and when we got back late, we found that Roger had locked the main hotel door. We hadn't a key with us so decided to throw some gravel up at John Woodcock's bedroom as we knew he never went to sleep early. He soon appeared at the window and we asked him if he would chuck us down his key. 'Wait a second. I'll go and get it. Just stand under the window, Roy, and I'll throw it down to you.' He came back but instead of chucking down the key, he poured a jug of water all over the waiting Roy. Unfortunately Roy had put on his best suit, and I have never seen anyone more angry. He shouted threats and obscenities at John who then threw down his key. When we got in Roy stormed up the stairs and rattled on John's door but he had wisely locked himself in. Roy, who was drenched from head to foot, went off cursing to his room and slammed the door.

About ten minutes later there was an almighty crash from Roy's room. By this time Roger Allen had appeared and he and I went along to find out what had happened. An even angrier Roy appeared almost speechless with rage. We managed to hear more threats from him and complaints that he might have been seriously hurt. We looked into his room and saw that his bed had collapsed. It had evidently happened when he threw himself on it (he weighed nearly twenty stone). We sympathised and swore that we had had nothing to do with it but he wouldn't believe us. We finally calmed him down and Roger went to get him a stiff drink. But dear old Roy, to his dying day he still thought that we were guilty. I must admit it *was* a coincidence. I hope he will forgive me if I admit that I still roar with laughter whenever I remember the incident.

I shall never forget the look on a policeman's face one afternoon in Richmond, Surrey. We were to record a *Down Your Way* from Brinkworth Hall, the retirement home for old variety artists. We weren't quite sure of the way so at about 10.00 a.m. we stopped to ask a policeman who was directing traffic at a road junction. We told him where we wanted to go and he very efficiently gave us detailed instructions, something like this: 'Go on to the top of the hill and turn left at the traffic lights. Go on past the next set of lights and then take the second turn to the left. Brinkworth Hall is about 200 yards up on the right.'

We thanked him and following his instructions easily reached our destination. We recorded our programme throughout the day and then at about 4.00 p.m. drove back into Richmond the same way as we had come. To my surprise when we came to the road junction where we had stopped to ask the way, the same policeman was still there directing traffic. (I hope he had had a break for lunch.) I just couldn't resist it. I stopped the car, wound down the window and said, 'Officer, excuse me, did you say the second or third turning to the left after the traffic lights?' You should have see his face! It cheers me up whenever I think of it.

Index

274